D1007522

MASTER OF DRAGONS

"Many thanks to Angela Knight for keeping this series sexy and unique."
—*Romance Reader at Heart*

MASTER OF SWORDS

"Fabulous . . . A terrific romantic fantasy that spins the Arthurian legend into a different, unique direction."
—*Midwest Book Review*

MASTER OF WOLVES

"Grandmaster of the paranormal romantic suspense."
—*Midwest Book Review*

MASTER OF THE MOON

"The author has certainly gotten inventive with her Mageverse series, and there's no denying it is something different among the current glut of paranormal books."
—*RT Book Reviews*

MASTER OF THE NIGHT

"A terrific paranormal romantic suspense thriller that never slows down until the final confrontation between good and evil. The action-packed story line moves at a fast clip."
—*Midwest Book Review*

WARRIOR

"A wonderful science fiction romantic suspense."
—*Genre Go Round Reviews*

"The character chemistry is gorgeous; the sex is searing hot; the world fascinating and a joy to explore. All in all, a great book!" —*Errant Dreams Reviews*

JANE'S WARLORD

"What an awesome, scintillating, and sexy book! *Jane's Warlord* is intriguing, extremely sensuous, and just plain adventurous. A star is born." —*RT Book Reviews* (Top Pick)

"Chills, thrills, and a super hero and heroine will have readers racing through this sexy tale. Take note, time-travel fans, the future belongs to Knight!"
—Emma Holly, *USA Today* bestselling author

"[Angela Knight's] world is believable and her plotting fast paced. Knight's fictional world seems to have a promising future." —*Booklist*

"Solid writing . . . sexy love scenes, and likable characters. I look forward to [Knight's] next book."
—*All About Romance*

"Exhilarating . . . Delightful." —*The Best Reviews*

Further praise for the novels of Angela Knight

"Nicely written, quickly paced, and definitely on the erotic side." —*Library Journal*

"If you like alpha heroes, wild rides, and pages that sizzle in your hand, you're going to love [Angela Knight]!"
—J. R. Ward, #1 *New York Times* bestselling author

Berkley Sensation Titles by Angela Knight

Mageverse Series

MASTER OF THE NIGHT
MASTER OF THE MOON
MASTER OF WOLVES
MASTER OF SWORDS
MASTER OF DRAGONS
MASTER OF FIRE
MASTER OF SMOKE
MASTER OF SHADOWS

The Time Hunters Series

JANE'S WARLORD
WARRIOR
GUARDIAN

CAPTIVE DREAMS
(with Diane Whiteside)

MERCENARIES

Anthologies

HOT BLOODED
(with Christine Feehan, Maggie Shayne, and Emma Holly)

BITE
(with Laurell K. Hamilton, Charlaine Harris, MaryJanice Davidson, and Vickie Taylor)

KICK ASS
(with Maggie Shayne, MaryJanice Davidson, and Jacey Ford)

OVER THE MOON
(with MaryJanice Davidson, Virginia Kantra, and Sunny)

BEYOND THE DARK
(with Emma Holly, Lora Leigh, and Diane Whiteside)

SHIFTER
(with Lora Leigh, Alyssa Day, and Virginia Kantra)

HOT FOR THE HOLIDAYS
(with Lora Leigh, Anya Bast, and Allyson James)

BURNING UP
(with Nalini Singh, Virginia Kantra, and Meljean Brook)

MASTER
of
SHADOWS

ANGELA KNIGHT

BERKLEY SENSATION, NEW YORK

THE BERKLEY PUBLISHING GROUP
Published by the Penguin Group
Penguin Group (USA) Inc.
375 Hudson Street, New York, New York 10014, USA
Penguin Group (Canada), 90 Eglinton Avenue East, Suite 700, Toronto, Ontario M4P 2Y3, Canada
(a division of Pearson Penguin Canada Inc.)
Penguin Books Ltd., 80 Strand, London WC2R 0RL, England
Penguin Group Ireland, 25 St. Stephen's Green, Dublin 2, Ireland (a division of Penguin Books Ltd.)
Penguin Group (Australia), 250 Camberwell Road, Camberwell, Victoria 3124, Australia
(a division of Pearson Australia Group Pty. Ltd.)
Penguin Books India Pvt. Ltd., 11 Community Centre, Panchsheel Park, New Delhi—110 017, India
Penguin Group (NZ), 67 Apollo Drive, Rosedale, Auckland 0632, New Zealand
(a division of Pearson New Zealand Ltd.)
Penguin Books (South Africa) (Pty.) Ltd., 24 Sturdee Avenue, Rosebank, Johannesburg 2196,
South Africa

Penguin Books Ltd., Registered Offices: 80 Strand, London WC2R 0RL, England

This is a work of fiction. Names, characters, places, and incidents either are the product of the author's imagination or are used fictitiously, and any resemblance to actual persons, living or dead, business establishments, events, or locales is entirely coincidental. The publisher does not have any control over and does not assume any responsibility for author or third-party websites or their content.

MASTER OF SHADOWS

A Berkley Sensation Book / published by arrangement with the author

PRINTING HISTORY
Berkley Sensation mass-market edition / August 2011

Copyright © 2011 by Angela Knight.
Cover art by Richard Jones.
Cover hand lettering by Ron Zinn.
Cover design by George Long.

ISBN: 978-0-425-24367-1

BERKLEY® SENSATION
Berkley Sensation Books are published by The Berkley Publishing Group,
a division of Penguin Group (USA) Inc.,
375 Hudson Street, New York, New York 10014.
BERKLEY® SENSATION and the "B" design are trademarks of Penguin Group (USA) Inc.

PRINTED IN THE UNITED STATES OF AMERICA

10 9 8 7 6 5 4 3 2 1

ACKNOWLEDGMENTS

First I want to thank my wonderful critique partners, Diane Whiteside and Shelby Morgen, who are always a huge asset when it comes to brainstorming plot ideas and checking the logic and flow of my books. I also depend on my incredible beta readers, Virginia Ettel, Markeeta Karland, Stephanie Burke, and Camille Anthony, who helped ensure *Master of Shadows* is as strong as possible.

As always, I want to thank my agent, Roberta Brown, who holds my hand when needed. My patient, long-suffering editor, Cindy Hwang, is always a source of encouragement and fresh ideas. Copyeditor Rick Willett slew various typos and other mistakes, and I am deeply grateful for his hard work.

Finally, I want to thank my family, especially my husband, Mike Woodcock, who is unfailing in his love for me, his support of my career, and his patience with my many neuroses. My son, Anthony, and our housemate, James Berg, did all those chores I was too busy writing to do. My parents, Gayle and Paul Lee, love, support, and believe in me whether I deserve it or not. My sister, Angela, and her husband, Chuck Patterson, cheer me on when I need it most.

Angela and Chuck also let me play with their gorgeous, clever grandbabies: Naomi Looper and Charlie, William, and Richard Patterson, who are good at teaching an obsessed writer what's *really* important. A new grandbaby should be joining the family any day now, to the delight of us all.

The babies' parents, my niece, Shanna Looper, and my nephew, Joshua Patterson, and his wife, Darah, have always been willing to pitch in and help whenever I need it.

I love you all, and I couldn't have done it without you.

ONE

"What do you do when they order you to kill?"

The conversation instantly died as every witch and vampire in the room turned to look at Davon Fredericks. Davon did not flinch under the weight of those incredulous stares. He'd been a trauma surgeon before becoming a vampire, and he'd never lacked balls. He just gazed at Belle, his chocolate eyes level and troubled. He was a big man in his jeans and dark blue oxford shirt, broad shoulders stretching the fabric as he leaned forward, elbows on knees. His curling black hair was cut close to his scalp, emphasizing the strong, handsome lines of his face—the full lips, the broad cheekbones, the wide swoop of his nose. His skin was precisely the color of milk chocolate, smooth and clear, with a faint, creamy gleam.

Belle looked up at him from the plates of hors d'oeuvres on the coffee table, a stuffed mushroom halfway to her mouth. "Why do you ask?"

A muscle flexed in his chiseled jaw, and he looked up at

the CONGRATULATIONS, DAVON AND CHERISE! banner hanging across the back of the den.

Belle had designed the room especially for the dinner parties she loved to throw, with two big white leather L-shaped sectionals arranged around a low, square coffee table. Davon's brooding gaze dropped to the table, flicking among the trays and bottles that crowded it. He chose a beer and opened it with a violent twist of one strong hand. "I was just wondering."

Now all twenty of her guests looked uneasy. Ten vampires and ten witches, Asian, black, Caucasian, Latino, all of them wet behind the ears. Though they were either in their early thirties, like Davon, or late twenties, none of them had been Magekind for longer than a few months. Well, except for Cherise Myers.

And Belle herself, who had been around one hell of a lot longer than that. She sighed and decided she'd better scotch this concern before they *all* started obsessing about it. "First off, none of you is going to be ordered to kill anybody." She dropped the mushroom on her plate and used a toothpick to skewer a couple of cheese cubes from a tray. "If someone needs killing, Arthur will send one of the Knights of the Round Table."

Like Tristan, who had been avoiding her for the past month. She curled a lip and stabbed a cheddar cube through its cold, imaginary heart.

"But . . ." Cherise began, only to fall silent with a glance at Davon, who sat beside her on the sectional. Each promptly looked away from the other, as if they'd synchronized their chins. Cherise looked delicate as a fairy next to big, broad Davon. She had a heart-shaped face, enormous blue eyes, and a tumble of blond hair that made her look like she'd just stepped off the cover of a romance novel. Yet a solid buzz of power radiated from her, and intelligence lit those blue eyes.

So what was with the grimness that thinned the line of her full mouth?

Frowning, Belle eyed the couple. They'd returned from their first mission a few days before, which was the whole point of this get-together. Belle always threw her boys a party to celebrate that first-mission milestone. *You're a real Magus now, kid.*

There was more to being a Magekind vampire—a Magus—than having a set of fangs. You had to save the world, too.

Whether the world liked it or not.

But Cherise Myers was no green recruit; she'd been a Maja for several years now. A steady, intelligent young witch, she had just enough power to handle most jobs without getting dangerously cocky about it. Belle had been pleased Davon had been assigned to her.

So why were they acting so twitchy now, when neither was the twitchy sort? "Look, Arthur doesn't make the decision to kill humans lightly. You've got to be a career asshole along the lines of a major terrorist leader to make him decide to take you out."

Richard Spotted Horse looked up from pouring himself a glass from one of the bottles of donated blood each of the witches had brought. He cocked a dark eyebrow. "But why not just cast a spell to make the bastard give up the terrorist business?"

"Wouldn't work," she said, and noticed that Davon was now pointedly avoiding her gaze. She'd have to pull him aside after the party and make him spill whatever was bothering him. Nobody had appointed Belle den mother to the men she'd recruited; she just couldn't help herself. "Once a murderous attitude becomes deeply engrained, you can't wipe it out of a subject's mind no matter how much magic you use."

"So why not kill 'em all?" Davon picked up a chocolate-covered strawberry, then dropped it back on the tray as if remembering he didn't eat anymore.

"Because we don't work that way. Not that we're not tempted, but . . ."

"Belle, we've got a mission." The familiar male voice rang across the room, cutting her off as a shaft of helpless longing stabbed through her. Which instantly pissed her off. *Tristan.*

The knight filled the doorway with his height and swordsman's solid brawn. He was dressed all in black. *He would be,* she thought. A black knit shirt tucked into black jeans over soft black boots, the darkness broken only by the glint of the silver belt-buckle at his narrow waist. His hair fell around his shoulders in thick, blond strands that gleamed like expensive silk.

Tristan had the face of a Renaissance warrior, long and square-jawed, his cheekbones precise juts, with sculpted hollows and a determined chin. His mouth was wide and far too sensual for her peace of mind. His eyes glittered vividly green under his thick blond brows, demanding and more than a little arrogant. "Sorry to interrupt your party, but I've got a nasty situation on my hands."

Belle gave him a smile sweet enough to rot the fangs right out of his head. The kids, of course, were staring at him in hero-worshipping awe. "Come on in, Tristan." *Since you already let yourself in my house without knocking.* "We're celebrating Davon's first mission."

"Congratulations." Tristan didn't even glance over at him. "Look, Belle, I've got a pissed-off werewolf waiting for me. It's kind of urgent."

She bared her teeth. They weren't fangs, but they apparently got the message across; he flinched. "I'll be happy to open a gate for you to go meet your fuzzy friend, but I'm a little too busy to accompany you just now. I'll join you once the party's over." Damned if he was going to stroll into her house and start ordering her around. Not when he'd been treating her like a Black Plague victim for weeks.

"Belle, if you need to go on a job, we can clean up," Cherise said earnestly.

"I think we can all be trusted not to get drunk and trash the place." Richard gave her a lazy grin, shameless flirt that he was.

Tristan glowered at him before turning the glare on her. "Look, I realize I'm interrupting fun and games with your . . . boys, but the Direkind needs us to investigate a murder. And they're convinced magic was involved."

Belle stared, making the instant leap. "Warlock."

"That's my thought."

"A murder?" one of the kids asked. "Who?"

"What happened?" Davon looked uneasy.

Tristan didn't reply, his gaze hard and demanding on Belle's.

Dammit, there was no choice in this one. She had to give him what he wanted. Again. Warlock and his daughter were the only Direkind werewolves who could work magic, and he was both immortal and incredibly powerful. He was also murderous, ambitious, and insane. Belle and Tristan had locked horns with him the month before, and had damn near died doing it. If he'd surfaced again . . .

Belle stood and looked around at the Majae. Unlike the vampires, they did eat, which is why she'd spent the day cooking for them. "There's more hors d'oeuvres in the kitchen, girls. Please finish them off. Stay as long as you want."

As Tristan stepped aside, she stalked past him through a chorus of good-byes. "All right, where am I opening this gate?" she said after he'd closed the door behind her. "And what the hell's going on?" *And why have you been avoiding me?*

Tristan shook his head. "Actually, I don't know many of the details myself. William Justice is my contact. He's the Wolf sheriff—the top werewolf cop, appointed by the Direkind Council of Clans. He's a good guy . . ."

"As opposed to the aristocratic nutjobs we dealt with last month," Belle muttered.

"Right. This guy fought for us during the Dragon War." He was referring to the battle the Magekind had fought a year or so ago, back when they'd been ass-deep in alien demons and calling in every ally they could find. The Sidhe, Dragonkind, and assorted werewolves had joined the battle against the Dark Ones, and a lot of them had died doing it. He's been contacting me for help on cases ever since, usually when he needs me to bring in magical firepower."

Like vampires, werewolves couldn't use magic beyond the limits of their own bodies; for spell work, they needed witch help.

"So where is this scene?"

"South Carolina. Some podunk little town." There were a lot of werewolves in South Carolina, Merlin only knew why. Tristan reached into a pocket to pull out an iPhone. "Hey, Justice? I found my witch. Help her with her gate, would you?" He offered her the cell, and she accepted it. The touch of his hand sent a flush of frustrated heat zinging up her arm.

Belle dragged her attention away from his stern, handsome face as she put the phone to her ear. Some Maja had enchanted it to carry inter-dimensional transmissions between Mortal Earth and the magical city of Avalon. She could sense the buzz of an active spell as she handled it. "Hello, Justice?" Good name for a cop.

"Look, you people need to get over here *now*," growled a deep voice with a distinct Southern drawl. "The kid's parents have called every wolf in the fucking county. The mood's getting ugly. I need to get you and the knight in and out before I have a riot on my hands."

"I'm sorry for the delay," Belle told him. "We're on our way."

"Do you want to gate directly to the scene?"

"Not if you want me to sense any magic cast by the killer," she told him. "A dimensional gate produces a pretty strong blast of magical energies that would destroy older traces. We're going to have to come in some distance from the scene if we don't want to contaminate it."

"You do realize that means you're going to have to walk through a pack of pissed-off family members?"

She shrugged. "Can't be helped."

"All right. How far out do you want me to get?"

"At least a couple of blocks."

"Okay. Give me a minute." She listened to the rustle of clothes and the murmur of angry voices, then the click of boots on cement. Silence fell, broken by the chirp of distant crickets. "I'm there."

Belle concentrated, drawing on the hot roil of the Mageverse as she used the phone's magical connection to home in on Justice's location. Magic poured from the tips of her fingers, conjuring a glowing point in the center of the hallway. A heartbeat later, it had expanded into a shimmering oval: an inter-dimensional gate.

Avalon, the Magekind's capital city, was located in another universe entirely, on a world that was a twin to Mortal Earth. Magic was a physical law in the Mageverse; both the Magekind and their werewolf cousins, the Direkind, drew on its energies to power their magic. Travel between the two Earths could only be accomplished with a magical gate, which meant Tristan needed Belle's help. Otherwise he'd probably still be avoiding her, the bastard.

Tristan ducked through the gate before it was even finished expanding. Belle followed, trying not to admire his ass as she went. Like the rest of him, it was a very nice ass.

Too bad his personality wasn't as pleasant as the view.

They emerged in a neighborhood straight out of a fifties sitcom. Middle-class tract homes, all very similar, nestled in small yards surrounded by azaleas and oak trees. A startled black cat crouched and hissed at them, before darting away to vanish under a wax myrtle hedge. William Justice must be the guy pacing the sidewalk. Lean as a fencer, dark haired, and starkly handsome, he wore chinos and a navy blue polo shirt. He carried a pump-action shotgun tucked under one muscular arm.

Justice wasn't fooling around.

"Clock's ticking here," he told them after a quick round of introductions. "I need you to check the scene so we can get the boy to the funeral home before some human cop shows up and starts asking questions. Or before there's a riot." His mouth tightened into a grim, flat line. "Could go either way."

"Tell us about this kid." Tristan frowned down the length of the sidewalk as though he'd heard something that worried him. Belle, whose Maja senses were less acute, heard nothing.

Justice swung the shotgun up across one shoulder. "Vic is seventeen years old. Name's Jimmy Sheridan. Just got through his transition successfully, so his mom and dad thought they were in the clear."

"In the clear?" Belle asked. "Of what?"

"A fifth of our kids don't survive their first transformation. The magic runs rogue and burns them alive. Just incinerates them to ash."

She stared at him, having never heard that particular horrific detail about the Direkind. "My God."

"Why do you think we call it 'Merlin's Curse'? It's hell on our families. Which is why we're a little nuts when it comes to our kids."

"Everybody's nuts when it comes to their kids." Belle cast a quick spell, opening a telepathic link to Tristan. *"This is going to get really, really ugly."*

"Yeah, I picked up on that."

"You are quick." Smart-ass. Belle curled her lip at him before turning to Justice.

"The Sheridans took their oldest son, Steve, out to dinner," the Wolf sheriff continued. "They left Jimmy at home because he had a term paper for summer school he'd been putting off writing. Paper was due tomorrow, so he was cutting it pretty close. Apparently, they had a little fight about that."

"And the parents are now suffering the agonies of the damned, wishing they'd taken the kid with them." Belle had been a parent once, a couple of hundred years ago. Never again. She had to deal with enough loss and grief as it was.

Genevieve had been her light and her pride, but like all Magekind children, she'd also been born mortal. The Majae's Council had ruled the girl wouldn't be able to withstand the Gift without going mad. Watching her die of old age had almost been more than Belle could take.

"Yeah, well, unfortunately, the family left Jimmy at home," Justice said. "They headed to Outback Steakhouse at 5:40 P.M. When they got back at 8:20, they found the den sprayed with blood splatter. Boy's body was sitting in an armchair with his Xbox controller in his lap. They found his head under the coffee table. Looked like he didn't even hear his killer walk up behind him. Sure as shit didn't put up a fight. He was just executed."

"Fuck." Tristan scrubbed a hand over his face.

"You haven't heard the worst of it yet. The weapon was obviously a sword, and the room stinks of magic." Justice eyed them, his face utterly expressionless. "Magekind magic."

Belle felt her jaw drop.

"Wait a minute." Tristan's eyes narrowed to green slits. "Are you suggesting one of *us* decapitated a seventeen-year-old boy? From behind?"

Justice didn't drop his hard gaze. "The evidence is pretty damned clear, Tristan."

"Fuck that," the knight spat. "We don't murder children, boy."

"Any of us with that kind of mental defect is discovered right after they turn," Belle said, laying a calming hand on

Tristan's tense shoulder. "We have to kill them on the spot. It could not have been one of us."

"You're assuming the killer is crazy," Justice said. "The family thinks this could be revenge for the attempted murder of Arthur's son a few months ago."

"You're suggesting *Arthur Pendragon* butchered that lad?" Tristan's voice dropped to a furious hiss Belle found more unnerving than a shout.

"That makes no sense." Belle shot a warning glance at her partner. Tristan's temper could be explosive, and they didn't need him to go off on the only ally they had. "Logan already killed the werewolves who tried to assassinate him." And prevented the deaths of three hundred humans in the process.

Logan's fellow cops had gathered at a funeral home to mourn the death of an officer murdered by the werewolves' hired assassin. "Those wolves strapped suicide vests on the human sheriff's grandchildren," Belle told Justice. "Everyone would have died if Logan hadn't disarmed the bombs."

Which he then used to blow up the werewolves. *Pissing off a Pendragon is never a good idea.*

"I'm aware of that," Justice said. "That's why I want you to check out the scene. I don't believe Arthur would kill a child either, but the family is pretty worked up."

"I don't bloody care," Tristan snapped. "Yes, Arthur has ordered deaths, but only terrorist leaders and military dictators. He's not going to murder an innocent boy to revenge himself on the Direkind. That's insane."

"But it's exactly the kind of thing Warlock would do," Belle said thoughtfully. "Especially if he's trying to trigger a war between the Direkind and the Magekind."

"Warlock?" Justice gave her a blank look. "Warlock's just a legend."

"Yeah, we've already heard that song and dance from every werewolf we've talked to," Tristan drawled. "Except your 'myth' damned near killed one of my best friends last month, so please believe us when we tell you he definitely exists. And he's a psychopath, so if anybody is butchering seventeen-year-olds, it's Warlock."

"But . . ." Justice stared at him, shaken out of his cool professionalism. "If Warlock really does exist, he's as big a hero to my people as Arthur is to yours. Why would he kill one of our boys?"

"Because he's a son of a bitch."

"Look, why don't you let us check the scene and see what we can find out?" Belle said. "If he's trying to frame Arthur, I can work a spell to prove it."

Justice took a deep breath and blew it out. "Fine. Come on then."

The scent of Belle Coeur was driving Tristan insane. Some of that cock-teasing smell was expensive perfume—probably French, knowing her. *Jasmine and moonbeams . . .*

And what romantic tripe was *that*? *Great. She's making me think in stupid poetry.* But it was hard to resist the scent of distilled sex, as female as the swing of her ass and the sway of her breasts.

Tristan had spent the past month trying to dig Belle and her scent out of his skull. There'd been the workouts with Arthur, both with blade and hand-to-hand, until his hair streamed sweat as his muscles cramped and shook.

"You're obsessed with that woman," Arthur had told him after listening to Tristan bitch about Belle one too many times. "She's worked her way under your skin all the way to the bone. Serves you right after all the women whose hearts you crushed."

So Tristan tried women as the cure. He banged every pretty young Maja he could seduce, the older ones being wise to his habits. Unfortunately, those green enough to be susceptible to his advances maddened him with their awed stares. He could say any rude thing he pleased, and all he'd get in return was a lip quiver that made him feel like a prick.

Belle didn't quiver her lip. Belle gave as good as she got, toe to toe and snarl for snarl.

And his mind was supposed to be on the murdered boy, not on Belle's admittedly luscious body. How did she do this to him? He never had trouble keeping his mind off the job. Distraction got you killed in this line of work. Worse, it could get innocents killed. Like Belle . . .

Jesu, look at all the werewolves.

Jarred out of his preoccupation, Tristan stopped dead in the center of the sidewalk, staring at the crowd gathered around the house at the end of the cul-de-sac. The brick colonial had a bigger yard than most of those on the block, with a long colonnaded porch, neatly trimmed holly hedges, and a yard shaded by a huge magnolia tree whose ghostly white blooms perfumed the night air.

The werewolves gathered under the magnolia's spreading limbs and clustered around the pickup trucks parked along the street. The smell of Dire Wolf magic rode the summer breeze, thick with the scent of fur and rage.

And beer. Coolers sat on the open truck gates, filled with cans nestled on piles of melting ice. *Just great. The werewolves are getting plowed.*

They were all still in human form, thank Merlin. The men were dressed for the weather in short-sleeved shirts and jeans or khakis, while most of the women wore sundresses or shorts. The females all clustered together on the porch, gathered around a woman who sobbed fitfully in utter despair.

The boy's mother, no doubt.

Every instinct Tristan had told him this was going to get nasty. For a split second, he considered asking Belle to conjure his armor and sword.

Then again, better not. The sight of an armored knight

would only light the tinder under the werewolves' rage. He simply couldn't afford to do that, even though it meant being seriously under-equipped if things went south.

So instead Tristan fell back a pace behind Belle, guarding her back as Justice led them up the walk toward the house. The big cop carried the shotgun at the ready, his black eyes moving in wary flicks. Evidently he didn't like the smell of the situation any more than Tristan did.

Sure enough, one of the werewolves stepped directly into the Wolf sheriff's path. "What the hell are you doing bringing *them* here, Justice?"

Tristan was instantly aware of being the focus of enough fury to light a bonfire. *Looks like we're about to be the guests of honor at a werewolf lynch mob.* Belle's voice rang out, cool and clear. "If one of the Magekind did kill that boy, I can work a spell to identify the source of the magic."

"Question is, will you tell us who it is—or will you cover it up?" another man shouted.

She turned and scanned every face in the yard. The Dire-kind was immune to magic, but Belle had another kind of power in her eyes, the kind that made even furious were-wolves remember she was a woman.

And decent men protected women.

"I swore to serve mankind when I became a witch," Belle said, her voice ringing calm and steady. "Anyone who would kill a child—especially from behind with a coward's stroke—deserves nothing but death. If it's one of the Mage-kind, I'll kill him myself."

"What if it's Arthur?" a hoarse voice shouted.

Tristan had heard more than enough of *that*. "Arthur Pendragon is no child-killing coward. And any man who says he is in my presence again had better be prepared to bleed!" The last word was a little too close to a battlefield roar, but damned if he'd back down.

Arthur might no longer be High King of Britain—he hated anyone calling him by that title—but he'd never be anything but king to Tristan. Even if Tristan would rather die than admit as much out loud. He'd certainly never say so to Arthur himself.

Silence fell, broken only by the crickets.

"Any more questions?" Tristan snapped.

Apparently the point had been made, because nobody said a damned word as the Wolf sheriff led the Magekind toward the house.

But as they climbed the steps to the porch, Tristan realized they had yet another gauntlet to run. The werewolf women glared at them, radiating an outrage that seemed to sting his skin like sparks raining from burning gunpowder.

One of them rose, the tracks of tears glistening on her cheeks in the moonlight. She wiped her eyes with a swipe of wadded Kleenex and managed a croak. "He was a good boy. Maybe his grades could have been better, maybe I had to ride him about doing his homework. But he cut the lawn every other Saturday without being asked."

It's the kid's mother, Tristan realized. *Just what we needed—a nice match to go with all this dynamite.*

Stopping for another swipe at her cheeks, she sniffled. "Somebody hit the neighbor's cat with a car last week, and he found it lying on the side of the road, all bloody and hurt. He took it to the vet himself and paid for it to be treated. He hates cats, but he said Bonnie—that's the neighbor's five-year-old—she loves that animal. And the cat made it because Jimmy took it to the vet." Sheridan's mother was crying so hard by this time, Tristan could barely understand her. "He didn't deserve this!"

"I know, ma'am." Belle reached out to lay a gentle hand on the woman's shoulder. "I'm so sorry this happened. We'll find out who's responsible."

The kid's mother gave them a look so pitiful, Tristan felt his chest ache. "That won't bring him back."

Belle dropped her hand. "No, I'm afraid it won't."

"Could you . . ." A sudden, horrible hope lit the woman's eyes. "They say you Magekind are really powerful. Could you bring him . . ."

"No," Belle interrupted, her voice catching. "If I could, please believe me, I would." She swallowed. "I had a daughter once. I know how . . . I'm sorry. Sorry for your loss."

Breaking off as if realizing she was on the verge of losing it completely, Belle whirled and headed for the house's front door. Justice pulled it open for her, and she started inside—only to recoil in the doorway.

Tristan realized why as the smell of blood rolled out in a choking wave. The boy's mother collapsed into her chair and began to sob. The women around her joined in, voices a rising wail that made Tristan wish he was any other damned place at all.

Helpless. He hated feeling helpless.

Belle straightened her shoulders and walked into the house, her head high, her spine erect. The two men followed. Justice closed the door behind them, muffling the wails and angry mutters.

In the foyer, Justice took the lead. Not that he had to. They could easily tell where the scene was from the bloody tracks on the polished wooden floor.

When they stepped into the small den, they saw it was every bit as bad as Tristan had known it would be. He was no stranger to the effects of a beheading, so he'd expected the blood spray. He'd expected the body, still sitting erect in the armchair, since the chair's cushions supported it.

What bothered him was the big screen television and the Xbox, which was still mindlessly running the kid's last video game. Two armored knights swung swords at each other, accompanied by the sound of ringing steel and cries of pain. "Christ."

"Yeah," Justice agreed. "But take a deep breath. Under the blood—isn't that the smell of a vampire?"

Tristan frowned at him, but dropped to one knee and took an obedient breath right behind the armchair, where the killer must have stood.

He expected some generic odor that Warlock had faked in an effort to trigger the war he wanted. Maybe even Arthur's scent, since Warlock hated the Magus with an insane jealousy.

But as he breathed in, Tristan recognized a scent he didn't expect. One he'd smelled just a few hours before.

Startled, he looked up at Belle, who was standing frozen at his side, her face pale as fine porcelain. "Merlin's cup, Belle—It's Davon Fredericks."

TWO

Belle stared at him in frozen horror. Her stomach rolled at the blood reek, and she tried not to breathe too deeply. "If that's your idea of a joke, Tristan . . ."

Hurt flashed across the knight's face, almost too fast to register. "I don't make that kind of joke."

"Wait." Justice gave Tristan a narrow stare. "You know this guy? You recognize his scent?"

"No way in hell did Davon Fredericks kill this boy. Christ, look at him!" Belle turned to gesture at the body. The game controller still rested in the teen's hands, though drying blood covered him so thickly, it was hard to make out the details. She had to swallow again, hard. "Davon would have had to be blood-mad, and I'd have noticed. Even if I'd missed it, Davon's been Magekind for two months now, and you can't hide something like that. He'd have killed somebody before now. Probably me."

Justice frowned. "What's blood-madness?"

"Merlin's Gift drives some Latents insane within minutes

of the spell being triggered," Belle explained. "They just can't handle exposure to the Mageverse."

"Does it always happen like that? Could it have come on later?"

She shook her head. "It's immediate. I suppose it's the same as what happens to your young werewolves when they burn. They just can't control the magic."

"I've been a Magus fifteen hundred years," Tristan added. "I've never seen it happen any other way. If your mind withstands the Gift, you don't lose control of it later."

Justice propped his hands on his hips and studied them, his head tilted in curiosity. "Actually, I'm not sure how the spell is triggered in you folks. With us, you get Merlin's Curse if you're born into a Direkind family or if a werewolf bites you. It's automatic."

"It's a different process with the Magekind." Belle had repeated this next bit so many times, she could recite it in her sleep. "Back fifteen hundred years ago, Merlin tested the knights and ladies of Camelot . . ."

The Wolf Sherriff nodded. "He tested our Saxon ancestors, too."

"Right. In our case, the winners drank from Merlin's Grail, and their DNA was altered by the magical potion the cup contained, transforming the men into vampires and the women into witches," she said. "But all of them were immortal. Though their children inherit the DNA containing the spell, the kids are mortal. We call them 'Latents.' A Latent only transforms if the spell is triggered when they have sex at least three times with one of the Magekind. Then they transform into vampires or witches, depending on their gender."

"Sounds a hell of a lot more pleasant than how we do it."

"Not if you go insane." Belle winced at a particularly nasty flash of memory. "A blood-mad vampire immediately tries to rip out the throat of the Maja who Gifted him. Since I'm the Maja who Gifted Davon, one of us wouldn't be here if he'd gone blood-mad."

"One of you? Are you implying you'd have . . ."

"Killed him? Oh, yes. I've killed sixteen blood-mad vampires."

The werewolf's eyes narrowed. "You make a habit out of killing men who sleep with you?"

"She's not a serial killer, dammit," Tristan snapped. "That's her job."

"It's your *job* to kill men who sleep with you?"

Tristan curled a lip. "Now you're just being an asshole."

"And if Tristan says you're an asshole . . ." Belle muttered. "Look, did you miss the part where they try to rip out my throat? I always make sure they're attempting to kill me before I . . . take action."

Justice eyed her, brows lifted. "You weigh, what? A hundred and twenty soaking wet? How the hell would *you* kill a vampire? Fry him with a spell?"

"Considering I'm usually on top of him at the time, no. I'm good with a knife. And none of this has a damned thing to do with the boy."

"Depends. You good with a sword, too?"

"Justice," Tristan growled, "you're beginning to piss me off."

The Wolf sheriff shot him a cool look. "I was a cop for ten years before I became a werewolf. I've made a career of pissing people off."

"Then you boys should get along fine." Belle rubbed the spot between her brows where a headache was taking root. "Justice, I've been the lead Maja court seducer for more than a thousand years. I've Gifted so many men, I have literally lost count."

He blinked. "A thousand years? You're a thousand years old?"

"We are immortals," Tristan said dryly. Unlike werewolves, who were as mortal as humans. Why Merlin set it up that way was anybody's guess.

"I was given this duty because I have a talent for determining whether a man is likely to go blood-mad," Belle continued, grappling for patience. "I've refused to Gift three hundred and twenty-three men the Majae's Council sent me to seduce, because I could tell they couldn't handle it. That's a damned crucial skill, because Majae have been murdered by insane vampires. Twenty-eight of them were my fellow court seducers."

"You have those stats memorized?"

"They tend to stick in my mind."

Justice examined her face with his cop's searching black gaze. "You take your job pretty damned seriously."

"Yes, as a matter of fact, I do."

"So you get paid to sleep with these guys?"

"If you take one more shot at her," Tristan growled, "I'm going to take a shot at *you*."

Belle felt her jaw drop. Tristan was usually the one to make the whore comments. She closed her mouth and said, "No, I don't get paid, any more than Tristan or Arthur do. First, Avalon isn't a cash-based economy. Second, I do what I do because it's my duty, and I'm good at it. If I quit, another Maja would have to take my place, and she might get herself killed. I'm already haunted by sixteen ghosts. I don't need any more."

Justice tilted his head and studied her. She wished he'd direct that piercing stare elsewhere. "Why do those guys haunt you if you were only defending yourself?"

"Because I should have realized they didn't have the strength to survive the Gift. If I'd left them the hell alone, they could have lived out their mortal lives. They were all decent men, and I drove them insane and killed them." She looked away, her hands curling into fists. "Now, could we drop this, please?"

A cold silence ticked by, broken only by soft female sobs and grumbling male voices from somewhere outside. Finally Justice said, "All this implies that if this Davon Fredericks killed Jimmy, he was in his right mind when he did it. That doesn't improve the situation."

"I don't believe it's him." Brooding, Belle studied what was left of the teen. "Maybe Warlock created a false scent. It wouldn't be that hard to do. I can think of a half dozen ways myself. If he got his hands on a sample of Davon's hair, for example . . ."

Justice shook his head, his mouth pulled into a hard line. "I don't understand why you're so convinced Warlock is involved. Assuming he even exists."

"Oh, he exists," Tristan said grimly.

"I fought him," Belle confirmed. "So did Smoke."

"Smoke?"

"Shape-shifting Sidhe warrior," Tristan said. "Damned near a god himself."

"Warlock used a spell to absorb the elemental who gives Smoke his power," Belle explained. "Smoke got him back, but the elemental still remembers what being in Warlock's mind was like."

Justice frowned. "Elemental? What's an elemental?"

"An alien energy being. This one uses Smoke as a host. Gives him a hell of a lot of power."

The cop huffed out a laugh. "You guys sound like an episode of *Star Trek*, you know that?"

Tristan glowered at him. "Bite me, furboy."

Justice bared his teeth. "Okay, but you're not going to like it."

"Down, boys," Belle told them. "Point is, Smoke knows Warlock pretty well after all that psychic contact, and he says Warlock is insane. *And* that Warlock hates Arthur and wants to destroy the Magekind so the Direkind can take our place. A war between us would serve that purpose nicely."

Especially since the Magekind would probably lose. Merlin had created the werewolves to destroy the Magekind if they became a threat to humanity. The Magekind had been unaware of Merlin's little insurance policy until a couple of years ago. The werewolves had managed to stay hidden until a group of alien demons forced them out into the open. They still weren't happy about being revealed to their magical rivals.

Justice shook his head. "But why would Merlin give Warlock so much power if he was that crazy?"

"Smoke says he wasn't insane in the beginning," Tristan explained. "But he's spent fifteen hundred years watching the Magekind, waiting for any sign that we're a threat to the human race. The job's made him paranoid."

Belle nodded. "Plus, he's convinced Arthur should take a more direct role in preventing wars and disasters. We just don't work that way, so he's decided to get rid of us and take over."

"Basically, he's become exactly what Merlin created you folks to prevent *us* from becoming," Tristan said. "He means to make himself a mystical dictator/god of the human race."

"Warlock thinks he'll create a utopia, but Smoke says all he'll really accomplish is a bloody Direkind war with humanity."

Justice stared at her. "That's completely insane. There are six billion humans and at most thirty thousand of us. The humans would wipe us out, no matter how many of them we bit and Cursed."

"Yeah." Belle shifted her feet, brooding. The red-soaked carpet squelched as she moved. "And in the meantime, the Magekind would be destroyed as a stabilizing force for humanity. We were all that got the planet through the Cold War. Without us around to make sure nobody triggers nuclear war . . ."

"Oh, fuck."

"Yeah," Tristan said. "That about sums it up."

He turned to Belle. "I just thought of something. What about the dimensional gate? Judging by the scent trail, whoever killed that boy did not come through the front door. They must have gated in."

"But not right into this room." Justice frowned thoughtfully at the boy's body. "Judging by what I felt when you arrived, a magical burst like that should have gotten the kid's attention, no matter how intent he was on his game."

"Would the boy have sensed him if he'd gated into the hallway instead?" Belle stepped back out into the foyer. The two men followed her.

"Maybe." Justice shrugged his broad shoulders. "Maybe not."

"So we'll see what I can detect." Belle closed her eyes and opened her senses, looking for the fading pulse of magic. An instant later, a faint glow lit up the darkness behind her lids. Turning in that direction, she opened her eyes and pointed. "There it is."

A ghostly golden oval hung in the air, gently pulsing.

Justice frowned. "I don't see anything. Don't sense anything either."

"You're not a Maja," Tristan told him.

"It's definitely there." Belle moved toward the gate's shimmering remnants, raising her hands to cast a spell designed to draw in the energy and determine its origins.

The identity of the caster leaped to her magical senses like a shout, so strong any Maja would have known at once who it was. She stared at the fading glimmer in shock.

It's got to be a frame. Warlock faked the magical signature somehow.

If she could just dissect it down to its component energy, she should be able to prove as much. Warlock's Dire Wolf magic operated on a different magical wavelength than the Magekind's.

Belle picked at the energy carefully, trying to unravel the fading pulse without destroying it completely, seeking the distinctive signature of werewolf magic. Sweat rolled down her spine as she struggled, and the headache that had been born during the argument began a full-fledged throbbing. Ignoring the pain, she manipulated the trace energy, looking for the proof of Warlock's involvement.

She didn't find it. There was no sign of his magic at all.

"Screw this." Belle dropped her hands in frustration. "There's a simpler way to clear this up."

"And that would be?" Justice leaned an elbow on the banister of the stairs that led to the second floor, his pose that of a man who'd been standing there for a while. His shotgun lay on the carpeted steps.

"We call the pair in here and question them. You can smell a lie, right? If you can't, Tristan can. They'll tell us what happened one way or the other."

"Belle, who cast the dimensional gate that brought the killer here?" Tristan asked quietly.

"Cherise Myers," Belle growled. "Davon's *partner*."

Davon turned away from the crowd heading back toward Joyous Gard, the dorm building the new recruits shared. He didn't have the patience to listen to laughter. He felt scalded, as if he'd been sprayed with a hydrochloric acid solution that was slowly eating through his skin.

If he heard one more chorus of "For He's a Jolly Good Fellow," he was going to start howling like one of the schizophrenics that wandered the streets of Chicago.

Damn, he wished he was back home, schizophrenics and all. Patching up gangbangers and their innocent bystanders would be better than this.

It had seemed like such a fabulous dream when Belle first appeared with her offer. He'd been in the middle of dictating notes on a case when she'd opened a gate into his private office at the hospital.

A beautiful blonde, stepping from a sparkling hole in the air right in front of his desk. Davon thought somebody had slipped something into his morning latte.

The story Belle had told was just as flatly unbelievable. She'd finally had to cast a spell on him to make him accept what she had to say.

Davon had known he was the descendant of slaves, but

he'd never have dreamed a Knight of the Round Table was also among his ancestors. It had been all he could do not to call his parents with the amazing news. Mary Fredericks was a teacher, while Davon's father, Jordan, was a cop. Being middle class at best, they hadn't had the money to send him to college. Davon got in by wrangling a a football scholarship, then worked two jobs and clawed his way to an academic scholarship that had paid for med school. Between studying and working, he'd put in so many all-nighters, he might as well have been a vampire.

Still, all that effort had paid off in the end. He'd made the dean's list and graduated with high honors. His parents had been almost incandescent with pride at his graduation.

Davon had loved the medical career he'd worked so hard for. The thought of giving it up had been wrenching, but this was an opportunity to take an active role in saving humankind from itself. He'd never be able to save so many lives as a doctor.

Besides, being immortal wouldn't exactly suck.

Belle had warned Davon he'd pay a personal cost if he became a Magus. He'd watch not only his parents, but his brother and sister, grow old and die, not to mention his nieces and nephews, their children, and their children's children in turn. All while he stayed the same apparent age he was now. He would lose all his friends, and he'd never be able to talk about his work to the mortals he knew and loved.

Knowing all that, Davon had still decided playing a role in the survival of the human race was worth the personal cost.

But he hadn't known that cost would be so high. This was only his second mission, and it had been the most horrifying experience of his life. Still, he'd done his duty. His ugly, bloody duty. Now the guilt was eating him alive.

God, I wish I'd said no. Being immortal no longer seemed like a blessing. Not if it meant he'd spend the rest of that very long life being haunted by the boy's ghost. No matter what the kid had done, he was still a kid.

Davon's gut insisted it was the Direkind who should have decided the young werewolf's fate. Not Arthur. And sure as hell not him.

The furious slap of high-heeled booted feet rang on the cobblestones behind him. Somebody was going to break her neck if she wasn't . . .

"Davon!" The woman's voice rang out, high and breathless with strain.

He looked around, frowning. "Cherise?"

Her lovely eyes were too wide, and her skin was far too pale. He reached out and took her hand as she ran to meet him. Her fingers felt fragile and icy. "Belle just called." Cherise panted. "She and Tristan are at that kid's house. They need us."

Davon's eyes widened, and a chill rolled over him. His hands tightened on hers. "Did we make a mistake? Oh, God, did we kill the wrong kid?"

She pulled free of him to glower. "No, dammit, it was the right kid. I checked with Arthur three times. He confirmed it. In fact, he was starting to get pissed at all my calls."

"Better we piss him off than kill an innocent." Davon frowned. It didn't speak well of Arthur that he'd gotten angry. "In my business—in medicine—we always double- and triple-checked that we had the right patient and we gave the right drug. I have no intention of killing anybody by mistake."

"*We didn't make a mistake, okay?* Now, come on!" Cherise gestured, conjuring a glowing point that grew into a dimensional gate.

Heart pounding, feeling sick, Davon followed her through the portal. And prayed she was right.

Belle's heart sank the moment she saw Davon step into the hallway from Cherise's dimensional gate. The young doctor's eyes looked haunted. And she had a horrible feeling she knew who was doing the haunting. "Merlin's Cup, Davon, what the hell did you do?"

Davon's chocolate skin went ashen and bloodless. "Oh, God, we did kill the wrong boy." Staggering to the stairs, he collapsed on the bottom step and covered his face with his hands.

"We checked with Arthur three times!" Cherise protested. Angry confusion rang in her voice, tinged with panic. "He confirmed we had the right house and the right kid! James Sheridan was the target."

"You saying *Arthur* told you to kill this kid?" Tristan stared in appalled disbelief. "What the fuck gave you that idea?"

"Arthur called us to his office," Davon said, his voice dull. He'd dropped his limp hands between his knees as he slumped on the steps. "He told us what Sheridan had done—how he murdered that child . . ."

"Wait—what?" Justice interrupted. "*What* child?"

Davon looked up at him. "Shaquilla Miller. Arthur said the boy raped and murdered Shaquilla Miller."

Justice straightened, glowering at him. "Jimmy had nothing to do with killing Shaquilla Miller."

"Who's Shaquilla Miller?" Belle asked, confused.

Justice gave her an impatient look. "Don't you guys get CNN? Shaquilla is a four-year-old girl who was found dead in the woods outside town. Wild animals had gotten to her body. It was a pretty horrific story."

"What the hell would that have to do with us?" When everyone looked at him, Tristan glowered. "Yeah, it's a horrible crime, but we're not cops. That's a matter for the mortal police."

If anything, Davon looked even sicker. "Arthur said the killer was a werewolf, which was why we had to act."

"Which would make it *his* job." Tristan jerked a thumb at

Justice. "It sure ain't yours. Dire Wolves handle justice for
their own crimes. The Magekind doesn't get involved at all."

"Not unless we're the victims," Belle added.

"Arthur said he'd told the werewolves, but they refused
to act." Cherise looked as sick as Davon now. "You mean
Arthur was wrong—that the boy didn't kill Shaquilla?"

"I mean whoever gave you the job, it wasn't Arthur." A
muscle rolled in Tristan's jaw as he ground his teeth. Belle
could hear the grit of molar on molar.

"Or maybe it was," Justice murmured.

Belle shot him an impatient glance. "We don't send green
recruits to kill people, Justice. Give us credit for intelligence
if not moral decency. The Round Table handles executions."

Justice met Tristan's gaze, his own narrow and intent.
"And if Arthur told you to kill that boy, would you have
done it?"

"Hell no, but he wouldn't have given the order to begin
with. It makes no sense."

"Unless he wanted revenge on us."

"I told you . . ." Tristan began hotly.

"But the boy didn't kill the little girl?" Davon asked. His
dark eyes glistened with rising tears. "I murdered an innocent?"

"You were used, kid," Tristan said, still glaring at Justice. "A werewolf sorcerer named Warlock wants to start a
war between the Magekind and the Direkind. He probably
cast some kind of spell to make you believe you were talking to Arthur."

"That's one theory," Justice drawled. "So you admit you
killed James Sheridan?"

"I wish I could say no, but we—" He broke off and
straightened his shoulders as he corrected himself. "No, *I*
did it. I . . . I cut Jimmy's head off."

Tristan stared at him, gaze hard and narrow. "Why did
you sneak up on that boy like a coward?"

Davon sighed. "Because I couldn't look him in the eye while I did it."

"But why?" Belle demanded. "I touched your mind, Davon. I'd have sworn that if Arthur himself ordered you to kill a kid, you'd have said no. No matter what Jimmy was supposed to have done."

Bewildered torment filled his glistening eyes. "Because I had to. And . . ." He frowned and added slowly, "I don't know why."

"Arthur gave you an order." Justice studied him, appraising, his nostrils flared as if he drank in the vampire's scent. Seeking the stench of a lie. "And you couldn't refuse Arthur Pendragon."

"Because Arthur's infallible," Belle suggested, playing a hunch.

"No, he's human just like anyone else," Davon said automatically. "Just because he's immortal, that doesn't mean he doesn't make mistakes."

"He could have been mistaken about the boy being a killer," Belle pressed.

"Well, yes."

Tristan followed her lead. "So why did you *have* to do it?"

"I . . ." Davon frowned. "I don't know. I didn't want to. It was like a compulsion."

"It wasn't like a compulsion," Belle corrected him grimly. "It *was* a compulsion."

"*No*. Arthur was the one who gave the order." Cherise's blue eyes went hard, something feral in their depths. Something a little alien. "It wasn't this Warlock casting some kind of spell on us. It *was* Arthur. I've met Arthur. I'd have known."

"Cherise, Warlock is a powerful sorcerer. He could have altered your memories, made you believe anything he—"

"No," Cherise snarled, her voice rising in agitation. "*It was Arthur!* He told me to make sure Davon killed the murdering bastard. He said the Direkind had to pay . . ."

Involuntarily, Belle glanced at Tristan. He returned the look with a grim head shake and turned to Justice. "Don't tell me you can't see what happened to these kids."

"It wasn't Warlock!" Cherise's voice spiraled.

Davon stared at her in shock. "Cherise, what the hell is wrong with you? What's this about the Direkind having to pay? He didn't say anything like that."

"He *did*, Davon. I know what I know."

"She's under a spell, kid," Tristan said, a note of gruff kindness in his voice. "You both are. Warlock's trying to . . ."

"Where is he?" The door crashed open as the werewolf charged inside, transforming as he moved, his body shooting up and up until he was over seven feet tall. Fur rushed over his twisting arms and legs like a tide, his face lengthening into a wolf muzzle, curving white teeth filling his mouth, ears shifting into triangular points on the top of his skull. "I know the bastard's here!" His voice grew louder until it thundered, deafening in the narrow hallway. "I know that scent—it's the son of a bitch who murdered my brother!"

"Shit," Justice growled. "It's Steve Sheridan, the kid's brother." Light flared with a burst of magic as he transformed.

More werewolves filled the door behind Sheridan, changing as they followed him inside. Claws clicked on the wooden floor, and voices rose in a rolling rumble of rage.

"You're going to die, you fucker!" The Dire Wolf charged Davon, fanged jaws open wide.

The doctor lifted his chin, as if inviting Sheridan to rip out his throat.

THREE

"Belle!" Tristan stepped in front of Davon. Knowing what he wanted, Belle sent a stream of magic whirling toward him, transporting his sword, shield, and armor from the Mageverse. Weaponry glittered into being around his big body as he braced to meet the werewolf.

But as he raised his blade, Cherise lunged into the werewolf's path, dressed in nothing more protective than jeans and a T-shirt. "Leave him alone!" A sword materialized in her hand, and she swung it right at Stephen's lupine head.

"Cherise!" Belle shouted. "Armor up, dammit!" Too late.

"Bitch!" Steve ducked her swing, popped up again, and sank his fangs into her arm.

Blue light exploded around his teeth as they crunched down. Cherise screamed in startled pain, and the werewolf jerked away as if he'd been shocked.

Tristan hit him hard across the muzzle with the flat of his blade. Steve yelped and ducked backward, helped along by a hard shove from the knight's shield. "Calm the fuck down! Davon isn't responsible!"

Behind him, Cherise collapsed, a hand clamped over her arm as she writhed in agony. "Oh, Chriiiisst!"

"Get up, Cherise!" Belle yelled, stepping over her to swing her conjured shield into another werewolf's. face. The big creature jumped back, snarling. "Get clear!"

But the girl only twisted helplessly on the floor, shrieking as if unable to do anything else.

Davon raced over to scoop his partner into his arms and carry her away from the knot of fighters. He lowered her to the floor at the rear of the hall and knelt beside her to check her pulse and examine the bite, his hands quick and skillful.

Now in werewolf form, Justice stepped between Belle and Tristan, looking big as a grizzly as he snarled at the crowd. An armed grizzly: he pointed the shotgun at the invaders and racked the weapon with a menacing clatter. "This is a crime scene. Get the hell out."

"It's my house!" A graying werewolf shouldered to the front of the furry mob. "And they killed my boy!"

"I don't care if it's Buckingham Palace," Justice roared back. "You're not going to lynch this man without a trial. Not on my watch."

As the sheriff distracted the werewolves, Belle opened a magical connection to Tristan's consciousness. *"We need to get out of here before we get overwhelmed."*

"Tell me something I don't know." His thoughts held a distinct snarl. *"We'll be lucky if we don't end up Kibbles 'n Bits."*

More werewolves were transforming, voices deepening from human yells to rumbling roars.

Belle whirled and cast a dimensional gate. The magic bloomed from her fingers, swelling into a rippling hole in the air. At the sight of it, the werewolves roared louder.

"They're getting away!" someone howled.

I certainly hope so, Belle thought, and turned to gesture

at the doctor and his patient. "Davon, get her through that gate. *Now!*"

He swept the blonde into his arms and cleared the distance to the portal in one vampire bound. The superhuman leap jolted her wound, and Cherise screamed in pain as they vanished through the gate.

Werewolves flooded the hallway, either already transformed or in the process of turning. "Don't let the bastards escape!"

Tristan stepped forward. "You're not killing my people," he snarled, blade pointed squarely at the muzzle of the nearest werewolf, who towered over him by more than a foot. "Back the hell off, Furboy."

Belle grabbed Justice by the arm and tried to shove him toward the gate. "You next!"

"I'm Wolf sheriff. I stay with my people. Get out of here, witch, and for God's sake, take Tristan with you before somebody dies."

She gritted her teeth in frustration and spun toward Tristan. He was swinging his sword in showy, threatening arcs. It was working. The werewolves hung back, reluctant to charge a Knight of the Round Table.

"Tristan!" Belle shouted. "Come on!"

Without taking his eyes off the werewolves, he backed toward her. She caught him by the shoulder and pulled him through the gate. Magic rolled over their skin with a welcome foaming tingle.

The moment they were clear, she let the portal collapse. It snapped closed on the werewolves' howls of rage.

Justice pointed his shotgun at the Sheridan kid, who snarled. Only a head shot would kill a werewolf, but a less mortal blast wouldn't exactly feel good. "That's enough. I won't tell you again. *Get the hell out of my crime scene.*"

"That bastard killed my brother." The kid lifted his lips to reveal an impressive set of teeth. "And you just let him go!"

Justice bared his own teeth as he stared the kid in the eyes, willing him to look away. "You don't know that."

"I know what I smell—it was him. That fucking vampire cut off Jimmy's head."

"Maybe. Tristan and Belle say there's something more going on, and I think they could be right. One way or another, I'm going to find out. If the murderer is Magekind, I'll arrest him and let the Council of Clans decide his guilt. But if somebody else did the killing, they're not going to use me to frame an innocent man."

"It's Arthur!" a voice shouted from the crowd. "Arthur sent them to kill Jimmy to get revenge for his son."

"Maybe, or maybe not. But I *will* find out. And whoever's responsible is going to pay."

"That," Tristan said as the gate collapsed, "was a little too fucking close."

Belle frowned at the last dying pulse of the interdimensional portal. "They weren't just pissed about Jimmy's murder. Someone's been working on those werewolves, to turn them against us. And I'll bet I know *which* someone it is."

Tristan shook his head. "I don't get this game Warlock's playing. He—"

"Belle!" Davon said. "Look at this!"

She jerked around at his urgent tone. Given Cherise's injuries, she'd transported them all directly into Belle's bedroom. Davon had put his partner down on the canopied bed, where the girl now twisted in helpless pain, clutching her bleeding arm. "Jesus." The Maja gasped. "It's burning me alive! It feels like acid . . . Oh, hell." Belle hurried over to the bed.

Davon sat by his partner's side, an expression of deep worry on his handsome face. "This bite—I've never seen anything like it. And I was an ER doc for four years."

"Let me see." Belle reached for Cherise, but the girl curled tighter around the injured arm.

"Let her see it, Cherise," Davon said, his voice deep, soothing, as he gently took her arm and stretched it out. He had a hell of a bedside manner. It was almost a shame he'd left medicine.

Then Belle got a good look at the bite, and every other thought vanished from her head. A set of deep punctures marked the woman's arm in a V, sparks of magic leaping around the ragged holes. "Jesus, Mary, and all the saints," she breathed. "What the hell is that?" Conjuring a basin of hot water, Belle went to work rinsing the blood away so she could get a better look. Her magical senses told her the bite had penetrated all the way to bone, shattering Cherise's forearm.

But what chilled Belle was the blue glowing lines that snaked up the length of the Maja's arm, following the tracks of her veins, as if carrying some lethal spell throughout her body.

"It hurts, Belle," Cherise gritted. "God, it's all I can do not to scream." Her eyes shone with a feverish glitter, and sweat streamed down her face and matted her blond hair.

"Call Morgana," Belle snapped over her shoulder at Tristan. "Have her bring a healer."

"She's going into shock," Davon murmured, both hands cradling Cherise's arm to support the broken bone. "Her pulse is thready—and the way that magic is following her veins is scaring the hell out of me. Whatever you're going to do, do it now."

"Please!" Cherise gasped.

"Calm, child." Belle closed her eyes, gathered her magic, and sent mystical energy flooding the punctures—only to slam right into a wall of magic so viciously cold, it seared her mind like an arctic blast.

Whatever this was, it wasn't just a bite. It was devouring Cherise like magical acid. Belle could feel the Maja's life force weakening as the spell ate away at bone, muscle, and blood. Gritting her teeth, Belle poured more power into the girl. Cherise cried out in pain.

But it wasn't working.

I don't care if you're hunting the grassy knoll shooter," Tristan growled over Morgana's protests. "Get your ass over here." He shoved the enchanted iPhone in his pocket and turned toward the bed.

Davon clamped his hands around the girl's wounded arm, blood running over his dark fingers as magic popped and flickered over the Maja's skin. Belle sat beside him, her hands tracing magical patterns in the air.

Tristan stared at them, helplessness grinding at him. Belle sat as if carved from ivory, delicate and rigid, her face bloodless in the blue light leaping around the bite. Her eyes were wide, staring intently downward as her hands moved in the intricate patterns of spell-casting. Cherise was no longer conscious, though he couldn't tell whether that was the bite or Belle's doing.

Davon looked up at him, dark eyes lost and helpless. "It's killing her, Tristan. Cherise was bitten trying to protect me, and it's killing her."

Tristan offered the only comfort he could. "Morgana and the healer are coming. They'll save her life if anyone can."

He sensed the flare of magic from an opening dimensional gate in the hall. Morgana swept through the door a moment later, tall and carnivorously beautiful in a gown of black velvet that made her pale skin seem to glow. Black hair fell to her hips in long swirls of ebony. The healer followed, a strawberry blonde in a T-shirt and jeans, radiating power like a searchlight.

"Move aside, Magus," Morgana told Davon. "You can moon at your witch when we've saved her."

Davon backed reluctantly away to join Tristan at the other end of the room. "I'm a doctor. I should be able to help."

"This is magic, Davon. Witch business." Tristan frowned. The healer, Morgana, and Belle joined hands and began to chant.

"What?" Davon asked, reading his expression.

"That's not good. Usually Majae just will the magic to do whatever the hell they want it to. Any time they start making an extra effort, something's wrong."

The lines of blue light were winding up the girl's arm now, and the bite itself blazed, just short of blinding.

Davon's big hands clenched into fists. "If it reaches her heart . . ." He didn't have to say the rest.

Tristan eyed the young vampire. Normally, he kept his nose out of other agents' lives, but this time he figured a little advice was warranted. A little damned *late*, true, but still. "It's not a good idea to become lovers with your partner, Davon."

"How did you . . ." He broke off. "It's that obvious?"

"It's a natural temptation." Tristan decided it was best to ignore the implied question. "Mutual hunger, adrenaline rush . . ."

"Guilt," Davon muttered.

"But it makes things messy. The heart follows the body's lead—or maybe one of you doesn't feel anything while the other goes nuts, so you're just fucked all around. I've found it best to do my rutting elsewhere."

Davon eyed him. "Rutting?"

Tristan shrugged. "It is what it is."

"It wasn't rutting with us." The doctor's expression turned stark with pain. "It may not have been very professional, but we both felt . . . something. Maybe not love, not so soon, but *something*."

Something strong enough to make Cherise dive between Davon and seven feet of pissed-off werewolf. Now he was

going to have to deal with the fallout from her self-sacrifice.
Which, in Tristan's experience, was pretty much the way it
went. Nothing could suck quite like love.

Tristan's mind brushed the acid memory of Isolde's
betrayal and quickly shoved the thought away.

The chanting broke off. The healer cried out in wordless
protest. Morgana cursed and Belle muttered something
guttural in French, as Cherise's slender body bowed against
the mattress. She gasped out a strangled cry of pain that
trailed into a wet rattle. Blue light flared.

The young witch collapsed, boneless, limbs sprawled,
her empty eyes staring blindly at the embroidered canopy.

"Cherise?" Davon whispered it, the sound raw with disbelief and pain.

"Oh, hell," Tristan said wearily.

Warlock moved around the bar, his orange eyes appraising its drunken patrons. His claws clicked on the uneven,
peanut shell–littered floor, but nobody heard them over the
death metal howling from the sound system.

He had cast an invisibility spell on himself, a necessity
given that he was eight feet tall, with the head of a wolf,
thick white fur, and long black claws that contrasted with
his even longer teeth. If the customers had gotten one look
at him, you'd have heard the screams clear to Texas.

Dave's Beer Shack was a long, low building located on a
frontage road off I-85. The lighting was provided by a few
dim bulbs and neon beer signs. The bar, like the tables, was
a slab of uneven wood scarred by knife gouges and sticky
with spilled beer. A couple of Harley-Davidson posters hung
on the walls in dusty black frames, and the waitress wore
Daisy Dukes she could barely zip.

As Warlock watched, somebody passed somebody a
twenty and got a Baggie containing what looked like dirty

rock candy. A sweaty man with a jailhouse build—all chest and arms, not much in the way of leg muscle—flashed a knife and roared with laughter as the waitress flinched. Pool balls clacked from a table somewhere off to the left, and somebody cursed with a distinct lack of creativity.

The werewolf lowered his invisible head and sniffed delicately at a brawny man's hands. Fresh blood. A lot of it, splattering his arms and the legs of his jeans. He'd done a half-assed job washing it away, as if he didn't give a shit if anyone noticed it.

Warlock tilted his furry white head. Careless bastard.

A poker game was in process at the next table. He padded around the foursome, eyeing the cards. A man with a tear tattooed on his cheekbone lazed back in his seat, his face expressionless despite the aces in his hand. He was six-four or so, more lean than bulky. Warlock suspected he'd be faster on his feet than most foes would expect. His shoulder-length hair was tobacco brown with streaks of gray at the temples, and his black eyes were cold and alert. When he spread his hand on the table, the others cursed as he raked in his winnings.

"Jesus, Dice, you've got the luck of fuckin' Satan, you know that?" one wiry, hard-eyed opponent said and threw himself back in his chair with a huff of disgust.

Wayne "Dice" Warner laughed in a rusty rumble. "But you keep right on playing with me, you dumb bastard."

"I may be dumb, but at least I'm *persistent*."

The four laughed as Warlock studied Dice's leather jacket. "Demon Brotherhood" was scrawled over the back in scuffed red lettering.

According to his sources, the Demon Brotherhood wasn't one of the larger biker gangs—not like the Outlaw Disciples—but its fifteen members had a vicious reputation. Murder, arson, rape, armed robbery, dealing drugs and guns—name it and the Brotherhood was said to have done it and gotten away clean. They were even rumored to have killed a Highway Patrol trooper, which was why every cop on the Eastern Seaboard was gunning for them.

And Dice was their leader. Warlock had heard interesting things about Dice over the past month. The biker might well be perfect for his purposes, once Warlock established who was in control.

He'd kill the waitress first, he decided. Female that she was, she was no good to him, but her shrieks should unnerve the cowardly. The bartender would go next—he was too fat and too old for Warlock's purposes.

Then he'd see.

There were fifteen of the bikers. Warlock always limited his team of Bastards to twelve, like Arthur's twelve Knights of the Round Table. But these men weren't going to become his Bastards, as he'd originally planned before getting a good look at Dice. In fact, the more of them he had, the stronger the spell would be.

The waitress jumped and giggled as a male hand pinched her ass. Warlock recognized his moment.

She turned right into the werewolf's lunge as he dropped his invisibility spell and let them all get the full effect of his teeth ripping out the little bitch's throat.

It made one hell of a view. Warlock's hands were big enough to engulf her whole head, and his claws were the length of the girl's fingers. The waitress didn't have a prayer.

Her dying screech was suitably shrill and nicely bubbling. He picked her up and dumped her bleeding carcass in the middle of the poker game, then vaulted the bar to deal with the bartender.

He got to the man just before the bartender could bring up the sawed-off, knocked the weapon up, and bit off the bartender's head. He spat it out like the tip of a cigar, and it rolled across the bar: *bump bump bump.*

Now there was a conversation stopper.

Warlock threw up a spell shield in time to block Dice's

nine-mil blast. One of the other bikers screamed, the sound thin and high. No nerve in that one.

He bounced back over the bar and took the first bite out of a biker who didn't scramble away quite fast enough. Magic sizzled through his jaws into the man's arm, and Warlock cuffed him hard across the face, tumbling him ass over heels. That would keep him down while the Curse took hold.

Wheeling, the werewolf took a judicious bite out of someone's shoulder, then clubbed the biker behind the ear. He fell as Warlock sought his next victim.

You had to be careful with the bite, he'd found over the years. Merlin's Curse could heal some pretty impressive injuries, but not if the target bled out too fast. And in this case, he needed them to survive as long as possible.

Generally Warlock liked to restrict himself to one bite per customer, though he did enjoy the sensation of his teeth ripping human flesh. He just loved the look in their eyes, the utter panic of staring Death in the face. It made him feel like a god.

Which he basically was, since feasting on Zephyr's intoxicating power.

One. Bite. Each.

He was particularly careful when he did Dice, sinking his fangs almost tenderly in the biker's hand before knocking the human cold.

In the aftermath of Cherise's death, Belle, Tristan, Arthur, and the others gathered in the Round Table chamber, falling into hunched poses of weariness in the carved oak chairs.

The room had a twenty-foot ceiling and, like its centerpiece, was circular. A massive chandelier hung over the table, its countless iridescent crystals shaped like swords. Gorgeous tapestries covered the walls, depicting knights and their ladies fair, unicorns romancing virgins and dragons trying to eat them. Though the hangings were hundreds of years old, the magical thread was so brilliant with shimmering color, each tapestry looked new.

But the Round Table dominated the room. The surface of the gleaming slab of oak was carved with images of Arthur and his original knights gathered around Merlin, the boy sorcerer, and his beautiful mate, Nimue. Twenty-four seats surrounded the table, enough for the twelve knights and their chosen ladies.

Davon sat slumped in one of the massive oak chairs, looking like the survivor of a plane crash. Stunned, disoriented, utterly overwhelmed.

Belle felt little better as she sat beside Tristan, who occupied the chair that bore his name.

Arthur paced around the room like a lion in a cage. For all his heroic reputation, he was not a big man, though his body was brawny and capable. He wore his dark hair curling around his shoulders, and a neat beard framed his angry mouth. His black eyes snapped as he glowered at Davon. "You say *I* sent you to kill that boy?"

"Yes, sir." The doctor spoke in a monotone. It was painfully obvious he didn't care if Arthur killed him on the spot in a fit of royal rage. Maybe Davon even hoped he would. "You told us Jimmy Sheridan had murdered a four-year-old girl and that the werewolves knew as much but weren't doing anything about it. So we had to stop the kid from killing again."

"It wasn't me." Arthur's hand flexed on Excalibur's hilt. He wore the magical blade hanging from a scabbard belted around his narrow blue-jeaned hips. Its jeweled magnificence clashed with the blue T-shirt that stretched across his powerful chest, emblazoned with a Superman logo.

Arthur was an unrepentant geek.

"I know that—now," Davon said, not looking up from the hands he'd knotted together between his knees. "But it seemed so real to us then. Cherise believed it, too."

"But it makes no sense!" Arthur snapped. "None of it. I

wouldn't have gotten involved in a criminal matter, particularly not one that was werewolf business."

"Cherise and Davon didn't know that," Tristan pointed out quietly. "They had no idea how the Round Table works, and they certainly didn't know you."

"Which was no doubt why Warlock chose them," Guinevere said as she sat next to her husband's seat at the table, as blond and delicate as he was dark and burly. Her level gaze was cool with intelligence. She'd always been the balance for Arthur's fiery temper.

"We were the perfect patsies," Davon said bitterly. "And now an innocent boy is dead, Cherise is dead, and I'm a murderer."

"Davon . . ." Belle began, her heart breaking for him.

Before she could say anything else, a young woman walked into the council room, a cat riding her shoulders. She was delicately pretty in a short blue-jean skirt and a pink tank top, her dark hair tumbling in thick curls around her shoulders.

The cat balanced on her shoulder was a gleaming blue-black, with silver striping his forelegs and haunches. His eyes burned an intense blue. "Is this the one?" His voice was deep, resonant, startling coming from such a small body.

Davon looked up, surprised, as the cat leaped down from the woman's shoulder to land lightly in his lap. Rearing, the little beast planted his forepaws in the center of Davon's chest.

Blue eyes met brown in a fierce stare. "Do you want us to discover proof of what was done to you?"

Davon blinked at him in astonishment. "You're not a cat."

"Well, not *just* a cat," Smoke said, in a massive understatement.

The doctor sighed, tired defeat in his voice. "Whatever you can do would be appreciated. Knowing I killed that boy . . ."

Smoke pressed a delicate forepaw against Davon's cheek

to draw his defeated gaze. "I believe we can help you. I know Warlock better than anyone. If he used magic on you, I should be able to detect it." He'd been held a psychic prisoner in Warlock's mind for more than a week.

Davon stared back at him, a flicker of hope ghosting through his eyes. "Do it. Please."

The cat extended his neck until he was nose to nose with the vampire. His eyes blazed a bright, shimmering blue.

The girl who'd come in with him stepped up behind the doctor and put her hands on his temples.

As Eva Roman touched Davon, a pair of ghostly antlers spread to either side of her head—the outward manifestation of her union with the soul of an elemental named Zephyr. A creature of pure magic, he'd inhabited the body of a white stag until Warlock had murdered him and drained his magic. The elemental's ghost had sought out Eva as the vehicle of his revenge, giving her his knowledge of magic in exchange for her help.

Magic flared in the room as the two went to work. Belle felt it rush over her skin like the brush of electric feathers, tingling and delicate. Her gaze met Tristan's, and she was suddenly, intensely aware of him, of his powerful body and sensual power. Sometimes the nimbus of somebody else's magic hit Belle like that, bringing her to an intense erotic awareness. Her nipples tingled, drew into hard points.

Oh, hell.

Tristan smiled slowly, as if he sensed her arousal, and she thought she glimpsed a flash of fang.

Belle swallowed hard, realizing he was as turned on as she was.

This is a very bad idea. The voice of rationality spoke from the back of Belle's mind. You didn't get involved with your partner. Too many things could go wrong, as Davon had just discovered.

True, it was rare to lose a partner to death, but the Magekind were just as vulnerable to stupid anger and pointless jealousy as mortals were.

And yet, Tristan's green eyes stared into hers with hypnotic sensuality. Belle forced herself to look away. *I don't even like him half the time.*

Yes, he was courageous and intelligent, and Merlin knew he was gorgeous, with those broad shoulders and that lean swordsman's build. But he could also be a raging jackass. Worst of all, half the time he acted as though he considered her the Whore of Avalon.

Belle could forgive anything but that.

The magic died. She looked around just as Smoke hopped out of Davon's lap and into the chair next to him. Power starburst around him like a mini Fourth of July. When the light faded, a tall, muscular man sprawled where the cat had been. Blue-black hair fell sleek and shining around his shoulders, marked with slashing horizontal silver stripes that echoed the cat's fur. His ears formed elegant Sidhe points, and his eyes were the same intense blue as they'd been in cat form.

Eva sank down beside the big man, and he reached out, capturing her hand in an absent gesture. Belle watched their fingers curl together and felt her own heart ache. She'd had so many lovers, yet she'd never known that kind of tenderness. She was beginning to believe she never would.

"His mind has definitely been interfered with." Smoke flicked a lock of hair behind one pointed ear. "The false memories are detailed—a little too detailed, more so than his other memories from the same period. But there's no doubt he believed those memories. He killed the boy because he thought it was his duty, but it caused him great pain. He suffers now because of it."

"Can you prove Warlock created the false memories?" Arthur asked.

"Now, that's a bit tricky," Smoke admitted. "The wizard

did a very good job of covering his tracks. If we could get the Direkind to believe he exists, we could probably convince them that he did this, but the evidence he left in Davon's mind wouldn't be enough."

"They're going to demand that we hand Davon over," Tristan said grimly. "They'll want to try him before their Council of Clans."

"I'll have to plead guilty," Davon said, his voice heavy with defeat. "I murdered that kid, no matter what my reasons were. The werewolves want justice, and I have a responsibility to give it to them."

"Forget that," Arthur said roughly. "You did what you thought was your duty. I won't allow the Direkind to execute you because their lunatic wizard is trying to start a war. You're as much a victim as Cherise and Jimmy Sheridan."

"But what if they do declare war?" Davon stared at him, dark eyes tormented. "I don't want anyone else to die because of me."

"Look, kid, I'm not giving you up to the Direkind, period. You believed you were following my orders." Arthur demanded loyalty, but he also gave it right back.

"We need to warn the other young Magekind about this." Morgana leaned back in her seat, frowning as she tapped a long nail on the table's gleaming surface. "We don't want any more of them falling into this trap."

"I'm not sure we can prevent it." Smoke steepled his fingers and touched them to his lips. "Warlock's spells are damned powerful, now that he's absorbed Zephyr's abilities."

"The first thing we need to do is stop sending agents from Avalon." Arthur's black eyes narrowed. "He's not snatching the kids through the city wards, is he?"

"He didn't get past *my* wards," Morgana told him flatly. "I would have known." The city's most powerful witches had worked for days to cast the magical shield that surrounded Avalon, and Morgana maintained an intense magical awareness of it.

Gwen tapped a pen on the table, frowning thoughtfully. "We need to reinforce the wards anyway, just to be safe."

Morgana grunted assent. "I'll summon the others and we'll start work tomorrow night." Sunlight interfered with magic, so major sorcery could not be worked during the day.

"In the meantime, we shouldn't assume the older Mage-kind will be immune to Warlock's spells." Smoke absently traced a glowing pattern in the air like a man doodling on a sheet of paper.

Morgana straightened. "Do you think he'd be able to overwhelm even the most powerful Majae?"

"We have to assume he can," Belle told her. "Cherise wasn't a weak witch, and he definitely warped her thinking. She said the Direkind 'deserved to suffer.' That's not the kind of thing she'd think on her own."

Tristan drew a dagger from his boot and absently tested its edge with his thumb. "He's probably going to make another attempt to frame us for crimes against the Direkind."

"That's going to be a problem, because the Direkind seem to automatically disbelieve anything we say," Belle added. "And since Merlin created them to destroy us if we ever went rogue . . ."

". . . We're fucked," Tristan finished grimly.

"I sincerely hope not," Arthur said dryly. "Either way, we've got to figure out how to keep any more of our people from falling prey to Warlock." He toyed absently with Excalibur's hilt, frowning as he considered the problem. "While still doing our jobs. We can't protect humanity from behind Avalon's wards, tempting as it might be to pull our heads in for a while."

"Double the size of the teams," Tristan suggested. "Warlock might be able to bespell two people, but four would be harder to handle."

Morgana nodded. "If nothing else, one of the Maja should be able to gate back and warn us."

Arthur considered the idea. "That works. It may give us

manpower issues and fuck up existing missions, but it can't be helped. We cannot afford to give that bastard an opening to use any more of our people like this. I'd rather avoid a war with the Direkind."

"Especially if we'd lose," Tristan muttered.

FOUR

Warlock clicked through the puddle of blood, watching the surviving bikers writhe in pain. He'd relieved the Demon Brotherhood of an impressive collection of weapons— everything from box cutters to an Uzi, stashed everywhere from boot-tops to shoulder holsters. He'd even found a garrote in Dice's jacket pocket. He'd put the weapons on the bar, then methodically kicked the ass of anyone who seemed to even think about going after the pile.

Between the magical pyrotechnics and all eight fanged and furry feet of Warlock, the bikers had been too damned intimidated and exhausted to try anything. Though Dice had given it serious thought, according to the magical link Warlock had formed with the biker's mind.

Now that the point had been made, it was time to go. A flick of the wizard's clawed hands opened a dimensional gate wide enough for the entire crowd. A second gesture swept them all up and blew them through the opening like autumn leaves in a windstorm.

Humming softly, Warlock sauntered after them into the cavern that was his mountain sanctuary.

The network of caves he called home inhabited the heart of one of the Appalachian mountains, deep in western North Carolina. He'd transported his victims into the cavern that served as his workshop.

He'd used his magic to dig niches in the stone walls marching from the cavern floor to its ceiling. They were filled with countless books, the magical tomes he'd both written and collected over fifteen centuries. There were jars, too, filled with the herbs and potions he used in his spells. A long worktable occupied the one wall empty of niches, its wooden surface scarred in places from Warlock's claws and blades. A few burns and stains showed where potions had spilled or spells had backfired.

The center of the room was dominated by an immense inlaid silver spell circle. He'd chalked the ancient sigils of his latest spell creation around the circle that morning, while he'd done the preliminary work.

Now he immobilized fourteen of the bikers on the floor, arranging them carefully inside the circle like the spokes of a wheel, their heads at its hub, heels just inside the silver ring.

He hung Dice in midair over his companions' heads, supported by a glowing framework of magic in the exact center of the circle.

"What . . ." The man gasped, blinking down at him, half blind with pain. "What are you doing to us?" Warlock had been forced to get quite firm with him, breaking several ribs and giving him a nasty little concussion. But under the circumstances, he'd have been disappointed if Dice hadn't fought.

"Solving a problem that has been bothering me for some time."

"What kind of . . . problem?" Not that Dice cared. Warlock

knew he was just trying to distract himself so he wouldn't give his captor the satisfaction of screaming in agony.

He really was perfect.

"I had originally intended to recruit you and your men as my new Bastards, since the last team was killed by my enemies. But it occurred to me that you'd fail just as they did, especially going up against the Knights of the Round Table. I needed a new plan." He gestured at the spell circle around them. "And this is it. Werewolf magic, combined with the elemental's sorcery to create a new kind of warrior."

"Knights of the . . . ?" Dice peered at him, bleary with pain and the bite's magic. "What the flying fuck are you talking about?"

"Patience, my son. Soon the pain will be gone, and you will see what a gift I'm about to give you."

"I ain't your son." Anger gave his voice strength. "What 'gift'?"

"Power." Warlock threw his clawed hands wide, sending magic dancing in the air around him. "More power than you can imagine. Enough to kill my enemies and help me fulfill my destiny."

Dice curled his lip in a sneer, though he looked a little white around the eyes. "I ain't gonna help you do shit."

There was admirable defiance, and then there was insubordination. "Now, that was not an acceptable remark." Warlock flicked his claws, and Dice screamed as pain ripped him like buzz saw teeth.

The wizard jerked the pain higher with another claw flick, then higher still. Finally Dice's will bent to his. It took a gratifyingly long time.

"Sorry!" the biker wheezed at last. "'M sorry."

Warlock smiled. "That's better. Mind your tongue and show proper obedience, and we'll get along fine."

Then he got to work.

* * *

When Tristan strode out of the High Council building, he spotted Belle heading home, her shoulders rounded and her steps weary. Something about her pose sent a painful little twinge through his chest.

She was worrying about Davon, and he couldn't blame her. The young doctor was obviously on the edge of doing something stupid.

Tristan set off after her. He knew he should go home, but the thought of his empty house held no appeal. Not compared to exchanging quips with his partner, who was damned good at it. He lengthened his stride until they were walking side by side.

"There's going to be trouble with the Direkind." Belle frowned at the toes of her boots without looking up at him.

"Well, Davon did kill that kid," Tristan said, purely to get a rise out of her. He hated to see her looking so defeated.

He was rewarded with an angry flash of her blue-gray eyes. "He thought he was doing his duty. Anyway, they already got their pound of flesh. Cherise is dead."

"But they're going to want Davon."

"They're not getting him. If they want justice, they need to execute Warlock. There's the bastard who deserves to die."

"If we could prove he exists."

Belle tilted her head back and studied the stars. "The key is that werewolf girl, Warlock's daughter, Miranda. If we could get her in front of that council of theirs, have her do some magic and testify to her father's existence, they'd be more likely to listen."

Tristan's eyes narrowed as he considered the suggestion. "That might work—if we could find her. Finding her is the problem."

Belle sighed. "And right now, we've got more than enough problems to go around."

* * *

Belle's house was two charming stories of gray stone and arched stained-glass windows. Stone was a popular building material in the Mageverse, since it held up to the centuries better than anything else. The stained glass protected any vampire guests against the sun, and was damned pretty to boot.

A blooming riot of flowers surrounded the cottage: red roses climbing trellises, pink and white azalea bushes, pansies in multihued beds, cherry trees and magnolias. Their scents filled the air, so rich to Tristan's vampire senses he could almost taste them on his tongue.

He followed her through the arched wooden door and through the foyer beyond, boots clicking on the red-ceramic tiled floor. As they stepped into the kitchen, his gaze lingered on Belle's delicate back and the sweet curve of her ass. Suddenly he was intensely aware of her, the grace of her walk, the rich female scent of her hair wafting in her wake.

"Want a drink?" She strode to the fridge, a top-of-the-line stainless-steel appliance which stood among the black granite countertops. Belle was serious about her cooking. "Because I've got to tell you, I need one after today."

"Sure. Got any ideas how we can find Miranda?"

She was silent a moment as she got a beer out of the refrigerator, then pulled a second bottle from a cabinet. As she poured a stream of deep red liquid into a crystal goblet, magic sparkled and glowed around the stream. The complex spell preserved the blood and kept it from clotting.

Majae needed to donate blood as desperately as Magi needed to drink it. There could be unpleasant health effects for both otherwise. Vampires would starve without the magic in a witch's blood, while Majae could suffer strokes from a failure to donate regularly. Most single witches like Belle bottled their blood and handed it out to whoever needed it.

"Here you go. Enjoy." She passed him the glass, corked the bottle, and put it away again.

"Thank you. It's been a little too long." He sipped, forcing himself to go slowly. The taste of her hit his tongue in a fizzing explosion of magical heat. Her eyes met his, and hunger rolled through his body like a lightning strike.

Belle caught her breath. Hastily turning her back, she headed into the den beyond. He had the distinct feeling she was running from him.

So, being a predator, he chased her in a slow, deliberate stalk, the glass of her blood cradled in his fingers.

Warlock paced around the circle, dressed for war in gleaming enchanted armor, the great double-headed magical axe he called Kingslayer in one big hand.

He could feel the Curse building in the bikers' bodies, its magic blazing from cell to cell, preparing for their transformation. He could see it swirling, cold and blue, as they shook and groaned in its searing teeth, filling the air with the smell of pain, sweat and ozone.

He'd been working on the spell for the past week. First there'd been the potion he'd brewed and drunk two days ago, a gut-burning concoction that had left him writhing in pain all yesterday.

But even as it had tortured him, the potion had altered both his saliva and the magic of Merlin's Curse.

Normally, anyone he bit would become a Direwolf, both immune to magic and unable to cast spells. And useless for his purposes.

The potion he'd brewed with Zephyr's stolen abilities was strong enough to change that, if only for a few precious hours. He'd never have been able to restructure Merlin's magic without the elemental's vast power and even greater knowledge.

Now he needed to work the second half of the spell, the

really delicate part. One mistake would blow Warlock, the bikers, and half the Appalachian mountain range straight to hell.

He began to chant, his voice weaving a new spell as Merlin's Curse built in the bikers, altering their brains, their bodies, their very DNA.

The men's moans and whimpers became screams as the power built faster and faster until their bodies began to glow.

Warlock barely heard their cries, his total attention on his chant. Each word built a lattice of power around Dice that would guide the energies of the bikers' change.

As always when involved in a Great Work, the werewolf's mind fell into a crystalline clarity where nothing existed except his purpose. There was no room for fear, anticipation, or even the driving whip of ambition that flogged him the rest of the time. There was only the magic.

One by one, the bikers' bodies vanished in the blinding glow of the spell.

Dice, who'd been utterly silent, began to scream. His voice cut off abruptly as his own transformation raced up his body, the glow sweeping from his feet toward his head in the space of a heartbeat.

Recognizing his moment, Warlock roared the last words of the chant, seizing the magic from the transforming bikers to send it spinning up the conduits of the spell lattice.

Right into Dice.

The human's glow became a blazing conflagration, so bright Warlock could see nothing but white.

At last the wizard fell silent, his throat aching savagely from the chant, a migraine pounding between his ears from the raw effort of casting the spell. Exhaustion weighed his body as the light vanished, leaving the cavern in darkness.

Utterly drained, Warlock dropped to his knees. The thud of his big body hitting the stone sounded loud in the sudden stillness. It would be hours before he'd be able to work magic again.

He blinked until his stunned eyes began to recover. Dark though the cavern was, his acute night vision picked out the outline of something massive that had appeared in the center of the cavern.

The huge, hunched thing that had once been Wayne "Dice" Warner lay limp in the center of the spell circle.

The other bikers were gone.

It wasn't the first time Belle had served her blood to a vampire guest. She'd done it at the party that very evening. But she'd never felt so intensely aware of the sensual intimacy of the act.

Maybe it was the way Tristan looked at her as he drank, as if he wished he were taking it from her throat as they lay naked in each other's arms.

Well, he was a guy, after all. Tristan might be an immortal Knight of the Round Table, but he was still most definitely male.

She sank down on the sectional couch and sipped her beer. She could have used something with a little more kick, but getting buzzed with Tristan giving her that erotic stare struck her as a very bad idea.

As he proved when he sat down next to her on the sectional. She thought about pointing out just how many other seats were available on the two L-shaped couches, but decided not to bother. He wouldn't move—and she really didn't want him to.

"So, Miranda." Tristan took another slow, sensual sip, closing his eyes as if savoring the taste. The faint smile on his face sent another little erotic buzz zapping through her body. "How are we going to find her? Justice said she'd disappeared."

Belle frowned, distracted from the heat swirling around them. "Do you think Warlock got her?"

He shrugged in a lift of those deliciously broad shoulders.

"It's possible. Justice said her parents were murdered and her house burned. Could be Warlock's work. But then again, she could have gotten away and gone into hiding. We need to talk to Justice and see what we can find out."

"Tomorrow night," Belle said. "It's getting a little late. The sun's almost up." Tristan would enter the Daysleep as it rose, whether he liked it or not.

"Yeah." He took another slow sip as if he had all the time in the world.

"Shouldn't you be heading home?"

"Trying to get rid of me?"

"Considering you'll be passing out in about twenty minutes, you need to find your own bed."

"Guess I do." Deliberately, he drained the glass of its last drop and rose.

Relieved, Belle escorted him to the door. "I'll talk to Justice in the afternoon, see what I can find out about Miranda. Maybe I'll be able to cast a tracking spell."

Tristan met her gaze, his own suddenly all business. "Don't go after her until I can join you. You don't want to run into Warlock by yourself."

"Not really, no." When he just stared at her, she sighed. "I'll wait for you, Tristan."

"See that you do." With that, he strode off into the pre-dawn gleam.

Tristan's house was a sprawling one-story building in the Arts and Crafts style, all beige stone and dark wood. Square wooden columns with stone bases supported the roof of a wide porch that wrapped around the front of the house.

The decor was just as aggressively masculine. The furniture was downright massive, tending toward big leather and wood pieces set off by wrought iron light fixtures and dark hardwood floors. Gwen had designed the house for him back in the nineteenth century after she'd convinced him that his Tudor-era monstrosity was on the verge of falling down around his ears.

Thing is, the house was just too damned big for one occupant, and it had a tendency to echo, especially on the rare occasions he was both home and occupying his bed alone.

Now, as he waited in his king-sized bed for the sun to rise, Tristan stared at the slowly brightening stained-glass window above his bed, remembering the vivid taste of Belle. *It was just blood*, he told himself. *I drink it all the time.*

Majae blood always had a kick, a delicious fizz of magic and vitality unlike anything he'd ever tasted in his mortal days. Every Maja's blood was just slightly different, in subtle, delightful ways.

But Belle's was more intense. More erotic.

More.

It seemed to burst on his tongue, distilled feminine sensuality, sizzling magic, and that lush something that was pure Belle.

He knew he must have tasted her before. Probably several times, considering that Majae often bottled their blood as gifts, donated it to the Lord's Club, or served it to guests. For God's sake, he'd known her for a thousand years.

But not really. Yes, he'd run into her at parties and served on the High Council with her, but there'd always been others around. And she'd been a court seducer, a job which had both kept her busy and encouraged him to keep his distance.

Besides, she'd always reminded him a little too much of Isolde, another beautiful blonde who'd been adored by every man who met her. He'd assumed Belle would have Isolde's darker edges, too.

So he'd steered clear. Until last month, when Morgana had forced him to accept Belle as a partner, after Belle had suddenly acquired an inexplicable need to work field missions.

He'd quickly realized she was far more dangerous than Isolde, magic notwithstanding. Yes, she had the same bright and flashing charm, but she also had a strength and intelligence Isolde had never possessed.

He really should have anticipated that. Belle was, after all, a Maja, while Isolde had failed Merlin's tests.

Isolde had also been a the traitor who'd left his soul in bleeding desolation.

Tris was coming to want Belle every bit as much as he'd ever wanted Isolde. Remembering the look in her eyes as she realized how the taste of her affected him was enough to get him hard all over again.

"It's not a good idea to become lovers with your partner," he'd told Davon. And it wasn't.

But he didn't always follow his own advice.

He was planning Belle's seduction when sunrise stole his consciousness.

The creature that had been Dice Warren snarled, sounding like a chainsaw in the confines of the cavern.

Warlock circled him warily. Dice was huge, easily the size of an Indian elephant. The wizard had been forced to gate them both into the largest cavern in the cave network for this little exercise. He wanted to give his monster room to learn who was dominant.

Warlock was looking forward to this. He hadn't had a really good fight since the battle with Smoke and his little werewolf whore.

Nothing made him feel as alive as spilling the blood of something that could kill him.

Dice could definitely do the job. The beast looked like a cross between a wolf and a tiger, with a long muzzle and triangular, upright ears. Yet his body was catlike, with thick, powerful legs that were proportionately shorter than a wolf's. Each of his forepaws was the size of Warlock's head, while his retractable claws were the length of daggers. His fur was long and bushy like a wolf's, in a shade of rich, dark sable that contrasted with the yellow glow of his eyes. He was both beautiful and terrifying.

Now all Warlock had to do was tame him.

"What have you done to me, you bastard?" Dice's voice sounded deep, growling. He also had an incongruous lisp, since he hadn't yet learned to speak through his carnivore's fangs.

Warlock gave him a taunting smile. "I've made you my perfect weapon."

Yellow eyes narrowed. "You made me a monster. And I'm going to rip you apart."

Warlock smirked and gestured. A snaking length of blue light appeared in his hand, spilling to the ground to curl around his clawed feet like the lash of a whip. "Come on then, boy. Try for me."

"I ain't a boy." Black lips lifted off white teeth. "I ain't even a man." And he charged.

Fortunately, he wasn't used to his massive body, and inexperience made Dice slow and awkward. Warlock stepped aside like a matador teasing a bull. A flick of his wrist sent the spell whip flashing out to bite into Dice's shoulder. The creature yelped in startled pain.

Dice wheeled and struck out with a clawed forepaw. If he'd connected, he would have ripped Warlock's head off his shoulders.

The wizard was too fast and experienced for that. Ducking, he sent his whip licking out to curl around Dice's foreleg. This time the creature's cry of pain was more howl of rage. He spun toward Warlock and gathered himself, narrow yellow eyes watching his enemy with feral intensity. Yet he held back, watching for an opening.

Warlock studied him with approval. He was beginning to think. He'd be deadly once he got used to his huge body and started using the advantages it offered.

But first he had to be broken.

"You are slow," Warlock growled, cracking the light lash

to send up an explosion of sparks. "You are clumsy and ignorant. You can't take me. You can barely keep from tripping over your own big feet."

"Fuck. You!" Dice exploded toward him in a furious blur of fangs, claws, and massive muscle. Big paws flashed out.

Warlock spun aside and flicked the whip to cut across Dice's unprotected belly. The beast roared and leaped.

Warlock dove clear, narrowly avoiding being crushed under the monster's weight. As he hit the cavern floor, the werewolf spun, flicking the whip to flay the length of Dice's ribs.

"Fucker!" In his fury and pain, Dice opened his fanged jaws wide and roared.

A torrent of flame boiled from his jaws and poured over Warlock like a blast from a blowtorch.

FIVE

"*You put me* in one hell of a position, you know that?" William Justice growled.

Instead of replying to that opening shot, Belle gave him a sunny smile and lifted the two venti Starbucks cups she held. "How do you like your coffee?"

"Black," he muttered. "Like my disposition."

"No wonder you and Tristan get along." She handed over one cup and kept the other. A quick spell doctored her coffee to her tastes: two sugars and a cream.

"My brother wolves want your vampire's head on a pike," Justice told her, taking a sip of the coffee.

"Instead they got the witch's."

"What?" He glowered at her, suspicious.

"Steve Sheridan's bite killed Cherise."

Justice lowered the coffee and frowned at her. "How? He didn't do that much damage."

"Apparently Direkind bites are poisonous to the Mage-kind. She died despite all our efforts to save her. We're having the funeral later this week."

"I'm . . . sorry." He looked taken aback. "We had no idea. I don't think any of us has ever bitten one of you."

"It was a shock to us, too." She studied the fire-blasted yard that stretched before them. Yellow crime scene tape meandered between trees and bushes, swaying in the light breeze as it surrounded the burned-out husk of what had once been a sprawling mansion.

Now all that was left was the brick fingers of a couple of fireplaces and a few partially tumbled walls. Jagged studs stood here and there, broken and burned black. The ground was covered in soaked piles of ash and debris—tumbled bricks, burned insulation, chunks of wallboard, and bits of blackened metal.

Belle sniffed. Charred wood, seared plastic, the chemical stench of God knew what. And something else, something like a cross between ozone and fur.

Watching her, Justice took a breath too. "Smells like magic."

"Not Magekind," she told him, frowning. "More like Miranda Drake. Tristan and I met her just the other day, and she had that scent."

Justice nodded. "At Joan Devon's Grieving. I heard all about that from the ladies. Most of them said it was 'tacky' of you and the knight to show up to such a private moment. Especially as one of your people killed the man Joan was grieving for."

Belle snorted. "I didn't get the impression Joan was doing much grieving. Which might be because the son of a bitch deserved it, since he died trying to blow up two kids and three hundred cops."

"Good point, but the ladies didn't see it that way. The general opinion is that whatever crimes Gerald Drake committed, he was driven to by grief over the death of his son."

Belle lifted a brow. "His son, the serial killer?"

"That's the one." Justice took another sip of his coffee and meditated on the taste. "I'd have taken Trey Drake's head myself if Arthur's son hadn't beat me to it. We still don't know how many women Drake killed and ate."

She shook her head. "I don't get those people at all. The Sheridans I understand. Jimmy's dead, he was an innocent, and they want revenge. But the Chosen . . ."

"Our aristocracy has never been the sanest bunch around. And they can rationalize the bloodiest fucking crimes you'd ever want to see, most of them against their own wives and daughters. What's more, the women just seem to accept it, as if it's the way things are supposed to be."

"Assholes," Belle growled, and stepped over the police tape. She was picking up a lot of power coming from a point in the middle of the ruins. Setting her feet carefully, she started picking her way through piles of ash.

"Yeah, but they're powerful assholes," Justice called, watching her. "And they'll turn this thing around and hang it on you guys before you can blink."

"What, this fire?" She glanced over her shoulder at him. "We had nothing to do with it."

"Since when has fact had anything to do with a juicy rumor?" He cradled his cup and leaned back on one leg, a pose that made his broad shoulders look even broader. "Especially when there are five Chosen aristocrats willing to swear you and Tristan were about to kidnap poor Joelle's daughter right in front of them."

"Miranda wanted to go with us, Justice. That's not kidnapping."

"The way they look at it, Miranda Drake had a duty to obey her parents, so she had no right to go with you. Which, to them, would make it kidnapping."

Belle grunted at him, concentrating on her footing in the treacherous remains of the house.

"Then an hour later, the Drake house burns to the ground," he continued. "Doesn't look good. Especially given that firefighters found Joelle's body in the ashes with a broken neck."

"Well, we sure as hell didn't break it," Belle snapped.

"So find me some evidence."

"Will anybody believe it if I do?"

"Probably not, but it will satisfy my curiosity."

Belle's magical instincts whispered, and she bent to dig carefully through the debris at her feet. When she stood, she held a fragment of a book. Most of the thing had burned away, but the left lower corner remained. Delicately, she fanned it open, casting a quick spell to keep the seared paper from crumbling to ash.

"What the hell is that?" Justice crunched across the ruins to join her.

"A magical gold mine." She grinned at him. "Miranda Drake's spell book."

It was very quiet in the cavern, especially after the howls and screams, the roar of flame and electric crack of the lash.

Dice lay in the darkness, trying not to whimper as he bled from countless slices from the whip.

Warlock stood watching him. There wasn't a mark on the bastard, though Dice had tried to fry him, slice him open, even bite his head off. The wizard had conjured energy shields to protect himself from the magical attacks, danced around the physical ones, and basically run Dice into the ground.

Exhausted, weakened from blood loss, Dice had finally collapsed after more than an hour of vicious combat.

"Are you done?"

Panting with pain and exhaustion, Dice opened his eyes and found the werewolf standing right in front of his nose. He considered breathing fire at his foe again, but he just didn't have the power. He'd drained himself dry.

He considered lunging forward to take a nice big bite, but he was too exhausted to move.

Worst of all, he found he couldn't meet Warlock's orange

gaze. He tried, but each time his eyes brushed the wizard's, he felt the impact of Warlock's will like the blow of a hammer.

"Are you done, dog?" The wizard asked the question again, the words soft, menacing.

"Fuck you," he growled, even as his eyes skated away from Warlock's.

The whip licked out, slicing across his sensitive muzzle and tearing a gasp of pain from his lips.

"Watch your tongue," the sorcerer hissed, "or I'll rip it out of your mouth." Warlock lifted the whip as if to strike. "I asked you a question. Are you done, dog?"

"I'm done." The words escaped him despite his determination not to say them.

Dice knew with a sinking heart that he spoke the truth. He could no longer fight. He no longer wanted to. Warlock would only hurt him worse and humiliate him more.

The sorcerer smiled.

Miranda Drake flipped off the lights and locked the restaurant's back door, the keys producing a cheerful jangle as she turned the dead bolt. It had been a good night for tips, and she smiled, thinking of the sexy pair of red boots she had her eye on at the mall. She'd been saving for weeks to afford those boots.

A hand hit flesh in a hard slap, and a woman's voice yelped. Miranda's head snapped up as she spun around.

Two figures struggled in a pool of light cast by the parking lot safety light. A wiry male figure gripped a woman's thin shoulders as he jerked her onto her toes and shook her hard. Her hair flew around her face, and she yelled again.

His roar sliced through her cry like a razor. *"I said give me the money, Hannah!"*

Hannah Davis was Miranda's fellow waitress at Flo's, a timid young woman with two children and a tendency to come to work spotted with bruises. "Eddie, Carey's shoes have holes in the—"

The crack of fist hitting flesh came louder this time. That was no slap. That was a punch, the kind that left bruises and fractured bone behind. Hannah cried out, her voice choked with pain. "Eddie! Stop it, let me go!"

Memory flooded Miranda's mouth with bile.

She skittered back, calling her magic as she retreated from her stepfather's snapping werewolf jaws. Her transformation raced over her body in a wave of fur, muscle, and bone contorting like soft clay in the grip of her power.

"You dare change?" As she met Gerald Drake's frenzied gaze, Miranda realized he'd lost control completely. And he intended to kill her. "You dare fight me? You dare?"

But Miranda was tired of cowering from these bastards. "Oh, I dare," she spat. "And if I get the chance to talk to Belle again, I'm going to tell her everything."

"Then I'll have to see you don't get the chance, you traitorous bitch!" He drew back a clawed hand as if to rip out her throat.

Joelle threw herself between her daughter and the blow. "Ger—"

His claws ripped into her face before she could get the rest of the word out of her mouth. She flew sideways, her body slamming into the base of the stairs with a crash. Something snapped.

The sound seemed to echo in Miranda's skull. "Mother!" Forgetting her father, she leaped to her mother's side, landing beside her in a coiling crouch.

Joelle's head lay at an impossible angle, the life draining from her eyes.

Miranda started across the gravel parking lot before she even knew what she was going to do, her strides long and angry as she headed for the struggling couple.

"Eddie . . ." Hannah gasped.

"Enough!" Miranda snarled, her hands curling into claws. She felt the prick of them on her palms, a warning that she was far too close to transforming. She struggled for self-control; it wouldn't do to change in front of humans.

Eddie Gibson shot her a glower over his shoulder. "Mind your own damned business, bitch!" He had a meth addict's bad skin and missing teeth, his long, thinning hair pulled into a stringy dishwater blond ponytail. "This is between me and my—"

He didn't get the last word out of his mouth before Miranda's magic jerked him off his feet.

"What?" Hannah sank back, staring with helplessly wide eyes as her boyfriend kicked and wheezed in the grip of Miranda's power. "Miranda, how . . . ? *What are you doing?*"

"Stopping *him*. For once. He's been beating you since I came to work here. You think I haven't noticed the bruises?" Miranda sucked in a deep breath, fighting the blinding rush of rage. She'd spent years at the mercy of a man just like Eddie. How many times had Gerald hit her, raked her open, threatened her mother to keep her in line?

After Gerald murdered Joelle, he'd come after Miranda, and she'd killed him. It had been self-defense—barely. Eddie Gibson was cut from the same cloth. Another abusive bastard who beat someone smaller and weaker, simply because he could.

So Miranda was going to teach the little creep how it felt to be on the receiving end.

There was a glitter in Belle's blue-gray eyes that completely infuriated Tristan. Primarily because she seemed utterly unaware of how much it turned him on.

Somewhere in the ruins of the werewolves' burned-out house, Belle had found the charred remains of Miranda's spell book. It was only the left lower corner, and only a couple of the badly burned pages had readable words. But it wasn't the spells Belle was interested in. She had plenty of magic of her own, and more spells at her fingertips than that poor werewolf girl would ever know.

No, the power of the spell book was that Miranda had once concentrated on it fiercely, using it as the focus of her words and her power. Which meant Belle could use it to find *her*, whether she'd been taken or had simply vanished on her own.

Which still wouldn't make it easy. Belle was taking the project very seriously, so much so she was using the permanent magic circle in the basement of her house—an inlaid silver design comprised of interlocking Celtic runes.

The circle lay in the exact center of the room's slate floor. The surrounding stone walls were lined with floor-to-ceiling shelves that held rows of mysterious jars and bottles filled with Merlin knew what. Other shelves were tightly packed with ancient books of spells written in languages that had been dead for centuries. There were magical objects, too: crystals, statues of stone or bronze or silver, blades of every kind, all of them humming softly with power.

Belle had dressed for spell work, in a loose, comfortable white gown that really had no business being as sexy as it was. It draped over the full swell of her breasts in a way that made Tristan's mouth water. If he concentrated, he could see the shadows of her nipples through the worn lace. It was cool in the lab, and both little peaks stood at proud attention against the fabric.

Her feet were bare and pink, and the gown's short sleeves revealed long, elegant arms. It had a simple scoop bodice with pretensions of innocence its cleavage missed by a mile.

Tristan all but drooled.

She'd lit candles around the perimeter of the design, slim white tapers that cast dancing yellow light over the otherwise dark room. Incense burned, sending up coils of cool blue smoke smelling of sandalwood and lavender.

Morgana had told him once that the candles and incense,

even the design itself, did not have true magical properties. But the process of entering the Celtic circle, lighting the candles, and smelling the incense acted to focus the mind into a trance state that intensified a witch's connection to the Mageverse.

Meanwhile it gave Tristan a hard-on.

He watched her, breath caught. Belle sat with her skirts in a white cotton pool around her long, slender legs. Her hair shimmered with highlights and mysterious shadows, blond and silver, gold and umber, and shades of sable, curling around her slim shoulders. Her long hands seemed to float over the seared pages of the book, slow as seaweed in an ocean current. Graceful fingers drew patterns in the air, and sparks of magic trailed them, gold shading into white.

Her eyes looked dark and endless, until sparks of power lit them bright gray-blue, like lightning flashes in the clouds. The candlelight painted soft shadows over her lovely face, tracing her angled cheekbones, full, seductive lips parted in gentle breaths, the straight line of her nose, the round little thrust of her chin.

If he concentrated, he could hear her heartbeat, trance-slowed to a steady thump. He remembered the taste of her blood, burning magic on his tongue, and it drove his pulse into a leaping bound. His cock lengthened in his jeans, pressing hard against his fly. He thought about tumbling her down in her spell circle, tasting her throat in the candlelight, thrusting deep between her legs as the incense wove blue patterns in the darkness.

Tristan wanted to take her so badly, his balls ached like a sore tooth.

"Randi, you're gonna hurt him!" Hannah licked her lips, her frightened gaze lingering on the distance between her boyfriend's feet and the pavement. "Please let him go!"

"Bastard needs to be hurt." Miranda didn't look away from Eddie's darkening face and rolling eyes as she dangled him well off the ground. "He's a snake, Hannah, and you know it."

"No, he's not really that bad. Randi, please!"

Miranda ground her teeth, caught between the pleading in the other woman's eyes and her own outrage. Hannah reminded her far too much of her mother. Joelle had let Warlock and Gerald Drake terrorize her for years. Miranda hadn't dared attempt escape for fear of what they'd do to her mother.

But Eddie wasn't Gerald. And Hannah wasn't Miranda.

With a snarl of disgust, Randi tossed the meth addict like a ball of trash. He hit the graveled parking lot in a yelping tumble of elbows and knees.

Hannah started to run toward him, but Miranda grabbed her arm. "No." She sent a curl of magic out to catch the human's thoughts and met the woman's gaze. "Do you want to leave him, Hannah?" Longing flashed in the woman's bruised eyes, there and gone so fast Miranda might have thought she imagined it. Luckily she knew better. "You do, don't you?"

"Eddie said he'd kill my babies," Hannah admitted in a voice low with defeat. "I can't go."

Little hostages. The same way Gerald and Warlock had used Miranda's mother. "He's not going to do a damned thing to your children, Hannah. I'm not going to let him." With a flick of her magic, she snapped the chains of fear that Eddie's fists and feet had forged in his victim's brain. "You go on home now. You take care of your boys."

Hannah wrung her hands. "But what if he . . . ?"

"He won't. You let me take care of Eddie."

Her hands twisted harder at one another, expressing her anxiety and ambivalence. "You're not going to kill him, are you?"

"Do you really care?" The woman opened her mouth, and Miranda sighed. "No. No, I'm not going to kill him."

"Hannah!" Eddie yelled, staggering to his feet, his jeans ripped from impact with sharp bits of gravel, his knees bleeding. "Don't leave me with her! She's some kind of witch!"

Miranda flicked a hand and he froze, locked in the grip of her magic. "Go on, Hannah." She put just enough will behind the command to make the waitress head for her beat-up blue Cutlass Supreme. Another thought struck her, and she called out. "Hannah?"

The woman froze and looked back at her, eyes wide, face pale.

"You won't remember this tomorrow," Miranda gestured, weaving another quick spell. "All you'll remember is that Eddie decided to leave, and he's not coming back."

"He's not coming back." With a dreamy, relieved sigh, Hannah got into the car and started it. She threw the Cutlass into gear and peeled out of the lot.

Leaving Miranda with Eddie.

Feeling her teeth lengthening into fangs, she sauntered toward her captive, menace in every step. A knife materialized in her palm, raining blue sparks. Eddie stared at it, his mouth forming an O of terror. His body twitched as he tried to escape, but her spell held him fast.

"How does it feel, you bastard?" Miranda whispered the words, soft and acid. "Being helpless. Being at somebody's mercy. Knowing they could kill you if they want. *I* could kill you—and I do want."

His fear smelled acrid as piss. *"What the hell are you?"*

"I'm exactly what you think I am. A witch. And I'm not human." Miranda grabbed Eddie by his T-shirt collar and jerked him close as she flashed her fangs in his face. "And you don't want to piss me off by talking about what you saw tonight. Do you?"

"No! I won't say nothin'!"

"And you certainly don't want to piss me off by bothering Hannah again. She's under my protection now, and I wouldn't like it if you came around her or her kids again. You don't want to do that, do you?"

"Okay! Okay, I'll stay away from her. I swear it! Just don't hurt me!"

"And you won't tell anybody about what I can do. Not that anyone would believe you if you did." Miranda let magic ignite her eyes with an eerie shimmer. "Hell, they'd probably think you're stoned. But you're not." She jerked him closer and pressed the knife against his throat until the sharp steel bit into flesh. A bead of blood welled and ran down his bobbing Adam's apple. "So you'd better run, Eddie. You'd better run and keep running. *Never come back.*"

When she let him go, he did exactly that, stumbling across the parking lot to dive into his Ford pickup. He started it with a roar and sped out, gravel flying from his spinning wheels.

Miranda watched him go, wondering why she felt so damned ashamed of herself. As if she wasn't any better than the man she'd just so thoroughly terrorized.

Maybe she wasn't.

Wearily, Miranda's fingers found the choker around her neck. Magic buzzed around it, generating a shield that should keep her father from sensing what she'd just done.

If Warlock detected her magic, he'd be on her like a cat on a mouse. She'd pay for protecting Hannah with her own life. Miranda had known that was a risk when she'd crossed the parking lot, but she'd also known she had to take that chance. Doing nothing while another woman suffered would have made her no better than Eddie.

Now at least Hannah and her kids would sleep safely tonight.

Even if Miranda didn't.

* * *

How the hell was Belle supposed to concentrate with Tristan staring at her like a cat at a birdbath?

He was sitting tailor-fashion, wearing jeans in a shade of indigo verging on black. A forest green shirt was tucked into the jeans, cinched by a belt tooled with intricate Celtic patterns, its buckle engraved silver. Soft black boots shod his big feet. His sword lay on the floor before his knees, gleaming unsheathed in case he should need to defend her while she was entranced. He'd bound his blond hair into a long tail, the severe style emphasizing the strong lines of his handsome face. His green eyes glittered in the candlelight.

And she was supposed to be finding the little witch werewolf, not ogling Tristan. No wonder she'd been working for two hours now with no luck at all. She couldn't concentrate.

Forcing her attention away from him, Belle focused her will on the charred fragment of the spell book, trying to use it to locate its creator. Despite its badly burned condition, the magic that clung to it was strong; Miranda had a great deal of power. Belle had known that from their brief encounter last month before Miranda's frightened mother dragged the girl away.

As Belle focused her will on the book, she sensed a definite pull.

That's it. I've got her!

Miranda crawled into bed and flopped over on her back. She knew she was going to have a hell of a time relaxing after her clash with Eddie.

A leaden depression lay over her like a fog, clinging and cold, and she didn't know why. After all, she'd made it possible for Hannah and her children to escape an abusive bastard who regularly beat her and threatened her kids. In the process, Miranda had struck a blow against Warlock and all the others who thought women were weak and inferior. She should feel a sense of satisfaction.

But she'd also terrorized Eddie Gibson and used her magic to alter both Hannah's mind and his. It didn't matter that she'd had good intentions. She'd still misused her power just as her father misused his. Was she any better than Warlock if she used the same methods? Was she just an abuser, striking out against those weaker simply because she could? She . . .

Magic.

Miranda froze in terror as the power brushed featherlight against her consciousness, touching her like a questing hand.

Warlock. Her father had found her!

Driven by pure panic, Miranda reached into the Mageverse and dragged in every bit of power she could, then blasted it at the source of the magical probe.

Die, you fucker.

"Arrgh!" Belle's blond head snapped back as if someone had punched her in the face. She flew out of the circle, banged into the shelves lining the opposite wall and collapsed in a heap of gold curls and white silk.

"Belle! Dammit!" Tristan leaped to his feet, charged across the circle, and dropped to one knee beside her. At least she hadn't been driven halfway through the wall, like the last time a magical search had gone bad. And she was conscious, he saw as she stirred. Relief made his voice sharp. "I told you to keep your fucking shields up!"

She slitted her blue-gray eyes open like an irritated Siamese cat and straightened her long, deliciously bare legs. "I did. Shielded just before she hit me. You can't find somebody and maintain a barrier against them at the same time."

Relief gusted through him, and he sank back on his heels. "Have you ever tried?"

"Funny." The word emerged as a groan that suggested genuine pain.

"Fix that."

Another Siamese glare. "I was going to." A slender hand touched her temple, and a faint golden glow danced. She sighed in relief.

"You okay otherwise?" He looked her over critically. "Nothing crispy anywhere?"

Belle laughed, which encouraged him. "No, nothing crispy. Would have been if I hadn't shielded in time, though." She started to sit up. He took her hand and helped, bracing his other palm against her warm, slender back to push her into a sitting position. The fact that she allowed it worried him, as did her weary slump when she was upright.

He frowned. "So Warlock has the girl?" If Belle had tangled with Warlock again, it was a miracle she hadn't been killed.

"No, the blast came from Miranda. Same magical signature as that." She nodded at the charred remains of the spell book.

"Then why the hell did she hit *you*?"

"God knows. Might have thought I was Warlock. I don't think she and Daddy get along."

"I'd wonder about her taste if they did. Gonna try again?"

"Oh, yeah. Really, reeeally carefully."

"You sure about that?"

"What are you, *my* daddy? Yes, I'm sure. Get your brawny self out of my spell circle so I can work."

He grinned. "Brawny?"

"Beefy? Muscle-bound?"

"I am *not* muscle-bound." Tristan got up and stomped

out of the circle, then sat down again to pick up his sword and glower.

After a moment, Belle growled, "Quit giving me that look."

"Your eyes are closed. How can you tell what kind of look I'm giving you?"

"I can feel it burning the outside of my eyelids. It's distracting."

But not as distracting as you are, Tristan thought, staring at her hungrily.

Half an hour later, Belle gave up with a disgusted grumble. "That girl's shielded tighter than a Crusader bride's chastity belt. She is definitely not taking messages."

"Maybe she's got a Facebook page, like every other kid in America. We could put something on her wall."

Her eyes lit up very briefly before she slumped. "No, she's far too paranoid for that."

"I was *joking*."

"Yes, but you know how kids are about Facebook."

"But she's hiding from an eight-foot-tall sociopathic werewolf wizard who can call down *lightning bolts*."

"We're also talking about *Facebook*."

Tristan contemplated her. "I think I need to feed you. Your blood sugar must be getting low."

Belle snorted, rose to her feet, and stretched, reaching her slender arms toward the ceiling and arching her back. "Yes, but I'll do the cooking. I have no taste for E coli."

He eyed the luscious jut of her breasts. "Hey, I can cook."

"How do you know? You haven't eaten anything since before the Norman Conquest."

"I've never had any complaints."

"Given the infants you date, I'm not surprised. You could serve them sawdust and they'd eat it with a smile, dazzled by the swing of your broadsword."

"What do you know about the swing of my broadsword?"

"More than I care to. Women talk."

Which shut him up, as he started wondering who'd said what. Tristan followed Belle into the kitchen and took up a position leaning against a counter, making sure to flex his biceps periodically. He'd spotted her eying them a time or two, though she always looked away when she realized he'd caught her at it.

Belle pulled out a carving knife and went to work. She chopped leeks, carrots, and celery with skill and speed, then put them into a stock pot to sauté. Intriguing smells wafted into the air as she moved around the kitchen, all competent grace and economical movement. Lentils, chicken stock, and tomato paste joined the vegetables as she turned up the heat.

Then she reached into the refrigerator and emerged with more than a foot of the most phallic piece of meat he'd ever seen. Giving him an evil grin, Belle pulled a huge carving knife out of a wooden block bristling with blades, and brought it down on the kielbasa with a *thunk*.

"Ahh!" Instinct took over. He cupped himself protectively.

She hooted in triumph at his reaction and went on chopping up the sausage with gleeful savagery.

"You're deadly with that thing," he told her. "I gather you don't let *your* infants see you with a knife."

The humor fled her face. "No."

Touched a sore spot there. Tristan winced as she grimly dumped the sausage into the soup. Hoping to change the subject, he asked her how her meeting with Justice went.

She described the whole depressing incident as the soup finished cooking. "So those damned Chosen bitches have everyone convinced we killed Miranda's parents, burned their house down, and abducted her for some nefarious purpose."

Belle handed him a glass of that wonderful blood, and he

followed her to the table. "Joy." He paused to sip, letting the taste of her roll over his tongue. His cock promptly sat up and took notice. He reminded it of the fate of that poor kielbasa.

It didn't seem intimidated.

SIX

"Who do you think killed the mother?" Tristan asked.

Belle paused to sample her soup and take a bite of a crusty French loaf. "My money's on the stepfather, that Gerald Drake character. Joelle certainly seemed afraid of him." So much so she'd turned into a werewolf in the middle of Joan Devon's tea party and threatened to attack Belle and Tristan if they tried to help Miranda leave.

"Wonder what happened to him."

"He's probably dead and magically disposed of. If he killed the mother, could be Miranda killed him."

"Then she burned the house down and took off?" He took another slow sip, trying to make the glass last.

Belle shrugged. "All the magic I detected on the scene had the same signature as the spell book." She poured herself a glass of Cabernet Sauvignon that was almost the same shade of red as her blood.

An unpleasant possibility occurred to Tristan. "Could Miranda have killed her mother, too?"

Belle slowly buttered a piece of bread while she thought about it. "I doubt it. She seemed to really care about Joelle. Otherwise she'd have accepted our offer to shield her from Warlock." Unfortunately, Joelle had been vehemently against the idea, predicting that Gerald would beat her, Joelle, if Miranda left. The girl had given in.

Pointlessly, as it turned out. Joelle had ended up dead anyway.

"Nasty piece of irony there." Tristan crossed his booted ankles and stretched out his legs to contemplate his toes. "Wonder why Miranda hasn't tried to contact us."

"How? She doesn't have a focus. Her mother wouldn't let her take one of my spell stones, so she's got no way to reach me in the Mageverse. It's like not having the telephone number."

"Dammit. I wish you'd been able to slip her one of those stones. It would make life one hell of a lot easier."

Belle snorted. "We're Magekind. We don't get easy."

Tristan took another one of those sensual sips. He was the only man she'd ever met who could look like he was making love just drinking from a wineglass. His lips shaped over the rim, and his eyes slid closed with an expression of pure erotic bliss. His head tilted slowly back. The overhead light gave his bright hair a glow and painted his hard profile with a rim of gold.

God, he was gorgeous.

"Quit performing cunnilingus on that glass," Belle heard herself say. "That's just *wrong*." *Oh, damn. Should have kept my mouth shut.*

He opened one eye. "Jealous, darling?"

"Actually, I'm wondering if I should leave you two alone."

"You taste good." The words emerged in a rough growl, stripped of the sarcastic sophistication of their usual banter.

To hide her erotic reaction, she gave him a sneer. "Does that line work on those Malibu Barbies you usually date?"

"It's not a line." Tristan stared at her, his direct gaze a bright, piercing green. He reached out to thread his hand through her hair, wrapping his strong fingers around the back of her neck. "It's the truth. I want to taste you." His eyes burned hypnotically into hers. Magi had no magic, but he seemed to work a spell on her just the same. "I need you."

"You spent the last month banging every Barbie in Avalon, Tristan," Belle said, but her tone lacked bite. "You never even gave me a hello."

"I seem to have lost my taste for plastic. I want a woman." He was so close to her, his lips brushed hers when he spoke. "How about you? Aren't you tired of seducing boys?"

God, yes. How long had it been since she'd slept with a man she wasn't afraid she'd have to kill? How long had it been since she'd been able to enjoy a touch, a kiss, without watching her partner's eyes for signs of blood madness?

Belle wanted to make love to Tristan. She ached to touch him, to kiss him. She'd wanted it for weeks. But . . . "You cut me dead, Tristan. I spoke to you at the High Council meeting, and you wouldn't even look at me."

"You have too much power over me. I was trying to fight you off." His tongue flicked out, traced the seam of her lips. "But now I'm tired of fighting. Aren't you?"

"*Dieu,* yes." Tired and stupid. She was being stupid. If she made love to him now, there was nothing to stop him from freezing her out again.

So what? a mental voice demanded. *This is just sex. I have sex all the time. It means nothing.* If he decided to freeze her out again, she'd probably be too busy to notice.

Belle was a court seducer and Tristan was a Knight of the Round Table. That was duty. And duty was all there really was. Moments like this were only a brief reward.

She opened her mouth and let him inside.

* * *

Tristan kissed Belle. Finally.

God, she was good. Her lips felt exquisitely soft, and her tongue welcomed his with a seductive little curl and swirl. She tasted of spices and Cabernet and Belle, pure Belle, and she flooded his vampire senses with the smell of sandalwood and arousal.

Tristan pulled her out of her chair and into his arms. Her breasts pressed into his chest, soft and tempting beneath the white cotton of her gown. Her nipples pushed against the lace, silently demanding his mouth. He wanted to bend her back over the table and suckle those little points through the fabric, but he wasn't a barbarian.

Though he was seriously tempted.

So instead Tristan hooked one arm under her shoulders and one under her knees, lifting her with a vampire's effortless strength. "Bed or couch?"

"Couch." She bit his lower lip gently. "It's closer."

He shuddered in arousal and turned toward the den, carrying her down the hallway. Her tapered fingers caressed the line of his neck, the rise of his pecs through his shirt, tracing teasing patterns over the cotton. His cock pressed hard against his zipper.

Spilling Belle onto the white leather sectional, Tristan came down on top of her, hungry for another taste. She felt exquisite beneath him, slim and surprisingly strong, her long legs wrapping around his waist, her arms around his back. He kissed her slowly, not wanting to rush. The advantage of being immortal was there was no hurry. He'd found when he got an opportunity like this, a smart man made it last. Not that he'd had many opportunities like this.

Tristan kissed with a surprising delicacy, his mouth soft as a whisper, one hand cupping her chin. His tongue slipped across her lips, tasting, stroking, tempting her to relax into him. He felt so warm and strong as he cradled her in his arms as if she weighed nothing at all.

He had a way of pushing every erotic button she had.

When Tristan eased off her and started gathering her skirts in his hands, she knew what he had in mind. She sat up, lifting her arms as he swept the gown off over her head.

Belle hadn't felt like wearing a bra—she really never did—instead putting a spell on her bodice to give her full breasts a little support. So when he stripped off the gown, she felt cool air touch heated flesh. It made her gasp. She felt herself cream in the white lace panties that were all she wore.

As he tossed the gown aside, Tristan rocked back on his heels, a knee on either side of her hips. His green eyes glittered hot and wild as he stared down at her bare breasts. "Jesu, you're beautiful." He had a way of saying things like that that gave them the ring of raw truth.

Belle tried to deflect his stinging honesty with a teasing smile. "That's what they tell me."

"They are not me." His stark gaze dared her to lie.

She couldn't. *"Non."* Her practiced English tended to melt into French as she became more and more aroused.

Belle rarely spoke French with the boys.

Tristan settled down over her, mantling her body with his big, brawny one. When he covered one erect nipple with his mouth, sensation bloomed through her in velvety delight, vivid as a rose. His lips suckled, tongue dancing over the sensitive peak of her nipple. Teeth tugged, carefully, so carefully, yet with just enough wicked little rake that she squirmed and threw back her head. His hands stroked breasts and waist and thighs, and she luxuriated in every brush of his sword-calloused fingertips.

Letting herself simply *feel*, as she never did with her boys.

Belle usually did all the work of seduction with her Latent lovers, in part to make up for the risk she was making them run. Their sanity and their lives balanced on the edge she danced them along. If she was wrong, if they didn't have the strength to handle the magic, it would destroy them. Then she'd have to use her knife. So Belle always made sure the pleasure she gave them was as exquisite as she could make it.

But she didn't have to do that this time. She could relax with Tristan. She could even climax, as she so rarely did with the boys.

She could do *everything* with Tristan.

As his tongue drew sweet patterns over her breast, Belle thought, *I forgot it felt so good.* Those big, warm hands of his, stroking her with the elegant precision of a man who knew how to make love from centuries of experience. His fingertips traced her skin, found hidden bundles of nerves, teased them into delicate bursts of delight.

"I love the way you smell," he rumbled in that deep male purr of his.

"Ummm. *Merci.*" She blinked at the ceiling, then gasped as his fingers slid between her thighs, stroked lips already slick with cream. He discovered the eager jut of her clit and circled it in a teasing spiral as his mouth suckled her nipple into rosy delight. Every nerve from breast to sex pulsed in warm syncopation. Tristan began working his way down her torso, licking, nibbling, stroking. Belle felt the points of fangs now, sliding over her skin in a ticklish rake. He pushed the thin fabric of her panties aside and slipped a finger into her sex, a deft little probe. One finger, two, in and out, thumb strumming clit. Another blinding little pleasure jolt.

"You're wet."

"Oui." The word emerged in a pant. She threaded her hands through his hair. God, it was soft. Long and bright as gold thread, yet as supple as raw silk, sifting through her fingers.

He looked up at her, those eyes burning up the length of her body. "You're going to get wetter, because I'm going to eat you."

Excitement spiked through her at the blunt, raw words. *"Oui. Mon dieu, oui*, Tristan. Do it."

Tristan rose over her, looked down at her lying sprawled and naked, rocked back on his heels, and stripped off his shirt as if impatient to be skin to skin with her. Then he stopped. "Fuck. Pants."

He sounded so frustrated, she chuckled.

"You laughing at me, wench?" One corner of his mouth curled up as he pushed to his feet. His zipper hissed.

"Oui." She licked her lower lip, watched his jungle eyes go dark. "What are you going to do about it?"

Tristan slid off the couch and jerked his pants and briefs down, freeing his cock. It sprang out, a length impressive enough to make her brows climb. "I'm sure something will occur to me."

"I'm terrified." She watched in appreciation as he shucked his jeans, toed off his boots, and somehow got rid of it all with a minimum of frustrated fumbling. He rose to his full height and stood there a moment, the light gleaming over broad, glorious shoulders, swordsman's arms, horseman's thighs, and all the deliciously chiseled brawn between.

Belle grinned at him. "Are you posing?"

Tristan flexed and grinned back. "Are you ogling?"

"Oh, *oui*. It's a damned nice view."

"Why, thank you." He moved to kneel between her legs. "Now, where was I?"

She lifted a brow. "Have you forgotten, old man?"

"Oh, now you're living dangerously, wench." He caught her thighs, spread them wide, and dove between with a low male growl.

Belle started to laugh, but then his mouth covered her sex and his tongue licked the length of her in one long, broad swipe. She almost catapulted off the couch. *"Tristan!"*

His only reply was a growl, rumbling and deliciously feral.

Tristan's tongue swept delightful circles, as his hands

reached up to claim her breasts for a teasing double caress of both her nipples at once.

The triple sensation of tongue on sex and fingers on nipples was startling in its intensity. Hot ripples of pleasure built to rolling pulses in her belly, then to a deep thrumming that seemed to vibrate up her spine right into her brain. "Tristan." She gasped, her hands clutching helplessly at the smooth, hard flesh of his shoulders.

He pulled away from her sex and started crawling up the couch, muscles bunching and rolling in his arms, his chest. His face was wet, and his green eyes burned with a wild glitter. "I love the way you taste. The taste of your pussy. The taste of your blood. I can't get enough of you." Bracing one hand beside her head, Tristan used the other to position his cock in her opening. He thrust the smooth shaft deep in one long drive.

She gasped, startled at his width, his silken heat.

Tristan froze. "Did I hurt you?"

"Non," Belle managed. *"Non.* There's just . . . a lot of you."

He grinned at that and faked surprise. "Is there?"

"Wretch."

"Is that any way to talk to a man with his cock in your—"

"Watch it, you."

"Oh, I intend to." And Tristan began to thrust, slowly, carefully, and those delicious pulses started again as he rocked and rolled against her with the wicked skill of a man who definitely knew what he was doing.

Belle sighed in a slow exhalation, wrapping her arms and legs around him, cuddling him close, taking him in. His ass worked under her calves, a strong, steady push, in and out.

The pulses strengthened, grew hotter, harder as he drove, until her climax roared out of some dark, feminine part of her and shook her until she screamed. Without fear. Without death. Feeling only the delicious heat of Tristan's strong male body surging into hers.

His teeth found her pulse and bit down as he drove right to the balls, and froze, growling rough male music against her skin. Somehow that extra little sting grabbed her climax and twisted it, sending it raging higher, hotter. She screamed again, letting herself go as Tristan fed.

Belle came. And came. And came.

Lying in Tristan's arms, she felt him suckle her throat in gentle pulls. A bead of blood rolled down the curve of her throat. He drew away before he had to, and licked the little punctures his fangs had left. She felt the dancing tingle of magic as his saliva began to heal her.

Belle half expected him to move away, perhaps make a joke to reestablish the cool distance between them. Instead his strong arms tightened, cuddling her closer as he rolled onto his side. They lay like that for a long, floating moment, sated and warm.

It crossed her mind that the sectional was wide and comfortable, but Tristan was a big man, and nobody would describe her as tiny. "You're about to fall off the couch, aren't you?"

He was silent just long enough to tell her she was right. "I think I'm agile enough to keep my ass off the floor."

"No doubt," Belle said dryly. "But there's a perfectly nice bed upstairs, wide enough for you, me, and the offensive line of the Dallas Cowboys."

She waited for him to make the expected joke about her bedding football teams. Instead he rolled to his feet, scooped her into his arms, and strode for the door.

"You know, I do have functional legs."

"You certainly do," he purred, and made no move to put her down.

It wasn't the first time Belle had played Scarlett O'Hara and Rhett, but she'd never had a partner step so confidently or carry her as if he didn't even feel her weight. Tristan even managed her long legs as he swept her around corners with a piratical flare she found herself thoroughly enjoying.

"Oh, *mon dieu*," Belle said as he strode into her bedroom. "You're a romantic. I had no idea."

"Don't be absurd." Tristan deposited her on her feet.

She waited for him to deny it, getting her joke ready.

"I'm a Knight of the Round Table. I'm romantic as hell." He pulled back the bed covers with a flourish. "We *invented* romance."

Belle eyed him. "You and Arthur have belching contests."

"We're guys. We drink beer." Tristan swept her up again and tossed her lightly on the bed, then pounced on her, gathering her into his arms with a certain gleeful greed, like a small boy with a stuffed toy that had gone missing for a little too long. "Come here, wench."

"Who are you calling a wench, Fabio?"

"Now you're just asking for it." He engulfed her in warm, hairy muscle and hugged her close, growling in mock threat.

Belle giggled. The sound startled her.

When was the last time she'd giggled like a little girl? She'd laughed, certainly—Belle had a fine, ringing laugh that turned male heads, and she used it ruthlessly in her seductions. She'd chuckled, even snickered a time or two, but she hadn't done much giggling.

Tristan had a talent for making her laugh. Of course, he also made her curse, snarl, and yell.

Which meant, she supposed, that this was not likely to be a long relationship.

Tristan curled around Belle and buried his nose in her hair. He was instantly conscious of her delightful scent— sandalwood and jasmine. The taste of her lingered in his mouth: the copper penny shimmer of her blood flavored with the fizz of magic and the musky tang of her sex. She pressed against him, firm, round ass nestled against his groin, her skin soft and smooth and warm.

He sighed. "As delightful as this is, if I don't brush my teeth, I'm going to have a case of vampire morning breath that would strip the paint right off an outhouse."

Belle hooted. "*Dieu*, you do know how to maintain a mood."

"Hey, I'm just a fan of the wake-up kiss."

"So am I." She gestured.

An electric tingle ran through his mouth, and he blinked, running his tongue over his fangs. "Minty fresh."

"Lunatic. I am going to sleep now."

And in surprisingly short order, she did just that.

Tristan was usually the first one snoring after making love, but this time he found his mind was churning too hard for sleep. His memory kept replaying the delightful buck of her body against his mouth, the scented silk of her breasts, the rich musk of her sex. The way her accent thickened into a throaty French purr that was sexy as hell. *Well,* he thought, *I did it. I seduced her.* And it had been amazing. So amazing, in fact, that he intended to do it again.

Tristan was still planning the next seduction when the sunrise put him to sleep.

Miranda swung into the restaurant's kitchen and picked up the order of fried chicken, mashed potatoes, and corn for table twelve. The cook grunted at her. She grunted back as she refilled her tea pitcher and hurried out again.

Flo's was a bare-bones establishment, with wooden booths and green checkered tablecloths made of tough plastic designed to be wiped down between customers. The walls displayed cheap prints of bowls of fruit and vases of ugly flowers. The vinyl flooring was cracked in places, though scrubbed ruthlessly clean thanks to Miranda's werewolf strength. The tableware was battered stainless steel the waitresses wrapped in paper napkins between meals. Still, a job was a job, and given the economy, Randi was glad to have it.

So she delivered the chicken and a charming smile to table twelve. "Here's your lunch, Mr. Williams. Enjoy."

The burly UPS driver smiled back and nodded at Hannah, who was practically dancing around the dining room. "Hannah's in a good mood."

"She threw out the Rat Bastard."

His smile took on a feral gleam. "It's about time. I was about to lay for the creep in the parking lot." Miranda wasn't the only one who'd noticed the bruises.

"He finally pushed her too far."

Williams frowned. "Hope there's not going to be trouble."

"He left town last night." *And he won't be coming back.*

"Good."

Miranda noticed table eleven's iced tea was getting low and headed over to refill it.

Hannah grinned happily at her on the way to the kitchen, and Miranda savored the warm glow she felt. At least one thing she'd done last night had turned out.

Unlike her panic at that magical contact. She'd blasted back at the source of that brush of power, then spent more than an hour heavily shielded. It was only after she'd calmed down that she realized the magical signature wasn't Warlock's. Though she did recognize it.

Dammit, she'd fireballed La Belle Coeur.

Miranda frowned, hoping the witch was all right. Luckily, Belle was very powerful, so she doubted she'd actually hurt her.

One way or another, Miranda had lost a valuable opportunity. If she'd been a little less paranoid, maybe she'd have been able to establish communication.

When they met at that damned tea party last month, Belle had offered to protect her from Warlock by taking her to Avalon. She'd have been truly safe for the first time in her life.

Miranda sighed. In retrospect, she should have taken Belle up on her offer, and dragged her mother along, kicking and screaming if necessary. Warlock and Gerald Drake could have kissed their asses.

At the time, Joelle had told her Warlock would declare war on the Magekind if the two of them accepted the protection Belle offered. Innocents would die, and they'd be responsible. Miranda had listened to her mother.

And Joelle had been the one to die.

After recovering from last night's scare, Randi had spent two hours gingerly reaching out, hoping Belle would attempt to contact her again. Unfortunately, she hadn't dared broadcast too strongly, because that might attract Warlock's attention. She sure as hell didn't want to do that.

Dammit.

Miranda would just have to hope Belle tried to contact her again. And next time, she'd make damn sure not to blast her.

In the dream, Belle rode him, her long legs straddling his hips, her sex gripping him in tight, liquid heat. He floated in the pleasure of the moment, savoring the sight of her lovely breasts bouncing with the rise and fall of her body. Her blond hair shifted and gleamed like strands of spun sunlight. Her skin glowed in the light of the candles that filled the room with dancing shadows. She looked pale and perfect in the dim light, an alabaster goddess of sex.

Tristan reached for her, unable to resist the temptation of those candy pink nipples. She purred in pleasure, but her head was tilted back, and he couldn't see her eyes. He wanted to see those blue-gray eyes.

"Look at me, Belle," he pleaded on a gasp. "I want to see you."

She dropped her head and met his gaze. But it wasn't Belle.

It was Isolde.
Her features twisted in hate as she raised the knife . . .

Tristan jerked himself out of the dream with a strangled shout, his heart pounding like a warhorse at a gallop. For a moment, he didn't recognize the intricately carved bed with its fairies and dragons.

Belle. He was in Belle's bed. They'd made love. But where the hell was she?

Tristan rolled naked out of the bed, his heart still beating hard with the aftermath of the nightmare. Sweat beaded on his upper lip, and he wiped it away.

Spotting a piece of cream stationery on the bedside table, he plucked it up and read the flowing lines in Belle's lovely handwriting.

Tris—

> *Morgana called to ask my help with Cherise's memorial service tomorrow night. Merlin knows when she'll let me go. Sorry. I was looking forward to feeding you breakfast.*

> > *Belle*

Implication being that he would have drunk said breakfast from her pretty throat. In retrospect, it was probably just as well. He wouldn't have enjoyed explaining why he woke sweating buckets and breathing hard. Isolde was not a memory he liked to share.

Feeling off-balance, Tristan looked around for his clothes. Thoughtful hostess that she was, Belle had conjured clean slacks and a fresh Polo shirt that matched his eyes. She'd left them stacked with his sword belt on the dresser, apparently knowing no Knight of the Round Table liked walking around unarmed. Tristan dressed, buckled on his sword, and wandered downstairs, feeling out of sorts and grumpy. *Fucking dream.* He hadn't had a nightmare about Isolde in years. Apparently his subconscious had noticed the resemblance between his former wife and his new lover, and had elected to sound the alarm.

Which was just too bad. Damned if he'd go running because of a bad dream. It had been fifteen hundred years. It was high time he got over Isolde.

For one thing, Belle was nothing like his wife, despite the slight physical resemblance. She was funny and intelligent, loyal and courageous. Betrayal was no part of her honest soul. She wanted to save every man she met, even the ones who went blood-mad and tried to kill her. She took responsibility for their weakness and flogged herself for her failure to recognize it.

It apparently didn't even occur to her to blame the Majae's Council, though eliminating weak candidates was its job. Anybody she made love to had been first vetted by that group of witches. If her lover went mad, it was because the council had failed to predict he would.

But Belle never blamed anybody but herself.

All true. So why did unease crawl through his mind like a worm eating an apple?

Dammit.

SEVEN

Tristan left Belle's house to find the night clear and almost painfully bright. Avalon stood around him in all its glory, its châteaus, castles, and palaces shimmering with moonlight and magic, surrounded by a riot of vegetation. Gardens, topiary, and old oaks were interspaced with burbling fountains and moonlit statuary. Vampires and witches walked the cobblestone streets, arguing and laughing and flirting, enjoying rare moments of downtime. Their happiness made him feel oddly empty.

Tristan frowned. He had no desire to go home to his silent house. It was too damned early for that anyway.

I'll head for the Lord's Club. Maybe Arthur would be there, or one of the other Round Table knights. He needed company to drive off Isolde's restless ghost.

The Lord's Club had been built in the style of an English gentleman's club—a purely male bastion of solid red-brick and cream cornices, complete with oxblood leather armchairs and dark wainscoting. It featured an impressive library, a magical wine cellar with bottled blood from every Maja in Avalon, and a movie theater that featured flicks dear to the heart of anyone with an XY chromosome: *The Three Stooges*, *Monty Python*, the entire Quentin Tarantino oeuvre, and various dumb but entertaining action movies. If your mood was more violent than that, you could usually find a sparring partner in the state-of-the-art gym and dojo that occupied the lower floor.

All of which sounded pretty good to Tristan.

But as he walked in the door, a shouted battle cry rang out, a raw howl of rage and despair.

Jolting, Tristan drew his sword and broke into a run, plunging up the sweeping staircase in vampire bounds, following his brother knight's voice.

Sir Bors stood at the top of the stairs, naked to the waist, a sword in his hands. Sweat painted glistening trails down the warrior's chest, and his dark hair was plastered around his shoulders in sweating strands. He wore an expression of frenzied rage on his flushed, bearded face, and his eyes were wild.

And he was alone. There was no enemy menacing him as he leaped and spun, swinging his weapon in great arcs around the broad corridor.

"Bors," Tristan snapped, "what the fuck is going on?"

His brother knight looked around at him, white surrounding his too-wide eyes. Like Tristan, Bors was one of Arthur's original knights. "What? I'm practicing."

"At what, giving me a heart attack?" Disgruntled, Tristan slid his sword back into its sheath.

Bors shrugged. "I needed a fight. There was no one here, so I thought I'd make do." His expression brightened. "Would you like a workout?"

Tristan had given him a closer look, and it wasn't hard to put the pieces together. "You've been drinking."

Bors shrugged. "Not all that much."

"Enough. Bors, you know what Arthur told you about this."

"I needed it." He sheathed his sword and turned toward one of the huge stained-glass windows that lined the hallway. "It's too quiet at home. I was hoping someone would be here, but there was nobody. So I hit the Majae's Cellar. God knows there's plenty."

"That's not the issue. It's not good to drink that much blood, Bors."

"Maybe not, but it makes me feel a hell of a lot better." He flashed Tristan a reckless grin.

It was called being blood-drunk, but it was much more like being high. Too much blood gave a vampire a sense of invulnerability, speeding up the mind and body like a dose of amphetamines.

Luckily, Magi were a fairly disciplined crowd. Overindulging in blood was considered a weakness, and most vampires were far too proud to become dependent on anything.

Bors had never had a problem with the addiction either. Not until his son, Richard Edge, had gone on a rampage.

Richard had been enraged that he hadn't been permitted Merlin's Gift and the immortality of a vampire agent. He'd turned to forbidden death magic he'd learned from demonic alien invaders called the Dark Ones. Eventually, he'd kidnapped Arthur and tried to sacrifice him as part of a spell that would have destroyed the Magekind. Bors had fought his son and helped Arthur and Gawain kill him.

Richard's betrayal had broken something in Bors, something that couldn't be fixed. Now when he fought, it was with a fatal recklessness, as if he was deliberately courting death. His blood addiction only made that recklessness worse.

For a moment, Tristan considered ripping a strip off his friend's hide. Then he sighed and drew his sword. "Come on, Bors. We'll burn it off."

Bors shot him a surprised glance. "I figured you'd give me a lecture."

Tristan shrugged. "Hell, I don't want to go home either."

If they had a prayer of avoiding war with the Magekind, Justice figured Carl Rosen was it.

Carl was the chairman of the Council of Clans, an upright, graying werewolf with stern features and cool hazel eyes. Of all the werewolves on the council, Carl was one of the few with the courage to give the Magekind a fair shake. Even better, he had the power to make it stick.

As the Justice Committee met, Carl sat, listening without comment as the members argued about the murder of Jimmy Sheridan.

The five of them met around an oval table in a quiet briefing room located in the depths of the Livingston Corporate Center. The company was owned by Elena Rollings, nee Livingston, who was both a werewolf and a member of the Council of Clans. She let the council use company facilities for meetings, held after hours so they wouldn't raise questions from the humans.

This particular room was a pleasant one, with thick blue carpeting and soft, gray-painted walls. It still smelled faintly of the coffee and apple Danish the company's employees had enjoyed during the day. The massive armchairs that surrounded the black laminate table were made of soft leather that cupped the butt and back in expensive comfort. Elena wasn't cheap with her employees.

Justice sank back in his very nice chair and eyed the other four members of the committee. With one exception, he didn't trust any of them worth a damn.

Elena, who sat to his right, was Justice's only real ally. Redheaded and delicately beautiful, she was married to a cop named Lucas Rollings, and held the Wulfgar Seat on the

Council of Clans. Which made her about as aristocratic as it was possible to get. Yet she wanted to improve the lives of the werewolves they served instead of simply increasing the political and economic clout of the Chosen.

Unfortunately, the committee's other members included a couple of assholes. Thomas Andrews IV always used his own full name, including the number, even though the other Thomas Andrewses had been dead for years. The tanned and manicured CEO of Andrews Oil, he was a werewolf aristocrat, and he didn't let anybody forget it.

Then there was Robert Tanner, who was worse.

"The Magekind have gone mad, just as Merlin foretold." Tanner tapped his fourteen-carat gold Cross pen on the council table in a continuous annoying rap that was slowly driving Justice crazy. "We have to stop them before it's too late."

"Merlin didn't 'foretell' that the Magekind would go mad." Elena visibly fought to maintain a cool, logical tone. "Yes, he was concerned there would be a problem. But we've got no reason to believe Arthur has suddenly gone insane with bloodlust."

Tanner leaned forward, a muscle clenching and releasing in his lean jaw. He was a handsome, older man, lean and fit, his graying hair clipped short, his gray eyes intense. "Elena, you know what they've done. Davon Fredericks himself said Arthur ordered the Sheridan boy's beheading."

"I don't believe Arthur gave any such order. Justice said . . ."

"My dear, don't be naive." Tanner dipped his lids and stopped just short of a sneer. "It's obvious our Wolf Sheriff has lost his objectivity. He's grown too . . . close to Tristan and the Magekind. He believes whatever unlikely tale they tell."

Justice had heard about enough of *that*. "Tanner, I am first, last, and only a cop," he growled. "Nobody influences me—including you. I look at the evidence, and that tells me everything I need to know."

Tanner lifted a brow. "Does it?"

"*Yes.* And yes, Davon Fredericks admitted he killed Jimmy Sheridan. He seemed to believe that Arthur gave him the order to do so. But judging by his scent, he was also deeply confused and apparently under some kind of magical influence at the time."

"From his own people, obviously." Triumph rang in Andrews's voice. "The Magekind are the only ones that work magic."

"Except for the Sidhe, the Dark Ones, the Dragonkind, and damn near everybody who lives in the Mageverse," Rosen pointed out. "Any of them could have cast some kind of spell to make Davon kill the boy in the mistaken belief it was under Arthur's orders."

There was a short, stunned silence. Tanner and Andrews exchanged a quick look; it was obvious neither had expected Rosen to enter into the discussion. The chairman usually remained aloof.

"But why?" Tanner demanded. "What possible reason would they have?"

"It would trigger a war between the Magekind and us, which wouldn't be good for anyone," Elena observed. "And it wouldn't do wonders for the human race either. Maybe someone on Mageverse Earth has his eye on invading this planet. It's happened before."

This time Tanner did sneer. "So the Magekind says."

"I don't think we can dismiss the testimony of the Magekind out of hand," Rosen said. "Don't forget, Arthur and his knights—including Sir Tristan—have been protecting mankind for fifteen hundred years. I find it difficult to believe that King Arthur would suddenly start murdering children."

"I move we have Tristan and Belle appear before the Council of Clans to testify about this incident," Elena said.

Realizing that the two might be able to turn the tide, Justice seconded. The vote passed three to two, with Tanner and Andrews looking frustrated.

The others filed out, leaving Justice and Rosen alone as they got their papers in order. As Justice slipped his into a folder, Rosen looked up from the briefcase he was closing. "Do you think Tristan and the Maja will agree to testify?"

"I believe so," Justice said cautiously. "Though they're justifiably concerned they won't get a fair hearing."

"They don't need to worry about that. I don't want a war," Rosen told him. "The death of this boy was a great tragedy, but I don't think Arthur had a damned thing to do with it. And I don't want to watch more boys die trying to avenge him."

Justice considered him thoughtfully. "Tanner thinks we'd win a war with the Magekind."

"Tanner's an idiot. We might be able to defeat the Magekind if we could get to them, but as long as they can open dimensional gateways, we're at a serious disadvantage. Think of the kind of damage they could do to us with the abilities they have. We may be immune to magic, but our young children aren't. Neither are our homes and businesses."

"And that kind of fight would be damned showy," Justice pointed out. He'd been worrying about the implications of such a war since Jimmy Sheridan died. "We could end up revealing ourselves to the humans, and then we'd all be screwed."

"We certainly can't afford that." Rosen shook his head. "Get Tristan and the woman to testify, Justice. I'll do my damnedest to get everybody calmed down."

Cherise Myers lay surrounded in great mounds of flowers. Roses, stargazer lilies, tulips, and orchids foamed around the gleaming mahogany bier in shades of white and pink, complementing the white silk gown she wore. Pearls and crystals shimmered on her bodice and sparkled from the folds of the skirt. A wreath of star lilies and white roses crowned her head, and more flowers had been woven through her long, shining blond curls. Her delicate hands clasped a great sword that lay the length of her slim body. To either side of the bier, candelabra burned, the ranks of candles illuminating the bier in a soft, golden glow. Overhead, the stars of the Mageverse night blazed in their brilliant glory, as if adding another layer of beauty to the service.

The Magekind surrounded the bier as it lay on the cobblestones of the central square, a solemn crowd of thousands dressed in medieval garb. Black velvet and silk trimmed in silver embroidery and jet beads rustled over the cobblestones.

Tristan stood with the other Knights of the Round Table to the right of the bier, an honor guard in full armor, swords at their sides. The men talked among themselves in low voices, heads bent together, expressions solemn.

Carefully managing her long silk gown with the practiced ease of centuries, Belle made her way through the crowd to join Guinevere and Morgana, both grimly beautiful in black velvet trimmed in pearls.

"I hate funerals," Gwen murmured. "At least mortal deaths are usually from old age. We never get anything but combat fatalities and murders."

"It doesn't help that this whole situation was a clusterfuck from first to last," Morgana growled. "First the mess with the werewolves, then this poor child's death. That magic bite of theirs is a development I could have done without."

"We'll find a solution. We always do." Guinevere gave Belle a wicked smile obviously designed to lighten the mood. "So, how's it going with Tristan?"

"Oh, fine. He . . ."

"You *slept* with *Tristan*?" They stared at her, eyes wide and incredulous. Belle cursed silently. The problem with being friends for a millennium was that your confidantes became all but telepathic. They could read every eye flicker and lip twitch, then decipher them in a blink.

"Why?" Gwen demanded.

There was no point in denying it. She gestured at Tristan. "Oh, come on. Look at him."

"Yes," Morgana protested, "but he's a dick."

"He also *has* a dick." Belle suspected her own smile was feline. "And it's . . ."

"I do *not* want to know about Tristan's dick." Gwen spread her hands as if to ward off any other information.

"You know it's a bad idea to get involved with a fellow agent."

"I get involved with agents all the time, Morgana."

"Recruits, not agents. This is different and you know it. This is Tristan."

"No, it's *sex*. Sex with somebody I do not have to worry about killing."

"Avalon is full of men you don't have to kill. Only one of them is Tristan."

"But Tristan is . . ."

"Shush," Gwen said. "Here comes the chorus."

The double line of twenty white-garbed Magekind filed into the square and moved into place beside the bier, opposite the honor guard. Utter silence fell, almost vibrating with anticipation. Avalon's City Chorus always gave gorgeous performances.

The choir began to sing an ancient Celtic dirge of loss and grieving, the women's voices soaring high, the men's a deeper, rolling rumble that made the old words echo across the city. As they sang to the infinite darkness overhead, the light of the moon poured down over Cherise's still form, surrounded by masses of flowers like sweet-smelling clouds.

The priest spoke next, since Cherise had been Catholic. Father John de Clairvaux had been a Templar knight before becoming a vampire, and now he served the spiritual needs of Avalon's many Catholics. He had a fine, deep voice, and he spoke with an elegant simplicity and a quiet faith. There was genuine grief in his voice when he spoke of his young parishioner.

Next her friends moved to stand before the bier, one by one, telling the story of the young Maja who had been with the Magekind such a short time.

When Davon started forward, Belle tensed. "Oh, great."

"What?" Gwen whispered.

"This is not good."

Davon looked haggard, as if he'd lost weight just in the three days since his partner's death. "Cherise was more than my partner," he said, his hoarse voice ragged. "We only went on two missions together, and one of them we shouldn't have been on anyway. Yet in that short time, she demonstrated her love of duty. She believed in the importance of Merlin's Great Mission to serve and protect mankind. Our oath wasn't just words to her. They were etched on her bones and written in her blood. And when a werewolf charged me"—Here his voice broke—"it didn't matter to her that he was seven feet tall and resistant to her only weapon, her magic. She stepped in his way and met his charge. And he bit her." A tear rolled down his cheek. He made no sound as he cried, made no move to wipe it away. "She died for me because that's how she lived. And there's no way I can repay her."

Morgana frowned as Davon walked away from the bier. "That one needs help."

"I've sent the healer to him," Belle whispered. "He refused care."

"Yes, well, he won't be able to turn her away if Arthur sends her. I'll see to it."

"Thank you."

She only grunted in response, but Belle wasn't fooled. Most thought her friend a cold-blooded bitch, but Morgana had a warm core of genuine compassion. True, it was locked under a mile of icy calculation, but it was still there.

Arthur stepped forward. "Once again, my friends, we face an enemy who has claimed the life of one of our own. Warlock and his agents have killed thirteen innocents, both Latent and mortal. Now he has used one of *us* to kill an innocent, preying on my agents' loyalty and sense of duty to do so. He's trying to start a war because he imagines he can destroy us. He is not the first to make that assumption, and he won't be the last. We have survived fifteen centuries of war, and we are not so easy to kill. He will pay for his crimes. This I so swear." Arthur drew Excalibur, the big blade ringing bell-like as it slid from his scabbard.

As one, his Round Table knights drew their weapons. Tristan's deep voice led the chorus. "This we so swear."

All the other vampires followed suit, thrusting their blades heavenward. "We so swear."

Morgana stepped forward. "The Majae join this oath as we send our sister home."

"We so swear," Belle said, her voice rising with the other Majae as she called her magic. The power burst from her hands, joining with the blazing magic the others summoned to blast into the flower-piled bier.

The bier flared white, glowing brighter and brighter until Belle wanted to shield her tearing eyes. Instead she raised her arms in concert with her fellow witches, sending the great globe of energy shooting skyward. It detonated, raining sparks of golden magic over the empty space where Cherise's body had lain. The Maja, her bier and her flowers had vanished, consumed by the raw magic of the spell.

She'd become part of the Mageverse again, returned to the source of all magic.

Darkness fell, a moment of dazzled blackness after the detonation. Belle sighed. It could just as easily have been her or Tristan on that bier. And one day it would be.

The Magekind might not age, but they weren't truly immortal.

Not in this business.

* * *

The Magekind started making their way to the Great Hall, where Cherise's memorial feast was being held. Cooking was considered an art form among the Majae, who actively competed to impress one another. Belle had worked all day on her offerings: roast pheasant with black truffles—she'd used her magic ruthlessly to obtain enough pheasant and truffles to produce the dish in sufficient quantity—and *Daube de Boeuf Provencal*, a complex beef stew she'd marinated for eighteen hours. She was looking forward to the reaction.

Tristan appeared beside her with astonishing silence for a big man dressed in armor. He opened his mouth, and she absently cast a spell before he could even voice the request. His mail disappeared back to his quarters, replaced by breeches, tooled black knee boots, a white shirt with flowing sleeves, and a black velvet doublet embroidered with Celtic designs in silver thread. A cape draped over one shoulder and under the opposite arm, fastened with a silver chain and a ruby clasp. He glanced down at himself, taking in the somber elegance of his clothing. "Very nice. Thank you."

The genuine pleasure in his voice gave her a warm little glow, and Belle smiled at him. She suspected her expression was a touch sappy, but she couldn't seem to help herself. To make up for it, she shrugged. "Well, you're a Knight of the Round Table. I can't dress you like a peasant. The other witches would talk."

A smile teased up the corner of his tempting mouth. "Can't have that, can we?" She took his offered arm and they started toward the Great Hall.

A few feet behind them, Arthur, Guinevere, and Morgana strolled along together. He was still brooding about the girl they'd just committed to the light when Morgana said, "Look at those two. 'Just sex' my pert little ass."

"Who?" Arthur asked. The two witches always seemed to pick up on whatever was going on with his men long before he did.

"Tristan and Belle," Gwen replied, nodding toward the couple walking along arm in arm, blond heads together. "She said they're 'just' having sex. Does that look like 'just sex' to you?"

Now that they'd brought it to his attention, he could see the tenderness in Tristan's hold on Belle's hand and the flirtatious way she looked up at him with a sassy little tilt to her head.

"Oh, shit," Arthur growled. "She's going to chew him up and spit him out."

"Who, Tristan?" Gwen stared at him. "I don't think so."

"It's more likely that ice-cold fucker will stomp her heart into pâté the way he does every other female he beds," Morgana growled.

"Oh, come on," Arthur protested. "This is Belle Coeur. Do you have any idea of how many male hearts she's ground into meatloaf?"

"That's different," Gwen said. "Those are the recruits. They're supposed to fall a little in love with her. She never lets it get too serious."

"Exactly. Tristan's too vulnerable for that shit."

"Tristan? Vulnerable?" Morgana hooted. "He's got his heart locked behind six feet of glacial ice. She'll never touch him. Meanwhile, she'll fall for him and he'll chew right through her. It'll be the *Titanic* all over again."

"Morgana, you don't know what the hell you're talking about. That wife of his left a hole in Tristan's soul that's never healed. If Belle's not careful, she'll crack him wide." Arthur glowered, staring as his friend's back. "And I don't want to have to put my best knight back together with spit and Super Glue."

"Yes, well, I think it's more likely that Belle will be the one hurt," Morgana said grimly. "And I'm not going to just stand back and watch."

Arthur was too busy making his own plans to be suitably alarmed at her tone.

Cherise's memorial feast was held in Avalon's Great Keep, a five-story granite castle surrounded by topiary knights and ladies. Inside the hall, banners from ancient battles hung from the vaulted ceiling, their colors as bright as the day they were captured thanks to the spells that preserved them. The stone walls were decorated with thousands of swords, pikes, and maces of all sorts, arranged in intricate geometric patterns that shone with a muted metallic gleam.

In contrast to all that cheerful barbarism, the Majae had decorated the hall with flowers and candles anywhere they found a flat surface to put them on. Several easels held Cherise's formal portrait, framed in heavy gold and wreathed in white roses. She looked heartbreakingly young, her smile bright with optimism. It made Belle's chest ache to look at her.

Gone now. Gone like so many others.

A string quartet played in one alcove of the Great Hall, magically amplified to fill the room. That was saying something, considering the sheer size of the space and the murmur of conversation from all the people that filled it.

The Magekind always went all out for memorial feasts.

Tables swathed in linen creaked under the weight of countless steaming dishes on sterling silver serving platters. Artful flower arrangements surrounded candles that cast a mellow glow over the food. The Majae strolled up and down along the tables as they chose whatever delicacies they planned to enjoy. A particularly large group swarmed around the dishes Belle had prepared. Smiling slightly, she wandered closer to the table, the better to enjoy the murmurs of praise and muffled sensual groans.

"Oh, God," Caroline moaned as she forked up a bite of pheasant and rolled her eyes in mock ecstasy. Her husband, Galahad, watched her indulgently. "I hate you. I really do. Every man in Avalon is in love with you, and you cook like a goddess. It's not fair. Aren't you ashamed, you greedy bitch?"

"Ummm." Belle pretended to consider the question. "Nope. Nope, really not ashamed at all." Then she smiled. "But it's sweet of you to suggest I might be."

"Excuse me," Caroline sighed, "I need to be alone with my pheasant." She wandered off, carrying her loaded plate across the shining checkerboard marble floor.

"I think I'm jealous." Galahad grinned at Belle. "I'd better go make sure she doesn't eat herself into a coma."

Though the group around the food tables was mostly female, the bar served both sexes. Satisfied at the reception her dishes had received, Belle headed in that direction, hoping to find Tristan and escape back home. She was in the mood for a bubble bath in her huge sunken tub.

With company.

"Belle?" Arthur spoke from her shoulder.

She turned around, but her smile faded as she noted the line bisecting the royal brow and the muscle flexing in his jaw. *Oh, God, what did I do to piss him off?* Aloud, she managed a more politic "Yes, my liege?"

"I would like you to take a little more care with my knight," he said in that low, careful tone that told her he was both furious and worried. Like everyone else that spent any time at all in Arthur's immediate presence, Belle had learned to read the finely calibrated signs of his temper.

"Your knight?" She stared at him warily. "You mean Tristan?"

"Yes, Tristan." There was an edge to the words now. "I know it will come as a surprise to you, but he is more vulnerable than he seems. Isolde's betrayal wounded him deeply."

"That was fifteen hundred years ago." Her temper started

to get the better of her. Arthur might be the Liege of the Magi, but that didn't give him a right to butt into her love life. "Tristan doesn't know you're talking to me about this, does he?"

"No, and I would take it as a great favor if you did not tell him."

Oh, boy. When Arthur got all formal and precise like that, he was dead serious. You didn't fuck with him in such a mood. You could find yourself missing favored body parts. Figuratively, if not literally.

"And with some wounds, it doesn't matter how long ago they were inflicted," Arthur continued. "Ask any amputee."

Okaaaaay. "So what, exactly, do you want me to do? Or not do?"

"Don't make him fall in love with you."

Belle opened her mouth, and he cut her off with an impatient gesture. "You know very well what I'm talking about. You make all of them fall in love with you—every one of your boys."

"They're *boys.* He's *Tristan.*"

"Exactly," Arthur snapped. "He's also my good right arm, as well as my dearest friend. Do not play your usual games with him, Belle Coeur. I won't appreciate it."

He turned and stalked off, his cape flaring wide at his heels.

"Well, *merde,*" Belle said.

EIGHT

The slug of Irish whiskey burned all the way down Tristan's throat. He sighed in pleasure. *Man cannot live on blood alone. That's why God made booze.*

"Why, hello there, Tristan."

Tristan turned at the seductive purr, brows lifting as he took in its source.

Sabryn Sans Merci wore a black velvet gown that seemed to have been shrink-wrapped over generous curves. Some skillful spell lifted her truly outstanding breasts and pressed them together like two scoops of vanilla ice cream in a very decadent sundae. The soft red shimmer of her hair was piled high on her head, a few curls cascading artfully down around her long neck. It was an arrangement designed to drive any vampire into a frenzy of lust.

Her eyes glittered, catlike and dark green above full lips slicked with something bronze and shimmering. She was flamboyantly beautiful, every line of her face in perfect relation to every other, as though God had mathematically plotted her features. Like Belle, she was a High Court seducer.

Unlike Belle, she had a tendency to leave wreckage in her wake.

She spoke in a throaty cat's purr. "Morgana tells me you're looking for a partner."

"Morgana tells you wrong." Tristan turned his back, having neither time nor patience for whatever game Sabryn was playing. He took another sip of his whiskey and started off through the crowd to look for Belle. Sabryn's high heels clicked after him, determination in every tap.

Two months ago, he'd have happily flirted with Sabryn in hopes of getting her into bed. She was reputed to be very good there, with an intriguing edge of kink. Belle, for all her impressive erotic skills, had no apparent interest in kink whatsoever.

Tristan was a bit surprised to find himself not in the least intrigued by Sabryn's wicked green eyes and whatever outré thought processes went on behind them. If he'd really wanted kink, it would have been more fun to coax Belle into joining him.

"Would you stop and talk to me?" Sabryn demanded, catching up at last to grab his arm and glower into his eyes. "What sort of game are you playing?"

"Do you find it so difficult to believe I'm not interested?" Tristan said lightly. "Better check your ego, darling. It's getting unwieldy."

"Are you trying to snow Belle into believing you're faithful? She's much brighter than that."

"I have no interest in snowing Belle into believing anything." Tristan eyed the witch like the dangerous beast she was. "What are you up to, Sabryn? When I told you I needed a partner six weeks ago, you wouldn't give me the time of day."

"I like Belle." Sabryn frowned at him, a militant light in her eyes. "She doesn't deserve to get hurt."

"I like Belle, too. Why the hell do you think I'm going

to hurt her? Besides, isn't that a little hypocritical coming from you?"

"I think you're going to hurt her because I've got eyes." She shifted close, almost within kissing distance, though from the glint in her gaze and the flash of her teeth, kissing was not what was on her mind. "And I've seen what you've done to other friends of mine. I don't like it. Neither does Morgana."

Ahhh. He'd wondered who'd put her up to this. Figured it would be the Ice Bitch.

Sabryn took a deep breath, and he watched raw seduction slip over her beautiful face like a mask. "You and I can have a very good time together, Tristan. And neither of us will get hurt, because neither of us has a heart to break. Think about it."

She turned with a roll of that remarkable ass and walked away. Tristan frowned, watching her stroll off. Was she right? Was Belle in danger of falling for him?

And why did the thought warm him?

Couldn't be. He was a cold-blooded bastard—not only a killer, but sarcastic, nasty and just plain rude. Why the hell would Belle Coeur, who was none of those things, fall in love with him?

The most you could say for him was that he did Arthur Pendragon's dirty work so Arthur didn't have to. And Arthur, for some unknown reason, seemed to view him as a friend.

It was far more likely Tristan would fall for Belle. And that would just be embarrassing.

Maybe he should take Sabryn up on her offer. She'd make a fantastic Maja partner. She had power to burn, she feared absolutely nothing, and as she'd said, she had no heart to break. Which meant she lacked that delicious warmth that so attracted him to Belle.

Everyone would be safe. Including him.

* * *

Belle strolled along the long stone balcony that ran around the Great Hall. Golden light, low and soft enough for vampire night vision, flooded down from ironwork lamps festooned with fanciful metal shapes. Hooking an arm around one cool post, she leaned against the low stone wall, stared out over the garden, and brooded.

Topiary knights jousted from leafy horseback or flirted with elegant green ladies. White roses and night-blooming jasmine perfumed the air. She could hear the laughter and music floating from the building. Moonlight poured down like bright fairy wine, shimmering over every leaf, petal, and branch.

It was all so romantic she could just spit.

God knew where Tristan was. She should go look for him, dance a little, improve her acid mood. Instead Belle kept thinking about Arthur and his threats.

But really, what the fuck was he going to do? Fire her? That ship had sailed when Belle drank from Merlin's Grail. Being Magekind wasn't a job you could be fired from.

True, Arthur was perfectly capable of maintaining discipline by kicking knightly ass—he'd done it more than once. But she was a lady, and he would never touch a lady. He might make her feel like an utter flaming bitch, but he wouldn't touch her.

Actually, Belle might prefer getting her butt kicked to suffering the royal temper. Not that she'd ever personally endured an Arthurian tongue-lashing, but she'd heard Morgana's accounts. Admittedly, every one of those dressings-down had been richly deserved. Morgana could be high-handed, duplicitous, and ruthless in the pursuit of whatever she considered just goals.

Belle loved her anyway.

Nobody, but nobody, called her the Whore of Avalon in

Morgana's presence, even in jest. The Liege of the Maja had always been her defender and her friend.

"There you are." Morgana's smoky voice purred from the darkness.

Speak of the devil.

She glided from the shadows, sleek as a cat in the black velvet gown that rode her curves like loving male hands, a silver belt swinging from her lush hips. Belle gave her friend a smile. "Hello there, darling."

"Hello, yourself." Morgana leaned a hip on the stone wall and studied her. "You look glum."

"Well, this is a funeral."

"True, but I get the impression it's more than that."

"Arthur just informed me that I'd better not break the delicate heart of his best friend, on pain of the royal wrath. Have you ever noticed he forgets he's not king anymore?"

Morgana snorted. "My dear, don't let his protestations fool you. He's still king. He just has delusions of democracy."

Just as Morgana had been elected to lead the Majae as liege, Arthur was Liege of the Magi. There'd been others over the years, generally whenever Arthur got sick of the job. But he was always reelected whenever he bothered to run.

They didn't call Arthur the Once and Future King for nothing.

Belle told her friend about the tongue-lashing she'd just endured. "I have no idea what he was talking about," she finished, frustrated. "He seems convinced that Tristan is still mortally wounded by whatever Isolde did, never mind that it was fifteen centuries ago . . ."

"And when did you kill your first blood-mad Latent?"

Belle went still. "That was a bit low of the belt, 'Gana."

Morgana sighed, tilting her head. Her dark curls rolled like foam from her shoulders to her ass. "I know, darling. I'm sorry for it. But I think you've made a mistake, and I feel the need to warn you."

Belle dropped her forehead against the lamp post and moaned in mock pain. "Not you, too."

"When you start hearing the same thing from multiple people, perhaps you should listen."

"Multiple people are not always right. There were no WMDs in Iraq. God knows we looked for them."

"Tristan is a lot more dangerous than a WMD."

"Oh, come on. Not even Tristan is a weapon of mass destruction."

"Perhaps not, but he could certainly destroy you."

"Now you're being melodramatic."

Morgana drummed her fingers on the parapet. "I sent Sabryn to offer him her services as partner. I had to order her. Even Sabryn was reluctant to poke her hand in that buzz saw."

Belle felt her face go icy, then blazing hot with sheer rage. "Sabryn has never been reluctant to stick anything of hers anywhere. At all."

Morgana blinked at her in slow, pretended shock. "My dear, that sounded almost catty. Are you all right?"

Belle bared her teeth. "Considering that my best friend just knifed me in the back, I'm just dandy."

Morgana studied her, genuine concern in her eyes. "He's going to hurt you, Belle."

"So you thought you'd beat him to it by sending Sabryn after him?" Belle was conscious of her own breathing. Too fast. She made a deliberate effort to slow it down, to fake a calm she was very far from feeling.

"He's crippled, Belle. You don't remember what he was like then . . ."

"Largely because I wasn't even born. Which is saying something, considering how fucking old I am."

". . . But I *do* remember. Tristan was vicious, Belle. He was dangerous. It was more than a century before he drank from anything but a bottle, because all the Majae were afraid of him."

"That was then. This is fifteen centuries later. He got over it."

"We have very long memories, Belle. We never really get over anything, because we never forget. It's part of the Gift."

Belle folded her arms and glowered. "I can't believe you sent Sabryn."

"And I was right," Morgana said, her gaze steady with that infuriating confidence. "If he wasn't beginning to get to you, it wouldn't hurt you like this."

"That's utter bullshit. But even if I were falling for him, it's still none of your business."

"Tristan's going to drop you for Sabryn, Belle. He'll do it to protect himself, because no matter how many centuries have passed, he remains that wounded beast everyone feared." She lifted her chin. "Eventually, you'll realize I've saved you a lot of pain."

Belle had heard just about enough. "Are you going deaf, Morgana? *My pain is none of your damned business!*"

"But it is, because you're my dearest friend. And I'm right."

"That's the thing about you that charms everyone so— *you're never wrong.*"

Belle turned on her heel and stalked back into the hall. She was going to find Tristan.

And fuck his brains out.

Tristan poured blood into a crystal goblet. The enchanted bottle had a name written on it in flourishing, beautiful calligraphy. The ink was pink. He didn't recognize the name, but it must be one of the new Maja recruits. No one any older would write her name in *pink*, for God's sake. What was she, sixteen?

His first sip confirmed that theory. She tasted new. It wasn't just power, since plenty of new Majae had power to burn. Her blood lacked that ineffable richness and depth that years gave to the magic in a witch's blood.

Belle had that. He would never mistake her blood for anyone else's. And to drink it from her throat . . .

He hardened.

The instant lust was astonishing in its intensity. Hot, feral, a burning rush that made him crave her, made him long to search her out and drag her off *right now*. Like some kind of barbarian instead of a Knight of the Round Table.

Not that anybody had ever accused him of being the beau ideal.

"Tristan." The purr made his eyebrow rise even as his cock twitched in randy anticipation. He turned to find Belle watching him with eyes that held an almost feverish glitter. "I don't know about you, but I've had about enough of this." She spoke in that slurred French accent she used whenever she was really turned on.

Oh, yes. He dipped her a bow out of sheer spinal reflex. "As you wish."

"Oh, I wish." She stepped to his side and twined an arm through his in a distinctly possessive gesture.

He looked down at their linked arms as his heart sank. *She's gotten wind of Sabryn.*

Well, fuck. How was he supposed to handle this? His general technique for dealing with jealous women—as he'd had to do more than once over the years—was to lift a frigid eyebrow and defy the woman in question to express a claim on him. Generally, if she had the temerity to start such a statement, she'd stutter to a stop pretty damned fast under his chilly stare. He did not, thank you, belong to *anybody*. Not since Isolde.

But this was Belle. Belle was not some random bit of tail. She was his *partner*, not just a wand for hire he used for transportation and the occasional spell. She'd fought beside him like one of his brother knights, only without the trash talk, Monty Python jokes, and belching contests.

She was also highly pissed about Sabryn. He could see it in those stormy eyes. Worse, he could tell she was hurt. The anger he could deal with, but he had no clue what to do about the pain. Apologize? But he hadn't done anything, hadn't approached Sabryn, hadn't even accepted her offer. He was damned if he'd apologize for something he hadn't done.

So he wouldn't say anything. *Wait for her to bring it up.* Which was probably not the best thing to do, but damned if he had any other ideas.

He braced himself for the storm.

Except there wasn't one. Instead, she chattered as they left the Great Hall and headed back toward her house. *What the fuck? Belle doesn't chatter.* But there she was, inundating him in bright gossip about people he barely knew and didn't give a damn about, until he wished she'd just let him have it about Sabryn. *Get it over with.*

He actually began to twitch.

Tristan looked so coolly expressionless Belle wanted to scream. *Are you dumping me for Sabryn?*

Damned if she'd ask.

Belle was too bloody old to act sixteen, but she also couldn't seem to help herself. She was mad enough to chew nails and spit daggers.

All right. Maybe he did intend to dump her. She had no claim on him. Not that she wanted one on the infuriating bastard, despite the way the moonlight silvered his blond hair and edged his hard profile in light. He was still a raging asshole ninety percent of the time.

And Belle was going to give him a fuck he'd never forget. No matter what pleasures Sabryn trotted out from her impressive repertoire of kink.

As they entered the house's front gate, Belle flashed him a smile that blazed so hot, it cracked his icy composure. For just a blink, she glimpsed outright panic in his green eyes.

You'd better be scared. Belle upped the heat in that lethal seducer's smile. "I've got something to show you." The words emerged in her best velvet French purr, the one that had been known to make men hard all by itself.

To her feline satisfaction, he swallowed.

Belle drew him around to the rear of the house, sure-footed in the moonlight as she sent a tide of magic ahead of them. Preparing the scene, the way she'd done so many times with so many men.

When they entered the garden, the tiny pool was already warm and steaming. A stream tumbled down the side of the rough gray stone fountain that thrust from the center of the water like a tiny cliff face. Roses and votive candles floated on the water's gently swirling surface, sending up golden light and sweet scents. Mounds of honeysuckle surrounded the pool's stone lip, spilling tendrils of pale white blooms to float on the water. The scent was so sweet it would have been overwhelming, had it not been for the herbs she'd planted here and there to add pungent green notes. The result was as precisely balanced as any Parisian perfume.

Tristan stopped to study the garden with admiration. "The poor bastards don't stand a chance, do they?"

"By the time I bring them here, they don't want one." Belle gestured, a deliberately lyrical wave of the fingers. A mist formed around her body, white and glowing in the moonlight. When it melted away, she stood naked.

Tristan's pupils expanded, his lips parting. "Ah."

She tilted her head. "I'm in the mood for a swim. Would you care to join me?"

He recovered enough to give her a rake's hooded stare. "How could I refuse?"

She stripped him with an offhand wave of magic. Rather than watch the revelation of his handsome body, Belle made herself turn away and stroll down the stone steps into the water.

He didn't come after her. Involuntarily, she glanced around, and found him standing on the lip of the pool.

Despite her steaming anger, Belle caught her breath. Tristan's warrior's shoulders were painted in the light and shadow that poured down his torso, revealing the scars he'd won before he'd drunk from Merlin's cup.

This was no steroid-plumped gym rat. His body had been forged in combat, built for speed and agility, without the bulk that would have gotten in the way of a sword swing or the weight that would have slowed him down. He was distilled masculinity, so pure she could taste the testosterone on her tongue.

Tristan started down the stairs, one slow step at a time, head lifted, all arrogant male animal. His gaze locked on hers, dark with hunger, defying her to look away.

Belle had lost count of the men she'd seduced, but suddenly she'd never felt so naked.

Stepping down onto the pool's floor, he reached for her. She went into his arms, catching her breath at the heat of his big body pressing against her much smaller one. Then his mouth covered hers, and she moaned between his lips.

No. I'm supposed to be in control.

Belle bit his lower lip, carefully, ruthlessly, teeth tugging, her tongue sweeping in for a hot lick that swirled between his teeth. She touched him, hands sliding slowly down his torso, pausing to explore, trace the rise of muscle, the dips and ridges of scars, the taut points of his small male nipples. She heard him inhale, once, sharply, the sound loud in her sensitized hearing. So she bit his chin in a press of teeth, a kiss and suckle. His head tilted back, and she found his pulse and pressed her mouth against it. Bit down, the pressure carefully calibrated just short of pain, a tiny, demanding nip.

His hands found her breasts. The heat of his fingers stopped her breath. He began to play with her nipples, tugging, twisting, teasing little flips and flicks that sent sweet scarlet pleasure feathering up her spine.

Tristan knew just how to touch a woman. He weighed

her breasts in his hands, purred like some huge cat against her ear. "Silk." That one rough word in his deep growl was more erotic than another man's poetry. His tongue swept into her ear in a quick, teasing lick. It made her shiver.

So Belle kissed him in challenge, biting and suckling, increasing the pressure with every move of her mouth until he growled in response. His cock lay against her belly, thick as a club. Somehow she resisted the urge to touch it, to taste it, to climb up his body and ride it like a stallion.

But she wanted to.

Belle felt slick and swollen, ravenous for cock as she hadn't been in far too long. She, who could play a man's body like a minstrel's lute, forgot all her clever songs and heard only the raging beat of her own pulse.

Pushing him backward, she guided him against the mini-cliff. There were jutting projections there for a man's feet, and he found them, just as she'd known he would.

Tristan braced his back against the rocks, in the bouncing path of the water, and waited. His cock thrust above the pool's churning surface, thick and flushed. Belle grasped him, bent with the deliberate grace of a geisha, tilted the shaft upward. And sucked him in.

He gasped, and she smiled around his cock in triumph.

The sensation of Belle's mouth on his cock was so intense, Tristan shuddered in hard, racking delight. She suckled him so fiercely, her cheeks hollowed as her tongue laved the exquisitely sensitive head. He let his head fall back and gasped. The fountain's blood-warm stream poured down on his head and rolled along his chest, adding to the stunning sensuality of the moment.

God, she knows how to drive a man insane.

Belle cupped his balls tenderly as she gripped his cock, pumping her fist up and down the thick shaft as she licked and nibbled and sucked. Hot lust and bright pleasure blinded him, and he curled his fists in her hair. His hips rocked help-lessly.

Tristan looked down, wanting to watch her. The water splashed over Belle's face as she sucked him, drops rolling down her shoulders and dancing over cheekbones. She drew his big shaft deeper in an effortless swoop, right to the balls. The sight seared him like a red-hot blade, a delight so intense it was almost painful.

Pleasure hit him, fierce, burning, pulsing through his cock from tip to balls. She rolled her eyes up at him, and they glittered, wild and triumphant.

Suddenly Belle pulled her mouth off him and rose to her feet, graceful as a hunting cat. She stepped backward, one hand still wrapped around his cock, pulling him gently away from the rock face. Dazzled, helplessly aroused, he let her guide him around by his shaft, until his thighs hit the side of the pool.

"Up," she ordered, her eyes sparking in challenge. "On your back."

Unease stirred in him, but it was a faint whisper in the roar of his arousal. He hoisted himself out of the pool and let himself fall back on the stone lip.

Belle vaulted out of the water with a Maja's supernatural strength and straddled him, knees on either side of his ribs, one hand pressing his shoulder as the other reached between their bodies to seize his cock.

She took him into her hot depths in one delicious rush. Her head fell back, the soaked tips of her honey hair tickling his hot thighs. She began to jog, up and down, faster and faster, a fierce little trot that sped into a breath-stealing gallop, each rise and fall of her body slick and tight, a feral pressure.

Leaning over him, Belle slapped both hands down on his shoulders, bracing herself as she rode, her angry eyes bright. "You can go to Sabryn, but you're not going to forget me."

She had said once she was always on top the last time

she rode her men. *I'm good with a knife.* She looked angry enough to use one on him.

As she had in the dream. The dream where she'd been not Belle, but Isolde.

Reality seemed to warp, dumping him into a searing vision. *His wife rode him, her face twisted in lust and rage. From the corner of his eye, he thought he saw steel flash . . .*

The blade.

Remembered fury rolled over him, drowning him without a gurgle. Grabbing Belle's shoulders, Tristan rolled with her and pinned her beneath him. He snarled as his fangs filled his mouth, and he lunged for her throbbing pulse as he'd done those long centuries ago.

Belle gasped in startled shock as Tristan struck—there was no other word for it—right for her throat, his fangs sinking into her skin as he began to drive in long, merciless thrusts.

It should have hurt. It felt glorious.

His hips circled as he drove, screwing her hard in a fierce and delicious possession that shook her and made her breasts dance. Her orgasm thundered out of nowhere in long, rolling pulses that shook her until she screamed, "Tristan!"

Belle went limp, her arms dropping away from his shoulders. He'd come as he drank, and his big body crouched over hers like a predator's, heavy and warm. She blinked in sleepy pleasure, enjoying the dazed aftermath.

Tristan jerked and froze, his mouth going still against her throat. Suddenly a vision lanced through her brain, bloody, violent.

He'd come out of his frenzy to find Isolde cooling under him, her throat torn, blood streaking her pale, pretty breasts. The knife she'd buried in his chest was buried now in hers . . .

He jerked away and pushed himself onto his elbows. "Belle?" Panic rang in his voice. "Belle?"

Jesu, that horrific vision had somehow leaped directly from his mind. "Tristan? Are you all . . ."

"Did I hurt you?" His eyes examined her, dwelling on her throat, sweeping down her body.

She stroked his hair and felt the fine tremble of his body against hers. "I'm fine, Tristan. All you gave me was a howling orgasm."

He said something Gaelic again as his head dropped against her shoulder in a gesture of sheer relief.

She hesitated a moment before she added cautiously, "Tristan, you did *not* hurt me." Belle threaded one hand through the gold silk of his hair. "I saw something there at the end. A vision. You and a woman. And blood."

"Yeah. Flashback. Bad flashback." He wrapped his arms around her and held on. "When you were riding me with such anger, I saw Isolde. And I . . ." He broke off with a groan of despair.

Being told a lover had thought of another woman while making love to her would normally piss Belle off. But this was a very different situation.

"What did she do to you, Tristan?"

His racking quivers had yet to subside, speaking of the depth of his trauma.

The term "post-traumatic stress" was a very recent one, but the Magekind had known of its effects for centuries. When people go into combat again and again, facing death in a variety of ugly ways, they're going to end up with personal demons that plunge them into hell without warning.

He still hadn't answered her. "Tristan?"

"She was on top. The last time."

Belle went cold. "You were making love when she tried to kill you?"

"Yeah."

"Nobody told me that."

"I never told anyone."

Belle had heard Isolde had turned traitor after she failed Merlin's test to become a Maja. Tristan had not failed, yet he'd chosen to drink from Merlin's Grail rather than remain mortal with his wife. She'd been furious, and she'd joined the rebellion led by Mordred, the bastard son of Arthur and Morgana.

The pair hadn't known they were half siblings when Morgana got pregnant. Merlin revealed their true relationship when he and Nimue appeared to test the inhabitants of Camelot.

Brilliant, proud nineteen-year-old Mordred had been one of those to fail Merlin's tests. Having been raised as Arthur's heir, he hadn't appreciated being denied the power and immortality the Grail conferred. He'd led other disaffected nobles against his father in a rebellion that left the kingdom in ruins. Arthur finally killed him at the Battle of Camlann, after a fight that nearly cost the king his life.

"Just before Camlann, Isolde sent a secret note saying she wanted to reconcile," Tristan said. "She hinted that if I met her, she'd spy on Mordred for Arthur."

"It was a trick."

"Yes." He said nothing for a long moment, breathing against her throat. "I still loved her. Despite everything, I remembered the girl she'd been when we fell in love as teenagers. We'd been married for twenty years by the time Merlin tested us, and she couldn't understand why I chose to accept the Grail when I knew she'd remain mortal. I tried to make her see it was a matter of duty. I was one of Arthur's knights and he needed me, but . . ." He lifted his head and met her gaze, silently begging her for the understanding his wife had denied him. "Some of our best fighters had failed Merlin's test, Belle. I couldn't let him go into combat alone against Mordred. We were too badly outnumbered."

"She seduced you." Belle's chest ached, a hard, deep throb that shot from her heart to her fingertips.

"Yes. She was on top, like you were a few minutes ago.

I didn't know about the dagger under the pillow. I'd closed my eyes, coming, and she slipped it out. I looked up just as she buried the blade in my chest."

"She didn't know it takes an enchanted weapon to kill one of us."

"No." His green eyes took on a tormented gleam. "I dragged the knife out, and I . . . It was instinct."

He didn't have to finish. They clung to each other for a long, shaking moment.

Belle felt sick. "Did you think I was going to kill you?"

Tristan's eyes flashed wide. "No! No, I just . . . saw her. It was a flashback. I saw her face. So many centuries gone, and I saw her face." He gritted his teeth. "Will I never be free of that bitch?"

NINE

Belle felt numb. The kind of numbness that follows a fatal blow, when you feel nothing but cold.

"I've never hurt a woman in bed since then, Belle. I swear it. I never would. But for a moment there, I was afraid I'd injured you with my bite." His green gaze searched hers, smoky with anxiety. "Are you sure I . . . ?"

"No. I'm fine."

Tristan looked at her for a long moment, and she stared back, feeling more helpless than she'd felt since she'd watched her daughter die.

"I'd better go." He drew away from her. With a start, she realized his softened sex had still been inside her.

A wave of her hand cleaned and dressed them both in jeans and T-shirts. Belle scrambled to her bare feet as he rose, every line of his body shouting of weariness. "Tristan, you don't have to leave. I want to talk . . ."

"I don't."

That stopped her dead. She stared at him for a sickly moment. "Oh."

"I've got too many devils, Belle. I thought I'd forgotten, but I haven't."

"You're going with Sabryn."

His gaze met hers. "I don't give a shit about Sabryn. And she'll never care about me. It's safer that way."

"Safe can kill the soul, Tristan."

"And sometimes you can't afford to care." He hesitated, slipping his hands into the back pockets of his jeans, his eyes on his toes. "You're a hell of a partner, Belle. There's nobody I'd rather have at my back."

"But not on top." The words emerged with a bitterness she hadn't intended.

"Demons just aren't that easy to kill." Tristan started out between the mounds of honeysuckle. Then he stopped and spoke without looking back at her. "I wish it were different."

"Tristan, dammit . . ."

He walked out of the garden.

"Well, Belle," she muttered to the fragrant night, "you really fucked that one up."

He'd hurt her. Physically, it could have been worse; Tristan had managed to arrest his dive at her throat like a man pulling back on a collared wolf.

Emotionally . . . the fear in her eyes when he'd told her about Isolde raked at Tristan like claws. It wasn't the first time he'd had a woman fear him; he'd had a very bad reputation after Isolde. Women had actively avoided him.

But then, he hadn't sought any out either. Bottles were enough for him then. It had been safer all the way around.

Until the minstrels had started in. Tristan guessed some Magekind's mortal child had whispered something in a bard's ear. The silly poet had woven so many lies around that kernel of fact, there was no recognizing it.

Isolde became his lady fair, and they were star-crossed

adulterous lovers. Apparently somebody had conflated the story with the mess between Arthur, Gwen, and Lancelot.

And Christ, what bad poetry was born.

Soon the new Magekind no longer feared him, for the true story was something the older ones considered too painful to repeat. So he was redeemed by minstrel lies. Women began approaching him again, and his dick decided it had had quite enough of celibacy, thank you.

Now here he was.

Tristan paused his long stride over the footbridge that arced across the River Nimue. He walked toward the stone handrail and leaned against it, looking down on the water. It rolled along, black as a stream of ink, with the white reflection of the moon dancing spectral-pale on its surface. The current looked almost lazy, as if a man could wade across.

In reality, it could snatch up a vampire and sweep him away between one breath and the next.

Like time. Like love. Tempting and treacherous.

Damn Isolde. She clung to him like a ghost, draining the pleasure from his life with icy, jealous fingers, making him a menace to the first woman he'd loved in fifteen centuries.

Tristan enjoyed nothing more than taunting death, but he'd finally found a risk he wouldn't take.

He wouldn't risk Belle.

She paced the garden, swiping angrily at her cheeks. *Damned if I'll cry for that bastard.*

Her tears felt cold, a slick, wet stream. Revolting.

In retrospect, Belle saw that she was the worst possible partner for Tristan. She killed her blood-mad partners in exactly the same way that Isolde had tried to slay him.

Not that she had a choice. When a vampire went blood-mad, he could rip your throat out before you even saw him move. Belle had learned that the only way to survive that third and final ride was to get on top, ready to pin her lover if he lost his wits. None of her Latent partners ever knew she fucked them all with a conjured blade in her hand.

So she adopted those that survived, treated them more like sons than ex-lovers as she guided them through the process of becoming veteran warriors. She celebrated their triumphs and comforted them after their failures, since not even the Magekind can learn without mistakes.

They never had any idea that she cherished them out of gratitude: *they hadn't made her kill them.*

She'd thought Tristan was safe. He would never turn on her. He was her equal, not a protégé to be carefully taught survival. Yet he'd turned out to be more vulnerable than any of them. Belle felt vaguely betrayed.

Morgana and Arthur had been right, dammit. Which should have been no surprise. Arthur was Tristan's best friend, had known him longer and better than anyone. When he said cracks ran through his friend's granite façade, she should have listened to him.

Something chirped. It took Belle a dazed moment to recognize the sound. Her cell. Probably Morgana.

But when she pulled the iPhone out of her pocket, Justice's deep voice spoke. "Hi, Belle. Listen, the Council of Clans wants you and Tristan to testify about Jimmy Sheridan's death tomorrow night."

"So they can call everything we say lies and declare war anyway? No thanks, Justice." Besides, she had no desire to see Tristan again for at least another century.

"Look, I've found out we've got the chairman of the Council of Clans on our side. He says he doesn't want war, and he wants to find a way out of this mess. If you testify, there's a chance we'll be able to talk sense into the council. Otherwise, war is certain. And a lot of people are going to pay with their lives."

When he put it that way, she didn't have much choice. "All right. I'll talk to Arthur and Tristan, see how we want to handle this."

"Nine P.M. tomorrow night, at Livingston Corporate Center. I'll message you from there to let you set up a gate."

"Fine. We'll be there." Assuming she could talk Tristan into tolerating her presence that long.

Hunger gnawed at Dice like maddening rat teeth chewing on his guts. He'd woken up that night healed of the countless cuts as if they'd never been. Ever since then, Warlock had been driving him, teaching him how to fight with his huge new body by stalking deer deep in the mountain woods. How to wheel and leap, bringing prey down with his size, his jaws, his quick, ripping claws. But no matter how much he ate of his prey, the tormenting hunger wasn't sated.

Weakness had set in as they worked, but he'd tried to ignore it. He'd wanted to make sure that the next time they fought, Warlock wouldn't take him apart.

But there was no ignoring the relentless gnaw now. Dice's legs shook under him like a weary old man's. "I'm sick, Warlock," he said, sinking onto his belly in the leaves. The wizard could fry him or not; he was done. "I gotta lay down."

Warlock cocked his head, orange eyes studying him. Clawed fingers flicked, sending a spell rolling across his furry flesh. The feel of the magic made his body go on point like a birddog catching sight of a grouse. "You're starving. Go hunt."

Dice stared up at his master. "Hunt what? Another deer?" He didn't have the strength.

"Magic. You need to kill something that has magic. I'd suggest one of Arthur's witches."

"Witches? What witches?" Dice stared at Warlock as he managed to reel to his feet. "Where the fuck am I supposed to find a witch?"

Warlock glanced at him appraisingly. "I'll give you the

first one, since you've burned through all your magic. After that, you'll have to do your own hunting."

His furred fingers sketched a shape, and a glowing point appeared, expanding into a hole in midair. "Through there. Wait. They'll be home in a couple of hours, and you can feed then."

Dice licked his dry, cracked lips. His tongue felt swollen. "How do you feed on magic?"

Warlock grinned, the expression chilling even to Dice. "You'll figure it out."

All in all, sitting next to a pissed-off Belle while surrounded by three hundred furious werewolves wasn't an experience Tristan would recommend. Even as she testified in that clear, ringing voice, she radiated cold at him like a dry-ice machine. Meanwhile wolves growled and rumbled all around them as if it was feeding time at the zoo. Tris was starting to feel like frozen Alpo.

"You set us up, Justice," Tristan muttered to his friend. "Thanks a lot."

"Not necessarily," Justice whispered back. "Carl Rosen— he's the chairman—is from an old family with a hell of a lot of pull. And Rosen doesn't want war. He can calm this bunch down if anyone can."

"You'd better be right, or things are going to get ugly." Having the job he did, it was hardly the first time Tristan had attended a meeting with a bunch of angry people. Generally, if you had a witch along, she could make sure the situation didn't spin out of control. But since werewolves were immune to magic, Belle couldn't cast a spell to calm everybody down. To make matters worse, there were one or two fuzzy bastards in the crowd who were actively trying to whip everyone else into a lynching, just for shits and giggles. His vampire hearing kept detecting incendiary comments, not that anyone exactly whispered.

Plus, there was plenty of room for a really good mob. The Livingston Corporate Center was a sprawling four-story cream building that occupied five wooded acres on the outskirts of Greenville, South Carolina. Livingston was one of the few remaining textile firms in the South that still operated manufacturing plants in the U.S., and the company used the center for its research and development. More than a thousand people worked in the building, so its auditorium was spacious, with comfortable theater-style seating facing a large stage. He, Belle and Bill Justice sat up there under the hot lights, at a table facing the longer one where the thirteen council members sat.

Twelve of them looked constipated, worried, or bloodthirsty, depending on their political leanings. Chairman Carl Rosen was simply expressionless.

Meanwhile the audience was SRO with people who wanted Tristan's head on a stick. Tristan wanted something sharp in his hand and a layer of metal between his hide and all those teeth.

"So you're saying this Cherise Myers died of one bite?" Robert Tanner curled a handsome lip, black eyes cold.

"Yes. We did everything we could to save her, but none of our healing spells worked," Belle said, completely ignoring Tanner's implication she was lying. Tristan wanted to punch in the bastard's teeth. "It was a very painful death, and it took her more than an hour to die."

"I've never heard our bites are fatal to Magekind." Linda Corley drummed her fingers on the table and looked nervously out over the crowd. She was a motherly, gray-haired woman dressed in a flowered polyester dress, who looked as if she should be baking cookies somewhere. Judging by her expression, she wished she was wrist deep in Toll House dough right now.

Tanner slanted Corley a look. "Where is the body?"

"Cherise died shortly after being bitten. We held her

memorial service last night, sending her body back to the Mageverse in accordance with our customs."

"How convenient."

Tristan glared, sick of Fido's attitude. "What do you mean by that?"

"We have no proof this woman died."

"Why would we lie?"

Tanner settled back in his chair and gave Tristan another lip curl. "To protect Arthur Pendragon. To protect the admitted killer of Jimmy Sheridan."

The audience growled in savage agreement.

Tristan opened his mouth to snarl a reply, but Belle's hand landed on his knee in a light, cautioning squeeze as she opened a magical communications link. *"He's trying to get a rise out of you, Tris."*

"I'll give him a rise. I'll rise out of this chair and cut that lip right off his face if he curls it at me one more time."

Belle spoke up before he could. "Arthur had nothing to do with Jimmy Sheridan's death, Mr. Tanner."

Tanner leaned forward like a prosecutor smelling blood. "But isn't it true that Arthur was furious his son was targeted by a grief-stricken werewolf trying to avenge his own son's death?"

She didn't even blink. "As we've told you before, Logan killed the assassins who tried to kill him. As far as Arthur's concerned, that was the end of it."

"You must think we're fools," Andrews spat. "Arthur wants Direkind blood, and he's having our innocent children killed."

"Got any proof?" Tristan demanded.

Tanner lifted a brow. "Davon Fredericks and Cherise Myers both said Arthur ordered them to kill the Sheridan boy."

"They were under magical influence at the time," Belle explained. "A spell compelled them to believe Arthur had given them that order when he did no such thing. It also convinced them the boy had murdered a little girl, or neither of them would have committed such a horrific crime."

Tanner gave Belle a chilly, triumphant smile and asked the question Tristan had been dreading. "And who cast this supposed 'spell'?"

Belle didn't equivocate. The sound system mic picked up her answer and set it echoing around the room. "Warlock."

Tanner stared at her, eyes wide. He was a lousy actor. *"Warlock?"*

"And Santa Claus cut off Jimmy's head," Anderson muttered. The audience hooted.

Belle ignored the laughter. "Warlock exists. I fought him last month after he tried to murder a friend of mine. He is evil and he is insane, and he's trying to manipulate the Direkind into going to war with the Magekind." Her eyes narrowed as she scanned the council table. "The question is, are you going to fall for the scam? Are people going to die while you play politics?"

Stunned silence reigned for almost a full minute. Tristan, knowing what was coming, had to fight the impulse to close his eyes in pain. *"Belle, you just maligned their hero. They're going to lose their collective minds."*

"Well, how would you explain what the bastard did?"

Right on cue, the crowd detonated into furious shouts. Wolves who'd been seated bounded to their feet, and those already standing shook their fists and roared.

"Warlock's a hero—he would have never killed a kid!"

". . . Crazy bitch . . ."

"Arthur's the killer!"

"Fucking Magekind murderers . . ."

"If you believe these liars, you're stupid as hell!"

"Warlock died centuries ago . . ."

"Enough!" Rosen banged his gavel down hard, though it was his growling roar more than the little wooden hammer that finally silenced the crowd. "I said that's enough!"

It took another five minutes of snarls and curses, but the

crowd finally subsided, staring at Belle and Tristan with contemptuous, hate-filled eyes.

Anderson spoke into the simmering silence. "You must take us for fools, witch. Warlock's been dead for centuries, assuming he ever existed at all. And everyone knows werewolves can't use magic, so it's impossible that any of us could have cast such a spell."

She didn't even blink. "Actually, werewolves can use magic, and I can prove it."

Rosen lifted a graying eyebrow. "Produce your proof."

Belle pulled her enchanted iPhone out of a pocket and punched a couple of buttons. "We're ready for you."

A dimensional gate spiraled open beside their table, drawing murmurs of amazement from those werewolves who'd never seen one before. Eva Roman stepped through the shimmering oval, dressed in black slacks and a black silk shirt that matched Smoke's fur so perfectly he seemed to grow out of her shoulder. The sight of him aroused a little growl from the audience; apparently some of them really didn't like cats.

He shot them all a blue-eyed glance and pointedly turned his head away with feline disdain. The tip of his tail flicked against Eva's back.

Smoke did do cat well.

Point made, he leaped down from Eva's shoulder, changing into his Sidhe form before he hit the floor. Straightening to his full height, he let the werewolves stare, taking in his pointed ears and elegant Sidhe features. Like his lover, Smoke looked as if he'd been painted in India ink, with that black raw silk shirt and black slacks, his hair gleaming like fur as it fell from his broad shoulders to his narrow waist. A few women in the crowd sighed. He gave them a slow, seductive smile.

Yeah, Smoke knew how to work it.

Belle stood, visibly suppressing a smile at his act. "This is Smoke, a Sidhe warrior and elemental." She nodded to the woman beside him. "And this is Eva Roman, who is a werewolf and Smoke's partner. She's also my proof."

Eva transformed in a bloom of power. Magic sparked blue around her body as she shifted, growing taller, her body broadening, head lengthening into a lupine muzzle, sable fur spreading over her body like a dark silk wave. When her transformation was complete, murmurs of astonishment rose at the ghostly blue antlers that spread to either side of her pointed wolf ears.

Tanner smirked. "What the hell is she—Rudolph the Red-Nosed Werewolf?"

The crowd laughed, the sound nasty with mockery.

Eva lifted her chin like a young queen. "Yes, I'm a werewolf. But I'm also a witch." She flicked her claws and sent a ball of blue light shooting at Tanner's head.

He yelped and automatically threw a hand up to ward it off. The little ball promptly burst in front of his nose in a harmless shower of sparks. This time the laughter was at his expense. Tanner flushed.

Go, Eva, Tristan thought. *Get the bastard.*

"How the hell did you do that?" Elena Rollings leaned forward, her long, curling red hair brushing the table in front of her. "I thought Merlin's Curse was specifically structured to keep us from being able to work magic. That was the only way we could be resistant to magical attacks." A power Merlin had known they'd need if the Magekind ever went rogue.

"It is," Eva told her. "And my new abilities have made me vulnerable to magical attacks again." She shrugged her furry Direwolf shoulders. "Nothing's ever free."

Rosen had produced a netbook from somewhere and had been typing. He looked up. "There's no Eva Roman in our database of werewolf families. You're unregistered. That's a serious violation of Clan law, Ms. Roman."

"Until a month ago, I never even knew there was a Council of Clans, much less that I'd be required to register by one."

"And why not?" Tanner demanded, his gaze predatory, obviously hoping she'd say something he could turn against her.

Smoke straightened. The look in the Sidhe's eyes said he was considering doing something to the werewolf a lot more painful than tossing a few fireworks.

Eva gave Tanner a long stare. "I was Bitten by a serial killer. He neglected to instruct me in proper werewolf etiquette before he abandoned me in the woods to die. Probably because he was more interested in eating me."

Elena paled, looking sick. "Did you survive?"

Eva shrugged. "The cops showed up and scared him off before he could finish killing me."

"I'm so sorry for what you went through." Genuine regret softened her voice. A few women in the audience murmured sympathetic agreement. "You must be talking about Trey Devon. We had no idea he was the one who was murdering humans." Elena sat back in her seat, eyeing Tanner as if expecting his next salvo. "He was Chosen, and his father used his influence to block the Wolf Sheriff's investigation of the killings."

"Fuckin' Chosen," someone in the crowd shouted. Tristan suppressed a smile.

"Trey Devon was an aberration," Tanner piped up right on cue. "And his father acted out of love."

"I knew George Devon and his son, and both of them were bastards," Elena said tartly. "His daughter was every bit as bad. And you know it, Bob. If you weren't so busy trying to cover the Chosen's collective ass . . ."

"We're off the subject," Rosen snapped, and turned to Eva. "How did you acquire the magic? And what's with the antlers?"

Eva tilted her head, and sparks danced around the tips of her horns. "Warlock attacked and murdered an elemental in order to rob him of his powers. His name was Zephyr, and though he occupied the body of a white stag, his powers were nothing short of godlike."

"A magic deer god," Andrews drawled, looking up from doodling on his notepad. "Riiiight."

Eva flicked a pointed ear and ignored him. "Stealing his abilities made Warlock immensely powerful. Warlock then tried to kill Smoke . . ."

"And damn near succeeded," Smoke rumbled.

". . . And Zephyr's ghost sought me out. He said he could teach me how to alter Merlin's genetic spell in my DNA so I could work magic and help Smoke. The catch was that I had to permit him to share my body so he could seek revenge on Warlock. Smoke was in danger, so I agreed."

"And saved my ass." Smoke gave her a slow smile and threaded his fingers with her clawed ones. Somebody gasped, whether in outrage or titillation, Tristan couldn't tell.

"Let me get this straight—you're possessed by a magical *ghost deer*?" Tanner turned to Rosen. "Don't tell me you believe this crap."

"You can turn into a seven-foot werewolf," Smoke observed mildly. "You're sitting in a room with a Knight of the Round Table, and discussing declaring war on King Arthur. And you say you find *us* unbelievable?"

The Sidhe warrior gestured, and a three-dimensional picture appeared in midair as if projected on a movie screen. Great stone blocks gleamed in the moonlight, providing cover as the figures of Smoke and Eva crouched behind them. "This is a projection of my memories of the battle that took place last month." A towering white figure stepped out from behind one of the blocks, glowing against the night like a ghost. "And *that* is Warlock."

The crowd murmured in awe, a sound that became a startled shout as the wizard hurtled a lightning bolt at Eva and Smoke. The flash was blinding, and the boom made the room shake. The recorded Smoke deflected the strike with an energy shield that lit up the room.

"Was that a lightning bolt?" Elena demanded. "Warlock tried to hit you with a *lightning bolt*?"

Smoke shrugged. "We were tossing around a lot of power."

Tanner blinked. "Can *you* throw lightning bolts?"

Smoke gave him a feral grin. "Why, yes. Would you like me to demonstrate?"

"No!" Rosen interrupted, in chorus with the council and half the audience. "That's fine, we believe you."

"Good. Then watch, and I'll explain."

Smoke started narrating as the image flared bright with thundering energy strikes. Tristan exchanged a satisfied smile with Belle and sat back to enjoy the show.

Dice had never been so hungry, not even as a child. But this time, it wasn't food he craved.

He wanted magic, needed it. *Craved* it like a crackhead craved rock. If he didn't feed soon, he'd be too weak to hunt.

There was magic inside the house. He could smell the sharp, ozone scent of it right through the walls: three stories of expensive cream brick that reminded him of a castle. He stalked along the perimeter of the house, drinking the smell, aching to taste its source. It was a damned good thing the place nestled in the middle of two acres of woods. Otherwise the neighbors might have spotted a certain bearlike monster and called the cops. Which would have been a bitch.

Especially for the cops. Rearing up on his hind legs, Dice braced his massive paws on the frame of a second-story window and looked inside. A child's room, judging by the bed shaped like the Batmobile. Magic glinted at him from the black plastic headboard. A spell to ward off bad dreams and give the kid a deep, healthy sleep.

The witch sure loved her brat.

He backed away from the window and dropped to all fours, wondering if he could use that love somehow. Take the kid hostage, offer to release him if she surrendered without a fight?

She might not love the kid *that* much. God knew Dice's mother wouldn't have taken such a deal. Hell, Ma had once traded him for a twenty-five dollar crack rock. He'd been all of eleven, and the bastard who'd bought him had been a big, beefy fucker. Dice hadn't had a prayer.

Wasn't the first time, wasn't the last.

He'd enjoyed shooting his mother. He'd made sure nobody ever found the body, either.

Dice padded onward, pausing at yet another rosebush that smelled deliciously of magic. It wasn't much of a spell, just something to ward off bugs, but it made the roses smell like ribeye to Dice's starving nose.

He ate the blooms one by one, then started nibbling the leaves, careful of the thorns. None of which was enough to fill his pit of a stomach. It reminded him of the pack of crackers he'd found at the bottom of his mother's purse once, when she'd been too wasted to feed him for a couple of days.

Even peanut butter on stale cheddar still tasted delicious to a famished little five-year-old.

Feeling a bit stronger, Dice continued around the house, sniffing at flower beds and windows for more magic. He was too big to fit through the door, but there were more magical items inside. He had to get to them.

Just to take the edge off until the witch got home.

TEN

The bastard council had blindsided them.

After Smoke and Eva had finished testifying, Tanner stood up and said, "All this is interesting, I'm sure, but it doesn't address the primary issue. Davon Fredericks has admitted beheading James Sheridan. He should be handed over to the Council of Clans for trial. I move that if Arthur Pendragon fails to surrender him, the council shall declare war."

Even the werewolf crowd had muttered in astonishment.

Elena Rollings had made an impassioned argument that Arthur had no reason to want Jimmy dead. She might as well have saved her breath. The outcome had been painfully obvious as each council member voted, aye following aye like the tolling of a grim bell.

"Aye." Tanner tried to look suitably grave as he added his vote to the rest, but his eyes glinted with excitement.

"Nay." Elena said looked sick.

"Twelve ayes to one nay." Rosen banged his gavel. "The motion passes." He looked down at Belle and Tristan. "You will inform Arthur that the Council of Clans demands that he hand over Davon Fredericks for trial. If he refuses, we will go to war against the Magekind."

"Dammit, we proved Warlock exists!" Tristan exploded. "He lied to Davon, tricked him into believing he was Arthur, and compelled him to kill Sheridan."

"But he did kill Sheridan. His reasons for commiting the crime are irrelevant." Rosen announced. "The boy is dead. Either he pays, or the Magekind does. The ball's in Arthur's court now."

"If we go to war," Tristan told him in a low, deadly voice, "Jimmy Sheridan will not be the only dead werewolf. I'd think twice about this if I were you."

Rosen lifted his chin. "Sir Tristan, we are not afraid of the Magekind. Hand over Fredericks and nobody has to die."

Except Davon, Belle thought.

"Man, it was sick the way Danger Man killed that monster!" Noah crowed, bouncing a little in the backseat. "He just opened up with his Starblast and zap! The monster was gone!"

Emma glanced back at her eleven-year-old son as they drove, a smile teasing her mouth. She hated to admit it, but she'd enjoyed the movie every bit as well as her son. The 3-D effects were impressive, and the creators had done a good job computer-animating Danger Man, his sidekick Dynamite, and their various evil enemies. Plus, there'd been just enough adult-level humor to keep her husband laughing, while sailing right over Noah's head.

Thomas tossed her a look as he drove their Camry into the development. *"You giggled just as hard as I did, and you know it."*

"Yeah, yeah."

"You also cried like a baby when Danger Man got shot."

"I did not."

"Hey. Truebonded here. Remember who senses your every thought and emotion? Can't lie to me."

"Didn't your mother teach you it's rude to eavesdrop?"

"Rude, but fun."

As he drove, Emma slid a hand over and rested it lightly on his knee, enjoying the shift of hard muscle under her hand. They'd been married for fifty years now, and Truebonded for most of that time. She'd never regretted forming the psychic link that bound them soul to soul.

And now they had Noah. She looked back over her shoulder at her son, who was still chattering about Danger Man. With Arthur's permission, they'd decided to take an eighteen-year sabbatical to raise the boy. Sometimes she missed the adrenaline rush of fighting beside her handsome husband for Merlin's Great Mission.

But hell, they were immortal. There would always be missions, but there was only one Noah.

The moonlight pouring in through the Lexus's rear window set her son's blond hair ablaze as it traced the line of the boy's snub nose and round little chin. He looked so much like his father, he made her heart ache.

Thomas turned into their driveway, and Emma glanced around just as the headlights swept across the front of the house. She stiffened. "What the hell happened to my roses?"

Which was when she realized there was something far more wrong than a few uprooted bushes. She froze. "There's something inside the house."

Tom's head snapped toward her, dark eyes going narrow. His mental voice reached out to her through the Truebond. *"What kind of something?"*

"Something with power." She reached for the door latch.

He grabbed her arm. *"Not without me, you don't."*

"We can't both go in and leave Noah out here by himself. And we're sure as heck not taking him inside."

"Then I'll go."

"This thing is radiating magic, Tom. You don't do magic. That's my job."

"Mom?" Noah's voice sounded crushed tight and small with fear. "Momma, what's wrong?"

"I don't know. You just sit here with your daddy and I'll go have a look."

"I've got a better idea," Thomas said in the link. *"Let's call Morgana and get some backup."*

"Tom, whatever it is isn't that powerful. We are not talking about a Dark One here. I can take care of it."

"You don't even know what 'it' is."

"So I'll go find out. I'll be back in a minute. If I need help, I'll give Morgana a yell."

"Dammit, Emma . . ."

But she'd already unbuckled her seat belt and thrown open the door. She was out before the Lexus had even rolled to a complete stop.

Emma moved fast and low toward the garage, adrenaline singing through her veins. She'd almost forgotten how much she loved this. She adored being a mother, but nothing made her feel so thoroughly alive as knowing *something* waited inside the house. Something with power. Not much power, true, but enough to be interesting.

It had been way too long since she'd fought anything interesting.

She conjured her armor and went in.

Tom watched his wife steal into the garage, moving like the warrior she'd been for more than eight hundred years. He ground his teeth, as sick tension gathered in the pit of his stomach.

Damn Emma anyway.

"Where's Momma going?" Noah asked in a shaking voice.

"She's just going to check on something. It'll be fine." If overconfidence wasn't about to bite her on the ass. Of course,

Emma had good reason to be confident. She'd fought and killed one of the powerful, demonic Dark Ones who'd tried to invade Avalon a couple of years back. She was no lightweight.

Neither was he. Between the two of them, they'd battled every nasty breed of human you could think of for half a century. Al-Qaeda, Nazis, communists, all kinds of spies, traitors, assassins, and serial killers. Emma herself had been at the job even longer, casting spells, shooting guns and knifing various bastards for centuries. Whatever was in the house was simply more of the same.

He just wished he was in there, too, watching over her. Just as he'd been doing for the past fifty years.

Keeping Emma alive had gotten to be a habit.

"Would you calm down?" Emma said through their bond. *"You're making me twitchy."*

"Yeah, well, I'm twitchy. And I'd feel a lot less twitchy if I could fucking watch your back."

"You're watching something far more important—Noah."

He couldn't argue with that. Noah had added so much to their lives as they'd watched him grow from helpless newborn to active little boy. Tom knew he'd die for his son without hesitation, just as he'd die for Emma. She'd already slipped into the house and was padding silently toward the source of the faint sounds she could hear coming from the living room. Tense, worried, Tom focused hard on their link, trying to identify those noises.

Was that . . . chewing?

Sword in one hand, the other ready to conjure an energy shield, Emma stepped into the house's two-story great room. With its fireplace, bookshelves, and soaring ceiling, it was her favorite room in the house.

She'd never expected to see a monster in it.

The beast crouched in front of her precious collection of

rare spell books. Huge, black, and furry, it looked like some kind of enormous bear. How the hell had a bear gotten into the house?

Emma felt a draft of cool night air and flicked a glance to the side. The glass door that led out to the deck was shattered into jagged chunks on the carpeted floor, as if the beast had rammed right through it. The animal had been injured in the process too; drops of blood snaked along the floor in a trail leading to the bookcase. What the hell would a bear want with the bookcase when the trashcan was right down the hall, complete with tonight's leftovers?

Books were scattered all around the creature's huge paws. The bear turned its head to look at her, and she realized it wasn't a bear at all, but the biggest fucking wolf she'd ever seen. It had to be ten feet tall at the shoulder. And there was a piece of paper hanging out of its mouth. She sensed a fading flicker of magic, and realized what it was doing.

"*You're eating my spell books?*" she demanded, outraged.

"Yeah," said the giant wolf in a growling rumble. "I'm sorry, but I'm so fucking hungry."

And then it lunged.

Tom gasped at the searing agony as the creature's jaws clamped onto his wife's forearm, which she'd thrown up in an instinctive attempt to protect her throat. He heard the crunch of bone through the link as Emma's shrill scream rang out.

"Daddy—Mommy's screamin'!"

"*I know!*" He threw the car door open and threw himself out into the garage, wanting only to rescue his wife from the thing that hurt her.

Then he heard the rear door open and the slap of Noah's little sneakers.

He wheeled. "No, Noah, you've got to stay—"

The pain chopped his legs right out from under him. He didn't even feel himself hit the cement floor. From somewhere very far away, he heard his boy yell "Daddy!"

Pain. Pain, a blazing pressure in his chest. Knowing he had only seconds, he fumbled his BlackBerry out of his pants pocket. "Call . . . Belle . . ." he panted, and the spell Emma had cast on the phone did its job.

"Hello." He could barely make out the familiar voice of his oldest friend.

"Emma . . . Some . . . thing's killing Emma . . ." Tom rasped, fighting to speak through the cold pressure that crushed his chest. "Save . . . Noah . . ."

Belle jumped up from the couch in Arthur's living room and cast a gate to the source of the cell phone's magic. She knew the sound of a dying man's voice when she heard it.

Which meant Tom's son was in one hell of a lot of trouble.

Tristan rose to his feet and grabbed his sword. "What's going on?"

"Did he say a 'thing' was killing Emma?" Arthur drew Excalibur as his wife summoned his armor, then did the same for Bors.

The six of them, including Morgana, had been meeting at the Pendragon home to discuss the Direkind's ultimatum. Eva and Smoke had remained behind at the Livingston Center so they could follow Tanner; Smoke thought the councilman smelled as if he'd been keeping company with Warlock. Which in retrospect sucked, since they could have used the powerful couple in the current situation. Belle conjured armor and weapons for herself and Tristan. "Don't know, but it's not good," she told Arthur. "Tom sounded hurt. Bad."

Tom was worse than hurt.

The gate took them to the long curving cement drive in

front of the Jacobs' big brick house. They could hear the boy screaming hysterically from inside the garage. "Daddy! Daddy, get up!"

Weapons drawn, the six fanned out and moved fast into the garage.

Noah's father lay on his back not far from his still-running Lexus. His empty eyes stared sightlessly at the ceiling, past the tear-streaked face of his son, who lay across his body. There wasn't a mark on him, but Belle's magic told her they were too late. Grief stole her breath.

Tom Jacobs was dead.

"Daddy, Daddy!" the little boy cried in a repetitive heart-breaking wail. His thin arms wrapped around his father's cooling neck, and his chest worked with furious sobs. "Don't die! Please don't die!"

Gwen swept forward and bent to place a hand on the child's bright blond head. "Shhhhh. We'll take care of you, baby."

The boy slumped sideways, and she caught him up in her arms. His body hung limp with the bonelessness of a child's deep sleep. Gwen's spell had put him out like a candle flame.

"I'll get him to the healer," she said, glancing up at them. "I'll be back as soon as I can." As she headed for the dilating spark of her dimensional gate, she added to her husband, "As I don't want to end up like that poor bastard, try not to get yourself killed."

When one partner in a Truebond died, the psychic shock tended to kill the other. That was one reason Magekind agents thought twice about entering the bond, though it did enhance one's strength and magical abilities.

All of which meant little Noah had lost his mother as well as his father.

Arthur turned to Morgana as his wife slipped through the gate. "Any idea what's in there?"

The witch frowned. She was Avalon's most powerful

Maja, so it was possible she sensed more than Belle did. "I'm not sure. There's something with power in there, but its magical signature is muddied. It reads like werewolf, but there's a strong Magekind signature too." Which couldn't be coming from Emma; her death had apparently killed her husband.

"Could we have anyone else on the scene?" Arthur asked.

Morgana's frown deepened. Belle sympathized. She couldn't tell what the hell was going on, either. "No. It's not a Maja."

"Then let's go in and find out what the hell it is." Arthur hefted his sword and started for the front door.

Tristan stepped into his path. "Arthur, we've had this discussion before. You don't take point. We can't afford to lose you." The point man had a tendency to get killed.

Sweat rolled down Belle's back, and it occurred to her she had no desire to lose Tristan, either.

Wait. Did she even *have* Tristan?

Arthur frowned, but he dropped back reluctantly. "Does anybody know the lay of this house?"

"I've been here several times," Belle told him, forcing herself to concentrate on a question she could answer. "I think whatever attacked Emma is in the great room. There's a deck with a glass door on that side. It might have gotten in that way." Which also made it a possible escape route for the killer.

Arthur jerked his head in that direction. "You and Bors go around and cover that door."

"Aye, my liege," Bors said, turning to lead the way.

For a moment Belle wished she'd been partnered with Tristan, but she thrust the thought aside. Tris was Arthur's bodyguard and right arm. He belonged with Arthur.

So she strode after Bors as he stalked out of the garage and around the back of the house. The night was clear overhead, the stars as sharp as bright needle pricks in black silk. As they went, she moved in close to the knight's back and cast an energy shield in front of him to protect him from magical attack.

Bors paused, frowning up the deck's wooden steps. "Looks like whatever it was broke in."

He was right. The glass door was not only shattered, its metal frame was warped out of shape as though something huge had forced its way through.

"I don't like the looks of that," Belle murmured.

"I do." Bors hefted his sword and gave her a reckless grin. "Suddenly I'm no longer bored."

Tristan frowned as Belle disappeared around the corner at Bors's heels. His instinct was to go after her, to protect her from whatever had killed Emma. But his duty was to watch Arthur's back, and besides, Belle was safer outside than inside with whatever was killing agents.

Still, he felt his stomach coil into a sour knot of anxiety. *Take care of her, Bors, dammit.* He hoped the bastard hadn't been drinking.

"We don't have all night, Tris," Arthur growled.

"No, my liege." Lifting his sword, he turned and slipped into the house through the garage entrance, Morgana and Arthur padding after him.

There was a rattling scrape, like something metallic being dragged across the floor. Inhaling, he tasted the air. Fur. Blood. And the heavy ozone reek of magic.

Lengthening his stride, Tristan moved through the dark, silent kitchen and stepped into the great room.

The armored figure of Emma Jacobs lay sprawled in the middle of the room, surrounded by a puddle of bright red blood that spread out across the cream carpet. An enormous furry beast crouched over her, its muzzle buried in her belly, past armor ripped open and peeled back like a tin can. The thing's jaws worked as it fed.

Red eyes rolled up to glare at him. A chill rolled over Tristan's skin as it lifted its bloody muzzle to snarl.

"Get the hell away from her!" Tristan roared, swinging his sword at the beast.

The creature jerked away from its victim and reared, its head hitting the ceiling fifteen feet overhead. There was a crunch, and plaster rained down around it as it swung a big clawed paw at Tristan's armored head.

He ducked back as the creature hit the shield Morgana had generated in front of him. Sparks snapped and danced from the blow.

Arthur stepped in, Excalibur glowing white with magic as he swung at the beast's massive chest. Tristan pivoted and thrust his blade at its exposed belly. Sparks popped. Apparently the thing had a shield of its own.

Not just a werewolf then, Tris thought. *Not that I've ever seen a werewolf that size.*

With a roar of fury, the monster whirled and plunged through the glass door's bent frame. The agents ran after it as it leaped off the deck and hit the ground with an earth-shaking thud.

Belle rounded the deck and shot a blast of fire at the monster's head. The beast opened its jaws and snapped up the fireball like a dog catching a treat.

Oh, Tristan thought, *that's just not good.* He bounded off the deck as the monster reared onto its hind legs and batted at Bors, who charged, sword swinging in wide arcs.

The knight roared a battle cry and dodged the swipe. Belle ran after him, her own blade raised as she shielded him. The monster fell on them like a house, hitting the hemisphere of her shield so hard, her knees buckled. Somehow she straightened under the creature's great weight, knocking it back on its rear legs. It balanced on its haunches and bit into the shield as if it were an apple. Sparks flew from its mouth. It pulled back and snaked a foreleg through the hole its jaws had created.

Bors swung furiously at the encroaching claws. Belle shoved him down the instant before the beast could rip off his head.

Jesu, Tris had to distract it before it had Belle for lunch. His heart in his throat, he darted around and slashed at the creature's elephantine haunches, hoping to hamstring it. Snarling, it twisted and lunged at him, jaws snapping down on the shield Morgana had thrown up around him. It ripped at the shield, pulling out a shining strand of magic, then gulping the energy down like a kid eating taffy.

"What the hell is that thing?" Tristan yelled at Morgana.

"Big," Morgana snapped.

"Thank you, Lady Obvious!"

The beast fell to all fours, and Bors went on the attack again with flashing figure eights of his sword, dancing around just beyond the creature's nose.

As she'd been trained to do, Belle stayed at Bors's shoulder, moving with him like a dancer so she could maintain the magical shield. Her eyes were wide and wild in her white face as she stared up at the thing.

"Bors, get back dammit!" Tristan bellowed. "You're too damned close!" *And so is Belle.*

Instead of retreating, Bors pressed closer, aiming blows at the creature's belly and forelegs. The blade glanced harmlessly off its shield, but that didn't stop Bors from continuing his attack.

Frustrated, Tris snarled at Arthur, "If that son of a bitch gets Belle killed, he's a dead man!"

"Keep your mind on the monster, not the girl," Arthur growled.

"Somebody just conjured a gate!" Morgana yelled. "And it wasn't one of us."

Tristan looked around as the gate dilated wide, far wider than any of them would have needed, but just the right size for Godzilla Furboy. The creature swung its head around and shot them a look, then stood up on its hind legs, opened its jaws, and breathed a gout of fire right at Belle and Bors.

"Belle!" Tristan bellowed, as the inferno hid her from view.

The monster whirled and leaped through the gate with a triumphant flick of its bushy tail. The flame winked out, leaving Belle and Bors unhurt. Thank God.

Tris felt Morgana's magic swell, then fade away again as she swore in a half dozen languages.

"Did you get where the gate went?" Arthur demanded.

She shook her dark head. "Something blocked my spell. Something with one hell of a lot more power than the furball."

"Who wants to bet it was Warlock?" Belle asked. She looked pale as a shroud, and blood streaked her armor. Tristan couldn't tell if it was her own.

"Anybody got a clue what that thing was?" Bors asked, flipping up the visor of his helmet.

Anger sizzling through him, Tristan flipped up his own and stalked over to his brother knight until he could stare into his eyes. Even as dark as it was, Bors's pupils were contracted into pinpricks. It was a miracle he'd been able to see to fight. "How much blood did you have tonight, Bors?" The words emerged in a growl so deep, he scarcely recognized it as his own.

Bors planted one hand in the middle of Tristan's chest and shoved hard, forcing him to step back a pace. "Get out of my face, Tristan."

"How much?"

"That's none of your damned business!"

"It is my damned business when you endanger Belle!"

"What, did you elope while I wasn't looking?" He raised his sword. "Get off my ass, Tristan, or I'll put you down."

"Did you have too much blood tonight, Bors?" Arthur asked the question softly, but with a dangerous note in his voice Tristan recognized. That Pendragon temper was on the verge of detonation. He raised his visor and stared into his knight's face.

Anguish and shame slid across Bors's handsome features. Which was all the answer any of them needed.

"See the healer," Arthur told him shortly. "You're not going back into combat until you kick the addiction."

The knight's broad shoulders slumped. "Yes, my liege."

Morgana opened a gate with a gesture. Bors looked through it, then glanced at Arthur, straightened his shoulders with an obvious effort, and strode through the gate.

After it closed behind him, Arthur sighed. "I knew he had a problem. I just didn't realize it was that bad."

"I did warn you," Tristan said.

"I'd hoped you were wrong." Shaking his dark head, Arthur turned toward the deck. "Let's see if our monstrous friend left any clues behind."

Belle stared down at what was left of Emma Jacobs, her stomach tying itself into a sick, sour knot. Morgana crouched beside the body, both hands spread wide as she conducted a magical autopsy, sensing both every injury the woman had suffered and when they'd occurred.

Justice stood just behind her, staring down at Emma with an appalled expression on his handsome face. Belle had brought him in so that he could report what he saw to his council, since they'd probably refuse to believe anything the Magekind had to say. Arthur stood next to the werewolf, looking grim as his hand rode Excalibur's hilt. He'd sheathed the weapon, but he looked as if he badly wanted to draw it and start hacking at something.

Morgana's fingers traced the air over the ragged edges of the hole in Emma's abdomen. "This bite was postmortem," she said, voicing the conclusion Belle had already drawn.

"It appears this is the wound that killed her." She gestured, indicating the woman's forearm. It was crushed and mangled despite Emma's armor.

"See those puncture wounds, Morgana?" Belle said. "It looks as though it bit her arm and just held on."

"She fought back pretty hard," Tristan said, gesturing at the arcs of blood that splashed across the room. "Judging by the smell, a lot of this blood is the creature's."

Justice crouched to eye the distance between the two puncture wounds the beast's fangs had left. "Damn. That's not a typical Direwolf bite. The thing must have a head the size of a grizzly's."

"No shit," Tristan growled, in a thoroughly foul mood. "We told you it did."

The werewolf leaned down over Morgana's shoulder and sniffed, frowning. "Does that bite smell like the one that killed Cherise to you?"

Morgana rose to walk around the body, studying it. "Could be the same death spell, though it worked far more quickly. Otherwise, this wound would not have killed her so fast."

"My human nose isn't worth a damn." Magic detonated around Justice as he shifted to Dire Wolf form. He didn't appear to notice how everyone else tensed. Going to one knee, he lowered his head over Emma's arm and drew in a deep breath.

He promptly jerked back his head, as if he'd smelled something rotten. "This wound smells corrupted, as if the bite was poison. And the magic is rank."

"Death magic smells like that," Tristan told him.

Belle turned away, grief weighing at her. *Poor Noah. Both parents gone.* She bent to pick up one of the books that lay scattered and crushed on the floor. As she opened it, she frowned. It was one of Emma's spell books. "Where's the magic?"

"What?" Arthur looked up at her.

"This is one of Emma's spell books, but the magic is completely drained from it." She traced the deep punctures in its cover. "It's as if the wolf drank its magic like a vampire drinking blood."

"You're right." Morgana's eyes widened. "There should be magic lingering around Emma's body even now, but there's nothing. It drained her dry."

"Remember how it seemed to bite into your shield?" Tristan asked. "The fuzzy bastard *eats* magic."

Arthur's lip curled. "Now, there's a twist we didn't need."

Even Justice looked appalled.

Dice stood in the cavern on shaking legs, blood streaming from a dozen cuts. He'd survived a battle with Arthur, his knights and his witches, but it had been too damned close.

And he'd eaten the Maja. Nausea curdled his triumph as he remembered the taste of blood and meat in his mouth. The human part of him had been revolted, but the wolf had been too hungry to care.

He'd drunk down Emma's magic in greedy gulps that had somehow sucked in her husband's, too. His name had been Tom Jacobs, he knew. And they'd had a son, Noah. A son they'd both loved.

Orphaned now.

Dice shook his head hard. He'd done some nasty shit in his life, killed men, even tortured when he'd had to, but none of it had meant anything to him. This was different.

When he'd eaten Emma's magic, he'd gotten her memories. Memories of the life she'd lived, the battles she'd fought, her dedication to the Great Mission Merlin had sold the Magekind on all those centuries ago.

Bullshit. It's all bullshit. Emma had been weak, and so was that husband of hers. Tom could have fought Dice, maybe avenged his woman and kept his kid from being orphaned. Instead his love had killed him.

It really wasn't Dice's fault. He'd only done what he had to do. Their weakness had done the rest. He was fucking well not going to moon about it. It wasn't even his guilt anyway. He'd caught it from Emma like a cold.

But damn, the woman had known her magic. She'd spent eight hundred years studying magic—how to draw on the Mageverse, how to make it do what she wanted with spells and chants and pure, raw will.

Now Dice knew what she'd known. He reached for the power of the Mageverse as Emma had done so many times . . .

And nothing happened.

Warlock's deep voice rumbled from the darkness. "You can't draw on the Mageverse the way they can. You get your magic from killing."

Dice whirled as the wizard stepped into the cave, claws clicking on the stone. "I did it." He wanted the bastard to know. "I fought them. Arthur and his knights. And I killed the witch and her husband."

"I know. I saw you. Good work. Although—" He bared his white teeth. "They would have killed you if I hadn't opened a gate for you and kept them from following. You're not quite up to their weight yet."

"I did well enough." He eyed Warlock hungrily. The fucker had so much magic. More than a hundred Emmas. If Dice could kill him, he could gorge. All that power would be his. Enough to kill any witch or vampire he wanted.

Which was the problem. Warlock had too damned much power, and he was mean as a snake. Not only would he kill Dice, he'd make it a long, nasty death.

Smarter to leave the bastard alone. And watch. Maybe an opportunity would come. Dice would damn well take it if it did. But only if he was sure he could kill Warlock and survive.

He realized that as he studied Warlock, Warlock was watching him just as intently, calculation in his glowing orange eyes. Creepy fuck.

"I need a war," the wizard announced. "Our people could accomplish so much—but unfortunately, the Magekind is in the way. Arthur will never allow me to make the moves that are necessary. Which means Arthur needs to die."

He turned away and began to pace. "The trouble is, I have to persuade my people that Arthur has gone mad. I managed to capture a couple of green agents and get them to light the kindling for my war. Unfortunately, Arthur is now alert to my plans, and I haven't been able to capture any cat's-paws since."

Dice frowned, watching Warlock stride from wall to wall. He moved with a feral grace, despite the odd anatomy of his legs, more like a wolf walking upright than a man. His voice rumbled in a deep growl that echoed in the cavern. Something in its feral timbre made Dice's hackles rise.

Many people are going to die, Emma's ghost breathed in his ear. *Magekind and Direkind will fall to his madness. And he is mad.*

Get the hell out of my mind, witch!

You're the one who put me here. You're the one who ate me.

Tasting blood and other things, Dice shuddered. And wondered if Warlock was the only one who was mad.

ELEVEN

Accompanied by Tristan, Arthur, and Morgana, Belle walked through the dimensional gate, following the bodies of Emma and Tom Jacobs, which floated along on a wave of magic.

They arrived at the Mageverse's clinic that served as a combination morgue and funeral home. A grim healer waited to take possession of the bodies.

"How's Noah?" Belle asked anxiously.

Aaliyah sighed, sadness in her large, dark eyes. She was a tiny woman who wore her black hair straight and shining to her hips. "Petra is with him," she said in her soft, Farsi-accented English. "He sleeps still while she works to take the edge from his pain. She will not be able to eliminate it, of course—she would not if she could, for she would have to blunt his love of his parents to do it. But by the time he wakes, it will be bearable for him."

Belle's heart ached for the boy. The idea of being a parent again jammed a hot needle into her heart, but she couldn't stand the thought of Tom's son being left alone. Any grandparents would be long dead, considering the age of Noah's parents. "Does he have a place to go?"

The healer nodded. "His parents left a will. Ria Tizia and her husband Michael have a daughter a couple of years older than Noah. Both couples had agreed that if anything happened, the other family would take in their child. The Tizias say Noah will have a home with them."

"Oh." Belle would have expected to feel relief that she didn't have to raise the boy. Her disappointment surprised her. She still grieved for her daughter, but she also remembered the joy of raising her.

Belle was still thinking about Tom and his family as she followed Arthur, Morgana, and Gwen back to the Pendragon home. Tristan fell in step beside her.

"You okay?"

She looked up at him, a little surprised at the rough concern in his voice. "I'm fine. Tom was one of my boys, you know."

"I could tell." When she blinked, Tris explained, "The expression on your face when we found him."

"It's funny. I gave him the Gift two centuries ago, but seeing him like that . . . It brought it all back." Belle stared down at the toes of her boots as she walked, remembering that first meeting. "I arranged an introduction at some ball or other. He was such a cocky young rakehell. Third son of a baron. Thought he was mad, bad, and dangerous to know. I half expected that learning he was a descendent of the Round Table would quite go to his head, but it didn't. He was oddly . . . humbled."

"You have that effect on a man when you want to."

She looked up to find his smile was a touch dry. "Really? Doesn't seem to work on you."

"Touché."

"I was so happy for him when he and Emma found one

another, I guess it was fifty years ago now. Emma was a hell of a lot older than he was, and God knows she was powerful. But they really loved each other. I wasn't surprised when they Truebonded. He was so damned happy afterward. And yet it killed him."

"There's always risk in love." Gwen lifted a blond eyebrow as they looked around at her. "And yes, I was eavesdropping shamelessly. I can tell you that if the same thing happens to me, I'll have no regrets. The Truebond Arthur and I share has added so much to my life, I'm willing to pay whatever cost it exacts. I'd imagine if you could ask Tom, he'd tell you his only regret is leaving Noah." She grimaced. "Though, admittedly, that's a pretty damned big regret."

Arthur folded her hand in his. "Since our son is grown, I can say I don't really mind the idea that Gwen's death would take me, too. I wouldn't want to live without her." He gave his wife a slow, intimate smile. "We've been together so long, she's gotten to be a habit."

"Yes, well, the rest of us don't want to lose either of you," Tristan told him tartly. "So try to stay alive."

Arthur shrugged. "Well, that *is* the plan."

Warlock was casting another spell. The magic burned over Dice's furry hide like acid, and he had to resist the urge to moan in pain. He didn't want to give the bastard the satisfaction, since Warlock hadn't exactly offered him a choice.

The wizard's deep voice chanted, twisting the hot energies of the Mageverse around him with every syllable. It reminded Dice far too much of the first time, when the werewolf had turned him into a monster.

God, what was he going to become now?

The energy built, sizzling over his skin, wrenching bone and muscle with ruthless force until the world went white around him.

The pain faded along with the light, leaving him shaking

and sick, every muscle twitching with remembered torment. It took long moments before he could see again.

When the purple spots finally faded from his vision, he stepped back in instinctive fear. Warlock stood far too close, towering over him. Which meant . . .

He glanced down and barely resisted the urge to shout in delight. *He had hands again!* He was human!

"Now, boy," Warlock said. "Work me some magic."

Dice shot him a look. He'd love to work the bastard some magic—like a fireball right in the face. *Better not.* Warlock would probably fry him like a piece of bacon.

So he gestured, casting the spell with the knowledge he'd stolen from Emma Jacobs. A ball of light appeared over his palm, floating there as demurely as a helium balloon.

"Smells like Mageverse magic." Warlock grinned in an intimidating display of teeth. "You're not very strong, but you can draw on the Mageverse now. Most of your power will still come from death magic, so I wouldn't advise you to get in any fights with Majae until you've killed someone. They'll kick your ass."

Now that he knew something about the Mageverse, Dice realized just how difficult it must have been to change his magical nature. "How did you *do* that?"

Warlock grinned again, until Dice wished he'd stop. "I'm powerful, boy—a lot more powerful than you. Keep that in mind."

Did he have a choice?

Smoke examined Emma's gauntlet, a frown on his handsome face. "He bit through the enchanted steel as if it were cardboard." The Sidhe and Eva had joined them at the Pendragon home.

"We noticed," Arthur told him dryly. "Do you know what the hell that thing is?" Given Smoke's millennia in the

Mageverse, they'd figured if anyone could identify Warlock's monster, it would be him.

He looked up at the three-dimensional image of the creature Morgana had magically created. "Never seen anything like it. Looks like a cross between a wolf, a tiger, and a grizzly bear."

"Bet fighting it was no fun at all," Eva observed.

"It wasn't," Tristan growled. "And if it had managed to bite one of us . . ." His gaze slid to Belle.

"You'd have ended up like Emma." Smoke put the punctured gauntlet on the coffee table and leaned back in his seat, frowning. "One thing is for damned sure: you've all got to reinforce your armor. None of you can afford to get bitten."

"It might be dangerous for you, too, Smoke," Eva pointed out. "We don't know how a bite would affect you, either."

"And I'd rather not find out the hard way."

"The question is, how much reinforcement is needed?" Arthur drummed his fingers on the arm of his chair. "It's going to add weight and reduce flexibility, even with an enchantment to lighten the armor. That's going to make fighting in it more difficult."

"We'll just have to experiment." Morgana took a sip of her tea, eyes narrowed in thought. "It's going to be a time-consuming process, so we'd better put out the word. I'll issue an order to all my Majae to get to work on armor, including suits for vamps who have no partners."

Arthur nodded. "And nobody goes in the field without the new armor." His expression turned even more grim. "I don't want to hold any more funerals."

Smoke and the witches started discussing armor weight versus flexibility ratios, spells to counter that effect, and speculating about the bite strength of Warlock's monster. To Tristan's experienced ear, this had the sound of a conversation that would go on past dawn. Since sunrise was only an hour or so away, he excused himself and headed home. He needed time to think, and he wasn't going to get it at Casa Pendragon.

He was no longer sure he should take Sabryn up on her offer. Yeah, doing so had plenty of benefits from his point of view, but he hadn't considered the implications for Belle. Watching her fight beside Bors had made Tristan sharply aware that abandoning her was not a good idea. Bors had damned near gotten her killed.

True, there were plenty of other Magi who weren't blood-addicted she could partner with. But the sad fact was, Bors fought better dog-drunk than most of those puppies did sober as a judge.

The only man Tristan really trusted to protect Belle was Tristan. If he could be sure she'd go back to seducing Latents, that would be one thing. But he knew Belle, and she wasn't going to take a safe job with the Magekind at war.

Assuming you could call being a court seducer particularly safe. After all, she'd be on mortal Earth, among the witch-eating werewolves.

No, thank you.

Unfortunately, dumbass that he was, he'd said a bunch of crap he couldn't take back. Now he was going to have to persuade her to ignore all that and partner with him again.

Oh, what fun. He'd rather have his fangs pulled with a pair of rusty pliers. Tristan headed into the house and up the stairs, still wrestling with the question of how he was going to talk Belle into taking him back. He was so preoccupied, he was outside his bedroom door before he caught the scent of a woman waiting for him. His heart leaped in anticipation. *Belle's realized she needs me.*

Then he took a second breath and swung the door wide. "Sabryn, what the fuck are you doing?"

A dozen candles ignited around the bedroom, revealing the witch lounging on a pile of pillows. She wore a wisp of red lace that barely shadowed her nipples and fell open across her thighs, framing the hot copper curls of her sex. She smiled, pure, wanton sex in human form. "I wondered when you'd get home. I was starting to worry we wouldn't be able to play before sunrise. But you're just in time."

Oh, shit. "Sabryn, go home. I'm tired, and I'm really not in the mood."

Her smile turned carnivorous. "Lord Tristan of the Round Table, too tired for sex?"

"No," he growled. "I'm too tired for the screaming fit you're going to throw when I tell you to get the fuck out of my house. I don't want to become your partner, in bed or out of it."

Shock flashed across her lovely face, followed an instant later by hot rage. No hurt at all. Good. "Are you telling me you're turning me down for that skinny little hag?"

"Hag? Belle?" Tristan laughed, a great whoop of amusement.

"You bastard!" She jerked up the nearest object off the bedside table and flung it at his head.

It happened to be a dagger. Tristan caught it out of the air and sighed. "Give it a rest, Sabryn."

"I'll give *you* a rest, you arrogant fuck!" She exploded off the bed, a ball of bright gold magic condensing over her palm. She fired it at his head with lethal speed, her face twisted in rage.

He barely ducked in time. "Now, wait just one damned minute, witch!"

But Sabryn was already conjuring another fireball.

Belle climbed the stairs to her bedroom with feet made heavy by grief. Tom's ghost seemed to float at her shoulder, a laughing young man with dark eyes, cocky and handsome. Her ears rang with his son's screams. *"Daddy, Daddy, don't die! Please don't die!"*

Jesu. Her eyes stung, and she swallowed a sob as she pushed the bedroom door open. And stopped dead.

Tristan sat in the armchair next to the bed, a cut-crystal glass full of something amber in one hand. A bottle of Jack Daniel's sat beside his booted foot.

She'd opened her mouth to tell him to get the hell out of her house when the condition of his face registered. A bright crimson burn marked one cheekbone, and his left eye was swollen shut. His right sleeve was wet with blood. "Sorry for dropping in like this," he said, "but there are some very big holes in my house."

"What the hell happened to you?" Forgetting her anger at his invasion, she hurried across the bedroom to catch his chin and angle his head up. A cut marred his lower lip with a drying smear of blood. She conjured a light with an absent gesture. "Let me see that arm."

His bloody sleeve vanished at a wave of her fingers, revealing a long slash that cut across his biceps. It was at least five inches long. To her experienced eye, it looked like a sword wound. "Tristan, who attacked you?"

One corner of his mouth quirked upward. "Sabryn has a very bad temper."

Her jaw dropped, and she stared at him in shock. "Sabryn did this?" The idea that a Maja would attack a Magus stunned her silent. Though vampires were far stronger than witches, they couldn't shield themselves against magical attacks. That was the whole point of having a Maja partner.

Too, a knight like Tristan would feel it was dishonorable to strike back against a woman. All of which would make it practically impossible for him to defend himself. Her gaze dropped to his bloody arm, and her rage flashed hot. "I'm going to kill that bitch. What happened?"

"I got home to find Sabryn in my bed," he said as she laid a palm across the wound and sent a wave of healing magic into it. "I told her rather bluntly that I'm not interested in a partnership. She didn't take it well."

Belle stared down at him, her brows rising. "Why did you change your mind?"

"After I watched you and Bors take on our large fuzzy friend, I realized I don't want anyone partnering with you but me." His green gaze met hers, dark and intense. "Please forgive me, Belle. I was wrong."

She cupped his burned cheek and sent another wave of power into his skin. The burn faded, smoothing into healthy flesh. "No, you *weren't* wrong, Tristan. I caused a bad flashback, remember? What if I do it again?"

His smile looked a bit twisted. "So you don't get on top next time."

She sighed. "It's not that simple, Tris."

"Yes, actually it is." He caught her hand in his. His fingers felt almost feverishly warm, and his gaze seemed to burn with its intensity. "I want you, Belle. We're probably going to go to war with the Direkind in the next few days. I want to be beside you when that happens."

Belle snorted. "You just want to make sure I don't get myself killed."

"That's not all I want." He hooked a hand behind her head, pulled her down and took her mouth. The kiss was as fierce as his eyes, a hungry plundering of lips and tongue that let her feel the points of his fangs.

Her head began to spin, and her knees went weak as he softly licked and bit at her mouth.

Finally he pulled away to rest his forehead against hers. "Forgive me for being such an ass, Belle. Take me back."

She knew she should say no. He'd hurt her, and he'd probably hurt her again. And yet . . .

Belle remembered Tom's empty, staring eyes and the heartbreaking sobs of his son. She realized she didn't want Tristan going into combat without her either. She wanted to be at his side, protecting him.

And she wanted to make love to him again. Wanted to feel his big body pressing into hers, hot and strong and hard. She breathed her answer against his mouth. "All right. We'll see how it goes."

"Thank you, Belle. You won't regret it." He combed his fingers through her hair. "The sun'll be up in a few minutes. Would you lie with me?" His lip quirked. "Though I wish there was time to do more."

Straightening away from him, she turned toward the bed, flipping the covers back. "You'd better get in before you end up falling on your face."

Tristan gave her a smile and shrugged out of what was left of his shirt. She watched him strip, shamelessly enjoying the ripple of dense muscle as he moved.

Her own clothing disappeared with a gesture, and she slid in beside him to seek that perfect spot between his left pectoral and the rise of his shoulder. Her arm curled around his waist as he drew her close. They lay there between the cool sheets, listening to the thump of each other's heart, enjoying the warmth of each other's skin. Just before the sun rose, she felt his lips against her hair. "Thank you, Belle."

Tristan was still deeply asleep when Belle woke some hours later. No surprise; it was only two in the afternoon.

Belle sat up and looked down at him. He lay sprawled in bed, as abandoned in sleep as a small boy. But there was nothing boyish about his big body. He had all the powerful muscle of a man who'd spent decades with a great sword in his hand, his legs long and powerful from years in the saddle and miles of running. He looked like the warrior he was.

She couldn't believe Sabryn had thrown a fireball at him. And that wasn't all, either. She'd be willing to bet money that wound on his arm had come from a sword.

Belle gritted her teeth and decided she'd drop by Tristan's place to take a look at the damage. Though if she'd had any sense, Sabryn should have magically cleaned up after herself.

Then again, Sabryn had never struck Belle as being all that smart.

And she wasn't. Belle stalked around Tristan's bedroom, eying the hole in the outer wall. Sunlight streamed through the opening, more than enough to ensure Tristan couldn't have slept in his own bed. Though Magi didn't really turn to ash in the light of the sun as vampire legend said, it could burn them badly.

The edge of the hole was singed dark, indicating Sabryn had used a pretty powerful fireball. "You were lucky you didn't burn the house down, you stupid bitch," Belle growled.

She pulled her cell phone out of the back pocket of her jeans and flipped it open. "Morgana!"

"Yes, Belle?" Morgana's velvety voice sounded bright this morning. She was in a good mood.

That was going to change by the time Belle got through with her. "Get over here and see what your pet slut did to Tristan's house."

Morgana's mood did indeed change as they studied the evidence of Sabryn's magical strikes. But it was the bloody sword they found at the foot of the stairs that really set her off. Picking up the great blade, Morgana examined it with her magical senses. "This is Tristan's blood."

"Looks like she took his own sword to him. And being Tristan, he chose not to fight back."

Morgana's lip curled. "A Knight of the Round Table wouldn't. Not against a Maja. He'd just duck and take to his heels."

"Which probably galled him no end. He wouldn't like

running from anyone." Belle picked up the remains of a colorful pillow lying on the floor. It was sliced in two and trailing stuffing, as though he'd used it to deflect an attack. The streaks of blood on the batting revealed he hadn't been entirely successful.

Morgana conjured a cell phone. "Sabryn," she snarled, "get over here."

"He insulted me." The witch growled, her arms folded over her generous chest, a glower on her face that made her appear much less pretty than usual. "And he had the gall to *laugh* at me!"

"So you tried to kill him?" Belle fought the impulse to slam her fist into the Maja's face.

Sabryn tossed her red hair. "If I'd tried to kill him, he would be dead."

"You blasted a hole in his bedroom wall, you psychotic cow! What if that blast had hit him instead?"

She shrugged one shoulder and glanced away. "I would have healed him. And it would have taught him a lesson."

"So why don't I teach *you* a lesson?" Belle spoke between her teeth. "I demand satisfaction, Sabryn Sans Merci. Choose your seconds."

Sabryn's head snapped back toward her as her jaw dropped. "Are you challenging me to a duel, you lunatic?"

"Lunatic? I didn't blast holes in Tristan's house. Will you give me satisfaction or not?" Duels among the Mage-kind were exceedingly rare, but they weren't unheard of.

"Not!" Morgana snapped, glaring fiercely at Belle. "Do I have to remind you we are on the brink of war?"

"She needs her ass kicked by someone who can honorably do it." Belle glared at the younger witch. "She wouldn't have dared attack Tristan if he could have fought back."

"Are you calling me a coward, bitch?"

Belle displayed her teeth. "And you're *clever*, too."

"Stop it, Belle." Magic sparked dangerously in Morgana's eyes, revealing how close she was to losing her own temper. "As your liege, I forbid you to duel. Sabryn, I will deal with you. Belle, don't you have armor to reinforce?"

"Yes, actually." She gave Sabryn another flash of her teeth. "Tristan's."

Sabryn stepped toward her, magic flaming on her palm.

"Enough!" Morgana roared. A wave of force rolled out from her palm, seizing Sabryn and flinging her against the wall of Tristan's living room hard enough to shake the house. That the blast had simultaneously cushioned her back was revealed by the fact that she was still conscious as she hung there, pinned like a butterfly by the older witch's power.

"Belle, get out of here," Morgana snapped, glaring at Sabryn. "You want Tristan that badly, he's yours. I wish you joy of him. Go."

Belle turned and stalked for the door. Just before it closed behind her, she heard Morgana say, "Now, about this habit of yours of attacking other agents . . ."

Belle's knees were shaking, and she took a deep breath as she walked home. The sun rose high in a clear blue afternoon sky, and the cobblestone streets were accordingly quiet. Avalon tended to roll up the sidewalks during the day, since many Majae followed the same sleeping schedule as the Magi did.

She'd challenged Sabryn to a duel over Tristan. Now that she'd left the scene, it was hard to believe she'd done it. But when she'd seen his burns and bruises, not to mention that sword wound, her temper had started smoking. It hadn't taken much goading from Sabryn to make it explode.

One thing was for sure, Morgana would never again stick her nose into Belle's love life. Which made the whole embarrassing incident worth it.

Now she intended to go home and curl up beside Tristan again. Tonight she'd start work on his armor.

Well, maybe not first thing.

When the sun set, Tristan's consciousness returned in a rush, as it always did. He could feel the delicate weight of Belle's lush body stretched across his.

Opening his eyes, he glanced down. She was curled around him like a fox stole, one long leg thrown across his hip, an arm lying over his chest. Her long blond lashes feathered her cheeks; she was still deeply asleep.

She'd forgiven him. With a sigh of relief, he wrapped his arms around her and relaxed back into a lazy doze.

Until, that is, Belle stirred and moved against him in a long, feline stretch. He heard her heartbeat pick up as she woke, and he was abruptly aware of the lush female perfume of her scent, tinged with magic and jasmine.

Just like that, he was as hard as Excalibur. His fangs lengthened, aching in his jaw, and he was abruptly starving for her, for the taste of her sex and the magic in her blood.

He rolled over with her and covered her mouth with his, moaning in hot need at the way she tasted, at soft breasts and hard nipples, the long, silken heat of her legs sliding apart for him. His cock came to rest against her firm little belly, and he imagined how she'd feel gripping him, tight and slick and ready.

His tongue slipped into her mouth. She opened for him with a moan, her arms sliding around his neck.

TWELVE

Nobody had ever kissed her like Tristan, Belle realized in that heady moment. He drew her close with arms strong and warm, and covered her in a body he'd forged as hard as any weapon. His tongue slipped into her mouth, swirling lazily, brushing over teeth and lips, teasing her into licking him back. She kissed him until the sheer heat of it grew to be too much, and she had to fling her head back and breathe.

That didn't discourage him. He only switched his attention to the angle of her jaw, the shell of her ear, the throbbing leap of her pulse. Belle quivered against him, loving every kiss.

His long swordsman's fingers discovered her breasts, stroking over them with fingertips rough with calluses that somehow made his touch even more arousing. When he pinched her nipples, she shivered, enjoying the delicate delight. He tugged her, twisted gently, even as he made love to her pulse with his mouth, teasing her skin with the gentle rake of his fangs. Not piercing, not breaking the skin, just running the points over her flesh until she tightened, imagining the sweet almost-pain of his bite. She loved the way his bite made her float, head spinning as he fucked her, his body thrusting hard and sure into hers.

Her dark lover. Her sweet bastard, with his fiery temper and utter lack of diplomacy. You always knew where you stood with Tristan. He never sugarcoated anything, never told pretty lies, no matter how badly you wanted to hear them. He was what he was.

And he was delicious.

She stroked her hands through the rough blond silk of his hair down to the hard planes of his shoulders. He'd kissed his way lower, and his mouth hovered over her nipples now, making her catch her breath.

His tongue flicked out to circle one hard point in a teasing little dance. Another lick, hot, wet, teasing, making her squirm with the pure intensity of sensation.

Tristan feathered his rough fingers over her breast as he licked her, a back-and-forth flick of his tongue. Until he engulfed her nipple for a good, hard suckle that sent streaks of golden fire running up her spine.

She raked her nails gently across his back, barely resisting the urge to dig in as he teased and nibbled and stroked. Belle shivered as he played his hands over her skin, until one hand found its way between her legs.

His fingers slid between her delicate lower lips, sending heat shooting through her like a lightning strike.

"God, Tristan!" she gasped.

"Yes?" he purred against her breast, his voice flavored with laughter.

"You know, two can . . . AH! . . . two can play that game!"

"Can they?" He bit down gently on the nipple, then laved it as if in apology.

"Yes—especially if one of them's a witch." An image

flashed through her mind: Tristan, tied to her bed with scarlet ribbons, deliciously helpless while she . . .

Uh, no. Not with his mental scars. The thought of the fear such a scenario might trigger washed over her like a bucket of cold water.

"I don't know what you're thinking, but stop." Rising to hands and knees, he slid between her legs, spread them with big hands, and settled his shoulders between them. Feeling his fingers spread her lips, Belle rose to brace herself on her elbows. His blond head bent as he contemplated her sex with a very wicked smile.

His first lick streaked fire across her clit. "Oooh!"

He rumbled back at her and licked again, treating her like a melting ice cream cone.

"No fair," she informed him. "I can't touch you all the way down there."

"Really?" His tongue swirled, sampled. "That is too bad."

She shivered, and her eyes narrowed. There was more than one way a witch could touch her lover. Belle let her power rise and sent it swirling down his body until she could feel him, the ripple of hard muscle under velvety skin, the silken curls of chest hair spreading across wide pecs and down his abdominals, the tight jut of his male nipples.

The width and heat of his cock.

Belle smiled, slow and wicked.

He threw up his head, startled, his wide eyes meeting hers. "Belle!"

Her smile only widened.

The grin on Belle's face was downright evil. As well it should be, because it felt as if her tongue was simultaneously licking both Tristan's nipples and the length of his cock.

"Now, that is just not fair." His attempt at a stern tone

shattered into a near-squeak when teeth closed over the head of his cock. Which was flatly impossible, since his dick was pressed into the mattress more than a yard from her talented mouth.

But Belle had a lot of talents, and she demonstrated every one of them on his hapless body. He went back to work licking her in sheer self-defense. She tasted delicious—salty, female, distilled, musky, sex. His cock lengthened and grew harder than his armor just from the taste alone—never mind the wet swirl of her tongue.

Suddenly he had the unmistakable sensation of his cock plunging to the balls into Belle's hot mouth, right down her throat to a depth he suspected was probably impossible. He was a big man, and taking him that far was not something most women could do.

Yet Belle and her tricky magic accomplished the job nicely. She dug her nails into his shoulders—that was real; he saw one hand out of the corner of his eye. But simultaneously, those nails bit into his ass while her heels rode the small of his back. His head whirled from the delightful intensity of her hands, her mouth, the heat of her body, until he had trouble telling what was real.

His body didn't particularly care. He felt lost in the taste of her, the perfume of her arousal, the flick of tongues and fingers, until he felt a climax pulsing in his balls, and he knew he was about to lose it. Just shoot like a green boy into the sheets, which he hadn't done since—ever, come to think of it.

"Enough!" Tristan lunged upward, gasping as he crawled up her lush body and took his cock in a shaking hand. Barely taking time to aim, he drove to the balls, hard and fast, managing at the last minute to drag back on his vampire strength. They both groaned at the sensation.

Which was when his gaze met hers, and caught helplessly in the blue-gray depths, in the pupils so huge and dark in the candlelight. He was conscious of her trembling mouth, her slow, dazed blink up at him, as if she was tracking about as well as he was. Which was not at all.

Tristan's arms shook, not with effort, but from the sheer sensory overload of being so deep inside her. His head spun with sensation. Every inch of her pressed to every inch of him. Warm. Fragrant.

He lowered his head and kissed her. The magic of it exploded in his awareness—not some trick she was doing, but the raw truth they made together.

"Tristan." She spoke his name, and the word trembled on her lips, quivered from her mouth to his.

"God, Belle," he breathed. He knew he should add something clever and romantic, but just then, that much intelligence was beyond him. He started thrusting, a slow in-and-out pressure that made stars light up his skull. One of her heels dug into his butt, and he picked up the pace, as obedient to her urging as a stallion.

He couldn't seem to look away from her eyes. They held him, blue-gray as storm clouds, deliciously inescapable.

This was *different* from every time he'd made love before. There'd been times he'd been more creative, times his partner had been kinkier, times there'd been riding crops and fuzzy handcuffs. Yet he'd never felt such stark intensity, as if something momentous was happening, something that went beyond mechanics and body parts and toys. As if he and Belle had touched.

Fuck if he knew what it meant.

All he did know was that the way she touched him reached parts of him no one had ever reached. Not Isolde, not any woman.

Her pulse leaped in her throat, and he lowered his head and took it. Something snapped in his head like a closing circuit, forming an intense connection with the throb of her heart and the taste of her blood. And they were, somehow, one.

He suspected he should be scared out of his mind.

* * *

Justice reported what he'd seen to the members of the Security Council in a carefully objective voice. He couldn't let them think his emotions had been affected by what he'd seen. It took real work; he still felt sick at the memory of Emma Jacobs's savaged belly. It wasn't the goriest corpse he'd ever seen; there'd been the ninety-year-old man who'd murdered his wife with a hatchet, plus a few shotgun killings and several traffic accidents that still gave him nightmares because of the kids involved.

But the idea of taking a bite out of another human being made his stomach rebel. He'd hunted deer in wolf form, and he could remember biting into hot meat, tasting the rush of blood. To eat a *human being* like that . . .

His mouth filled with bile. He dropped his eyes to his notes and struggled to keep his voice level.

"The smell of death magic was unmistakable," Justice told his four fellow members. Only Elena Rollings and Carl Rosen looked sympathetic, and he now knew better than to believe he had Rosen on his side.

"And how would you know what death magic smells like?" Andrews demanded, lifting a contemptuous eyebrow.

"I fought with the Magekind in the Dragon War," Justice told him, keeping the temper from his voice. "I saw the Dark Ones fight, and I smelled their magic. It's a stench you don't forget. Like a corpse that's been dead a week. In July. In a closed house."

Even Andrews winced at that.

So he went on. "When I examined Emma Jacobs, the fang punctures on her arm were seven inches apart."

Tanner's jaw dropped. "A wolf that big would have to weigh four thousand pounds."

Justice nodded. "Which would agree with the Magekind's description of the creature they fought."

Andrews sniffed. "The creature they *say* they fought."

"Well, *somebody* sure as hell killed Emma and Tom Jacobs," Justice snapped, thoroughly out of patience. "Unless you want to suggest Arthur killed his own people."

Andrews opened his mouth, and Justice knew he was about to do just that.

"Oh, give it a rest," Elena snapped. "This is getting ridiculous."

Andrews's icy eyes narrowed at her in displeasure. "How much did the Magekind pay you, Rollings?"

"If anybody's been paid off, it's you." His mouth opened and closed like a landed carp's as she snarled, "You won't be happy until you get thousands of people killed—on both sides. And do you really think the humans won't notice a magical war going on under their collective noses? Or do you *want* to be on CNN?"

That shut everybody up for a full forty-five seconds.

"Arthur may not give us a choice," Rosen said solemnly. "We will do what we must."

"If the humans discover us, we all die," Justice said. "It'll be our Holocaust. There are six billion of them and only thirty thousand of us. We don't have the numbers to survive, no matter how many humans we bite. And unlike the Magekind, we won't be able to hide from our hunters in the Mageverse."

Elena looked grim. "By that time, I doubt Arthur will be in the mood to give us shelter in Avalon, even if we beg."

Tanner sneered. "I'm not begging for *anything* from Arthur Pendragon."

She lifted a red eyebrow. "Not even to save that little boy of yours?"

He eyed her in sullen rage and said nothing.

"So you're saying we should ignore Jimmy Sheridan's murder?" Rosen asked coolly. "That will not go over well with our constituents."

"Neither will the deaths of their wives and children if the humans start hunting us," Justice pointed out.

"Merlin believed Arthur would eventually go mad, or he would not have created us!" Andrews's perfectly tanned face reddened with temper.

"I've explained this so many times, I've gotten sick of doing it," Elena growled. "So I'll just say you know what utter crap that is."

"I have seen no evidence that Arthur is mad," Justice said carefully. "He has a temper, but he seems perfectly aware that war with us would cost his people. I don't believe he would put them in that kind of danger over something that has already been avenged. He's told me he considers it over and done with."

Rosen gave him an appraising glance. "We already know what you think, Bill. I'm just not convinced you're objective. You're far too passionate in Arthur's defense, considering he's a suspect in that poor boy's murder."

It took Justice more than a moment to wrestle his temper back under control. "Look, I'm a cop. I've dealt with guilty people. I know the difference between a killer and an innocent man, and you can believe me when I tell you Arthur is an innocent man. *He didn't do it.* Period."

"But Davon Fredericks did do it. He admitted as much. Unless Arthur delivers him to our justice, I *will* recommend war."

"Yeah," Justice said, eyeing him coldly. "About that. I keep asking myself why, but I never come up with an answer I like."

Rosen stared at him. "What the hell do you mean by that?"

Justice stared back. "Take a guess."

Sitting on his haunches beside Warlock's throne, Dice watched the werewolf named Carl Rosen pace the cavern, fury in every step.

"Justice knows," the werewolf snarled. Rosen was in wolf

form, as Warlock required of his visitors. His fur was grizzled, and age streaking his muzzle with silver. "He knows too fucking much."

Rosen looked soft to Dice. An easy kill. Tempting, given the magic in him. Dice managed not to lick his chops, but it was a near thing.

Warlock had ordered him to transform into a four-legged wolf rather than his usual monster form. He was still roughly the size of a horse, and Rosen kept giving him disquieted glances. He'd have been even more freaked had he known what Dice was thinking.

Then again, he'd probably figured it out.

"I fail to see how this sheriff of yours is a problem," Warlock said, putting a hand over to stroke Dice's head as if he were a dog. Dice knew better than to jerk away and snarl. He'd be punished, and Warlock's idea of punishment was not something he wanted to experience. Ever again. "Or rather, I don't see how you think he's *my* problem."

Rosen shot him an angry look. Idiot. Warlock punished looks like that. "It's a problem for you if he starts spreading around that Arthur and his Magekind are being framed."

"You mean it's a problem if he tells people I've bought you off," Warlock said, giving Dice's head another infuriating stroke. "The incorruptible Carl." He laughed softly.

"This thing could easily become a civil war if too many people believe whatever Justice decides to spill. Or do you want war among your own people, too?"

Warlock's hand stilled on Dice's head, and Dice held his breath, sensing the fury in his master. "My people will do what I want them to do, Carl."

"How are you going to make sure of that? Magic doesn't work on us, Warlock, and you can't bribe everybody."

Warlock sprang to his feet and that big-ass axe was in his hand, so fast even Dice hadn't seen him reach for it. *"Watch your tone!"*

"If you kill me, who will declare war for you?" Rosen

tilted up his chin as if daring Warlock to take his head. Not a dare he should make. "Tanner and Andrews aren't exactly subtle about being bought off. I don't think enough Direkind will follow them. Elena Rollings, on the other hand, is Wulfgar's descendant, and there are plenty of werewolves who'll listen to her."

"A woman?" Warlock turned and spat on the stone floor. Dice half expected it to sizzle with his rage. "Who'd listen to a woman?"

"Most of the Direkind don't follow the old ways the Chosen do. They'd listen to Rollings. And they'd listen to Justice."

Warlock turned to Dice. "Then kill them. Kill them both."

"That thing can't do it," Rosen said contemptuously. "It needs to look as if the Magekind did. That would really seal the deal."

"Oh, Dice can do that. Can't you, my boy?"

Dice knew his cue when he heard it. Concentrating hard, he transformed in a spill of magic, dragging the Mageverse in around him like a golden cloak, hiding his lupine essence. It had taken him hours to learn the trick, with Warlock disciplining him every time he got it wrong.

When he was done, he stood beside Warlock's throne, a tall, armored man with a sword.

Carl stared at him with his mouth hanging open. "Magekind," he whispered in astonishment. "He smells exactly like Magekind."

Dice grinned. So did Warlock.

Noah Jacobs didn't cry as he approached his parents' funeral biers. Somehow that made it worse.

Belle watched the boy walk toward the twin biers carrying a pair of white roses. The bodies lay dressed in white and crowned with roses, surrounded by a jungle of flowers and flanked by tall golden candelabra with white beeswax candles. Noah's eyes were huge and dark, eating the light, and his face was as pale as his mother's flowing gown. He placed the first rose on her chest, where her hands clasped her sword, then pivoted on legs that visibly shook as he placed the other bloom on his father's still chest. He swayed when he turned back to face the crowd, and Belle was afraid he'd fall.

Instead the boy squared his narrow shoulders in the black velvet doublet and walked back toward Ria and George Tizia, who waited for him with their daughter, Jenna. The couple reached for him and drew him in, hugging him hard as he shook, his face pressed to Ria's chest.

"Jesu, this sucks," Belle murmured to Morgana and Gwen. "I'm going to kill that furry bastard if it's the last thing I do in this life."

"And I'll help." Gwen sighed, her gaze lingering on the boy. He was crying now, great racking sobs that carried across the square even as the chorus began a soaring hymn. "At least the Tizias have taken him in. I know that couple. They'll love that boy like their own."

The service continued. Finally the Majae aimed their magic at the biers and sent Emma and Thomas Jacobs into the sky on a wave of magic that detonated into the air overhead. Noah's glassy dark eyes followed the shower of sparks.

Belle's chest ached as if she'd been punched in the heart.

Dice considered himself something of an expert when it came to cops. He'd watched every forensic show he could find, and he'd observed them from a safe distance as they worked to solve the crimes he and the Demon Brotherhood committed. Which was why they'd never actually managed to catch him.

Yeah, he'd been suspected plenty of times, but it took proof to put a guy in jail. He'd been good at getting rid of proof.

This time, though, he wanted the cops to show. Or rather, a particular cop. William Justice, the man he needed to kill.

Which meant he had to do some other killings first. He needed the strength and power they'd give him.

Besides, he was hungry.

Warlock found him a set of targets he considered perfect for his purposes, a family of Bitten descendents. Which meant, Dice gathered, that they were not politically well placed, since their ancestors had become werewolves by being Bitten. As opposed to the Chosen, who became werewolves by being the descendents of the original Saxon nobles Merlin had chosen to make Direkind. Warlock had told Dice very firmly that he was not to kill any of the Chosen.

Unless Warlock told him to.

Dice stalked around his targets' home surrounded by an invisibility shield and his Magekind disguise. It wasn't much of a house, being one of those little one-story shotgun shacks the textile mills had thrown up in the twenties to house their employees. The mills were long gone, and the years had not been kind. A recent bright-yellow paint job was beginning to peel away from the wooden siding, and the grass needed mowing, whispering around Dice's armored boots as he slipped through the night.

A red and yellow Big Wheel was parked on the sidewalk, left by one of the family's brats. Dice stopped and stared at it. Emma Jacobs's ghost whispered urgently in his ear. *Don't do this. You can't do this.*

Fuck off, he told her, and forced her back inside her box in the back of his head.

His werewolf hearing picked up the TV blaring from the tiny living room as Jon Stewart gave his opinion of the day's news. Somebody hooted in laughter.

Dice strode up the cement-block steps to the front door and kicked it in. A skinny young man yelled, jumping off the couch as his wife screamed and cowered. Dice leaped at them with such speed, both went down under his sword before they had time to transform.

Then he crouched beside the closest body, put a palm on her chest, and began to feed, drawing her lingering magic in through his hand.

"I'm getting damned sick of funerals," Tristan growled to Belle.

"Maybe this will be the last one for a while," she said, sending a warning glower to Sabryn, who glared at her from across the room. The little bitch had the good sense to come no closer, and Belle turned her attention to Tristan again.

He headed toward Bors, who stood beside the vampires' table looking as if he was about to jump out of his skin. Tristan caught his fellow knight by the shoulder and steered him firmly away from the array of bottles. "How're you feeling, brother?"

"Like shit." Bors sent a longing glance toward the table. "But Petra says she's making progress with my therapy. Another three or four days, and I should be through the worst." His voice dropped. "If I live that long."

"You're a strong man, Bors," Belle told him quietly. "You'll make it."

"I hope so." He swallowed hard. "It just took me by surprise, you know? I knew I had a problem, but I didn't realize how bad it was." His eyes met Tristan's, and he looked haunted. "You think Arthur will kick me off the Table?"

Tristan started. "Oh, hell no. You're one of us, Bors. Always have been, always will be. Everybody's got problems."

"Look at Tristan," Belle said with a smirk, hoping to lighten the moment. "He's an asshole."

Bors laughed, then gave her a curious look. "Hey, is it true you challenged Sabryn to a duel?"

Tristan's eyes widened. *"What?"*

"Ummmm," Belle said. *Dammit, busted.*

Luckily, her cell picked that moment to blare the theme from *Hawaii Five-0*. "It's Justice. Wonder what he wants." She plucked out her iPhone, ignoring Tristan's *we're-not-done* frown.

"Hi, Justice," she said. "What's going on?"

"Nothing good. I need you and the knight. Now. Before the human cops show and this situation really goes to shit."

Fabulous.

"You're fucked," Justice told Tristan.

"Yeah, I picked up on that. Not as fucked as these poor bastards, but close." He surveyed the house's small living room grimly.

Tristan judged that before the killer's arrival, the room had been shabby, but clean, as if the lady of the house was a conscientious homemaker. The furniture looked as if they'd bought it at the Salvation Army thrift store, with wooden frames covered in an ugly brown fabric that was probably supposed to look like velvet. The coffee table was a cheap laminate that matched the entertainment center in the corner. They'd spent what money they had on the thirty-inch flat-screen television.

Now all of it was blood splattered, including arterial spray from the beheadings. The soaked carpet squished underfoot, and the whole house stank of gore.

Over fifteen hundred years, Tristan had become familiar with all the shades in the spectrum of violence, from *completely lost-it* butchery to *just-doing-my-job* professionalism. This he mentally labeled Goading the Civilians.

First the killer had beheaded the couple, which was one of the few ways to really be sure of killing werewolves. Then he'd gotten artistic, painting the living room like a psychotic Jackson Pollock in arcs and whirls of blood, probably from his sword blade. Tristan, however, had seen real psychotics in action, and this bastard was just a shade too controlled for that.

No, he was aiming to piss people off. And to frame the Magekind, since the whole house smelled like Maja spell work.

"We've got one chance to avoid a war, Tristan," Justice told him. "You're going to have to persuade Arthur to surrender Davon to the High Council."

THIRTEEN

"Fuck that." Bors's lips peeled back from his teeth. His hands shook and his glittering eyes darted around the room, less like a wary warrior than like someone in the grip of acute paranoia. "I've got a better idea—they want war, let's give it to 'em. Fuck 'em all!"

The knight had insisted on coming along, and Tristan had decided not to waste time with an argument. He was beginning to regret it. Bors was obviously in withdrawal. It was a good thing the killer was long gone—they'd conducted a thorough search—since the Magus would be useless in a fight.

Belle gave Bors a long look before turning back to Justice. "Surrendering Davon would only make him another victim. Don't you think enough people have died?"

"Not nearly as many as are going to get killed if my people declare war on yours," Justice told her. "Which is exactly what Carl Rosen has in mind. You're going to play right into his hands. Davon admitted it; he's toast. It's better to lose one man than thousands of innocents."

"That's not the way we work, Bill," Belle told him quietly. "The lesser evil is still evil."

"But it's also *lesser*." He thrust a finger toward the bedroom where the smallest body lay. "Or didn't you see what was in there? You want more like that? I would personally put a bullet in Davon Fredericks's brain if it meant I didn't have to look at any more butchered five-year-olds."

"Neville Chamberlain much?" Bors spat, referring to the British prime minister who'd tried to make peace with Hitler.

Justice glared. "Fuck you, Bors."

Belle stepped between them and threw up a hand, arresting Bors's lunge. "You're not helping," she told him.

"Sorry," the knight muttered, sounding abruptly tired. "My head feels like it's about to detonate like an IED."

She moved to rest a palm on his forehead. Bors slumped as her spell relieved his pain.

Tristan mentally growled at the jealous demon that reared in his skull. *Don't be an utter ass.* Trying to drag his attention back to business, he looked at Justice. "So let me get this straight. You got a call from here?"

Justice nodded. "A woman's voice. She could barely speak. Said she was dying. Name came up on caller ID, so I got the address from the Internet and called you for backup."

"Good thing, too." He nodded at the dead woman. "No way she called anybody."

"Yeah." Justice grimaced. "Had to have been the killer."

"Well, he's gone now." Bors put a hand on the hilt of his sword, stroking the weapon as if longing to draw on someone.

"Maybe," Tristan told them. "Maybe not."

Belle had knelt beside the woman's body, her hands spread wide over it as she used some spell or other. When she looked up, she'd gone pale, her blue-gray eyes huge. "It's the same killer."

"What?" Tristan stared at her.

"Whoever killed these people is the same as the creature

that murdered Emma. There's no magic left in either of these people, and there should be at least a fading trace. They're not even cold yet. He fed on their magic just as he did on Emma and Tom's."

Tristan frowned as he studied the corpses. "But this was done with a blade."

"He's a shifter," Justice said, hands on his hips as he appraised the scene. "He shifted to human form and used a sword on them."

"But the magical signature he left here is Magekind. He left nothing at all at the other scene." Belle seemed to be thinking out loud. "He did it deliberately to frame us, but it's really obvious if you look."

"You think we can use this to convince the council not to declare war?" Tristan asked Justice.

"Normally I'd say yes. If I had an honest council, definitely. But Warlock has bought at least three of the members off—Tanner, Andrews, and Rosen. God knows how many of the others he owns. The only one I'm sure is honest is Elena Rollings, and that's because her father's death left her with more money than God. And she's got the Wulfgar Seat . . ."

"What's that?" Belle asked, interested.

"Wulfgar was one of the Saxon warriors Merlin chose to create the Direkind. The legends paint him as our Arthur, a courageous warrior and brilliant leader. He supposedly accomplished all these amazing feats. Elena is a direct descendent of Wulfgar's, so she inherited his seat on the council, which traditionally represents the Chosen. Actually, her son inherited it, but he's two years old, so she holds it in his name."

Belle shook her head. "Your system is screwy."

"Tell me about it."

Tristan suddenly got that crawling sensation on the back of his neck that told him something was about to bite him on the ass. "Belle, call Arthur and the rest of the Table. I want to conduct another search for that bastard. We know he's not in the house, but there's one hell of a lot of woods out back." He glanced at the werewolf. "He called you for a reason, Justice, and my gut says he's not done."

Dice wrapped himself in an invisibility spell deep in the shadows of the woods, a thick blackness not even a vampire's eyes could penetrate. He watched in sizzling frustration as Tristan divided up the Magekind search teams and sent them off into the woods.

With Emma's memories, he recognized the Knights of the Round Table, counting them off silently and cursing to himself. Arthur, Lancelot, Galahad, Bors, Gawain, Tristan, Percival, Marrok, Kay, Cador, Lamorak, and Baldulf. They weren't all brawny bastards like Tristan and Bors; some were lean as marathon runners, while Marrok was a dark, towering brute who looked like a professional football player. There were witches, too: Belle, Guinevere, Morgana Le Fay, and three of the knights' wives, Grace, Lark, and Caroline. Lark looked about four months pregnant, which was probably why her husband, Gawain, shadowed her like a protective wolf.

But each and every one of them moved with a professional silence as they fanned out into the woods. Justice accompanied Tristan and Belle, and Dice ground his teeth. He'd hoped to get an opportunity to slip up behind the fucker and slit his throat, but the cop was staying too close to the Magekind.

If only he'd move out alone, like some of the knights. You'd think they were invulnerable. Though considering the skill they'd acquired over fifteen hundred years of combat, he'd hate to challenge one of them. They'd take him apart. He knew a little about swordplay from Emma's memories, but a Knight of the Round Table would simply gut him.

He froze as a thought hit him, reckless and daring. It was a good way to get himself killed, but if it worked . . .

Dice chose his target and moved after the man wrapped in a deep, tight shield of magic. He had to burn some of the power he'd acquired when he'd killed the werewolves, but it was worth it if the spell kept the witches from sensing him. He walked quickly through the moonlit woods after his target's broad armored back, his magic keeping the leaves from rustling under his boots. Excitement surged through him as he approached his victim.

This is wrong, Emma whispered. *You must not. He'll kill you. He's one of the oldest of them, and he's incredibly skilled with his blade.*

But he's weak. Look at the way he moves, as if he's in pain. And once I kill him, all that skill will be mine.

No. No. No! she chanted the word in his brain, a rising wail of anguish.

Be silent, witch!

Not like this! Not like a coward . . .

Do you think I'm stupid enough to warn him?

Dice stared at the expanse of Bors's back, covered in gleaming plate armor. Probing with a delicate curl of magic, he sought the spot where the metal was thinnest.

And found it.

Dice stepped in close to the knight and rammed his magical blade through the steel with all his werewolf strength, skewering Bors like a cocktail shrimp on a toothpick. The big man stiffed in agony as the sword broke ribs, sliced muscle and lungs to pierce his heart. The knight died before he could make a single sound.

Still shielded by his invisibility spell, Dice wrapped an arm around the man and began to feed, absorbing the knight's magic and memories in a hot rush of power.

Belle smelled the magic first—a carrion reek she first assumed must be coming from the house. Until she realized the source was closer than that.

Much closer.

She glanced around, frowning, every hair on the back of her neck coming to attention with that *oh-merde* feeling she got whenever everything had gone to hell.

Wait, where was Bors? He'd been walking to their left, but now he was gone.

"Bors?" She started toward the spot where he should be.

"Belle?" Tristan asked, following as silently as a ghost despite the leaves underfoot. "What's wrong?"

"I smell death magic. And Bors is gone." She gestured, weaving a spell designed to disrupt illusions.

The smell instantly hit her face in a gagging wave as the illusion shattered. Bors sagged in the grip of an even bigger man, blood sheeting down his armored torso, his eyes wide and blank in a corpse-white face. A full foot of sword blade protruded from his chest.

His assassin wore black armor that seemed to drink the light. Eyes glared at her through the slit in his visor, red as a hell hound's. "Bitch!" he snarled, and jerked his sword out of Bors, dropping the knight, who went down in a clatter of armor and a tangle of limp limbs.

The killer thrust his blade right at Belle's chest. She knew her parry would be too late even as she swung her sword.

Tristan's blade hit the assassin's with a clang of steel on steel and a rain of magical sparks. "You *fucker!*" Tris snarled, and Belle heard killing rage in his voice. "You're a dead man!"

She spun out of the way, her training telling her to get the hell back. No witch was fast enough for this kind of fight. Her best bet was to stay just close enough to shield Tristan when he needed it, but far enough back not to get in his way.

The killer swung his blade at Tristan's head, magic flashing down the sword in a blue blaze. Death magic.

Tris parried, and the spell leaped from the assassin's blade to his. But before it could run right into his hands, Belle cast a shield to block it. The spell raged, black and hungry, fighting to reach Tristan and stop his heart, but Belle poured more power into her barrier, more and still more, until the spell finally snuffed out.

"A moi!" she screamed, a knight's ancient cry for help. *"A moi!"*

"Tristan!" Arthur roared, charging between the trees like a destrier, all muscle and armor and hot rage, his wife flying at his heels. His sword flashed, and the assassin leaped back, parrying with a ringing rattle. Tristan pressed closer, and Belle followed, magic ready.

"Fuck this," the assassin snarled. "You're too late anyway. I have what I need."

And then he was gone, bounding like a deer through a dimensional gate that snapped shut before any of them could follow. Belle threw her power at the gate's fading pulse, but something hurled her spell back at her. She tried another spell and felt Guinevere's magic probe alongside it. But her casting bounced off the block as the last of the gate vanished. "You get anything?" Belle asked Gwen as the men watched in helpless frustration.

The witch shook her helmed head. "Something blocked me. Something damned powerful."

"Me, too." She turned toward the armored body in the leaves and hurried back to his side. Her magic told her it was too late even as she dropped to her knees. "Oh, Bors."

"Morgana!" Arthur bellowed as the other Knights of the Round Table gathered around.

"Here, dammit. Get back, you lot," the Maja snapped as she knelt next to Belle. Gwen and Caroline joined them. "Give us room."

The men stepped back reluctantly as the witches began to probe Bors's corpse with their magic, trying to determine what had been done to him.

"We were too late," Gwen said at last, sitting back on her haunches. Tears roughened her voice. "There's nothing left. The bastard ate him."

"What do you mean, 'ate him'?" Arthur demanded. "That's a sword wound."

"He devoured his magic and his spirit." Morgana pushed a lock of black hair away from her face, revealing the defeat in her eyes. "That bastard got it all."

Dice's knees buckled under him, and he hit the cavern's stone floor hard enough to jar his back teeth. He fell forward to land on his hands and knees. Shudders racked him.

Fifteen hundred years. Bors had been a Knight of the Round Table for fifteen hundred years. Dice felt his pride in being chosen by Merlin himself for the Great Mission of protecting mankind He remembered what it had been like to fight for the innocent, to use his vampire strength in acts of courage and accomplishment. He'd been a hero.

And Dice had killed him with a coward's stroke. From behind, because he never would have been able to take the knight any other way.

Self-loathing such as he'd never known filled Dice, so black and bitter that he wanted to take up his sword and slit his own throat.

"Get up," Warlock growled.

He paid no attention, staring blindly at the blood on his gauntleted hands. Bors's blood. For a moment he felt a sense of dizzy dislocation. He knew he was Dice, but Bors's memories were so incredibly strong, pressing down on him with the weight of centuries.

Warlock snatched off Dice's helm and fisted a big hand in his hair, dragging him to his feet. "I said, get up!"

"Oooww! Goddammit!"

"Listen to me, boy." The wizard thrust his fanged muzzle so close, Dice wanted to jerk away from the hot, stinking breath gusting into his face. "I've absorbed creatures like that before. If you are not careful, the sheer weight of his life will snap your mind like a twig. And his . . ."—Warlock's lip twisted—"*goodness* will make you loathe yourself. But you listen to *me*, boy. You are not evil. He and his kind are weak, gutless idiots. A true leader is willing to sacrifice a few lives to save thousands, to clamp down with an iron fist in order to create peace and plenty. I have that courage. So do you. Together, we will serve the greater good."

Dice blinked up at the werewolf as he struggled with thoughts that were alien to everything he'd ever known. "How can acts of evil create good?"

Warlock released his hair and grabbed his jaw, forcing him to meet the wizard's orange gaze. *"Because I will it so."*

Dice felt the wizard's consciousness slam into his, seizing those fragments of Bors, Emma, Tom, even the werewolf couple he'd killed. Warlock's lips moved, chanting a spell, binding the ghosts in chains of magic. Moans of pain rose, sounding weak and distant.

"There." Warlock studied Dice with satisfaction. "You'll be able to access their memories and abilities without being overwhelmed. Now, come." Turning on a clawed foot, he started deeper into the cave. "We have plans to make, and I must tell Rosen to find another way to deal with his sheriff." His lips lifted in a feral smile. "I have other missions for you."

Belle poured magic into her hands, adding it to the burning stream that rushed toward Morgana, who knelt beside Bors's murdered corpse. The knight still lay where the assassin had dropped him. Morgana crouched with one hand on the center of the dead man's chest, the other lifted as she led them all in a chant.

Eleven other Majae surrounded Avalon's most powerful witch, feeding their magic into her so she could use it to search for the killer. The circle included not only the witches who had accompanied the search team, but several additional Majae Morgana had called in from Avalon. She sent all that power blazing out like a searchlight, a ferocious beam of magic and will that blazed through the night, seeking some trace of the killer, some echo of a spell they could follow back to its source. Belle's palms burned as if she held them too close to a furnace, and sweat streamed down her face, despite the predawn chill. Her head throbbed savagely, and she could feel her power faltering.

"Enough." Morgana let her arms drop as though they'd grown too heavy. "If we haven't found him by now, we're not going to. Not before sunrise." One could work spells in daylight, but they weren't as powerful. And power was what they needed now.

The Majae groaned in a combination of relief and disappointment. Relief that the grinding effort was done.

Disappointment that they had failed.

Belle felt her knees start to buckle and braced them with an effort. God, she was tired. Between fighting and searching for the assassin, she doubted she had the juice to light a candle.

Arthur spoke in a low growl that jerked her shoulders straight. "Before the sun rises, I have one more little job I need to take care of." He gave Morgana a burning look. "Get me Carl Rosen."

Morgana's next words revealed just how tired she really was. "You mean on the phone?"

"No," Arthur snarled. "I mean right here. Right now."

Not even Morgana would argue with him when he used that tone. She turned to one of the witches who was a bit less thoroughly drained and nodded. Apparently Belle wasn't the only one who doubted her ability to light a candle.

Morgana looked around for Justice. "Get out your phone and call Rosen. We need a homing signal."

It took all Justice's persuasive skills to convince Rosen that yes, he did have to get out of bed at 5 A.M. because the shit truly had hit the fan.

The man still bitched and complained bitterly, right up until he stepped through Morgana's gate and saw Bors's body lying in the leaves, surrounded by glowering warriors.

"Now," Arthur growled, striding to meet the werewolf, "I don't want to hear one fucking word about 'Where's the body?' " His tone turned savage. "One of my best knights was *murdered* by one of you furry bastards, and now you can by God tell your fellow council members that *Bors is dead*."

Rosen blinked like a rabbit. "But I don't smell werewolf. I don't smell anyone but Magekind."

Arthur stepped so close to the werewolf that they were literally nose to nose. Neither was a tall man, but somehow the Magus seemed to tower over Rosen. "I *know* you're not calling me a liar."

Rosen's eyes widened, and he took a step back out of what looked like sheer reflex. "Ah, no."

"Because my people saw the killer, and they say he was one of yours. Which means one of yours butchered that family in there." He thrust an armored finger toward the little house just visible through the trees.

"A family is dead?" Rosen blinked. "An entire family?"

"A man, his wife, and their five-year-old daughter," Tristan said, his arms folded as he, too, glared at Rosen. "Killed by a werewolf who tried to make it look like one of us."

"Which is horrible, but beside the point. One of *your* people did kill James Sheridan." Rosen lifted his chin and managed to meet Arthur's blazing gaze. "If you don't surrender him so we can put him on trial, we will use whatever means necessary to . . ."

"Don't you threaten to declare war on me, *boy*." Arthur's lip curled. "When it comes to war, I do not fuck around. Your lot may be immune to magic, but you're not immune to steel. I'll cut off your damned head and mount it over the Round Table."

"Don't . . ." Rosen had to lick his lips before he could finish. "Don't threaten me, vampire."

"It's not a threat, *werewolf*. I've been killing men for

fifteen centuries. If you're stupid enough to declare war on me, you'll pay for it."

"Then hand over . . ."

"No."

"Our committee met . . ."

"Fuck your committee. I'm not giving you Davon Freder[-]icks. Warlock cast a spell on that boy and turned him lose on your little werewolf. I'm sorry for it. But Davon is as much a victim as all the others Warlock has murdered, and you're not killing him."

"I . . ."

Arthur looked at Morgana. "Get him out of here."

Five minutes later, Carl Rosen stood shaking in his own living room, having been pushed through a dimensional gate by one of Arthur's thugs.

He'd believed Warlock's portrayal of Arthur as an ineffectual medieval fop living in a fairy tale. Now he realized just how thoroughly he'd been deceived.

The man he'd met tonight had been every bit as scary as Warlock. Actually, more so. Warlock was surrounded by a cloud of magic so strong, you could almost taste it in the air like ozone before a storm.

Arthur exuded a different kind of power, the pure, distilled authority of a man other men followed without question. Had followed since Rome fell. It wasn't a power that had been conferred on Arthur by some election, or that he'd seized with military might. Merlin hadn't bestowed it on him when he drank from the Grail. Arthur had literally been born to lead, and now that authority informed every gesture, every thought, permeated every cell of his body.

When he chose, that raw dominion blasted out of Arthur's eyes with such force, it made even Carl want to drop to his knees.

Carl, who'd sold himself to Warlock.

There's good news, and there's bad news, he thought with a flash of semi-hysterical humor. The good news was that Arthur would provide them with the excuse they needed to declare war: he wasn't going to hand over Davon Fredericks.

The bad news was that Arthur would provide them with the excuse they needed to declare war. And having met Arthur, Carl was no longer sure they'd win.

But win or lose, a lot of people were going to die.

Belle was so tired, she was stumbling. Yet she still found the energy to worry, because the Knights of the Round Table were seriously pissed off. And that included Tristan.

Some of them raged and cursed as they stood guard around the house under an invisibility spell as several Majae worked the crime scene inside. Morgana had summoned fresh witches from Avalon for the job, which needed to look like a human shooting rather than beheadings by a sword-wielding attacker.

Now, *there* was a tidbit nobody wanted on CNN.

But as some of the knights swore vengeance, others were dangerously quiet. Tristan was one of the quiet ones. She wasn't sure why that worried her more than the others' vows of bloodshed, but it did.

Belle threw another glance up at his face as he stood next to her among the knights and exhausted witches milling around the house's shaggy lawn. His handsome profile was expressionless, but there was a look in his eyes she didn't like at all.

"I'll be glad when they wrap this up so we can get home," she said, hoping to pull him back from whatever evil place he'd gone. "We're cutting it close to dawn as it is." The eastern horizon was already going pale.

Tristan might as well have been the statue of David for all his reaction. Belle gave up on subtlety. "Are you all right?"

He looked down at her. Now she saw emotion, but it was

so stark, so tormented, she wanted to look away. "I just got one of my dearest friends killed. What do you think?"

Her jaw dropped. "Tris, how in the hell was this *your* fault?"

"He was walking not ten feet away from me, and I never even noticed when that bastard ran him through." His lips twisted. "I was too busy worrying about you."

Belle felt as though he'd slapped her.

"Yeah, and?" A petite blonde marched over to join them, a glower on her pretty face and Gawain at her heels. Lark was Tristan's great-granddaughter, as well as Gawain's wife. She'd also been eavesdropping—and didn't care if they knew it. "Belle is your *partner*, Tris. You're supposed to worry about her."

"She's got a point," Gawain observed. "You have a duty to look out for your lady."

"Yeah? And who was looking out for Bors?" Tristan growled.

Their raised voices had attracted Arthur's attention. He stalked over to join them. Judging from his expression, Tris wasn't the only one who'd booked a flight on Guilt Air. "There were unmated knights in the party. Bors could have been partnered with one of them. Which *I* should have seen to, but didn't." One big hand clenched around the hilt of Excalibur as the sword rode at his hip. "So if anyone is responsible for Bors's death, I am."

"Stop it!" Gwen snapped. They'd attracted quite a crowd by now. "Yes, Bors is dead. It's a tragedy, and he will be missed. But flogging ourselves only distracts us from what we should be doing—catching his murderer. Because if we don't, Bors won't be the only agent we bury."

Arthur gave her a faint smile. "As usual, my wife is right. We'll meet tomorrow night at the Round Table to discuss our next move."

"In the meantime," Morgana said, "we Majae should concentrate on reinforcing everyone's armor."

Along with planning yet another funeral, Belle thought grimly.

A couple of exhausted-looking young witches stepped out of the house and gave them all a nod. "We're done."

Arthur glanced at the reddening horizon over the houses across the street. "Just in time."

Belle lay in the curve of Tristan's big body as he spooned around her. He felt wonderful—all warm, hard muscle and smooth skin, with a soft ruff of hair clouding his broad chest and fluffing around his cock.

But even as her body warmed to his, she could sense the grief that lay over him like a heavy weight. She rolled over to look into his eyes. He promptly turned his face into his pillow, but not before she saw the tear tracing a path down his cheek.

Belle sighed and kissed him. His tears tasted salty. "I'm sorry."

"Bors was a good man," Tristan said.

"Yes."

"That bastard ran him through from behind because he knew he couldn't take Bors in a fair fight."

"Yeah." She kissed him again. Gently, tenderly. "Definitely a coward."

Another tear traced a slow, shining path down his face. "I'm going to kill that fucker."

"I'll help."

He laughed, soft and rough. "Considering his powers, I'll need all the help I can get."

"Tristan," Belle began, before breaking off again, not sure how to put what she had to say without making his pain worse.

Tris stroked his knuckles slowly down her cheek. "Yes?" he prompted, when she said nothing else.

"I think the Beast is doing more than simply feeding on

the magic of those he kills. I think he's taking on the abilities of his victims. That's how he left traces of Magekind magic at the scene."

Tristan considered the idea, frowning. "If you're right, he could have absorbed Bors's ability as a swordsman." He thought it through before shaking his head. "Doesn't matter. I'm still going to kill him, no matter how good he is with a blade."

"Yes." She cupped her fingers around his hand where it lay on the sheets. He turned it palm up and wrapped his fingers around hers. It felt good to hold his hand. Such a simple gesture, yet it said so much. Basking in the sensation, she brushed her lips over his mouth in a soft kiss. His arms slid around her, and he rolled over onto his back, pulling her against his side. With a sigh, she cuddled into him, the top of her head nestling under his chin.

"Thank you."

Belle wrapped one arm around his narrow waist. "What for?"

He shrugged. "Being here."

Belle smiled and snuggled against him. A moment later, the sun came up and his arms went limp around her as he lost consciousness.

It wasn't long before she joined him.

FOURTEEN

Belle opened her eyes to the glowing image of a unicorn, its golden horn lifted, its emerald eyes wicked. They reminded her of Tristan's.

She'd become adept at reading the light that poured through the stained-glass windows of her bedroom. Now she estimated that it was probably noon.

Belle stretched lazily, enjoying the waterfall of rainbow light pouring in. The windows weren't just pretty, they were a necessity. The bright colors filtered the sunlight so it wouldn't harm her vampire guests.

Like Tristan. He lay utterly still as his body drank in the magic of the Mageverse, an energy he needed every bit as much as he did blood. A vampire could die if he stayed away from the Mageverse for too long.

Tristan's blond lashes feathered his cheeks like thick gold fans, and his sensual lips were parted, as if waiting for a kiss.

God, she was tempted.

He looked as deceptively innocent as a boy in sleep, though there was nothing boyish about the hard, masculine angles of his face. His hair tumbled across her pillow in bright skeins that shimmered in the light from the unicorn window.

He could have been the one to die last night instead of Bors. As skilled and powerful as he was, even Tristan could fall to an assassin's blade in the back.

He needed better armor. Something without the chinks and weaknesses Bors's killer had exploited.

Belle rolled out of bed, conjured a cup of coffee and a muffin, and went to work.

She tried gauntlets first. They needed to be strong enough to resist a Dire Wolf's bite, yet light enough not to restrict mobility.

The armored glove she conjured incorporated sheets of titanium she folded and shaped with her magic into dense layers. Next she used her magic to create a disembodied Dire Wolf head that could bite with the same force as the creature they'd fought the day Emma died. A flick of her fingers, and the glowing avatar bit down on the gauntlet.

Crushing the glove like a beer can.

"Merde," Belle growled. She flung up her hands in disgust, and the failed glove vanished.

She tried four more designs as the afternoon went on, but all of them either failed the bite test or were too heavy to fight in.

This isn't working, she thought, pacing the bedroom in frustration. *And if I don't solve the problem, Tristan's next battle could be his last.*

Irritated, needing a break, Belle dressed and went out to her garden. The scent of roses and the tinkle of falling water never failed to soothe her frustration.

She began to pace as she struggled with the problem. There had to be some combination of magic and metal that would protect Tristan without keeping him from defending himself . . . A pair of huge winged shadows passed across the garden. Alarmed, Belle jerked her head up, then relaxed with a sigh.

It was only Kel flying with his wife, Nineva. Both were in dragon form, riding the thermals that rose from Avalon's sun-heated cobblestone streets. He was a rich iridescent blue, while she blazed gold in the sun. Each was more than forty feet long from tapered nose to whipping tail tip.

They were magnificent.

Belle remembered watching Kel land, the way his iridescent scales rippled over the thick muscles of his shoulders and long, flexible neck . . .

Dragon scales.

Belle's mouth fell open as the solution to the armor problem popped into her mind as if it had been waiting for the right moment to appear. She turned and hurried inside, detouring through the kitchen long enough to grab a blade from the set of chef's knives.

For this, she was going to need blood.

Davon swung his sword with a grunt of furious effort, his eyes narrow, sweat rolling down his muscular torso. He parried and spun, sending a bead of sweat flying. His heart hammered in his chest, and his breathing rasped in desperate heaves of his chest.

He'd started working the moment the sun set and dragged him from the blessed oblivion of the Daysleep. Davon had promptly dressed in a pair of loose cotton shorts, picked up his sword, and padded barefoot into the sitting area. He'd already moved the couch and chairs into the other room to give himself space to work.

Now he ticked through every sword move he'd been taught, every parry, every attack, every retreat, until his muscled ached and a stitch cramped his side.

Not enough. Not nearly enough. He wasn't shaking yet. He had to wear himself out until he couldn't think.

Thought had become Davon's enemy.

He leaped into full extension, driving his sword through the imaginary heart of his opponent, then slashed, taking his foe's . . .

Head.

Nausea twisted his stomach into a sour knot as guilt slapped him like a hard palm.

He'd murdered Jimmy Sheridan. He'd slipped up behind a seventeen-year-old boy who was playing a video game and hacked his head off his shoulders. Never mind that he believed Arthur had told him the boy was a vicious serial-killing pedophile. *He'd decapitated a child.*

The memory kept playing in his head in a nightmarish loop. *The* thunk *of the sword hitting bone, sending Jimmy's head rolling off his shoulders, to spray blood like a garden hose, painting the walls scarlet, splashing Davon's face. . . .* Now the boy's parents and brother were left with an aching hole blasted in their lives where a handsome young man used to be. All his intelligence, all his potential. All gone.

I swore to save lives. Instead I killed an innocent.

The head rolled, spraying blood. It splashed across his face, hot and sickening. He'd staggered into the bathroom to throw up.

I swore to save lives. Instead I killed an innocent.

He'd slipped up behind Jimmy, unable to look into the boy's eyes and kill him. He'd swung the sword, felt the *thunk* of steel biting bone. Jimmy's head rolled, splashing blood across his face as it painted the walls.

I swore to save lives. I killed an innocent.

Davon shuddered. He'd been caught in the same vicious mental loop since he'd learned the boy hadn't been a serial killer. The only thing that helped even slightly was working out until he so thoroughly exhausted his body that he was beyond thought. Even then, if he let the thought of Jimmy in, it instantly triggered another cycle. And the memory would roll over and over again like an endless, looping nightmare.

He should go back to the healer Arthur had ordered him to see, but Petra made him feel *too* good. Almost as if he'd never murdered the boy at all. That wasn't right either. He was a murderer, whether he'd intended to be one or not. He should pay some kind of price. After all, the boy's blameless family was suffering, and they'd done nothing whatsoever to deserve it.

The trouble was, this . . . obsession he'd developed was growing dangerous. He knew he was clinically depressed to the point of being suicidal. If Davon had discovered a patient this bad off in his emergency room days, he would have hospitalized him for his own good.

I swore to save lives. I killed an innocent.

"Davon? Well, hello there." The woman spoke in a rich female purr, the kind that would have brought Davon's senses on alert before Jimmy.

He looked around without much interest and saw Sabryn, who had stopped out in the hallway to peer in at him. Her mouth, slicked with bronze gloss, curled into a seductive smile.

"Hello, Sabryn." He gave her a curt nod and waited for her to go away.

Instead she prowled into the room like an oversized cat. "Have you heard the latest?"

Like he gave a shit about gossip. But his mother had raised him to be a polite Southern gentleman, so he forced a smile. "I've been sticking close to home."

"One of the werewolves killed Sir Bors. You know, the Knight of the Round Table?"

Davon hadn't been an agent long, but already he knew the importance the knights had in Avalon. He tried to make himself care, but the thought barely pushed its way through the mental fog that surrounded him. "That's terrible."

"Arthur was furious. He called the leader of the were-wolves and ripped him a new one. Do you know the man still demanded that he turn you over? Arthur told him to fuck off. The wolf said there'd be war if Avalon didn't—"

"Wait—what?" Davon frowned, trying to focus through the bloody mental loop playing in his head.

"Didn't you know? The werewolves are threatening to declare war on Avalon if Arthur doesn't turn you over for trial immediately, but Arthur says you're just as much a victim as Jimmy Sheridan, and the wolves can go to hell."

"Are they serious?"

"Oh, yeah." Sabryn eyed him. "A lot of people are going to die for you, Davon. I hope you're worth it."

Davon stared at Sabryn in horror. It seemed he couldn't breathe, as if all the air in the room had turned to lead. He shoved past the woman and reeled down the hall, desperate to get outside, find some fresh air before he passed out.

I swore to save lives, and now more innocents are going to die because of me.

Sabryn watched the young Magus shove open a door and escape into the night. She winced. Probably should have kept her mouth shut, but when she'd walked past and seen Davon working out, all big, thoughtless rookie, she'd re-membered Bors. Bors, who'd been kind to her. Thought of all the other agents who'd probably end up dead because of Davon.

It figured he'd be one of Belle's pampered boys.

If Sabryn was honest—and she was many things, but dishonest wasn't one of them—the thought of sticking it to Belle through one of her pets was irresistible. True, it was petty and beneath her, but Belle had humiliated her. Worse, she'd shamed her in front of Morgana.

And she'd stolen Tristan right out from under Sabryn's nose. That stung.

Besides, there was no permanent damage done. The rookie would probably run crying to Mommy, and Belle would have to spend all night calming him down and convincing him that nobody blamed him for the mess with the werewolves.

And they didn't. If Davon hadn't provided the excuse, someone else would have. That was just the way people were when they were intent on going to war.

People were bastards.

Tristan woke to find himself hanging upright, supported in midair by a column of golden sparks. He was also naked from the waist down.

Bewildered, he glanced around. He was still in Belle's bedroom, which was reassuring, since that was where he'd fallen asleep.

His arms were spread wide, clad in the most remarkable armor he'd ever seen. It was formed of countless tiny scales, each about the size and shape of a fingernail. When he moved, the scales flexed, shimmering silver. Each scale had edges of brilliant scarlet, so that bright crimson rippled across his body with every flex of his muscles.

"Belle?" She had to be around here somewhere.

A long fingertip stroked over the curve of his ass in a trailing little tickle.

And there she is. "Belle, darlin', what the hell are you doing?"

"Shhhh," she breathed, and the finger drew a rune over his butt with something wet. Belle hummed, the notes seeming to wrap around his body. He felt something move on his skin.

Craning his head to look over his shoulder, Tristan saw a wave of scales materializing in the wake of her moving finger, armor growing like something organic everywhere she touched him. He moved, stretching out his arms, testing the fit as best he could, pinned like this. It was lighter and more flexible than any armor he'd ever worn. Tris grinned, eager to try it out in combat, see if it was as perfect as it seemed.

Still humming, she circled him, sliding one delicate forefinger along his thigh, whatever paint she was using radiating those amazing scales. Belle was completely naked. Her eyes were wide and glowing, and he realized she was in the kind of deep trance Majae used to work major magic.

This was going to be one hell of a suit of magic armor when she got it finished.

Tristan frowned, realizing Belle held a knife. What was she . . .

Humming, she lifted the blade and drew it down her right breast, inflicting a shallow cut. Transferring the knife to her left hand, she ran a finger down the cut, then used the bloody digit to paint a rune of protection over his groin. Again, scales bloomed.

Holy God. No wonder they were edged in red. They were conjured from her blood.

Tristan stared down at her, stunned speechless. It wasn't unheard of for Majae to use their own blood in major spells. It was the strongest kind of white magic you could work, in fact—an enchantment which drew its power from the witch's own life force. It was said Gwen had done something similar to create Arthur's armor.

But Gwen and Arthur were Truebonded. Of course she'd be willing to spill her own blood to protect him. He strengthened her in turn.

But Belle had given Tristan a priceless gift for *nothing*. It wasn't the kind of thing you did for someone who was nothing more than a combat partner you sometimes bedded.

It was a gesture of love.

Isolde would never have done such a thing for him, even when they were in love. She wouldn't have tied her own life force to his protection.

He had no idea what to say. Except . . .

I love you.

The words lay on his tongue, filling his mouth, desperate to be spoken. Yet some other part of him refused to say them, as if they'd leave him vulnerable. The last time he'd loved a woman, she'd stuck a knife in his chest.

Which was ridiculous. With each stroke of her bloody fingers, Belle told him just how much he meant to her, just how far she was willing to go for him.

How far was he willing to go for her?

At last the spell was finished. Tristan's feet, shod in armored boots, touched the ground as Belle's magic lowered him to the floor.

Standing before him, Belle held out both bloody hands. Across her palm lay the knife. In a flash of magic, it became a great sword—almost four feet long from pommel to point, the kind of weapon it took two hands to use. Reverently, Tristan accepted the big blade.

"The sword controls the armor," she told him. "You only have to will it, and the armor will vanish back into the sword. You won't need me to conjure it anymore, so it will always be available."

"That's amazing." Tristan stepped back to take a short practice swing. Despite the blade's length, it was so perfectly balanced, it seemed to weigh nothing at all in his hands.

"Send the armor back into the sword," Belle urged. "I want to see if it works."

Obediently, he closed his eyes and willed the scales away. When he opened them again, he was as naked as she was, and the sword wore an elegant scale scabbard that shimmered in the candlelight. "Jesu, that's beautiful," he told her, examining the weapon reverently. "Thank you!"

Belle grinned at him, happy as a child on Christmas morning. "You're welcome. I tested the prototype with a mock Dire Wolf bite while you were asleep. The scale didn't so much as dimple. The magic dissipates any force applied to the armor out into the Mageverse. You could step on an IED without getting so much as a hangnail."

"Amazing." Tristan reached out, hooked a hand behind her neck, and pulled her in for a long, slow kiss. Belle purred into his mouth. He drew away just long enough to hang the strap of the scabbard over the bedpost. Then he bent, swept her into his arms, and put her down on the cool sheets. His eyes glinting with sensual hunger, he came down on top of her.

The long cut on her breast was still bleeding—she'd sliced herself a bit too deep. Carefully, Tristan ran his tongue the length of the wound, letting his saliva go to work healing it.

One by one, he found each cut she'd inflicted on herself, then kissed and licked them until she moaned and twisted in helpless arousal. The feel of her soft body writhing against his made him burn. His balls grew tight as his shaft rose to full erection, heavy and thick between his thighs.

Belle was every bit as hot as he was. When he slid a finger between her lower lips, he discovered she was as juicy as a fresh peach. His cock twitched in lust.

I love you. The words echoed in his head, but when he opened his mouth, they refused to emerge.

So instead he kissed her cuts some more, tongued her hard little nipples, and ignored the demanding ache of his cock.

Tristan's tongue drew a long, wet line along one of her cuts, then paused to lick and tease her breasts.

God, it felt good.

Eyes half closed, Belle combed her fingers into his long hair and hung on tight, enjoying every stroke and touch. She could tell from the way he looked at her that he knew why she'd used her own blood in the spell.

Maybe she was an idiot. Maybe he didn't feel the same

way. She kept waiting for the words, but he didn't say them. Instead he stroked and fondled and licked until she thought the pleasure would drive her out of her mind.

But he didn't say *I love you*.

She'd realized the gravity of what she was doing when she'd prepared to make the first cut on her palm. This was serious magic, and it could take a deadly toll on her if the armor was destroyed.

But then she imagined Tristan lying in the bloody leaves in Bors's place, and she realized she'd do anything to make sure such a thing never happened to him.

God help her, she loved him. Arrogant asshole that he was, he'd managed to steal her heart. Her life would be dark and empty without him. It was no wonder she was willing to bleed to ensure he survived his next clash with the Dire Wolves.

Belle wanted him to keep right on driving her crazy with his relentless honesty, his love of Arthurian belching contests, his flaming temper—and his mind-blowing talent for making love to her until she barely knew her own name. A little blood was a small price to pay.

Even if he couldn't say those three exquisite little words.

Tristan spread her legs wide, lowered his blond head, and began to lick, stroking the very tip of his clever tongue around her clit in slowly tightening spirals. He paused a thoughtful moment, then closed his mouth around her and suckled so hard she almost convulsed off the bed with an ecstatic shriek.

Tristan laughed softly and went back to licking, back and forth, in and out of her tight core, around and around her clit. At the same time, he tugged and pinched her nipples, the two pleasures weaving together like a golden braid, tightening slowly until she felt the first pulses of her orgasm.

Then he stopped again. And ignored the frustrated fist she smacked down on his shoulder. "Tristan!"

This time his laughter had a slightly sadistic note. He

went back to teasing her—nipples, pussy, clit, teasing and suckling until the swirl of sensation grew into a thundering storm that made her shake and scream.

She looked up to find him on top of her, guiding that delicious cock into her swollen sex. Belle gave a welcoming little yip as he drove home every last, luscious inch. Wrapping her calves around his thighs, she held on tight.

He started moving. In and out and innnn and ouuuuut, so slowly she thought she was going to detonate like a Roman candle. Moaning, she dug her nails into his back, and he took the hint, speeding up his rolling thrusts.

He reached between their bodies, clever man, and stroked a thumb over her clit as he ground. Her climax finally hit like the breathtaking slap of an unexpected wave, dragging her along as it spun her deep and stole her breath. When it finally retreated, she lay limp and panting with battered pleasure.

Tristan came with a shattering roar. Belle smiled.

Okay, so maybe he couldn't say the words. Neither could she. They seemed so damned huge, she couldn't wrap her tongue around them. Later. Later they'd say them. Right now, she was too busy holding tight to his delightfully sweaty body and enjoying the feeling of that big cock.

She'd made him safe. For now, that was enough.

"Are we sure we want to do this?" Rosen asked uneasily the next night. "People are going to die."

"Of course people are going to die," Andrews said contemptuously. "That's why they say war is hell."

"Not just the Magekind," Rosen pointed out. "Our people, too."

"Commoners." Tanner sneered into his whiskey glass. The three of them had gathered at his mansion in advance of the night's meeting to discuss how to handle the vote.

Rosen had to admit it was a beautiful house with its ivy-covered redbrick walls and arched windows, not to mention the marble floors and fireplaces everywhere you looked. Lots of fussy Louis XV antiques, gilded wood and rose velvet upholstery that made him think of a really expensive whorehouse.

Tanner's library felt more masculine. Leather-bound books filled floor-to-ceiling bookcases, interspaced with bronze statues of naked nymphs in poses of abandoned sensuality. He, Tanner, and Andrews sat in gilded antique chairs clustered around the crackling fireplace, sipping their drinks from Waterford crystal.

The only off note was struck by the painting that hung over the fire. A pretty young girl in Renaissance clothing sawed the head off a bearded man. The blood spurted realistically from her knife as an old woman looked on. The man looked horrified. Tanner swore the painting was a genuine Caravaggio, whoever the hell that was. It was all too damned gory for Carl's taste. But that was the Chosen for you.

Bloodthirsty.

Carl hid his expression in his glass. It irked him, the way the Chosen dismissed Bitten descendents like himself as inconsequential. The Direkind might be werewolves, but they were also Americans, dammit. The lives of commoners were just as valuable as those of the Chosen.

He managed a civil tone with effort. "Commoners or not, we have a responsibility to the people we lead not to waste their lives."

"That's what they're for," Andrews said with a disdainful snort.

"No good cause has ever been won without shedding a little blood." Tanner sipped his whiskey and smiled. "And protecting our way of life is a good cause."

"But is it good enough?" Carl had been asking himself that very question all night.

"Don't be ridiculous," Andrews snapped. "This modern world has strayed dangerously far from the path over the past forty years. Look at all the people that consider themselves our equals now—blacks, Hispanics, the Irish. Not to mention *women*."

"And what's been the result?" Tanner put in. "Crime, divorce, illegitimate children, pornography, and illiteracy. If we don't put a stop to this now, God knows where it will lead."

Like, oh, maybe a decent world, Carl thought, but he didn't say it. Between them, Tanner and Andrews controlled more money than God, and they had Warlock's ear besides. It wasn't in his best interest to piss them off.

"Don't curl your lip at us, Carl," Tanner said, and Carl winced, realizing he'd given himself away. "We are the Chosen. Merlin himself selected our ancestors to preserve humanity. If we don't act now, we will fail that responsibility. One day Merlin will return . . ."

"That's what worries me," Carl muttered.

Tanner ignored him. "I, for one, don't want him to come back to a world in chaos."

"Arthur actually knew Merlin, Tanner," Carl said. "He doesn't seem to believe Merlin held the Chosen's traditions in all that much esteem."

Andrews sneered. "Arthur Pendragon is Celtic trash. We are the descendents of *Anglo-Saxon* warriors. It's our job to preserve our ancient bloodlines."

He might be the descendent of warriors, but Arthur *was* a warrior. Carl remembered the look on the vampire's face—that royal fury and steely determination. "Declaring war on King Arthur is a good way to get a lot of people killed. That's not preserving your bloodlines."

"Warlock will not let our people fall to the Celts," Andrews said, a fanatical gleam in his eyes. "He will lead us to victory, first over Arthur, then over the politically correct weaklings of Modernity. That's our destiny."

Tanner eyed Carl and asked in a silky tone, "Are you losing your nerve?"

Rosen swallowed, recognizing the danger he was in. If

Tanner told Warlock he wouldn't play ball . . . "Of course not. I just want to make sure we're doing the right thing."

Tanner rose and sauntered over to the bar to pour himself another whiskey. "Of course we are, Carl. Vote with us, and unborn generations of Chosen Direkind will applaud your courage."

"Or vote against us," Andrews added in a low, nasty voice, "and your own grandchildren won't even know your name."

"Don't worry." Carl had to stop and swallow before he could add, "You have my vote."

Tanner smiled. "Of course we do."

"Before they left, the Magekind magically altered the bodies of the Green family to make it appear they had been shot," Justice told the members of the Council of Clans. "Given Jimmy Sheridan's beheading, we didn't want another set of deaths from a blade."

"No, we wouldn't want that," Andrews said snidely.

Justice ignored the comment. Andrews and Tanner had been making snarky little asides through his entire report on the murders. "Judging from the article in the paper this morning, the police have concluded the Greens were the victims of a home invasion." He paused and scanned the council. Almost all of them avoided his gaze. Shit, that wasn't good. "Are there any questions?"

Justice braced himself for another grilling about his every move during the investigation. He'd already answered a blizzard of such questions, but if he knew the council, they'd probably ask the exact same ones all over again.

"No," Rosen said, "I think it's all fairly clear."

"Indeed it is," Tanner said. "I move the council fire William Justice from the post of Wolf sheriff."

"Seconded," Andrews said, smirking.

Yeah, Justice had figured something like that was coming.

He asked the obvious question anyway. Damned if he'd roll over for the bastards. "On what grounds?"

Tanner assumed a sober expression completely at odds with the sadistic pleasure in his eyes. "You knew Arthur was suspected of involvement in these murders, and yet you called the Magekind to the scene, corrupting the evidence . . ."

"Corrupting what evidence?" Justice demanded. "I needed an expert in magic to evaluate the scene. The only ones I had access to were Magekind."

"The Magekind are our enemies!" Andrews snapped. "You've been *consorting* with our enemies!"

"They are not the enemy! They . . ."

Rosen banged his gavel. "That's enough, Justice."

"A motion has been made and seconded," Andrews said. "I'm calling the question."

"We haven't even started debating this yet!" Elena protested. "I think Justice has legitimate points . . ."

"Yes, we're all aware of your affection for Justice's . . . points," Andrews said.

Her jaw dropped. "How dare you!"

"Oh, don't pretend outrage, Elena. We all know you're involved with the man."

"What we all know is that Warlock bought you off . . ."

"There is no such thing as Warlock!"

"Tell that to the Chosen who have been worshipping him for fifteen hundred years . . ."

The meeting went downhill from there.

FIFTEEN

Justice walked toward the office building's exit feeling numb. Elena had been the only member of the council to vote against firing him. He'd turned in his badge and weapon, and they'd kicked him out of the meeting.

Now they were probably voting to declare war on the Magekind.

Pushing open the front door, Justice stepped out into the parking lot as he dug the enchanted cell phone out of his pocket. Tristan answered on the third ring. Justice told him the news as he headed for his car.

Listening to the knight swear, he scanned the lot warily. The office building was located well off the main road, and thick woods surrounded it. It would make a dandy place for an ambush—and Justice wouldn't put it past Tanner and his cronies to arrange one.

"You do realize they did this just to shut you up and get you out of the way," Tristan said.

"That did cross my mind, yes." He clicked his key fob to open his car door. "I . . ."

Justice broke off, hearing a metallic slither behind him. He'd hung around Tristan long enough to recognize the sound of a sword being drawn. He spun.

The stranger wore black plate armor that threw off faint sparks of magic as he moved. He grinned at Justice through his open visor in a sharklike revelation of teeth. "Yell for help, boy. Bring Tristan running. I want to kill him. And I'm really looking forward to eating that pretty little girl-friend of his."

Justice threw the phone at the assassin's head.

Dice ducked out of sheer astonished reflex as the cell spun past his ear. Even as he recovered and lunged into an attack, magic exploded around his target. Dice braced, expecting the cop to shift to werewolf form and attack him.

Instead, when the magic faded, Justice had become a huge black wolf. Whirling, he raced away, running like a jackrabbit in long, soaring bounds. Dice swore and transformed into a wolf, knowing he'd never catch the man otherwise.

"Shit!" Tristan rolled out of bed. "We've got trouble," he told Belle. They'd been in the early stages of foreplay when his phone rang.

Belle gestured, conjuring the new armor around them both. Hers was constructed from the same dragon scale design, except without the strengthening blood spell. "Another murder?"

"Not if we get there in time."

But when they stepped through Belle's dimensional gate, there was no sign of anyone in the parking lot. "Where the hell did he go?" Belle said, scooping up Justice's cell and glowering down at the little object. She'd almost stepped on it when she'd come through the portal.

The case was cracked, as if he'd thrown it. Her stomach

knotted as she imagined everything that could have happened to the big cop.

"I don't know, but I can track him." Tristan closed his eyes and called his own magic. It burst around him in a display of golden fireworks. Belle blinked away the dazzle.

One of the abilities Magi rarely used was the ability to shape shift, a trick they usually reserved for healing particularly deadly injuries.

Tristan makes a gorgeous wolf, Belle thought. His thick fur was the same shimmering gold as his hair, and he was enormous, with an elegant tapered muzzle, pointed ears, long legs, and saucer-sized paws.

No sooner had he put his nose to the pavement than he set off at a brisk trot. He'd obviously caught a scent.

"Wait, Tristan!" Belle shouted. "Let me call for backup!"

But instead of pausing, he broke into a lope, apparently afraid Justice was a dead werewolf if they didn't move fast. He was probably right. She ran after him as she dug out her own cell. "Morgana?"

Justice ran hard through the thick woods, leaping brush and ducking around trees, his Direkind night vision rendering the light of the quarter moon almost as bright as day.

The assassin crashed after him, bulling through the brush rather than around or over it, a furry guided missile intent on ripping him apart.

Justice had no intention of being ripped. He ran faster, knowing he'd better not get caught. The killer was the biggest damned wolf he'd ever seen. The beast looked like he weighed five hundred pounds, with massive shoulders and a head easily three times the size of Justice's. And his claws looked like straight razors.

Luckily, all that mass meant he couldn't run as fast as Justice. But if he ever caught up . . . Well.

A fallen tree blocked the path. Justice soared over it—and

saw a patch of something wet gleaming just below his paws. He twisted in midair, but his forepaws hit the slick mud and slid right out from under him. He went down in a tumble of long wolf legs, found traction as he skidded beyond the mud, and clawed his way back to his feet . . .

Too late. The assassin fell on him like a thrown car, slamming him into the earth so hard he saw stars. Before Justice could wrench free, the beast bit into his shoulder. Justice yelped in agony.

Twisting like a fish, he caught one of his foe's thick forelegs in his jaws, and crunched down until he tasted blood. The killer only growled and locked his teeth tighter.

I am so screwed, Justice thought, pain searing his senses like a blowtorch.

King Arthur was in Davon Fredericks's apartment, pissed and glowering. Davon could barely bring himself to care. Arthur and the healer sat facing him in the apartment's tiny sitting area; he'd dragged the chairs back into the room in their honor. "Petra tells me you're refusing to let her treat you."

"I murdered a man, sir. I really don't want to feel good about it."

"I have no intention of making you feel 'good' about your situation," Petra told him tartly in her sweetly lyrical voice. Petite, darkly lovely, the East Indian woman's hair fell around her shoulders in a shining black cloak. "I just want to treat your clinical depression." Her black eyes narrowed in irritation tinged with genuine worry. "You're a doctor, for God's sake. You know what kind of effect depression has on the brain. You . . ."

"A patient has a right to refuse treatment."

"Look, kid," Arthur told him impatiently, "you're not an American citizen anymore. You're a Magus, and that means you follow orders. *My* orders. And I'm ordering you to let Petra treat you. You're no good to me like this. You . . ."

Suddenly a man's voice sang out, "I'm a lumberjack and I'm okay!"

"Excuse me. I've got to get this." Arthur dug the cell phone out of his pocket. "Yes?"

His ringtone was a line from *Monty Python*?

But then Davon's sharp vampire hearing picked up the conversation, and he forgot all about Arthur's taste in entertainment.

"The Council of Clans just fired Justice," Morgana Le Fay's voice snapped. "They threw him out, and Warlock's assassin jumped him in the parking lot. Now Justice is running for his life, and Tristan and Belle are chasing him and the killer. Through the woods. In the dark. I've got our people meeting in front of the building to organize a search. We have to get to them before the bastard eats them."

"I'll be there." He handed the enchanted phone to Petra. "I need a gate and my armor."

As Petra conjured Arthur's gear, a wild plan flashed through Davon's mind. He surged to his feet. "Let me go with you."

Arthur glanced up from checking Excalibur's scabbard. "Petra says you're suicidal. Forget it."

Davon caught Arthur's forearm. The vampire looked down at his hand with a lifted brow. Davon refused to move his hand. "I *need* this, sir. I need to redeem myself." He pointed to the gleaming suit of plate armor standing on a rack in the corner of the room. One of the new Majae had created it just that afternoon, hoping to cheer him up. "I even have armor."

Arthur's hard black eyes searched his, then softened. "Dammit, all right." He poked a finger in the center of Davon's chest. "But you'd better not make me regret this, or I'll have your ass on a stick."

Petra's magic washed over Davon, and he was abruptly

clad in the new armor. Rolling his shoulders under its unfamiliar weight, he watched the Maja conjure a gate in the middle of his Spartan apartment. His stomach clenched in a combination of excitement and dread as Arthur led the way through the wavering portal.

They emerged into a crowd of armored agents, muttering and jostling. Arthur immediately moved off to start bellowing orders.

Everyone was too busy listening to the Magus's battle plan to notice when Davon made his way through the crowd to the cream brick office building. When the teams started trooping off toward the woods, he opened the double glass doors and slipped inside.

Acute vampire hearing detected the rise and fall of arguing voices. Davon followed the sound.

"Arthur refuses to hand the killer over," one man shouted. "We have no choice except to declare war!"

Which sounded like his cue. Davon swung the door open and stepped inside. Thirteen heads turned toward him, and jaws fell as they took in his armor. He straightened his shoulders and forced himself to meet their incredulous stares. "I'm Davon Fredericks," he said, ignoring his hammering heart. "I killed James Sheridan, and I'm surrendering myself to you. You don't have to go to war."

But as he stood there, he wondered why three of the councilmen looked so incredibly frustrated.

Belle raced through the dark after Tristan's bushy blond tail. It was a damned good thing her night vision was almost as acute as his, or she would have face-planted in a tree trunk a dozen times. As it was, she had to ignore the slap of branches across her face as she ducked and twisted and leaped like a deer.

She just prayed she was fast enough, because the assassin had caught Justice. Growls, snarls, and yelps of combat sounded from somewhere ahead of them. They had to get to their friend before the killer ate him.

Suddenly the darkness seemed to open up into a clearing just ahead. Unfortunately, she was concentrating so hard on Tristan's flicking tail, she didn't notice the tree trunk that lay across her path. Belle hit the obstacle hard enough to knock the breath from her lungs.

Tristan sailed right over the tree, hit a patch of mud beyond it and damn near skidded right into Justice and the killer.

The ex-cop had transformed into his biped Direwolf form, the better to rake and claw at the huge thing that held him down. The killer had shifted back into the creature they'd fought at Emma's, and was doing his damnedest to eat Justice like a burrito.

Justice had no intention of being eaten. He'd locked both huge hands around the thing's jaws and forced them away from his neck, holding the beast's head at arm's length with sheer brute strength.

"Let him go!" Magic exploded around Tristan as he shifted back to human form. Armor sheathed his big body, and he held a great sword in both hands as he stepped forward, heaving the giant blade up.

Only to stop with a muttered curse. Belle saw why; Justice was squarely in the path of his blade. He couldn't kill the Beast without hurting the cop.

So Belle flung a fireball at the two werewolves.

As she'd known it would, the blast splashed off Justice's magically resistant hide, while setting the killer's fur on fire. He reared off the cop, roaring in pained outrage.

"Get away from him, Bill!" Belle yelled, but Justice was already scrambling clear. As he moved, she saw something liquid go flying.

Blood.

Justice was hurt. His black fur was slicked to his ribs in the moonlight, though it was hard to see how bad the damage was.

As he jumped clear, Belle shot another fireball at the assassin. This time he snapped the blazing globe out of the air like a Scooby Snack and gave her an evil grin. "Yum."

Well, merde.

Opening his fanged maw, he exhaled a searing blow-torch gust of flame. Belle barely got a shield up in time.

Taking advantage of the monster's distraction, Tristan darted in and swung his sword at the Beast's head. The thing twisted with surprising agility and hit the flat of Tristan's blade, knocking it aside. "Okay," the creature said. "So I'll eat *you* now and the girl later."

He lunged, sinking those gatorlike teeth in the scale armor covering Tristan's chest. Belle heard the crunch of the scales cracking, and agony stabbed her like a dagger in the heart.

Oh merde, she realized, *I forgot that thing eats magic. And the armor* is *magic—my magic.*

Tristan felt the killer's lethal teeth sink into his armor as if it were a candy apple. The scales crackled, but by some miracle, they still kept the assassin's teeth from sinking into his chest.

Which was a damn good thing, since the monster's bite would probably kill him in seconds.

Belle gasped, a strangled sound of pain. *Oh, Jesu, the mail's blood magic is linked to her.* He had to get the bastard off him before the assassin did serious damage.

Gritting his teeth, Tristan smashed his sword down on the beast's skull with all his strength. Blood flew in a red rain, but not nearly enough. By all rights, the blow should have shattered the thing's skull. As it was, the killer growled and shook him like a dog with a rat. The world jerked back and forth with nauseating force until it was all Tristan could do not to vomit. The armor crackled as if the bastard's teeth were breaking through.

Tristan started hacking at the Beast. Blood flew and the thing growled, but Tris had no damned leverage at all.

"Give me a sword!" Justice bellowed, presumably to Belle.

The Beast slammed Tristan down on the ground so hard, stars wheeled around his head. The killer's jaws began to work, trying to chew through the armor.

Magic sizzled across his skin from some blast coming way too close. *Belle's throwing fireballs again*, Tristan thought, smelling burning fur.

The monster jolted, jerking its massive head up, tearing its jaws free of his armor with a brittle crunch.

Whirling, the Beast lunged, teeth snapping at Justice and his new sword.

Tristan wanted to spend a few minutes just lying there breathing, but he was a Knight of the Round Table. He forced himself to roll to his feet, pick up the sword he'd dropped, and go after his foe before the thing ate one of his friends.

The Beast snapped at Justice, who danced around it with impressive speed even by vampire standards. The boy had no idea how to use the sword Belle had given him, but he was trying.

Before Tristan could charge into the fight, magic hit him in a flesh-tingling wave. He looked down, startled, as the hole in the middle of his chest mail began to heal, sealing with incredible speed.

Tris threw Belle a smile. "Thank you." And leaped at the Beast, swinging up his sword for an overhand blow.

The monster leaped away, opening its jaws as if to breathe fire at him. He ducked back, hoping Belle would shield him.

But instead of attacking, the creature looked around, ears swiveling.

Which was when Tristan heard it, too. A crashing in the distance, the sound of voices lifted in shouts, Arthur's battlefield bellow ringing over it all.

The Beast whirled and ran. Before Tristan and Justice

could take more than a few steps in pursuit, he darted through a dimensional gate that promptly vanished with a soap bubble pop.

Tristan glanced at Belle. "Did you get a fix on him?" It would certainly be useful to know where the monster had his lair.

Instead of answering, her eyes rolled back and she fell to her knees. Tristan barely managed to catch her before she hit the ground. Her head lolled, eyes fluttering closed.

"Belle! What's wrong with her?" the werewolf demanded. It was hard to read the expression on Justice's furry face, but that looked like worry in his eyes. He was covered in blood from countless bites, and claw marks scored his body.

"The bastard hurt her when he savaged my armor," Tristan explained as he stroked her face. "Then she used whatever was left repairing the damage." He looked up and roared, "Morgana! *A moi!*"

"Hold on!" More crashing coming closer through the brush. It sounded as if Arthur had brought every agent in Avalon. Which just might be enough to do the job.

Tristan arranged Belle more comfortably in his lap and gently pulled off her helm. Her face was white, her eyes closed.

Magic detonated beside him, and Tristan looked up, alarmed. But it was only Justice, reassuming human form. The change healed his injuries, but he dropped to his knees and slumped, obviously exhausted.

Tristan examined him, concerned by his pallor. "You okay?"

"Fight took a lot out of me." Justice eyed Tris's face through the raised visor. "You, too, looks like."

"Narrow escape. If that thing had gotten his teeth into my skin . . ."

"You'd be dead."

"Yeah. That's about the size of it."

* * *

Davon thought about dying. How would they kill him? Would it hurt?

Little damned late to start worrying about it, he told himself, impatient with his own sudden fear. Whatever they did to him would still be better than watching that boy die in his mind over and over and *over* again. He'd do anything to stop that endless loop. Anything at all.

Something rattled, and he looked around as one of the councilmen walked in carrying a reel of thick steel chain. He'd gone out to get it when Tanner announced they needed to bind the prisoner. Apparently the man was a landscaper in his day job, and he used the chain to pull up tree stumps.

Tanner took the reel away from him and started winding it around Davon, who ignored them both. The landscaper shrugged and went to the corner of the room where the council was huddled, arguing in fierce, low voices about what to do with him.

"You just had to go and be a hero, didn't you?" Tanner snarled, and jerked the chain viciously tight. If not for Davon's armor, the thick steel links would have chewed into his skin.

"What the hell is your problem?" Davon demanded. "I did what you wanted. I surrendered. I'll plead guilty. I'll even let you execute me for my crime."

"But Arthur didn't surrender you," Tanner growled. "We should declare war anyway."

A spark of spirit flared through the doctor's leaden depression. "So basically, you're pissed because you're not getting your war." Davon shook his head. "Man, you really are an idiot. Arthur and his knights would go through you guys like a chainsaw. They . . ."

He saw the punch coming, but bound as he was, there wasn't a damn thing he could do to block it. The impact rocked his head and sent light exploding through his skull, and he tasted blood.

"Tanner, you son of a bitch!" A female werewolf stalked across the room and stiff-armed Tanner with both hands. He stumbled back, then jolted forward, fist cocked.

Davon instinctively jerked in his bonds, trying to break free and protect the girl, but the chain was too thick. "Leave her alone!" he roared.

The little redhead danced back and snarled in Tanner's face. "That's right, asshole. Hit me. Show everybody here exactly what you are—the kind of man who beats bound prisoners and women six inches shorter."

Tanner's face contorted with such savagery, it was obvious he was fully capable of killing her. Davon writhed in his chains, fighting desperately to break free.

"That's enough, Tanner!" Carl Rosen snapped, taking a long step toward them. "Don't hit . . ."

He swung anyway. The redhead ducked, and Tanner stalked her as she danced away. "Oh, yeah, you're a *real* man," she spat. "If my husband was here, you wouldn't dare look at me funny."

Tanner bared his teeth. "If Lucas was any kind of man at all, he'd teach you your place!"

"Dammit, Tanner!" Rosen and two other men grabbed the werewolf, jerking him away before he could hit her. "Have you lost your mind?"

"Well," Davon drawled, licking the blood from his split lip, "if we're done displaying our collective heroism, maybe you should consider getting me out of here before Arthur realizes I'm gone and sends a team to get me back. Much as I'd love to watch the knights kick Tanner's ass, it wouldn't get the Sheridan family their justice."

The werewolves stopped and stared at him, open-mouthed. Rosen went pale. "You mean Arthur's *here*?"

Great, Davon thought. *I'm going to be executed by idiots. This'll go well.*

* * *

Belle still hadn't regained consciousness when Arthur led his merry band into the clearing. Tristan, still cradling his lover, did a quick head count and realized his liege hadn't fooled around. There were fifty-one assorted witches and vampires in the crowd, all armed, armored, and looking grim. Justice edged closer to Tristan's shoulder, as if unconsciously seeking protection from all the pissed-off Magekind.

"Tristan!" Lark cried. "Are you all right?" His great-granddaughter hurried over and dropped to her knees in front of them. "What happened?"

Tristan gave her a weary smile. "The usual. A monster tried to eat us."

"That's what you get for teasing them," Morgana said, striding into the clearing in a swirl of black velvet skirts embroidered in silver. "Get out of the way, child," she told Lark, who still knelt at Tristan's feet. "I need to see to Belle."

Instead of moving, Lark examined his face. "Tris, are you hurt?"

"I'm fine." He looked down at the woman draped over his lap. "Thanks to Belle."

"Well, that's a relief." Lark blew out a breath and rose, stepping aside so Morgana could take her place.

"What happened?" the witch demanded. Arthur stalked over to stand behind her and fold his brawny arms, a glower on his bearded face. His wife joined him, concern knitting her brows.

Tristan began his report as Morgana took Belle's face between her palms. Her palms ignited in a glow, golden with healing magic.

Tris found himself a bit surprised at Morgana's obvious concern. Evidently Belle had the Ice Bitch charmed, just like everyone else.

At last she stirred and opened her eyes. Tristan relaxed and exhaled a breath he hadn't realized he was holding.

"Oh," she said, looking up at Morgana. "Hi."

"What the hell were you thinking, using blood magic to make his armor?" the witch demanded. "You're not even Truebonded, for God's sake. That thing could have killed both of you with one bite."

"I just . . ." Belle began.

Morgana turned her glare on Tristan. "And you! Why did you let her do something like that? You know better!"

"You're right," he agreed. "I knew the Beast ate magic. I should have realized it would eat magical armor."

Belle frowned and struggled to sit up. Tristan automatically pulled her back against his chest. "The point is, the thing wasn't able to bite through his armor," she said, her tone stubbornly defiant. "It saved his life. I don't mind sacrificing a little magic for that."

"You could have ended up paying a lot more than a little magic, you silly twit, and you damned well know it." Morgana glowered at Tristan. "What did you do, put a spell on her with your magic dick?"

Tristan choked.

"Morgana!" Belle snapped. "My sex life is none of your business!"

"It is when I have to clean up the mess. Now, let me finish." She caught Belle's face between her palms again. Once more, Tristan sensed the fizz and pop of magic.

Belle's slumping shoulders straightened. "Thank you," she said to her friend, a shade reluctantly. "I'm fine now."

"That's debatable." With one last glare at Tristan, Morgana rose to her feet. "But your strength is back to normal— at least until you try to kill yourself again." Pivoting on one armored high-heeled boot, she stalked away.

"She's got a point," Arthur told Belle. "Gwen may have created my armor with blood magic, but we're Truebonded. You really shouldn't . . ."

"Arthur!" Petra interrupted, pushing through the crowd, dark eyes wide with concern. "We have a problem."

He sighed. "We have any number of problems, Petra. What's your addition to the list?"

"Davon's gone. Since I've touched his mind in my healing, I was able to do a locate spell on him." She turned and pointed. "He's about two miles that way, moving fast. In a car, I suspect."

"The council must have captured him," Justice said grimly. He'd been so quiet since the Magekind had arrived, Tristan had almost forgotten he was there.

"Captured, hell. The suicidal idiot probably gave himself up. I'm going to kick his ass!" Arthur snarled. "He swore to me . . ."

"Rant later, darling," his wife murmured. "Get him back now."

"But should we?" Morgana asked, frowning. "He did, after all, kill an innocent. If he gave himself up to them voluntarily, and it prevents them from going to war against us . . ."

"Don't kid yourself," Justice told her. "They'll find another excuse. Smoke and Eva provided the council with concrete proof of Warlock's existence *and* the fact that he's an evil son of a bitch, and they still threatened war. I'd bet you dollars to dog chews the fucking wizard's bought half the damned council off, and the other half is too witless to do anything but follow where they lead. Except for Elena Rollings, and one vote is just not enough."

"I'm not letting them have Davon regardless of their threats," Arthur said. "I know the man is eaten up with guilt, but that comes with the job. He's going to have to get over it. Warlock mindfucked him, and I refuse to let the bastard get him executed on top of it."

He swept an eye over the crowd and started picking out vampires with thrusts of one gloved finger. "Gawain, Galahad, Lance, Reece, you go with Petra and recover our idiot doctor . . ."

"And me," Belle said as the men stepped closer.

"Forget it. You've done your bit for the day," Arthur told her, without even glancing around. He looked at his waiting agents. "Now, I want you to—"

"He's one of my boys, Arthur." Her delicate jaw set in a way Tristan recognized all too well. "Besides, I think I can talk him into coming back without being dragged kicking and screaming."

"Merlin's balls, woman . . ." Arthur began hotly.

Guinevere leaned in. From the look in her eyes, Tristan suspected she was talking to him in their Truebond.

He broke off in mid-rant and sighed. "Dammit, Gwen. All right, Belle, you can go. Tristan, go with them. And don't get bitten by anybody. I'm tired of holding funerals."

SIXTEEN

The werewolf's clawed hand wrapped around Davon's entire head the way his own could encircle an infant's. Except *his* fingers didn't have three-inch claws.

"I want to kill you," Stephen Sheridan whispered, his breath hot and rank, his eyes yellow with lupine rage.

"Yeah, I can see that," Davon said.

The Council of Clans had moved him to Howard Sheridan's church while they decided what to do. Apparently Jimmy's father was a pastor. Why that somehow made it all worse, Davon didn't know.

The one-story brick building had stained-glass windows and the traditional pointed white steeple. The white wooden sign out front read: HOLY RAPTURE BAPTIST CHURCH.

It reminded Davon of the church his family had attended when he was a child. His backside had occupied a pew every time the doors opened, which was usually at least twice a week.

Now the members of the Council of Clans huddled

together at one side of the soaring sanctuary, arguing in low voices as they tried to decide how to handle the situation.

Stephen Sheridan looked over at Carl Rosen and licked his chops. "Let me bite him," he demanded in a rumbling growl. "If Justice told the truth, he'll die just like his girlfriend."

Davon looked up at the kid—a long, long way up. Stephen was more than seven feet tall, with dagger-length claws and teeth that would make a crocodile weep with envy.

He should probably be terrified, but all Davon felt was a kind of weary fatalism. "Go ahead."

Stephen blinked. "What?"

He shrugged, despite the weight of the chains still wrapped tight around his arms. He'd long since lost the feeling in them. "You're certainly entitled. If it helps, it will be a lot more painful than what I did to Jimmy. It'll take me longer to die, too. He never even saw it coming."

The kid tightened his clawed grip on his captive's head. "You *don't* talk about Jimmy!"

Davon shrugged. "Okay." His voice dropped to a whisper. "But I'll still think about him. I think about him all the time. I can't stop thinking about him . . ."

The kid jerked back, letting go as if burned. Or as if he'd been unnerved by whatever he'd seen in Davon's eyes . . .

"I would like to satisfy my curiosity, though." Davon lifted his voice. "Hey, Tanner. Come here a minute."

By all rights, Tanner shouldn't have come anywhere near him, but they had an audience. A very large werewolf audience.

After Elena Rollings had convinced Reverend Sheridan to let them use his church—figuring the knights might hesitate to attack them there—every werewolf in the area showed up to watch. Now the pews were full of Direkind, staring and whispering. Even in Davon's current fatalistic mood, it was unnerving to be the focus of so much concentrated hate.

Apparently, though, Tanner loved the crowd. He swaggered over to Davon. "What do you want, killer?"

"I'm curious, Tanner—how much did Warlock pay you to sell your vote for war?"

Tanner's face went slack with shock, then flushed with furious rage. "You little . . ."

"Smell that?" Davon asked Stephen. "Guilt. I thought so."

Tanner lunged for Davon's throat, but Stephen stiff-armed him, knocking him back a pace. "What the hell do you think you're doing?"

"Giving me another black eye, I'd imagine," Davon said dryly. "He's got a nasty temper. Thanks for the save."

Stephen studied Davon's bruised face. Something dangerous glittered in his yellow werewolf gaze. "Was that before or after they chained you up?"

Davon shrugged. "After."

Howard Sheridan rose from the front pew. "You *hit* a chained prisoner?"

"He had it coming." Tanner rolled to his feet and tilted up his chin in defiance. "He mouthed off to me."

Andrews looked around at them and glowered. "Tanner, shut the fuck up."

Sheridan stiffened. "I'll thank you to remember this is a church."

Andrews opened his mouth, registered the watching crowd, and thought better of whatever he was going to say. "Of course, Reverend. Forgive me."

"Weasel," Davon muttered under his breath.

"You're not kidding," Stephen whispered back. "What a pair of jerks." The boy hesitated, before adding thoughtfully, "And you were right—Tanner did smell guilty."

Davon concealed his smile of satisfaction with an effort. He might be a dead man, but maybe the seeds he'd planted could prevent the war Warlock was so determined to bring about.

That had to be worth something. Didn't it?

Miranda contemplated the expanse of floor she needed to mop and sighed, greatly tempted to just cast a cleaning spell over the whole kitchen so she could go home.

Yeah, and you'd get a visit from Daddy Dearest fifteen minutes later. She'd far rather do it the hard way than face Warlock's savage temper. Again.

Sighing, Miranda headed for the corner where the wheeled mop bucket waited. She pushed it over to the stainless steel utility sink, grabbed the faucet spray attachment, cranked the hot water on high, and began filling the bucket.

She was just reaching for the bottle of cleanser when she thought she heard a cry coming from the restaurant's dining room.

Miranda frowned. "Hannah?" Her fellow waitress was closing out the front counter register. Concerned, she turned off the thundering water.

"Goddammit," a male voice roared, "I said hand over the money unless you want a bullet in the brain!"

"I'm trying! The key won't . . ."

"Fuck it." *Boom.*

The sound of the echoing gunshot hit Miranda like an electric shock. She transformed before she even realized she was calling her magic, fur racing over her skin, bones and muscles jerking painfully with the change.

She spun and ran on soft, silent paws, darting through the kitchen toward the swinging door into the dining room. Sliding to a cautious stop, Miranda pushed the door silently open.

The short counter with its cash register stood facing Flo's front door. Which was a damned good thing, because that meant she could come up behind the two armed robbers who stood with their backs to her as they struggled to open the register.

Hannah lay on the floor at the men's feet, her breathing harsh with agony and effort. Blood pooled on the floor around her as she stared blindly at the ceiling.

Dying. She was dying.

Miranda's thoughts flew to Hannah's two children, who would probably be sent to live with that abusive bastard Eddie if she died.

Oh, hell no. No way was Miranda going to let that happen. Not to Hannah, gentle Hannah, who adored her children and blueberry pie and watching *SpongeBob SquarePants* with the kids.

Miranda stepped up behind the two robbers, grabbed each man's head in a hand, and slammed their skulls together before they even realized she was there. She dumped the unconscious duo on the floor and shifted into human form.

Two transformations so close together were agonizingly painful, but she gritted her teeth and ignored the muscle spasms. All she cared about was saving Hannah.

Miranda dropped to her knees beside her friend, swallowing hard at the bloody hole in the woman's chest. "Hannah? Hannah, can you hear me?"

"Randi? Is that . . . you? Thought I saw . . . monster." The pool of blood around her torso was getting wider, and the hole in her chest produced a sucking, bubbling sound. *Oh, not good. Not good at all.*

"No monsters here, doll." Miranda spread her hands and prepared to cast the healing spell.

And hesitated. *If I do this, Warlock will know.* Healing a gunshot wound this bad was major magic, and it would take time. She'd be lucky if she finished before her father's assassins showed up to kill her.

And they would. She'd run away after killing not only her stepfather but also the werewolf Warlock had sent to rape and impregnate her. That was the kind of defiance the wizard would consider punishable by death.

Well, tough, Miranda thought grimly. *I'm not letting Hannah die.* Taking a deep breath, she let her magic roll from her hands to cover her friend in a glowing wave of sparks.

The shimmering blue whiplash wrapped around Dice's torso, sending hot-white agony jangling through his body like an electric shock.

"Failure is not acceptable, dog!" Warlock snarled. "When I send you on a mission, I expect you to accomplish it! Instead, all you've given me is failure!"

He decided he had nothing to lose and dared to protest. "Arthur and a whole pack of knights were on the way. I couldn't fight that many."

"Then you should have killed Justice before they arrived!" the wizard thundered. "You . . ." He broke off, his eyes widening slightly as if listening to someone Dice couldn't hear.

What now?

"Well, well, well." Warlock smiled slowly. "My darling daughter. I knew if I waited long enough, you'd use your powers."

What? Dice blinked. *Daughter?* Warlock had a daughter? *Who'd he rape?*

"It seems you have an opportunity to redeem yourself, boy. Go kill my daughter for me." He smiled in a chilling revelation of long white teeth. "And make it as painful as you can for as long as she lasts."

When the cavalry arrived, Davon opened his mouth to curse. Then he remembered Reverend Sheridan and swallowed the juicy phrase, contenting himself with a frustrated glare.

A veritable parade of armored Magekind agents charged

through a dimensional gate into the sanctuary, swords and shields in their hands.

Yelping in dismay, the werewolves started shifting to Direwolf form. Magical detonations rolled over the sanctuary as panicked werewolves jumped up from the pews.

Great. Just great. His heart sank as he wondered how many people were going to get hurt in this mess.

"Davon!" Belle leaped onto the stage and strode over to him.

Cocooned in chains, he watched her with resignation. The witch made one of those dramatic sweeping gestures, and the steel links rained around his feet, each abruptly disconnected from the others.

"What have these bastards done to you?" Belle frowned up at his bruised face and touched his swollen eye with a delicate finger.

He felt the tingling heat of a spell, and the pain faded from his battered face. More importantly, feeling flooded back into his numb arms. "Thanks, Belle," he growled. Then he moved her gently out of his path and strode toward his target, who still dithered on the stage as the knights streamed into the sanctuary. Tanner's eyes were wide with panic as he watched the armored fighters.

"Let me guess," Davon growled. "You're all for war until somebody actually expects *you* to do the fighting."

Tanner wheeled at the sound of his voice—right into Davon's truly beautiful right cross that laid him flat on his back.

The doctor shook his stinging fist. He'd scraped his knuckles, but it was worth it. "All right, you lot!" he roared, the fury in him suddenly overflowing its emotional dam. "Listen up!" He turned toward Belle and Tristan, who'd joined her on the stage. "And that includes you two."

The rest of the knights spread out, a wary wall of armor, crouching behind lifted shields. His gaze slipped past them to the werewolves, most of whom had already changed. The females knelt, their arms curled protectively around crying children. The males stood over them, obviously determined to defend their families to the death.

The sight of all those kids only added to Davon's frustrated rage. "Now, what the *hell* do you people think you're doing?" he asked the werewolves. "You brought your children to this? Are you out of your minds?"

"We didn't know the knights would come!" one woman cried, her voice surprisingly deep and growling. Even so, it quavered.

"You knew I'd been accused of murder!" He shook his head. "Well, fortunately for you, there's not going to be a fight. The Magekind do not put innocents in the line of fire."

"Davon, you're in enough trouble," Tristan barked, annoyed. "Would you shut the fuck up?"

"You're in a church, Sir Tristan!" Davon snapped back. And damn, it felt good. He looked out over the crowd as several people escaped out the sanctuary's rear doors. Nobody moved to stop them. He ignored them. "Merlin gave you people a gift, even if you do call it a curse. It's an honor to carry his magic . . ."

"Who the hell are you to preach to us, murderer?" somebody shouted.

Davon froze. "Yes." The word emerged in a low voice, and yet somehow it seemed to fill the room. "I did kill an innocent boy. That's why I surrendered myself to your justice."

His dark hands curled into fists. "But since I've been your prisoner, I haven't seen any justice. I've seen cowardice. I've seen corruption. I've seen people who'd better pray neither Merlin nor Jesus ever comes back to Earth."

"That's enough!" Rosen snapped.

"No, it's not! Come over here, Carl. Let everybody take a sniff while you lie and say you weren't paid to vote for war."

The chairman took an angry step toward him, then hesitated, eyeing Tristan. The knight stood just behind Davon wearing an evil grin. "Nobody paid me! And there is no Warlock."

Davon looked out over the audience. "Take a deep breath, folks. I can smell the stink from here. Can't you?"

"Are you going to listen to a murderer?" Tanner shouted. "He cut off a boy's head—from behind! Like a coward! And he has the *gall* to accuse us of anything?"

"I was under a spell," Davon snarled. "Though you're right—it doesn't matter why I killed that child. It doesn't matter that I thought I was saving other children." He stalked up to Tanner through the blinding red haze of his rage. "But the difference between us is that I killed because I thought it was my duty. I didn't sell other people's blood for money."

He poked a stiffened index finger into the werewolf's chest. "If you take these people to war, you will be just as guilty of murder as I am. But you'll do it deliberately, because you have no more conception of honor than a dog."

"Kid sounds like Arthur when you get him on a roll," Lancelot observed in the boiling silence.

"Shut up," Gawain told him. "I'm enjoying this."

Tanner growled, the sound dropping into a throbbing rumble as magic detonated around him. A heartbeat later, he loomed over Davon, better than seven feet of fur and claws. "You little fuck," Tanner snarled, "you're a dead man."

He lunged. And Davon thought, *One bite and it's all over . . .*

Miranda dropped her hands to the floor and sat there, so weary it was all she could do to breathe. Healing the damage the bullet had done had left her dangerously drained.

Hannah opened her eyes and blinked up at her. "Randi?" She licked her lips and frowned. "Randi, what happened?"

"Robbers." Miranda pulled her shoulders back and

managed a smile. "Robbers happened. They must have hit you on the head or something. When I came in, you were unconscious."

"Really?" Terror widened her eyes, and she tried to sit up. "Oh, man! Are they still here?"

"Don't worry about those guys." Catching her friend by the shoulders, Miranda gently pushed her back down and sent magic rolling with a flick of her fingers. A moment later, both men lay beside the register just out of Hannah's sight, trussed up in electrical cord. "They're still out cold," Miranda said brightly. "They were trying to figure out how to get the register open when I walked up behind them and hit them in the head with that big ol' heavy mop we use in the back. Boom goes the dynamite, *et voilà*—unconscious idiots."

"Wow." Hannah lifted her head with an effort, obviously still dazed. Miranda might have healed the worst of her injuries, but she still wasn't clicking on all cylinders. "That was really brave. You saved my life."

Alarmed, Miranda said hastily, "Oh, don't be melodramatic. I hit the silly bastards with a mop. Big deal."

"It *is* a big deal," Hannah insisted. "People get on CNN for that kind of thing."

"More like *America's Dumbest Criminals*. Look, the one thing I don't need is fifteen minutes of fame . . ."

"Oh," Hannah said wisely. "You're running from someone."

Miranda blinked at how close this was to the mark, started to deny it, then changed her mind. "Yeah, I am. I've got this ex-boyfriend who put me in the hospital a time or two." Almost true, except for the boyfriend part. And the hospital part; she'd had to heal herself.

"I know what that's like."

"I know. Thing is, he swore if he couldn't have me, nobody else could, so the one thing I don't want is airtime. So don't say anything about me to the cops, okay?"

"But how will I explain the robbers?"

"Say you hit 'em. Then you can be the hero. You'd probably enjoy fifteen minutes of fame. God knows you deserve it after the crap you put up with."

Hannah looked doubtful. "Well, I don't know . . ."

"What a pretty lady," a male voice purred just before the sense of power hit Miranda: huge, dark, and as threatening as a hurricane. Her heart shot into her throat as she whirled to see a man move out of the kitchen as silently as a snake.

He was tall, better than six-five, and his shoulder-length brown hair was streaked with gray. He had angular, sharply cut features that might have been considered handsome—until you saw his eyes. They were cruel and black, and magic burned behind them, blazing hot with glints of werewolf orange.

"Warlock sent you." It wasn't a question.

His mouth twitched into a smile, as though he found her funny. "Yeah. Seems you've really pissed Daddy off, little girl."

"Who the hell are you?" Hannah demanded.

Panic stabbed Miranda. "Go to sleep!" she snapped, and her friend's head dropped back so fast, it bumped the floor. She'd probably have a lump in the morning, but that was better than being dead.

The assassin grinned, and Miranda snarled at him. "She's got no part of this. She's just a human. Let her be. I haven't told her anything about Warlock."

He shook his head. "You didn't get that soft streak from Daddy, that's for damned sure."

"No," Miranda said. "But I did get this." Reaching into the Mageverse, she seized the magic, dragged it into her soul, and sent it blasting into the assassin's face.

The bolt picked him up like a paper doll in a tornado and blew him through the swinging kitchen door. He slammed into the solid steel freezer unit and slid limply to the floor.

Miranda whirled and bolted, banging through Flo's front door into the night beyond. The killer wouldn't waste time hurting Hannah if Miranda wasn't around to watch. He'd come after her instead.

And with the kind of power he had, he'd kill her.

Miranda raced across the dark, empty street and down the first alley she came to, then zipped left up a side street, then right down an alley barely wide enough for her shoulders.

Her objective was to put as much real estate between her and the killer as she could. She'd need time to work the spell she had in mind, which meant she had to hide and shield herself.

Flo's wasn't located in a particularly nice part of Derry, South Carolina—not that there were many nice parts of Derry, South Carolina, aging textile town that it was. The route Miranda chose took her into a section that was even worse. Graffiti marked every building she passed, some written in the code used by the local gangs, some just poorly spelled obscenities. Half the streetlights were dark, and windows were broken out or boarded over. The smell of rotting trash was so strong she wanted to gag.

She swallowed hard and ran on, knowing she hadn't put enough distance between her and the killer.

Normally her father sent his Bastards to discipline those who'd displeased him. But when Miranda extended her senses, she could detect only one magical creature in the area—the one she'd just blasted halfway across the restaurant.

He was already coming after her, and he was moving fast.

Miranda figured she had one chance at survival: La Belle Coeur. She'd been trying to come up with a way to contact Belle since she'd accidently blasted the Maja.

Fortunately, Miranda had touched the witch's mind once before, during that disastrous tea party a month ago. If she concentrated on the memory of that mental contact and gave it all the power she had, she might be able to make contact. Maybe. If she got lucky.

She'd hesitated to try it before because that kind of psychic bellow was just the sort of thing Warlock was bound to notice. But since that was a moot point now . . . *Time to find a hiding place and launch the spell.*

And pray.

Davon watched fanged jaws shoot right for his throat. One bite . . .

A big hand fell on the edge of the gorget that protected the back of his neck, gripped it, and jerked him backward.

Tanner's teeth snapped on empty air the instant before Tristan's shield hit the werewolf hard across the side of the head, sending him spinning. "Bad dog!"

But seven-feet-plus of fur, fangs, and temper does not add up to wimp. Tanner caught himself and lunged at Tristan, his yellow eyes crazed. The knight spun into a kick that would have done Jackie Chan proud and landed an armored boot upside the werewolf's skull. Tanner staggered backward, shaking his head hard, blood flying from his muzzle.

"Stop it!" Reverend Sheridan cried. "This is a church!"

But no one was listening. Women and children wailed in fear over male shouts of rage and wolf howls of fury. Fights had broken out between the knights and the werewolves, mostly fists and feet, but it was only a matter of time before somebody bit somebody and somebody else used a sword. Then the shit would really hit the fan.

Davon turned his back on Tristan and headed for the preacher. "Sheridan!" he shouted, bounding down from the stage. The reverend gave him a panic-stricken look and backed up, looking as if he was trying to decide whether to transform.

"No!" Davon yelled. "I don't want to fight. We've got to stop this before somebody gets killed!"

A complex expression crossed Sheridan's face—relief? Fury that it was his son's murderer trying to come to his rescue? It was hard to tell.

And it didn't matter anyway. Davon caught the man by the shoulder and drew him toward the front of the sanctuary. "Stop it! There are kids here! Somebody's going to get killed."

Sheridan added his deep bellow. "Break it off! Now!"

Nobody paid them any attention at all—except for Belle. The Maja studied them for a heartbeat and nodded as if coming to a decision. One hand swept in a graceful gesture toward the sanctuary's soaring ceiling, and a blast of fireworks exploded over their heads in a thundering salvo. Everybody ducked for cover with yelps of alarm.

"This is over!" Davon shouted into the sudden silence. "There are too many children here—one of them's going to get hurt."

"We're not giving you up, killer!" a werewolf roared back.

"I'm not asking you to. I came here for justice, and I'm not leaving. But the rest of the Magekind are."

"Kid . . ." Tristan began.

"I'm not a kid," Davon snarled. "But I did kill one, and his family deserves justice. And if you keep trying to take me back, somebody's going to end up dead."

It was so dark even Miranda had trouble seeing a damned thing. A dog had turned over a garbage can, scattering reeking debris the length of the alley.

Perfect.

Both the smell and the shadows would help hide her from the killer long enough to give her a few more crucial seconds to cast her spell.

Miranda headed for a stack of rotting wooden crates and slipped behind them, pressing her back against the rough brick wall of the building. Closing her eyes, she centered herself and worked to control her breathing. Between the robbers, healing Hannah, and blasting the killer, she'd used a lot of magic. Casting this spell with enough power to punch through to Belle was going to drain what little was left. If it didn't work, she was dead; she wouldn't have enough left to defend herself.

Miranda remembered the moment she'd touched Belle's mind. She called up the taste of the tea her werewolf hostess had served, the smooth, cool texture of the communication stone Belle had teleported into her hand. She recalled the moment when she'd met Belle's blue-gray eyes and sensed the power burning in them.

Then she flung her will and her magic out into the night. And *called*.

Dice ran through the darkness, grinding his teeth in fury, his stomach a burning, anxious knot in his belly. The little bitch had disappeared. She must have shielded herself somehow. If he lost her and she got away, Warlock was going to kill him—literally. At the very least, his master would torture him again with that damned magical whip.

And Warlock *was* his master. He was no better than a slave—or a dog. He . . .

Magic.

It blazed across his consciousness like a comet, a shriek of power that dragged his head around. He stopped his headlong race and scanned the darkness, locking in on the pure, ringing note of the spell.

There.

Whirling, Dice ran back the way he'd come, shot across a side street, and hung a left down a stinking alleyway. At this range, the sheer power of the girl's spell was almost deafening to his magical senses.

And all that energy was coming from behind a stack of rotting crates.

He padded around the barricade and found her crouched there, pressed against the wall, her eyes squeezed closed as she concentrated.

"Hello, you little bitch," Dice snarled. "Daddy says hi."

Her eyes flew open, terror flooding them.

He grinned. And shifted.

SEVENTEEN

That idiot Davon stared at them from the middle of a crowd of werewolves, his gaze so calm Belle wanted to scream. "If we don't want them to believe we're evil, we need to show them we're just," he said. "So I'm not leaving with you."

"God, I hate rookies," Tristan muttered in her ear.

At the moment, so did she. "Davon, don't you see that you're . . ."

BELLE! It was a magical scream that hit her like a hammer to the center of her forehead. She staggered, and felt Tristan steady her.

"What the fuck?" he demanded.

"Miranda," she told him thickly. "It's Miranda. The assassin has her cornered. We've got to go."

"But what about Davon?" Tristan demanded.

The open mental link transmitted a flare of agony before winking out. Belle bent double, gasping. "He's got her! *Jesu!*"

"Fuck it. Gate us."

She dragged herself upright, opened the gate, and staggered through, Tristan's hand steadying her elbow.

"Where the hell are you going?" Lance's voice floated through the gate after them. Then he, too, stepped through. "I hate rookies," he announced.

A menacing snarl rumbled out of the darkness. A female voice cried out, high and breathless with pain.

"And I'm not real fond of you either," he told the massive shadow.

Belle conjured an illumination spell, its glow revealing a huge black creature crouched over Miranda. One big paw pinned her to the ground like a cat's captured mouse. Blood shone black in the dim light, soaking the T-shirt and jeans the girl wore.

Tristan, Belle, and Lance started forward. The beast growled, the sound vibrating Belle's breastbone. She swallowed, staring up at it. If it bit her—or, oh God, if it bit Tristan . . .

"Hey, fleabag," Lancelot called, swinging his sword in a showy revolution that glittered in the light of her spell. "Ready to get your ass kicked?"

The creature laughed, a startling bellow that made Belle's ears hurt. "Not even on your best day."

"No?" Lance looked at Tristan. "Think we can take him?"

"Big and slow as he is? We'll turn him into dog chow."

The beast charged. Belle spun aside as Tristan and Lancelot danced backward, leading it back up the alley, taking turns darting in close and slashing with their swords. The creature snarled and struck at them, too focused on the knights to realize Belle had slipped down the alley to his victim's side.

"Miranda?" she whispered, conjuring another illumination spell. What she saw in its glow made her wince. The thing had damned near disemboweled the girl.

"Belle?" Miranda's eyes opened and blinked at her hazily. "*Ah!* Hurts."

"I know." She cupped the young werewolf's cheek and breathed magic into the girl's mind. Instantly, the strained lines of pain slackened in Miranda's face, and she sighed in relief.

"Thanks God, thanks." She gritted her teeth. "If I could just . . . transform, I could . . ." She had to stop to pant. ". . . Heal this. But I've drained myself too far . . ."

Unfortunately, Belle wasn't in terrific shape herself. Which sucked, considering that healing an injury this complex would take a lot of power she just didn't have. She reached for her cell phone. "Petra?"

An instant later, the healer answered. "Where the hell did you go?"

"I got a distress call from a werewolf friend of mine. Warlock's killer has hurt her badly, but I don't have the power for a healing spell. Can you . . . ?"

"Of course. We aren't getting anywhere with Davon and his werewolf friends anyway."

A moment later, a dimensional gateway appeared, and Petra stepped through, followed by a parade of armored agents.

The beast roared, the sound bloodcurdling in its fury even a block away. Galahad grinned. "Sounds like Tristan's making friends again."

"Man's a little ray of sunshine," Reece Champion agreed, straight-faced. "Let's go play."

The agents broke into a run and raced off around the corner. Belle waved to catch Petra's attention, and the healer hurried over.

"Oh, that thing did rip her up, didn't it?" Petra spread both hands wide and began drifting them in a circle just above Miranda's savaged abdomen. As her hands moved, she sang in musical Hindi, a prayer for healing and wisdom.

Belle had to admire her concentration. Out in the street, shouts and growls sounded as the men fought the creature, who roared back with all the volume of a sonic boom. She really should be with them, providing magical backup in case the killer decided to start breathing fire again. Unfortunately, in her current condition, there was very little she could do to help. *Don't get killed, Tristan.* "There." The glow faded from Petra's hands as she nodded in satisfaction, studying her patient. There was no sign of the bloody wound at all. "That should do it."

Belle eyed the girl's belly, now smooth and whole. Even the blood had disappeared, cleaned away by Petra's magic. "You're a miracle worker."

The healer gave her a pleased smile. "We all do our duty, do we not?" She sobered. "But we should get her back to Avalon before Warlock sends another killer. I'd better stay and help the boys with their playmate."

Belle nodded. "If you can open a gate for me, I'll carry her through."

Petra grimaced as the beast roared. "I'd better cast a noise-suppression spell while I'm at it. I can't imagine why nobody's come to investigate."

"People probably figure what they don't know won't eat them."

"Which is wise of them." The healer helped Belle lift Miranda into a fireman's carry, since the girl was still out cold from the healing spell. Steadying the werewolf with a hand on her ass, Belle started for the gate. Though not as physically powerful as vampires, Majae were still stronger than humans, so she was able to manage Miranda's weight with little trouble. Just before she stepped through, she paused. "Petra, Tristan . . ."

"I'll watch out for him for you."

Belle gave her a smile for her understanding. "Thank you."

Elena Rollings walked into her house on weary feet, exhausted and depressed.

A broad-shouldered shadow loomed over her in the

kitchen doorway, but she didn't jump. Her husband had stayed home with their young son, and she knew he'd be waiting up for her.

"I was getting worried," Lucas said, his voice velvet in the dark.

"For once you had reason." Elena dumped her purse on the marble counter and walked over to the stainless-steel refrigerator to retrieve the bottle of white Zinfandel she always chilled for the nights she had a council meeting. She usually needed a drink afterward. Or two. Or four. "Tonight that idiot Davon Fredericks decided to surrender himself to the Council of Clans."

Lucas frowned, watching her pour the wine into a pair of glasses. He was still as dark-haired and ridiculously handsome as he'd been when she'd met him two years ago. "Why isn't that a good thing?" He accepted the glass she handed him. "Doesn't it mean you get to avoid declaring war?"

"They'll just find another reason." She drained her glass and poured herself another. Elena rarely drank but it had been that kind of night. "Too many people on the council have been bought off. Though they may find it harder to vote the way Warlock wants, considering the scrutiny they'll be under."

Carrying her glass in one hand and the bottle in the other, Elena led the way into the living room. They settled onto the rose and cream couch as she started telling him about the events of the night.

"Where is Fredericks now?" Lucas asked, as she cuddled into his side.

Elena sipped her wine, enjoying the warmth of the strong arm he'd thrown around her. "Linda Corley and her husband have him locked in their basement until tomorrow night."

"Poor bastard."

"Yeah." Weary to the bone, she looked up at him. "Let's go to bed."

They headed upstairs to the master bedroom. Elena was

getting undressed when she felt something hard and round in one pocket of her slacks. Digging the object out, she found a small moonstone wrapped in a slip of paper. Frowning, she smoothed out the note.

"If you need me, just hold this gem and call my name. —Belle Coeur"

"Well," Lucas said, reading the note over her shoulder. "That's an interesting wrinkle."

"Yeah," she said. "Especially since we're holding Davon's trial tomorrow night—right before the planned execution."

Lucas winced. "Not real big on appeals, are they?"

"Nope. I think they're trying to piss Arthur off."

"That'll do it."

Tristan wasn't back yet.

Belle paced, walking restlessly through her house. She was tempted to call out to his consciousness—she could do that easily enough, given that he was wearing her blood armor. But what if he were still fighting the Beast? If she distracted him at the wrong moment . . .

No.

Normally she'd gate there to help fight, but she'd be less than useless, drained as she was. She needed sleep and several hours of meditation in her spell circle to rebuild her magic.

So she had to wait. Assuming he'd come back to her . . .

Belle sighed and raised both arms over her head, trying to stretch the aches out of her back. She'd settled Miranda in a guest room, where the girl was still deeply asleep, probably soaking up magic to rebuild her body's reserves. By morning the werewolf should be up and around, which meant Belle would need to haul ass out of bed to cook breakfast for her guests.

Justice occupied the third upstairs bedroom. She'd persuaded him to stay on the grounds that he was now just as much a target as Miranda. He'd agreed only because he was determined to help bring Warlock down; he hadn't gone on the rescue mission only because his presence was more likely to set the council off than anything else. After all, they'd just fired him.

"Belle." Tristan spoke out of the darkness, his beautiful voice sensual and deep.

Wheeling, she threw herself into Tristan's arms with the solid thump of sheer relief. "Jesu, you had me scared. Are you all right?" Belle examined him anxiously. His armor was smeared with blood, but all the scales seemed to be in one piece. He hadn't taken any more serious hits.

"I'm fine," Tris told her. "I suspect there are some interesting bruises somewhere under all this steel, but I'm a hell of a lot better off than the beast."

"Did you kill him?"

"No, unfortunately. But apparently the way to handle the bastard is to surround him with knights and poke him with sharp objects. Kind of like baiting a bear. He finally had enough and gated the hell away."

"Damn. I was hoping you'd killed him." Belle brightened as an amorous thought crossed her mind. "Want a bath?"

"That depends. Will you share it with me?"

"I planned to."

"Then hell yes."

The master bathroom was located off her bedroom, and had obviously been designed with seduction in mind. The bath itself was an oval seven feet long and four feet wide. When Tristan followed Belle into the room, he was unsurprised to find it already filled and gently steaming.

Magic was a damned convenient skill to have.

When he stepped down into the tub and sat on the raised marble bench, he found it was ringed with jets that pounded his sore muscles just hard enough to make him groan in relief. The water was chest-deep and smelled faintly of sandalwood. Enhancing the romantic mood, candles ringed the tub, their dancing light casting soft shadows. Plants stood everywhere the candles didn't, clusters of gleaming green leaves and fragrant flowers. A huge stained-glass window running the length of the tub depicted a woman bathing nude in a forest pool, smiling at a watching armored knight as if inviting him to join her.

"Mmmm." Tristan let his head fall back against the cool marble tiles of the wall. "The advantages of loving a court seducer. You do know how to make a man feel like a prince."

"That's fair," Belle said, slipping into the water beside him, her accent gone liquid and French. "Since you make me feel like a goddess."

Which sounded like an opening to Tristan. He sat up and swallowed. So much rested on what he said next. He didn't want to screw it up. "I have something I want to talk to you about."

She straightened, her nipples peeking over the water at him. He had to drag his gaze back to her eyes. "That sounds serious."

"Well, yes. But it's not something you won't like." *I hope.* "I want us to Truebond." Dammit, he hadn't intended to blurt it out like that.

Belle's big blue-gray eyes opened wide. "But—why? Not that I'm automatically against the idea, but you've never indicated that you even wanted to marry me, much less . . ."

"But I've been thinking about it. Especially after the fight with the Direkind yesterday. I . . ."

She frowned and hooked an arm over the side of the tub, absently stirring her fingers through the bubbling water as she studied him. "Wait, you decided you wanted to do this just yesterday? I don't think it's a good idea to enter into something like this on the spur of the minute. After all, what if something happened to me? You could *die with me.*"

"Which is why I'm thinking about it." He traced a wet finger along the back of her hand. "Belle, we're probably going to go to war in the next couple of days—"

"Which makes it exactly the wrong time to—"

"Let me finish," Tristan interrupted, catching both her hands in his. "Yes, Truebonding would mean the death of one of us could kill the other. But look at Arthur and Guinevere, or Simon Marin and Kathryn, or Garret Montessor and Felecia. How many times has the Truebond saved them? Arthur's told me he's drawn on Gwen's magical strength in a crisis. She's done the same. Together, they have more power than either has separately." He leaned close and met her gaze, his wet fingers gripping hers. "I want to know that if your strength ever runs out the way it did today, you can draw on my magic."

Belle shook her head. "Tristan, I'm touched, but . . ."

"Think of the benefit to Arthur and the Magekind." He let the passion he felt ring in his voice. He had to convince her. "Not only could the bond save us, it could save those we love. Arthur, Gwen, your boys . . ."

"But what about Isolde?"

He'd known that was coming. "You are not Isolde."

"Obviously, but you did love her, and she hurt you so badly, you still haven't healed." Her gaze was earnest, doubtful. It was the doubt that stung the most. "What if we bond and that pain is exacerbated? You can't break a Truebond, Tristan. You'd be trapped."

"That won't happen."

"You don't know that."

Tristan raked a wet hand through his hair and groped for the words to make her understand. "I'm not a kid, Belle. I know what I can handle and what I can't. I wouldn't ask you to bond with me if I didn't think I could hack it." Searching her gaze, he found she still looked torn. "Or is it that you just don't want a permanent connection?"

Belle gave him a cool look. "I've already shown you exactly how much you mean to me, Tristan."

Yeah, creating the blood armor *had* been a pretty vivid demonstration. It was time he was as brave. Blowing out a breath, Tristan said the words he'd never expected to say again. "I love you."

Joy lit her eyes so brilliantly they seemed to blaze with a pure, incandescent light. Only to fade into heartbreaking doubt again.

"I'm not lying," Tristan said, working to control his frustration. "I wouldn't lie to you. For one thing, you'd know the truth as soon as we bond. You'd feel my emotions as clearly as you feel your own."

Belle sighed. "I'm not accusing you of lying, Tris. I just need to think. Let me have some time."

He nodded, suddenly weary. "I'll give you whatever you want. But don't take so much time that you take too much."

"I wouldn't do that to either of us." Belle leaned in and kissed him. It was no little peck either, but a kiss so hot, so hungry, that his body leaped in response. Suddenly he was acutely aware of her nudity, her delicate grace, the scent of her skin . . .

Pursuing her advantage, Belle threw a leg across his thighs and straddled him, delightfully naked, her breasts beaded with glistening drops of water as they bounced with the movement. Her sex pressed down over his trapped cock, her lower lips so soft and slick, he hardened under her in a hot rush. She gave him a smile and wound her arms around his neck. "I do love you."

"And I love you." His eyes dropped to the pretty pink-tipped breasts bobbing in the bubbling water. God, he loved those nipples.

She laughed in a surprisingly girlish giggle. "Yes, I can tell." Her mouth swooped down on his, her tongue stroking past his teeth, then retreating to trace his lips, entering again to explore his mouth in gently erotic thrusts. The last of Tristan's anger drained away as his senses filled with Belle. She tasted exquisite, her lips delightfully soft, her clever tongue so hot and promising he wanted inside her *now*.

Even more delightful was the pressure of her sex caressing his cock, gone hard as a brick in the luscious captivity of her thighs. It occurred to him that this was the kind of pose that could trigger a flashback. Normally he'd find some way to change positions so that he was on top, in order to keep his errant mind from turning his partner into Isolde.

He felt none of that panic now. Belle was not Isolde. Whether she knew it or not, she'd exorcised his wife's vengeful ghost with every soft stroke on her hands, with every kiss and whisper.

Isolde was dead. And Belle was very much alive, as she proved with a hot little wiggle. The friction as she rocked over his cock made Tristan groan. Resting his hands on her slim thighs, he felt the lithe muscle work as she rolled her hips against his, teasing his cock with every soft glide of her pussy along its length.

He wanted *in* her. He imagined the hot, tight squeeze of her juicy inner grip and wanted to howl like a werewolf with need.

Instead he cupped her soft breasts and leaned forward to taste a delicious nipple. Circling his tongue over the hard little nubbin, he closed his lips and suckled her, drawing hard. He loved the way the tip jutted inside his mouth as he teased it with his tongue. Reaching below the water, Tris slipped a finger into the clinging folds of her sex. She dropped her head back and moaned, one of those erotic purrs that shot lust through him like a drug.

Belle reached down with one hand and caressed the head of his cock as she straddled him, teasing the sensitive glans. She kissed him lazily, licking at his mouth, tracing the line of his lips, nibbling his tongue.

Finally she drew away to stare into his eyes, hers gray-blue and bright. Leaning forward, she began to nibble her way down the tendons of his neck, and used her free hand to tease one of his tiny male nipples. Tris couldn't take any more. He reached past her to shove candles and plants out of the way, then grabbed her waist and sat her down on the marble edge of the tub. Belle laughed. "Tris, what the hell are you doing?" She sounded very French, and he grinned even as he slid off the bench, draped her thighs over his shoulders, bent to her sex, and took a good, long lick. She yelped, a sound that made his cock twitch.

Belle braced her back against the chill tile and clung to his blond head as he used his tongue and fingers on her clit. The pleasure stung her with its pounding intensity until she writhed against the tile, gasping as she rolled her hips, desperate for that one . . . last . . . touch . . .

Tristan pulled her off the lip and fell back into the tub, splashing water over the edge and sending it rolling across the bathroom in a little wave. Not that she gave a damn, because he pulled her down right onto his cock, impaling her with a powerful roll of his hips.

And began to fuck her. He gave her no quarter—not that she wanted any—rolling hard, thrusting with such power, Belle could do nothing but brace her hands on his hard belly and hold on for dear life.

She loved the deep, grinding thrusts he gave her, the water sloshing around them as he braced back on his elbows. His green eyes sparkled up at her, wicked with humor.

And then it hit her. "Wait!" she gasped. "I'm on top!"

He grinned, all roguish good humor. "I noticed."

"But Isolde . . ."

"Is not in this tub."

And he thrust even harder, his cock probing deep as he lifted her and let her fall and lifted her again. She stared into his eyes, frantic, afraid Isolde's ghost would overwhelm him.

But as she met his passionate stare, she realized he was right. His dead wife no longer haunted his heart. The scars she'd left were gone, healed by some miracle of love.

Her climax took her by surprise, a fierce, deep pulsing that shook her to her soul. Belle screamed in feral pleasure. He roared back at her, a cry of triumph and delight.

"Do you still want to Truebond?" she gasped.

"Yes!" he gasped back, still grinding into her. "God, yes!"

She reached for his mind and threw her own open to him. Together, they drew hard on the Mageverse, letting its wild energy rage through them. But instead of using its magic to shift or create, each shot delicate strands of power into the other's mind, slowly weaving a lattice of magical connections between them. More and more strands bound them, until each could feel the other's thoughts, see the other's heart. Until the web they wove hit a critical mass of magic.

It burst around them, golden and blinding, binding them soul to soul until they *knew* each other, body and brain and heart.

One. *"I never realized I was so alone before,"* Tristan said in wonder.

"This is going to take some getting used to," Belle murmured, her eyes half-closed as she enjoyed the velvet touch of his mind. Through his senses, she could feel her own sex gripping his cock like a juicy vise. The sensation was so deliciously exotic, she started grinding down on him, sending more sensation volleying back and forth between their minds, growing more intense with every searing pass.

Another orgasm rolled over her like a sensory hurricane, throwing him into another climax, though he'd barely recovered from the first.

When it was all over, they climbed out of the tub, dried each other off, and staggered to the bed. As they snuggled under the covers, Tristan asked the obvious question. *"How the hell are we going to fight like this?"*

"We'll figure it out." After all, they'd defeated Isolde's ghost. "But we'd better do it fast," Tristan muttered. "The shit is about to hit the fan."

Warlock found Dice lying in one of the caverns in a pool of his own blood. Black eyes watched the wizard, gleaming dully in the light of his spell.

"Kill me and be done with it," the beast rumbled. "I did all I could."

Warlock sighed and conjured a gate. "I can see that. Come."

Dice didn't bother lifting his head. "I can die as well here." He let his eyes drift closed.

"Well, I don't choose to let you. I've spent a great deal of effort and magic on you, boy, and I have no intention of seeing it all go to waste." A clawed hand closed over one of his pointed ears and dug into a bundle of nerves. The pain jerked away his breath, forcing him to his feet as the wizard pulled him ruthlessly toward the gate.

Seething with resentment, Dice followed his master through the dimensional portal.

The minute he stepped on the other side, the scent of magic hit him in the face, a warm wave of ozone and seduction, a delicious promise of power.

Dazed, suddenly ravenous, he stared at the source of the smell.

A lovely little pool lay in the center of the forest clearing. A cliff rose over the water, black against the starry sky. A waterfall tumbled down the black stone face, glowing gently, smelling of magic more powerful than anything he'd ever sensed. "What is this place?"

"Your salvation. Wade in, boy."

Dice didn't need to be told twice. He staggered into the pool, hissing in mingled pain and delight as the magical water touched his wounds. Instantly, they began to heal with a hot, stinging tingle he barely noticed as the pain vanished.

"There's a permanent dimensional gate over the falls, though no one knows why," Warlock called over the gentle sound of falling water. He nodded at the top of the cliff. "The universe there has magic even stronger than that in the Mageverse."

Dice glanced up at the unfamiliar stars. "The Mageverse," he said in wonder, as Bors's stolen memories whispered. "That's where we are."

"Of course. And once you've spent the day here, you'll have more than enough magic to fight Arthur and his knights. Now, let me tell you what you did wrong," Warlock said, wading into the water with a sigh of pleasure. "And how you'll win against them the next time."

Davon sat with his back up against the cement-block wall and waited for daybreak to steal his consciousness.

He wanted this over.

Linda Corley had volunteered her house as a makeshift jail, then had locked him in the basement under werewolf guard. As basements went, it was pleasant enough, with dark green shag carpet that probably dated from the 1970s. An artificial Christmas tree stood in one corner, covered with a plastic sheet, while a couch and armchairs upholstered in dusty flowered chintz crowded in beside a washer and dryer.

Reverend Sheridan and his son had guard duty at the moment, sitting in metal folding chairs beside the wooden stairs. They'd gossiped quietly for a while about people he didn't know, so he ignored them.

The silence that had finally fallen since then had a particularly glum quality. Davon wasn't sure why. They should be happy justice for Jimmy was within reach.

"Why?" Stephen asked suddenly. "Why'd you do it, Davon?" He'd reverted back to human form, and his voice was a full octave higher than the one Davon was used to. Tall, blond, and athletic, he was a handsome kid with earnest hazel eyes and a wide mouth. His hands and feet looked a bit too big for his body, reminding Davon of a puppy who had yet to grow into his paws.

"I've been through this, Stephen. I'd been told he was a pedophile . . ."

"Not that," the teenager said impatiently. "Why didn't you go with the knights when they came to rescue you?"

"Steve, he already explained that to the congregation," Howard Sheridan said. "He wants to atone."

"But they're going to kill him, Dad!"

Davon let his head fall back against the wall. "God, I certainly hope so."

Howard eyed him. "Is this repentance, or are you just using us to commit suicide?"

He shrugged and closed his eyes. The angry energy that had allowed him to speak with such furious eloquence and humor at the church had abandoned him. He felt as if his body had turned to solid lead. It seemed he was sinking slowly into the floor, weighed down by his sins. Even fear required more energy than he had.

"Or maybe," Sheridan's voice dropped to a deep, lupine growl, "you want me to kill you right now."

A huge clawed hand grabbed his gorget and hauled him into the air as if he weighed no more than a toddler. Davon's eyes snapped open in surprise to meet the preacher's, gone bright yellow in a Direwolf's lupine skull. Sheridan's lips rippled, revealing a great many shining white teeth, and his jaws opened as if to bite.

"Dad!" Stephen cried.

"Don't sweat it, kid," Davon said, his feet hanging a foot above the dated carpeting. "He's not going to kill me. He's not a killer."

Howard stared into his eyes. "Neither are you."

"Your son would beg to differ."

"You won't goad me into killing you, Fredericks, no matter what you say." The preacher lowered him carefully back down in his chair. "I was hoping to scare some sense into you. Guess not."

Davon snorted. "If I scared that easily, they wouldn't have made me Magekind."

"Yeah?" the pastor asked shrewdly. "How do you feel about hell? Does *that* scare you?"

He stared without hope at the ceiling. "I'm not real thrilled about going, but there's not much I can do about it."

The werewolf shook his head in disgust. "For such a smart man, you are profoundly dim. Ever thought about asking God for forgiveness?"

Davon snorted. "I'd think you'd want to see me fry."

"Yeah, well, I'm evidently a good bit brighter than you are, because it's obvious to me Arthur's right. You're as much a victim as my boy was." He folded his arms and stretched out his legs, then he directed a brooding stare at his toes. "I'm going to speak up for you tomorrow, but my people are probably gonna kill you anyway. I'd like to try to at least give you some peace."

He wasn't sure it would do any good, but he managed a smile. "Would you pray with me, Reverend?"

The werewolf looked up and gave him a genuine smile. "It'd be my pleasure."

So they knelt together on the green shag, and Davon placed his right hand in the pastor's clawed one. Stephen took the left hand, and they bent their heads.

EIGHTEEN

Miranda watched Belle practically dance around the well-appointed kitchen, humming in pleasure as she diced vegetables and cheese for omelets. *Whoever heard of a witch who's a morning person?* Her obvious joy made Miranda miserably aware of her own dark mood.

The sound of boot heels on the stairs alerted her just before she caught the scent of another werewolf. Miranda tensed as her instincts howled a warning.

The man paused in the doorway, tall and lean and so powerfully masculine her body purred approval. His hair was thick and curling over dark brows, and his eyes were black and shrewd.

His nose was a hawkish blade that suggested something exotic somewhere in his family tree, an idea enhanced by his coloring. She wasn't sure if the copper tint to his skin was a tan or genetics. His upper lip was a bit too thin, while the lower one had an intriguing fullness that made her imagine biting it. His cheekbones were broad—that exotic ancestry at work again—with deep hollows beneath them.

His long jaw was a fraction broader than his temples, which gave him a caveman kind of vibe. None of which should have been appealing.

But it was.

He looks like a thug, she told herself. Precisely the sort of man she shouldn't trust. Just like Warlock and her stepfather, the kind willing to use fists and claws and teeth to keep her and her mother in line.

"Good morning, Belle," he said, his voice surprisingly smooth and pleasant. She'd expected a Clint Eastwood rasp.

"Ah, Justice." Belle turned from the cutting board to flourish her knife in Miranda's direction. "Miranda, this is William Justice. Bill, Miranda Drake."

He gave her a long, assessing look that made her straighten her shoulders and lift her chin. "You're Warlock's daughter. The werewolf witch."

She gave him a smart-ass smile. "Yeah. And you're the Wolf sheriff the Council of Clans just fired." Belle had told her that much when she'd mentioned she had another guest. *Both of you have had to deal with idiots. Maybe you'll find you have a lot in common.*

Like a shared talent for pissing people off, Miranda had muttered. *Yeah, that'll go well.*

"Satisfy my curiosity," Justice said, walking over to accept the mug of coffee Belle offered. "Did you kill both your parents, or just your mother?"

Belle growled something in French. "Dammit, Justice . . ."

Miranda refused to let her gaze drop. "My stepfather broke my mother's neck after years of abuse. So I stuck cut off his head and burned the house down."

He lifted a dark brow. "Way to make a statement."

"All he loved was that house and the money Warlock paid him." She curled her lip over her coffee cup. "That's all the Chosen *ever* care about. So I got rid of it all and took the money. God knows I bled for it long enough."

He took a slow, deliberate sip of his coffee. Steam rolled

up around his barbaric face. "You know, you could have called me at any time to report you were being abused. I would have arrested the bastard and put a stop to it."

"Uh-huh." She leaned a hip against the marble counter and cocked her head over her mug. "And what would have happened when the case went before the Council of Clans for trial?"

He didn't flinch. "Hopefully, we would have found the evidence to obtain a guilty verdict."

"You and I both know better than that. The Chosen members would have voted not guilty because my stepfather was Chosen, and he'd have bribed the rest. Then he'd have killed my mother the minute they let him out of jail."

"I'd have protected you if you'd given me the chance." Justice put the mug down on the counter with an irritated clunk. "Instead, you took the law into your own hands. Which makes you as much a killer as you claim he was. And your mother still ended up dead. I'd bust you, except—"

"You're not a cop anymore." She smirked. "Isn't that too bad."

"Okay, that's quite enough of that," Belle snapped. "I've been working my butt off on this breakfast, and we're all going to sit down and chew on it instead of each other."

Ouch, Miranda thought, with a belated thought for the manners her mother had drilled into her head. She'd been rude to another guest in a friend's home. Joelle would have been mortified. "Of course, Belle. I'll set the table."

"I'll help," Justice said, biting off the words.

"I don't need your help." Miranda stalked to the china cabinet to get the dishes.

"Isn't that too bad?" Justice said, deliberately echoing her earlier snark as he got the silverware out of the drawer Belle indicated. "Because you've got it anyway."

Somehow they managed to set the table without breaking into outright combat, then sat down to eat. Which distracted Miranda nicely from her fellow guest, because Belle's omelets were light and deliciously fluffy, while the bacon had a perfect smoky crunch. Between that and the canned peach preserves the Maja served with her scratch-made biscuits, Miranda hadn't had a meal so good in ages.

But even as she ate, she was acutely aware of Justice's dark gaze flicking over her face. Miranda lifted her eyes to give him a defiant glare in return.

God, he was a handsome bastard.

The key word there is "bastard," Miranda told herself. He might not be Chosen, but he was male. Which meant that like every other male she'd ever known, he couldn't be trusted.

And yet part of her wished he was the hero he seemed: a man willing to fight to protect the weak. A man she could trust to have her back so that she didn't have to struggle every single minute. She was so damned tired of being alone and afraid.

Okay, that was self-pitying, Miranda decided, suddenly impatient with herself. *And the rest was just plain stupid. Stupid and stupidly romantic.*

She really needed to hunt down that part of her mind and bludgeon it to death before it got her killed.

Belle walked around the two suits of armor she'd arrayed on a pair of mannequins in the center of the spell circle: her own and Tristan's much larger one. The scales glittered in the candlelight like ancient treasure in a dragon's horde.

"The problem with these suits is they're magic, and that damned beast of Warlock's eats magic," she told Miranda. The girl had accompanied her into the basement to tackle the problem right after breakfast. "And since I used my blood to make Tristan's, if the beast bites the suit, it also gets its teeth into me. Tris and I are now Truebonded, so we've got to fix that or we'll both end up dead the first time Beastie starts to gnaw."

"Yeah, that would definitely suck." Miranda cocked her head, considering the armor. Tall and pretty, she had red hair as brilliant as a fox's coat and eyes that seemed to glow against the cream of her skin. Her oval face had an Art Deco delicacy, with its long, thin nose and cupid's bow mouth. You'd never guess she could become a seven-foot werewolf.

Today she'd conjured herself a pair of snug blue jeans and a black T-shirt with the words ONE OF LADY GAGA'S LITTLE MONSTERS scrawled across her generous breasts. No wonder Justice's eyes had glazed when he'd seen her this morning.

Too bad they got along like two badgers in a burlap bag.

Belle muttered and paced around the armor again. It was early afternoon, and she needed to solve the problem with the suits before the vampires woke at sunset. They'd likely end up going into battle tonight, which was no doubt when the Council of Clans would put Davon on trial. She wouldn't put it past them to try him during the day, but being a vampire, he'd be unconscious. Trying a comatose man would make for poor political theater. She hoped.

The key to the rescue was Elena Rollings. If only the councilwoman would use the communication gem she'd magically slipped her. Petra could find Davon again in a pinch, but it would be a good sign if Elena contacted her. For one thing, they'd know she, at least, hadn't drunk the werewolf Kool-Aid. Or eaten the kibble, or whatever.

Abruptly Miranda turned to her with a wicked grin on her face. "I think I know how to put a kink in Beastie's tail."

After the girl described the spell she had in mind, Belle grinned back. "Oh, child, I do like the way you think."

They were going to try him in a state park, for God's sake. Davon stared out the window of Linda Corley's SUV, watching the dark forest roll past, splashed here and there with silver pools of moonlight. He might have enjoyed the trip, but his wrists lay heavy in his lap, wrapped in chains and secured with a heavy padlock. You'd think he was a gate.

The truck stopped, and he looked around to see a wiry man in a state Department of Natural Resources uniform standing beside it. Linda rolled down the window and Davon caught a whiff of fur as the man leaned in to study him avidly. "That him?"

"Yes, that's the accused," Linda said, a bit primly.

"Figures he'd be black. Go on in."

Linda obeyed, the set of her shoulders suddenly gone stiff.

"A racist werewolf," Davon drawled. "Interesting. Gives the whole thing a lynching aspect I hadn't considered."

"This is not a lynching," the woman snapped, glowering at him in the rearview mirror. "Marvin's just a dick."

"No? White folks taking a black guy out in the woods to kill him . . . Y'all gonna get out the hoods and bedsheets next?"

"Shut *up*, vampire." Davon went to work cultivating an uncomfortable silence to give her a chance to think about what she was really involved in. He might have made his peace with God, but he wasn't above pointing out the hypocrisy of his werewolf captors.

He did wish he'd been able to call his parents, but he had no idea what to tell them.

The caravan of council vehicles snaked on along the mountain road between towering dark trees. Finally they pulled into a parking lot marked with a sign that read, FAMILY PICNIC AREA.

What, are they serving—vampire? Davon wondered. Well, at least his sense of humor was back.

An hour later, it was gone again, mostly because the end of his wrist chains had been padlocked to a stake driven into the ground, as Rosen announced, "for the safety of our audience."

What the hell did they think he was going to do? There had to be two thousand werewolves in the crowd.

Guess it's time for Kabuki theater, doggy style.

Judging by the snippets of conversation he heard, some of the wolves had been driving for hours to attend the trial. Evidently some kind of order had gone out that morning. *Lovely. Just in case everyone isn't in a bad enough mood.*

Then, as Davon watched in bemusement, the werewolves spread picnic blankets out on the grass and proceeded to wander around catching up with old friends.

Somebody started a bonfire. He eyed it nervously. *Are we planning to roast vampires and make s'mores?*

At least they'd left the kids at home this time.

That reminded him. *They'd better get this show on the road if they expect to kill my ass before Arthur shows up with the marines.*

What the fuck am I doing? Davon thought suddenly. Why had he turned himself in to these lunatics? Had he been high?

Shit. Too damned late now. His stomach felt like his half-blind grandmother's embroidery: one big knot. He shifted his booted feet and wished they'd let him take off his armor. Guess they wanted to play up the Knight of the Round Table aspect, though Davon was hardly one of the elite.

A man in Dire Wolf form walked out into the center of the picnic area, not far from where Davon stood. He stopped, came to attention, and lifted a large silver hand bell he began to ring in clanging peals. The crowd quickly fell silent, and he bellowed, "Hear ye, hear ye! The Council of Werewolf Clans meets to deliver justice to the vampire Davon Fredericks and the family of James Wendel Sheridan, his alleged victim."

Moving slowly in single file, the members of the council emerged from the trees. Like the guy with the bell—the bailiff?—they were all in Dire Wolf form.

They moved to the massive wooden table a pair of brawny wolves had earlier unloaded from a rental truck. It and its accompanying thirteen chairs were crudely built, in a way that suggested both tradition and great age.

The wolf who'd sat down in the center chair lifted a large mallet and brought it banging down on the table's dark wooden surface in three steady raps. Must be Rosen. "Who brings this case before us?"

"I, Galen Vanderberg, Wolf sheriff of the Council of Clans." It was the guy with the bell. Okay, apparently not a bailiff. Also not Justice either.

"Present your evidence," Rosen said.

Feeling the knots in his stomach tighten even more, Davon shifted in his chains and prepared to listen.

Belle and Tristan stood at attention under the starry Avalon sky as Arthur inspected the ranks. There were five hundred warriors assembled for the rescue mission—every experienced agent Arthur could pull in from the field without causing chaos in operations.

To Belle's delight, Elena Rollings had indeed used the spell gem to contact her with the location of the scene. She was there now, the moonstone gripped in one furry hand, ready to guide a gate.

"I hope the kid appreciates what we're doing for him," Tristan said in the Truebond.

Belle suspected the smile she gave him was a little goofy. She loved feeling his consciousness brush hers. Banishing the expression as inappropriate for an inspection, she replied, *"Unfortunately, Davon's probably going to get just as pissy about it as he was last night."*

"I hate rookies."

"Me, too."

"Oh, bullshit, Court Seducer."

"Not anymore." The thought sounded more than a little smug. She'd handed in her resignation to Morgana that afternoon. Once you Truebonded, you were no longer eligible for the office. Morgana had accepted the letter with a sigh. Evidently, she'd been expecting it.

Retired or not, though, Belle fully intended to visit and encourage her boys. She just wouldn't have to sleep with any of them.

Or, for that matter, kill them.

"Tonight we go to save one of our own," Arthur said in his ringing parade ground voice, jerking her from her preoccupation. "Davon's young, and his judgment leaves something to be desired . . ." His dry tone won a laugh. "But he's also a victim of an ancient enemy we didn't even know we had. Warlock is the self-appointed god of the Direkind, and he means to lead them to war against us."

He fell silent, his dark gaze sweeping the lines of agents, his mailed hand riding Excalibur's hilt. His armor shone in the moonlight, and he'd tucked his helm under one mailed arm. His wife stood just behind him, serenely beautiful in her own armor. "But remember, these people are our cousins—created, like us, by Merlin. They were to be humanity's guardians in case we ever forsook our vows and attempted to victimize humanity."

Arthur pivoted and began to pace along the line of warriors. "But we never did. We have done our duty faithfully all these centuries. Unfortunately, it seems Warlock has gone insane from jealousy and paranoia. He means to destroy us, and he's using Davon Fredericks as his excuse."

He stopped and swung to rake his eyes across the line. "*I will not allow it.* Warlock dies tonight, before he has the opportunity to poison his people any further. We will kill as few of the Direkind as possible, though we will defend ourselves when necessary. And we will bring Davon Fredericks home."

Silence fell, seeming to vibrate like struck crystal in the moonlit darkness.

"Now," he said, "as to the order of battle . . ."

"You have heard the evidence against you, Davon Fredericks," Rosen said. "How do you plead?"

Davon licked his dry lips. That was the question, wasn't it? Yesterday it had all seemed so very clear: he had killed Jimmy Sheridan, and that was all that mattered.

But then he'd prayed with Howard Sheridan and his son, and somehow that had changed everything. He'd felt God's forgiveness. The self-hate that had haunted him for days had lifted like a dark cloud, and a sense of peace rolled over him. He could plead not guilty because now he knew he really *wasn't* guilty. But if he did, the Council would howl betrayal and declare war on the Magekind, then execute him anyway.

If he pleaded guilty, however, maybe he could make the werewolves see that the Magekind were committed to justice, even if they had to pay the ultimate price for it.

Davon swallowed and lifted his chin. To his relief, his voice rose in clear, even cadences, without the tremor he'd half feared. "It was my hand that killed Jimmy. But I was the victim of . . ."

"We did not ask you for an explanation," Rosen snapped. "You've admitted your guilt. That is sufficient for these proceedings."

Howard Sheridan rose. "As the father of the victim, I claim my right to speak."

Rosen hesitated, obviously worried about what the preacher might say. Finally he admitted, "You have that right."

Sheridan paused, his gaze flickering across the faces of the watching werewolves. His eyes lingered last on the gaunt face of his wife, hollow-eyed and sleepless. The crowd went utterly silent.

Until at last he spoke. "I do not believe that Davon Fredericks is guilty of murder."

A gasp rolled over the audience, along with a broken cry of protest. Davon winced; it had come from Sheridan's wife. "But my boy is dead!" she wailed. "He's dead, and he never did anything to anyone! *I want his killer dead!*"

Sheridan flinched, but he lifted his voice over his wife's protests. "Fredericks told me that when he killed my son, he did so because of a spell cast on him by Warlock. He believed Arthur had told him my son was guilty of raping and murdering a four-year-old child. He wasn't, of course, but Davon had no reason to doubt the man he believed to be his leader. A man who told him that unless he killed Jimmy, Jimmy would kill again. I believe he was as much a victim of Warlock as Jimmy, and I have forgiven him for what he did."

Astonished whispers swept over the crowd. Some seemed surprised that he'd believe Warlock existed at all, while others were outraged that he'd suggest their mythic hero would commit such a crime.

"And why would I do such a thing?" The voice was all velvet seduction, tinged with a note of fatherly sorrow.

Davon jerked around and stared. The huge white werewolf stood at the edge of the trees, an armored warrior in human form standing just behind him like a bodyguard. He was the first werewolf Davon had ever seen in armor. Mailed gauntlets covered his hands and forearms, a chest plate stretched over his massive torso, and long tassets swung at his hips. The armor was black, with intricately engraved silver panels. He carried a huge battle-axe with rubies inset in the point between the blades. A helmet that resembled a crown covered his head.

"Warlock!" someone gasped. "It's Warlock!"

Oh, shit, Davon thought.

"Merlin gave Arthur a great trust—to guide mankind into a bright future." Warlock paced forward on clawed feet, his white fur seeming to shine with its own light. "But

Arthur has failed. Anyone who has ever watched CNN knows that much. Chaos wracks this world—mad assassins, terrorists, religious fanatics killing anyone who doesn't believe exactly as they do. Is this the world Merlin wanted?"

Warlock turned toward the crowd and spread his clawed hands. "Is this the world you want to give your children?"

"No!" a man yelled.

"Of course not." Warlock paced on. Davon's gaze slid to the bodyguard following the werewolf like a shadow, a two-handed great sword sheathed across his back. His plate armor was matte black; he was barely visible even to Davon's vampire vision. A helmet covered his face completely, making him appear menacing and faceless.

A chill made gooseflesh rise on Davon's arms. Something told him he was looking at his executioner.

"This world convulses with war, thousands starving while others die of obesity," Warlock continued. "Countries lurch along guided by fools and costly bureaucracies that accomplish little beyond giving idiots work. Meanwhile, what does Arthur do?"

He pivoted to face the crowd, and his voice lifted into a contemptuous roar. "I'll tell you what he does—*nothing!* Yet he has the means to take the chaos in hand instead of allowing it to thrive. Think of the power at his disposal. Thousands of witches who could make humans believe whatever he pleases, who can transport his vampire warriors wherever he likes to kill terrorists and madmen and murderers. Arthur's witches give him the power to ensure the hungry are fed, to heal diseases of the body and mind, to persuade leaders to follow him. And he does *nothing.*"

His voice dropped, forcing the crowd to strain to listen. "Nothing except send his killers to kill our children. And blame *me* for his crimes. Me!"

A rumble of outrage rolled over the listening werewolves, and Davon's heart sank. His gaze flicked to Warlock's silent bodyguard shadow, and sweat broke out along his spine. Bound as he was, he could do nothing to defend himself.

But damned if he would stand here any longer and listen to this self-serving shit. "Arthur wouldn't do such a thing!" Davon yelled. "He . . ."

"Silence, murderer!" Warlock flicked his fingers, and Davon's vocal chords locked, producing nothing more than a strained croak. "You've admitted your crime. The rest is lies. I will not allow you to hoodwink my people the way you did that poor boy's father."

Why didn't Warlock smell like the liar he was? Davon wondered in helpless fury. Tanner's lies had burned the air, as sharp and obvious as the stink of urine, but Warlock smelled like a man speaking the absolute truth. *He must be using magic to mask the odor. Werewolves can resist magic, but if he's not casting the spell* on *them, but on himself . . .*

"Arthur blames me because he knows I have the strength he lacks." Warlock curled a hand into a massive fist. "He knows my people have the strength to lead the humans, instead of cowering in the shadows like his." His gaze swept across the audience, blazing with a fanatic's certainty. "You all have so much potential, more than you even dream of. You are the descendents of warriors—my bold Chosen knights who fought at my side so many centuries ago. I can help you realize that potential, become the fighters Merlin intended you to be. And together, we can lead Humanity into a new future . . ."

"I have never heard such a stream of bullshit in my entire life."

Davon's head whipped around, and his heart leaped in joy.

Arthur Pendragon had just stepped through a dimensional gate. He was dressed in full plate armor, the enchanted steel shining in the moonlight, faint golden sparks trailing him as he moved. The Knights of the Round Table strode behind him, like a wall of steel at his back. Their ladies moved alongside them, also in armor, all silent, gleaming beauty.

More gates appeared around the picnic grounds, making the air dance, big shimmering ovals that disgorged armored knights who immediately moved into position around the werewolves.

"Hey, they're surrounding us!" someone shouted. The werewolves sprang to their feet with cries of alarm.

Magic exploded across the grounds in a series of blue detonations. In moments, the area was packed with Direwolves who glared at the warriors in defiance. Growls rumbled, and the light wind carried the reek of fear and fur and rage.

Oh, sweet Jesus, Davon thought. *This situation is about to go straight to hell.*

Belle stood at Tristan's side, just to Arthur's right. The werewolves, realizing they were surrounded, backed away from their armored foes, some of the women whining softly in anxiety as the men growled. It was like listening to a huge chainsaw.

"Oh," Belle thought into the Truebond, *"I don't like the way this looks."*

"They don't say war is hell because it's a great way to spend a Friday night."

"Smart-ass."

"Sorry." But it was absently said. His attention was focused on Warlock. "I think Fido there is about to make his move," he murmured to Arthur.

"Yeah. He's letting 'em stew. Then he's going to come to the rescue." There was a note of lazy cynicism to Magus's voice. "Funny how dictators always follow a pattern."

They sound so damn calm, thought Belle wildly.

We've been at it a while, darlin', Tristan said in the Bond. Evidently he'd picked up the thought. She was going to have to learn to shield the ones she didn't want him to hear. *"And we're not really all that calm."*

Actually, he was. Through the bond, it felt as though Tristan stood in the eye of a hurricane, his mind cool and crystalline in the face of all the violent emotion swirling among the werewolves. When Belle glanced up and down the line of Round Table knights, she saw the same watchful stillness in their faces.

Tristan's mind touched hers, enveloped her fear like comforting fingers clasping a shaking hand. She felt her battle nerves drain away. *"You've done this before, Belle. And I won't let anything happen to you."*

"We have no intention of harming any of you." Arthur's battlefield-trained voice cut over the werewolves' fearful growls. "All I want is my agent returned safely from this farce of a trial. Warlock played him just as he's trying to play you. But I assure you, the last thing Merlin would want is to see us killing each other over anyone's lies."

"I am not lying!" Warlock threw up a hand. A bolt of searing white energy burst from his fingers, arched high over the heads of his people, and slashed down toward Arthur and his knights. Belle threw a defensive shield up out of sheer reflex.

The curving field she created interlocked with the shields springing into place above all the other witches, forming the magical equivalent of a Greek shield wall. It was a move they'd all been practicing for years, and it had saved their collective asses more than once.

The bolt slammed into the shimmering golden wall and danced along its surface as if looking for some chink, some weak spot.

"Fuck, he's powerful," one of the witches gasped.

Belle, too, gritted her teeth, fighting to maintain her section of the barrier against the raging energy. Warlock definitely wasn't playing games.

"Did that son of a bitch just throw a *lightning bolt* at us?"

Gawain demanded, his worried gaze on Lark's strained, white face.

"Yeah," Smoke gritted, as he and Eva reinforced the Majae's shield wall. "He does that."

At last the bolt faded away as its energy dissipated. The witches sighed in relief, but they didn't let the shield drop.

"How long do you think you can keep that up?" Warlock called, mockery in his voice. "Because I have plenty more where that came from." He spun his battle-axe in a showy revolution. "I'm more than a match for all your little witches, Arthur."

"Fuck that," Arthur growled. "Kel, shut the bragging bastard up."

The tall knight on his left threw himself into the sky, blasting upward on a wave of foaming blue magic. The moment he had room, power flashed over the intricate cobalt scales of his armor, and he transformed.

Forty feet of blue dragon hovered in the air over them all, tail lashing, great wings beating, creating furious downdrafts that hit the grass like a rising storm. Papers flew and blankets tumbled across the picnic area. Werewolves screamed.

Kel winged over the cowering Direkind, straight for Warlock. By all rights, the werewolf wizard should have looked at least a little anxious.

Instead he smiled. Which was really chilling with all those teeth.

"Oh, that's not good," Belle told Tristan.

"Have faith, darling. Kel will send Fido yipping for home."

As the dragon approached Warlock, the civilian werewolves, trapped, fled as far in the opposite direction as they could before the encircling Magekind stopped them.

"Let 'em go!" Arthur roared to the fighters on that side. "I don't want them in the line of fire!"

"Stay, you cowards!" one of the werewolves howled. "Will you leave our lord to face his enemies alone?"

"Nay!" Warlock bellowed. "I want none at my back without the courage to fight!"

Which statement had the predictable effect of stopping about half the crowd in its collective tracks. Nobody wanted to be thought a coward.

Then Kel blew a gust of flame down on Warlock. The blast hit the werewolf's shield with a roar like the Space Shuttle taking off.

On the opposite end of the field, the agents formed a corridor to allow the werewolves to escape. Belle noticed that most of those who fled were females, who probably had no idea how to fight anyway. The males stopped as other wolves blocked their way, yelling insults.

"Let them go," Belle muttered. "Damned if I want to fight a bunch of hapless civilians, claws or no claws. Especially considering Merlin created them, too."

Looking across the field, she saw Petra hurrying forward with two brawny vampires at her heels. The three reached Davon without anyone trying to stop them. A quick burst of magic freed him of his chains, and they hustled him back to the ranks of Magekind.

Now if only we can kill Warlock, we can all go home, Belle thought.

A roar went up from the watching Magekind, echoed by a despairing cry from the Direkind. Belle jerked her head around and saw that Warlock was down inside his shield, as though he could no longer withstand the pounding pressure of Kel's flame.

The dragon dove like a hawk and slammed into the shield, attempting to batter through it with his scraping claws and pounding wings. His jaws opened wide, and his head snapped forward . . .

Warlock dropped his shield and hit him full in his open mouth. The blast of raw magic gave Kel no time to shield as it picked him up and flung him over the trees. He hit the ground somewhere out of sight with a boom that shook the ground.

NINETEEN

"Kel!" cried Nineva, his pretty blond Sidhe wife. She threw herself into the air and took dragon form, flying hard toward the impact site. Belle watched her go, feeling helpless and sick.

"Gate over there," she heard Morgana snap somewhere to her left, apparently talking to a healer. "Help her."

"Oh, hell," Tristan muttered.

Warlock was moving toward them, both hands gesturing a spell as magic flared blue around his fingers.

"Shields!" Morgana shouted.

Belle threw up another barrier, fitting it to those of the Majae on either side. The wall had barely formed when the blast seared into it with such raging force, Belle was terrified they wouldn't be able to hold it back.

A savage roar rose from behind her. Tristan swore and spun.

"What the hell is going on?" Belle demanded as werewolves howled in chorus.

"Direkind! They're sweeping down out of the trees. And

they're armed with swords. It's an ambush." She felt the jolt roll through his body as he used his great sword to block an attack. Steel rang on steel.

Grimly, Belle poured all the power she had into her shield as Tristan pressed his back against hers and fought their werewolf attackers. She could feel the roll of his powerful shoulders, the leap of muscle in his arms, the grim, cold intensity of his mind.

But she didn't dare let any of that distract her. He would defeat his opponent while she kept Warlock from frying them both. Otherwise they were dead.

It was as simple as that.

Somebody had taught these bloody werewolves how to fight. These were not the clueless civilians the Magekind had surrounded so easily. Every one of the furry bastards attacked with a savage abandon, long curving blades in either hand, ready to stab or parry with powerful arms.

In terms of sheer skill, Tristan knew he'd be able to take any of them apart. Unfortunately, this fight was about more than skill. The werewolves were huge, and their height and muscle gave them a far greater reach than Tristan had. The werewolf he fought was so tall, he could have stood back and cut Tris to bits while keeping him from getting close enough to do any damage with his sword.

Worse, the creature had the strength to match, so that every attack rattled Tristan's teeth. None of which mattered one damned bit. Tristan was still going to kill him. Because Arthur Pendragon fought at his side, grimly battling an eight-foot wolf with fur the color of sable. And he could feel Belle pressed against his back, dragging power from the Mageverse and flinging it into her shield, maintaining their only hope against Warlock's savage attacks. The two people he loved most. The two people he would not fail.

Tristan sensed the opening in his opponent's flashing

blades with some whisper of warrior's instinct. He struck even as he felt the weakness, stabbing his blade through the breach, knocking aside one knife and shattering the other. His sword rammed into the werewolf's chest and out the other side, pushing bone fragments into heart and lungs.

The wolf's orange eyes flared wide, and for an instant, Tristan glimpsed the man's hopeless realization that his death was upon him. Tris jerked his blade from the body, spinning to block another werewolf's hacking strike at Arthur's skull. Arthur used the opening he'd provided to chop through the wolf's neck with Excalibur.

Somewhere down the line, a vampire screamed in agony. He'd been bitten. The screams went on and on, until some endless time later, they fell silent. Tristan snatched a glance at the fallen vampire and saw that his pauldron had flapped out of position. His opponent had simply grabbed the armor section and jerked, breaking the straps. Then the bastard had bitten him on his unprotected shoulder.

The healers were all busy shielding them along with the rest of the Majae, keeping Warlock from frying them with a lightning blast. There was nothing Tristan could do for the dying vampire.

So he gritted his teeth and fought on, sweeping his sword left and right, fighting the damned werewolves as they surged at him, with those long, long arms and flashing blades.

"Enough!" Smoke's voice rolled across the field, deep and resonant with power. He stepped out from the shield wall's protection, lifted one hand, and sent a lightning bolt shooting across the picnic grounds straight at Warlock. The wizard barely blocked its searing white impact in time. Its crackling boom deafened Belle, and she jerked, resisting the urge to duck.

Smoke had one hell of a lot of power. Maybe as much as Warlock. And then there was his wife, who had changed to werewolf form. She looked tall and regal as she strode at his side, the great rack of her ghostly antlers spreading to either side of her wolf's head.

As Warlock focused on the couple, Belle blew out a breath and flexed her aching hands. Her skin burned from all the magic she'd been using, and her head ached savagely. But even as she tried to shake the circulation back into her numb arms, she was acutely aware of Warlock. She had to be ready with her shield when he returned his attention to attacking them.

Then Eva spoke in a voice far too deep and masculine to be her own, even in werewolf form. "You have misused my power, Wizard."

With a chill, Belle realized it was Zephyr, ghost of the murdered elemental, speaking through Smoke's wife.

Warlock laughed at her, a savage bark of amusement. "And what are you going to do about it, stag? You, in the body of a woman? I killed you once and took your power. I'll slay that little bitch as easily and devour what little is left of you."

"Oh, you really shouldn't have said that," Smoke snarled. "Now you've gone and pissed me off." Magic exploded from his hands in a golden bolt that tore across the field, lanced through Warlock's shield, and blasted his chest. The impact picked him up and blew him backward into the forest with a crash of breaking wood. He kept going for quite some time, trees toppling in his wake.

"Merde," Belle murmured in awe. It was damned disconcerting to realize your friends were all but gods. Especially when the friend in question spent half his time in the form of a seven-pound talking house cat.

Eva and Smoke broke into a run, sprinting toward the tree line, apparently hoping to hit Warlock again before he recovered. Smoke shifted on the run, sliding into the massive form of a great tigerlike beast, black as a lake of ink except for the silver stripes on his haunches.

Belle spotted movement as Warlock staggered to his feet to meet Smoke's charge. The weight of the big beast drove him back as Smoke raked scimitar claws into fur and flesh. Warlock roared and ripped his talons across Smoke's powerful chest. Blood flew around them in arcs.

Eva lowered her ghostly horns and threw herself into Warlock's side, driving him away from her husband with a punishing jolt of magic.

Belle opened her mouth to cheer—only to swallow a scream as a huge black werewolf suddenly soared over her head, landed in front of her, and jerked the helm off her head. Opening its jaws wide, the thing lunged for her face. She couldn't fireball the beast—they were immune to magic—and she'd never draw her sword in time . . .

Tristan whirled around her, slashing his great sword in a vicious diagonal blow that beheaded the werewolf as if he were lopping a peach off a tree.

Belle blinked at him as he spun like a bullfighter, meeting the charge of another werewolf and plunging his weapon into the beast's chest.

She had her own weapon out now, and she lunged, hacking the arm off a werewolf who was going for Tristan's helm with his claws. Pivoting, she took the Dire Wolf's head with another swing of her sword, though her gorge rose as his skull tumbled one way and his body fell the other.

Swallowing bile, Belle conjured a new helm to replace the one the werewolf had snatched. And spun, bringing her weapon around in a hard slash. The move drove back the werewolf who had attempted to sneak up behind her, jaws gaping wide for a lethal bite. She could hear other Mage-kind screaming, having been bitten in similar attacks.

Panting, Belle glanced around. Her gaze fell on Smoke, who had shifted to his werecat form. He'd swept his wife into a fireman's carry as he backed away from Warlock, one hand lifted to project a shield against the wizard's blasts.

Blood rolled down Eva's side in a slick black sheet that shone in the moonlight. Belle swore. Losing that much blood could kill even a werewolf. A female werewolf broke from the line of Magekind, a big male loping at her heels as she raced to defend the couple from other werewolves. Miranda and Justice. Belle had suggested they put aside their differences just for this evening, and it seemed they'd done just that.

The girl fired a salvo of crackling electrical blasts at her father, forcing him to retreat and giving Smoke the chance to get his wounded wife to safety. A healer ran out of the ranks to meet the couple.

"Fuck you, Daddy!" Miranda howled, and shot another blast at him. He barely shielded in time.

"Traitorous bitch," he spat, and backed away, hurling a fireball that looked less savagely bright than those he'd been tossing before. Miranda blocked it easily and fired back.

He's weakening, Belle realized. *Exchanging all those blasts with Kel and Smoke, not to mention pounding us with lightning bolts—it's drained him.*

She wasn't the only one who'd noticed the wizard's weakness. "Warlock, you faithless whoreson!" Arthur bellowed, swinging Excalibur up and starting across the field. Gwen moved after him, slim and blond and brave. "You've made a grand speech and gotten a lot of people killed. I wonder if you've the balls to face me blade to blade."

"Oh, fuck." The thought rang through the Truebond. Belle couldn't tell if it was her own or Tristan's.

Not that it mattered. She started after the Once and Future King, Tristan striding beside her, his sword swinging in threatening arcs to keep the prowling werewolves from jumping them.

Belle knew she was as bound to Arthur as she was to Tristan. She could feel her lover's fierce determination to protect his friend and leader. It was a role he'd held through fifteen centuries, through blood and war, through times when he'd been all but mad. No matter how bad things had been for him, Arthur had remained his dearest friend, never wavering in his support.

"You do realize Warlock will cheat," Tristan growled to Arthur as the other knights and their ladies ran to join them.

Arthur flashed him a boyish grin. "Oh, yeah. But I can cheat rings around him."

Gwen glanced at Belle and rolled her eyes. Belle swallowed a hysterical giggle.

Warlock waited for them, swinging his huge battle-axe in circles with an easy rotation of one wrist. "Do you know what I call my axe?" he shouted.

"No, and I don't particularly care." Arthur stepped to face the wizard. The Knights of the Round Table arrayed themselves at his back, as werewolves appeared to form the other half of the great dueling circle. Warlock's black-clad bodyguard moved into his habitual post at his master's side, silent and menacing.

Warlock grinned. "I call her Kingslayer."

Arthur snorted. "You're getting ahead of yourself, asshole."

"There's no poetry in you, Celt."

"I save my poetry for my wife." He raised Excalibur. "She's a hell of a lot more inspiring."

"And there's your weakness," Warlock said, his orange eyes blazing with arrogant hate over his axe. "You've tied yourself in that little whore's apron strings. No wonder you're weak."

The humor fled Arthur's face. "Oh, you just signed your own death warrant, Fido." Excalibur flashed in a glittering sweep aimed right for Warlock's head. Axe met sword in a ringing parry, and the two magical weapons shed an explosion of sparks as their power fields clashed.

Instinctively, Belle moved up next to Gwen, offering silent support to the woman who watched her husband fight to the death. Tristan joined them, planting the point of his sword in the bloody grass as he watched the fight with cat-like attention.

Tristan loved watching Arthur in action. His friend moved with surefooted grace and a vampire's breathtaking power, swinging Excalibur in elegant arcs, the magical blade shining with its own white-gold light. He'd never seen anyone who could match Arthur with a sword.

Until now. Warlock used his axe with awe-inspiring strength and all the skill his centuries had given him. He wasn't quite as fast as Arthur, but his reach and power made him a force to be reckoned with.

The werewolf and the vampire circled each other, eyes cold and watchful. Warlock struck like a snake, his axe arcing straight at Arthur's head. Arthur ducked and spun aside, swinging Excalibur up and across in a diagonal stroke intended to gut Warlock like a rabbit. The wizard leaped back with a curse, his powerful legs carrying him five feet back.

Arthur charged in as Warlock landed, thrusting for his enemy's heart. The werewolf brought his axe slashing down, catching Excalibur and driving the sword's point into the blood-soaked soil in a shower of magical sparks. Any other sword would have broken under the impact of the heavy axe, but Excalibur only chimed like a great bell. Arthur disengaged, jerking his blade free, spinning in a blur, Excalibur aimed for the Dire Wolf's neck.

Warlock caught the blow on the double-headed blade, then twisted his weapon against the sword, trying to break it with his greater strength and leverage. Arthur kicked him in the gut and jerked free.

Belle glimpsed a blur of movement from the corner of one eye and spun to see Tanner, in werewolf form, grab Gwen's helm and jerk it off, pulling her head down in the process. Before the witch could throw him back with a spell, the werewolf dove for the base of her neck and bit down. Magic flared blue around his teeth, and she screamed in agony, falling to her knees, both hands wrapped around the back of her neck.

"Gwen!" Arthur roared, whirling toward her, taking a single staggering step before his legs gave out beneath him. He fell to one knee with a grunt of pain.

"Tanner, you fucker!" Tristan jerked his sword out of the ground and swept it up in a merciless diagonal slash that cut the werewolf in two. The bisected corpse tumbled to the ground as the rest of the Round Table surged into the dueling circle, roaring battle cries.

Warlock laughed at Arthur as he struggled to rise. "Weakling," the werewolf shouted. "I told you the whore would be the death of you." He raised his axe to behead his opponent. "Now I rule!"

Lancelot spun in out of nowhere, his blade catching the descending axe. Lance muscled his sword up, throwing the bigger weapon aside so that he could ram a shoulder into Warlock's side, driving him back from the fallen vampire.

The knights hit Warlock en masse, Morgana, Caroline, and Lark at their heels. The werewolf roared and fired a blast of energy at them, but the witches' shields sent the attack splashing harmlessly away.

Apparently unaware of all that, Arthur started crawling toward his wife. Tristan snaked an arm around his torso and hauled him upright, half-carrying him to his mate as their comrades attacked the werewolf.

Belle dropped down beside her friend. "Healer!" she screamed. "I need a healer!" God, not Gwen. Her loss would kill Arthur and rip the heart from the Magekind.

"Let me!" A towering female werewolf as red as a fox loomed out of the dark, another wolf at her heels. Belle almost blasted them both before she recognized Miranda and Justice.

"I know werewolf magic better than you do," the Dire Wolf said, kneeling to cup Gwen's face between her furry palms. "Maybe I can work out how to take the spell apart."

"Fine, do it," Belle said as Gwen gritted her teeth in pain, her blue eyes glazing. "Do whatever you can." *Before she dies and takes Arthur with her.*

The werewolf went to work, Justice standing behind her, scanning the battlefield around them with the acute paranoid focus of a bodyguard.

At least they're not fighting anymore, Belle thought. *And I'll take all the help I can get.*

Tristan strode toward them, half-carrying Arthur. Despite his gritted teeth and sweat-slicked face, the Once and Future King clung to Excalibur with a white-knuckled grip.

Warlock's black-armored bodyguard charged in out of nowhere, slamming into Arthur's right shoulder so hard, the vampire lost his grip on his weapon. The assassin wrenched Excalibur from Arthur's hand and raced away like a rabbit, heading for the trees with the magical blade.

"No!" Arthur gasped, and almost fell on his face. He could barely speak.

"I'll get it back," Tristan growled, lowering his king to the ground beside Gwen. He bounded after the thief like a stag.

"Morgana!" Belle shouted, but the witch was already there, white-faced with fear for Gwen. "Help them. I've got to go with Tristan, or that fucking assassin will eat him."

"Go," Morgana snapped. "And get that sword before Warlock does. God knows what spell he'd cast with it."

Which was a damned good point. Bors's son had almost destroyed the Magekind by working death magic using Excalibur. Belle sprang to her feet and ran, sprinting across the field after Tristan and the fleeing assassin.

The men vanished into the trees, but Belle could feel Tristan in the Truebond. She didn't even break step as she hit the woods, leaping brush and ducking overhanging limbs, desperate to catch up before the killer turned on Tris.

Something roared, a deep, echoing bellow of animal fury. Belle's heart slammed into her throat as she hurdled a jagged stump and slid to a stop.

The biggest Dire Wolf Belle had ever seen had Tristan pinned to the forest floor with one clawed hand around his throat.

The beast's other hand gripped Excalibur.

Belle could feel Tris's fury as he bucked against the killer's hold, but the damn thing had to be twelve feet tall, with the strength to match. She flung up her hands for a blast . . .

Too late. The assassin dove for Tristan's chest, jaws opened wide, and bit down hard.

BOOOOOM!

The magical blast detonated straight up from Tristan's chest in a tightly focused beam that hit the the big monster and sent him flying like a ping-pong ball. *Oh, yeah,* Belle remembered, watching him tumble through the air, *Miranda booby trapped Tristan's armor.*

He came down hard, crashing through the limbs of a nearby loblolly pine to hit the ground with a meaty thud and a yelp of pain.

"Yes!" Belle pumped her fist in triumph. The spell had worked exactly the way the young werewolf had predicted. The kid might be young, but she knew her stuff when it came to Dire Wolf magic.

Unhurt, Tristan rolled to his feet. All the force of the blast had been aimed outward at his attacker; he wasn't even singed. "Let's go get that sword," he growled.

Stunned, Dice stared up at the tree limbs he'd crashed through, his body aching from countless bruises and what he suspected were a couple of broken ribs. For a moment, he had no idea how he'd gotten there.

Then he remembered. Tristan's armor had blown up in his mouth. He was lucky he still had a head.

Running footsteps approached, and Dice shook off his confusion to scramble to his feet. His skull shrieked in pain at the movement, and he had to swallow hard to keep from vomiting. His helm was gone, lost somehow during the tumble through the loblolly's branches.

The blast had not only hit him like a train, it had drained the magic he'd absorbed at the enchanted pool. He'd even reverted back to human form, though at least he'd retained his armor. *What the hell kind of spell was that, anyway?*

Excalibur! Fuck, he'd lost the sword!

He looked around desperately, spotted a silver gleam lying among the leaves, and pounced on the weapon a heartbeat before Tristan and Belle charged out of the trees.

As his fingers tightened around Excalibur's hilt, he felt strength flood his body, and his aches and pains instantly vanished. He looked down at the weapon, brows lifting. No wonder Warlock was so determined to get his hands on it.

"Are you going to give that sword back," Tristan snarled at him over his own drawn weapon, "or do I take it off your corpse?"

"Neither." Dice gave him a wild grin. "I'm going to kill you with it." He swung Excalibur up and charged.

Miranda winced in pity as Gwen gasped, fighting to breathe despite the bite's magic raging through her body. Her normally pretty face was so grotesquely swollen as to be unrecognizable. Arthur lay in the gory grass next to her, sucking in desperate breaths in concert with her struggles. He, too, looked swollen, his eyes slits in his distorted face. One hand clasped Gwen's hard, as though trying to lend her strength. His gaze caught Miranda's, silently demanding. *Save her.*

Miranda took a deep breath, caught Gwen's wounded neck between her palms, and sent her will questing into the punctures, seeking out the magic that was killing the former queen. She found the spell in the werewolf's saliva easily enough, wound tightly in the DNA.

Carefully, she explored the structure of the ancient magic, trying to tease out how it did its killing. Yet no matter how carefully she probed, she kept coming up with the same frustrating answer.

"Damn it to hell!" she snarled, jerking out of her trance. "This makes no sense at all. That spell isn't designed to do anything but turn humans into werewolves. It shouldn't kill anyone!"

"Yeah, well, there are a half dozen people lying dead on that field who could tell you differently," Morgana said grimly. "It also tries to fry me every time I attempt to probe anyone who's been bitten."

"Well, of course," Miranda told her absently. "The spell is locked against the kind of magical energies you people use. Dire Wolf magic works on a different frequency, has a different structure. But that still shouldn't kill anyone."

"Morgana . . ." Davon moved out of the group of helplessly watching witches to crouch beside Gwen's laboring body. "I have an idea. I—"

"I think you've done enough, don't you?" Morgana snapped. "Get the hell away from her and let her work."

"I'm a doctor, Morgana!" Davon rapped back. "And I know why these people are dying. This looks exactly like a massive allergic reaction. I should have seen it when Cherise died, but I was too rattled."

"It's a spell, Davon, not a bee sting," Morgana growled.

"Open your eyes and *look* at her, witch! See the way she's swollen? She can't breathe because her windpipe is swelling shut. It's a histamine reaction!"

Miranda's jaw dropped as she stared at him. "The Direkind magic is fighting the Magekind magic, and her body is reacting as if the spell is an invader. If I neutralize the spell . . ."

"We tried that. It didn't work."

"Because you're Magekind. I'm not." Miranda laid both hands over the punctures again, closed her eyes, and sent her power burning into the werewolf DNA, wiping the spell away. Then she whispered a new spell, reversing the lethal allergic reaction and shrinking the swelling in Gwen's airway. Distantly, she heard the witch suck in a relieved breath. Next to her, Arthur began breathing more easily, too, the Truebond carrying her healing magic to him.

Miranda opened her eyes to give Morgana a tired smile— just as a strange werewolf came racing out of the darkness to hit her like a runaway train. She didn't even have time to scream.

Belle watched in horror as Tristan jolted backward, reeling from the brutal impact of Excalibur slamming into his sword. The assassin pursued him, raining blow after blow against his guard, trying to force his sword aside so he could bury the enchanted blade in Tris's heart.

Yet somehow Tristan kept parrying, kept meeting the killer blow for blow, spinning aside, ducking back. Staying on the move because if he slowed down, if he gave his opponent the slightest opening, the killer would take him apart.

"The bastard's fighting with Arthur's strength. What's worse, the way he fights reminds me of Bors," Tristan snarled in the Truebond.

Belle cursed silently. She knew Excalibur enhanced Arthur's speed and power, as well as healing almost any injury he suffered. It even allowed him to sense an opponent's intentions so Arthur could beat a foe to the punch. Not that Arthur had ever been a slouch on the battlefield. He was counted one of the Round Table's finest warriors even without Excalibur.

The other champions of the Round Table were Lancelot—and Bors.

She clenched her hands into fists and ached to wade into the fight. *"Don't even think about it,"* Tristan warned her. *"He'd eat you alive."*

Belle wanted to charge in anyway, but she knew she was more likely to prove a lethal distraction for Tristan than anything else. She had nowhere near the skill of a Knight of the Round Table, and she certainly didn't have a vampire's strength.

An expression of horror flashed across the killer's face. He bounded straight upward and brought Excalibur smashing downward toward Tristan's head, obviously meaning to cleave the knight's skull in two.

Tristan spun aside and rammed his elbow into his foe's face, sending him staggering back, shaking his head as if stunned. An odd smile twisted the Dire Wolf's mouth before his expression shifted into lethal determination again. "You can't beat me, Tris, you never could."

"Fuck you," Tristan said, and hacked his blade at the werewolf's head.

The assassin jerked back, then slammed the flat of his own sword against Tristan's head, sending the knight staggering back. He fell to one knee. Again, horror flickered over the killer's face, replaced an instant later by savage determination as he brought Excalibur flashing down toward Tristan's neck. Tris threw himself into a backward roll, avoiding the stroke.

Tristan's friends call him Tris, Belle realized suddenly. *Bors had called him Tris.*

Suddenly the pieces slotted together with a click she could almost hear. Those horrified expressions right before every attack, the twisted smiles whenever Tristan hurt him. Her mind skipped to the glowing antlers Eva wore, outward manifestation of Zephyr's ghost, who had possessed her after the stag's death.

. . . The way he fights reminds me of Bors . . .

Bors, Belle realized. *When he ate Bors's magic, he ate Bors's ghost.*

She knew the beast's mental shields would block any magical attack she launched. But what if it wasn't an attack?

Reaching through the Mageverse as though opening a communication link to another agent, Belle slipped past his shields to touch the killer's mind below the level of conscious thought. *Careful,* she thought. *I can't let him know I'm here, or he'll block me.*

There, in the depths of the beast's consciousness, she found Bors. And the Magekind couple Emma and Tom Jacobs, and an entire family of werewolves, and the criminal members of a biker gang. All of them bound behind a spell that tasted of Warlock's work, a bit of minor magic designed to keep them from interfering with the killer's conscious mind.

So Belle broke the spell.

Tristan was tiring, Dice realized. His parries were slowing, his attacks losing their clean, hard snap. Any minute now, Dice could . . .

Howls of rage and pain exploded in his ears, so shatteringly loud Dice jolted. *What the flaming hell . . .*

The ghosts boiled up from the depths of his brain, screaming in fury at a child left orphaned, a man murdered with a coward's blow, a little boy butchered in his bed, bikers betrayed by their own leader. Dice saw them in his mind, their faces ringing his, pale and twisted as they howled for vengeance. Their fury blinded him, and Excalibur dropped from fingers gone suddenly numb. He started to bend down and retrieve the sword, but he couldn't move.

The ghosts had locked his muscles.

Tristan met his horrified gaze and smiled as something metallic flashed toward Dice's face. "Payback's a bitch." And so am I," Belle said, watching in satisfaction as the killer's head tumbled almost lazily off his shoulders, hacked off by Tristan's sword. His body toppled into the leaves with a meaty thud.

Tristan blew out a hard, relieved breath and bent to pick up Excalibur with his free hand. "No, darlin', a bitch is the one thing you're not. Let's take Arthur his sword."

Justice fisted a hand in the werewolf's mane and dragged him off Miranda before the bastard's claws could do any more damage than the long, raking strike he'd inflicted. "Andrews, you bastard, I am really sick of you." Wrapping one arm around the councilman's throat, he grabbed his foe's head and jerked hard to the side. The werewolf's neck snapped.

"Traitor!" Rosen spat, galloping out of the darkness at an awkward run, apparently following on Andrews's heels. He drew back a sword he must have stolen off one of the bodies. "I should have known you'd throw in with the vampires."

"Hell, who can blame him?" Davon growled, thrusting out a hand toward Miranda. Knowing what he wanted, she gestured, and a sword appeared in his palm. He closed his fist around the weapon and struck in one blurring motion.

Rosen's headless body hit the grass.

"Well," Morgana drawled, eying the doctor. "Decided you're one of us after all, did you?"

Davon gave her a wolfish grin. "How could I resist? You've got such a great medical plan."

She shook her head. "You must be feeling better. That joke was terrible."

"I kind of liked it," Tristan announced, walking up with Excalibur in his hand and Belle at his side.

"You would," Morgana muttered.

"So did I," Arthur said, a wheeze lingering in his voice.

He sat up, though he was still a little blue around the lips. Gwen's eyes were open, but she looked even worse than he did.

Tristan scanned the battleground. "Where the hell is Warlock?"

Morgana pointed toward the crest of a nearby hill. "That way somewhere, still fighting Smoke, Eva, and the Round Table."

"So Eva's okay?" Belle asked anxiously.

"Right as rain, thanks to Smoke's magic."

Miranda shook her head. "I'm amazed they've been able to hold their own against Warlock like this. He's got a *lot* of power."

"They probably couldn't have, if Kel and Nineva hadn't softened him up." Morgana looked upward as a shadow fell across their faces. Kel soared by overhead, Nineva winging along beside him. "Speak of the devil."

"Wait for it . . ." Miranda said, watching them disappear over the hill. "Wait for it . . ."

A moment later, a chorused shout of disgust rang out in the distance, sounding like several knights and a couple of infuriated dragons.

". . . Aaaand Daddy cuts his losses and gates for safety," Miranda announced. "He always did have a finely honed sense of self-preservation."

"Dammit," Arthur snarled. "I wanted a piece of him."

"Right now, you'd have choked," Gwen told him tartly, and coughed. "We'll get a big bite later . . ." She paused to pant. ". . . When we're all feeling more up to it."

TWENTY

The Magekind agents were home at last. They streamed through Morgana's dimensional gate, weary, battered, and solemn. Nobody felt triumphant, considering the procession of casualties who floated after them, carried on a wave of magic by the team of healers who followed. Most of the dead were bite victims who'd succumbed before Miranda realized how to cure them. The young werewolf had been working like a demon ever since, casting spells to heal the rest.

Belle was one of the last through the dimensional gate, Tristan striding beside her. One big hand rested on the small of her back with a possessiveness that made her lips curl into a smile of anticipation.

"I can't wait to get you alone," he told her through the Bond. *"I have plans."*

"Unfortunately, we also have house guests," Belle pointed out. Justice and Miranda were still staying with them, since they were both likely targets of Warlock's rage.

He snorted. *"Knowing them, they'll be fighting too hard to notice if we swing naked from the chandelier."*

Belle smiled. He was probably right. The two trailed them, having some kind of argument in low, intense voices. *"I give them a month before they're in bed."*

"You're on." He grinned. *"I figure they'll be shagging by Wednesday."*

"Ah, young love."

"I prefer old love." He dropped his hand to her ass and gave it a delicious little squeeze.

"Speak for yourself," she said, and bumped his hip with hers.

"I did save your ass," Justice pointed out, his strong jaw tight with irritation.

Even pissed looked good on him, Miranda thought. "You could have moved a little faster." She touched her belly. "Andrews damn near ripped me into confetti." The councilman had raked his claws across her abdomen, tearing so deep she'd had to transform to heal. "But thank you." The last was reluctantly said. She wasn't sure owing the big werewolf was a good thing.

"You're welcome," he growled, his tone less than gracious.

She sighed. It was obvious he was going to be a pain in the ass. Unfortunately, they were the only werewolves in Avalon, except for Eva, and she was busy with Smoke.

Which meant they were stuck with each other.

The next night, Belle cuddled closer against Tristan's side as he licked the tiny bite wound he'd left in her neck. She stroked her fingers through his blond hair, savoring the possessive male pleasure he radiated into the Truebond.

He was truly hers at last. Isolde's angry ghost would no longer torment either of them.

Tristan cupped her breast, his thumb flicking delicately

across her nipple, sending warm little jolts of delight ringing through her body. Smiling lazily, she reached down and curled her fingers around his cock. He was soft now, but he wouldn't stay that way if she had anything to say about it.

And she did.

Belle scooted down and delicately licked one of his tiny male nipples. The warm heat of the sensation echoed through the Truebond, adding to her building desire.

Slowly, tenderly, she began to nibble her way down his warm, sweaty chest. His cock went hard and hot in her hand. When she flicked her tongue over the sensitive head, he growled in delight and rolled his hips, thrusting his shaft in the grip of her hand.

"I love you." The thought rang in the Bond, so stark and true that Belle caught her breath.

"I love you, too" She curled her hand tighter around his cock and gave him a wicked grin. *"All of you."*

"All eight inches?"

"All six-foot-three of grumpy immortal," Belle corrected. *"I love the way you love me."*

"Wasn't that a song?"

"Jackass."

The werewolves were pissed.

Almost three hundred of them had gathered in the moonlit field to hear Warlock speak. He surveyed their angry faces with satisfaction.

The sacrifice of the werewolves had been regrettable, but necessary. And so far, Warlock's plan was working exactly as he'd intended.

"This is an outrage," shouted an older man whose potbelly stretched his white T-shirt. "A dozen werewolves dead . . ."

"And three members of the Council of Clans." This one

was in his twenties, young, muscular, and eager to prove himself. His hazel eyes kept taking on an orange glow, as if he teetered on the edge of transforming. Just the kind of cannon fodder Warlock could use.

"Not to mention all the Chosen." Grayson Corban clenched his big fists. He'd been one of the aristocrats who'd staged the ambush, sweeping down on the Magekind as they tried to get all those idiot civilians to safety. "So many of our best and brightest, dead at the hands of the Celts."

Warlock gave the big werewolf a slight smile. Corban was proof that even soft, twenty-first-century Americans could be taught to use a sword. Like the other members of the wizard's cult of Chosen males, he'd been training for years, and he'd fought well against the Magekind.

Much better than the idiot councilmen Warlock planned to portray as heroic martyrs. Distasteful, but necessary.

The one loss he regretted was Dice. The Dire Wolf had been a promising agent. He'd even managed to seize Excalibur just as Warlock had planned, though he hadn't made it back with the magical weapon.

Well, there'd be other opportunities.

The rest of the plan had gone off like clockwork. He'd known even his best Chosen werewolves couldn't defeat experienced Magekind agents in equal combat. So he'd told Rosen to call in as many civilians as possible, knowing they'd panic the minute the fighting started. Sure enough, some of them had been trampled.

Given the Magekind's delusions of heroism, they'd been distracted as they tried to get the Direkind to safety—which had set them up for the perfect ambush.

All in all, the plan had worked well. Warlock had noted the elements that needed tweaking so he'd be able to compensate for them the next time.

Best of all, now that he knew how to create warrior beasts like Dice, he could do it again. And again. Perhaps he'd create an entire team, though that would mean using a great deal of death magic. Warlock was willing to do whatever it took.

After all, he had a war to win. And Arthur Pendragon to kill.

Now Available
from *New York Times* bestselling author

Angela Knight

GUARDIAN:
The Time Hunters

When Riane Arvid—a superhuman cop from the future—
is trapped in the year 2009, the only one she can turn to
is a handsome twenty-first-century warrior, Nick Wyatt. In
an attempt to discover the other's true intentions, both decide seduction is the best tactic. But as both their lives are
threatened, their only chance at survival is to learn to trust
each other...

penguin.com